BURN

ALSO BY JULIANNA BAGGOTT

PURE
FUSE
BURN

JULIANNA BAGGOTT

BURN

headline

First published in 2014 by
HEADLINE PUBLISHING GROUP

1

Cataloguing in Publication Data is available from the British Library

ISBN 978 0 7553 8556 0 (Hardback)
ISBN 978 0 7553 8557 7 (Trade Paperback)

Offset by Avon DataSet Ltd, Bidford on Avon, Warwickshire

Printed and bound in Great Britain by
Clays Ltd, St Ives

Headline's policy is to use papers that are natural, renewable and recyclable
products and made from wood grown in sustainable forests. The logging
and manufacturing processes are expected to conform to the
environmental regulations of the country of origin.

HEADLINE PUBLISHING GROUP
An Hachette UK Company
338 Euston Road
London NW1 3BH

www.headline.co.uk
www.hodderheadline.com

For David Scott.
Sometimes all I want to do is lie down—blur-blind, life-weary—
and survive with you.

Prologue

BRADWELL

He knows the ending. He can see it almost as clearly as he saw the beginning.

"Start there," he whispers into the wind. His wings are bulky. The quills ruffle; some drag behind him. He has to tighten his wings against the wind as he walks through the stubble fields toward the stone cliff. He wants to go backward, to tunnel and dig to the little boy he once was.

This is what he's never told anyone.

He didn't sleep through his parents' murders; he willed himself to believe he did.

After the men broke into his house, he was woken up by a scuffle, his mother crying out, probably just before she and his father were shot. Bradwell had been warned about people breaking into the house. He scrambled from bed and hid under it.

He saw a set of boots in the inch between the bed skirt and the floor. They stalled beside his bed, and then one of the killers—his would-be killer—knelt, lifted the bed skirt, and for a moment, they were face-to-face.

Bradwell didn't move, didn't breathe. The man's face was long and angular with a slightly crooked jaw. He had blue eyes.

Finally, without a word, he dropped the skirt.

He said to the other man with him, "The boy must be at a sleepover."

"You checked the room?"

"I checked the goddamn room."

He listened to them leave and then still didn't get up. He pretended to sleep, still there under the bed. He pretended to dream. And then he opened his eyes and this is the part that he has confessed: He walked down into the kitchen as if it were any other morning; that might have been all his brain could handle. When his parents weren't making breakfast, he called for them, and only then did he start to panic. Finally, he found their bodies still in their bed.

He could have run toward his mother's cry, but instead he hid. He told Pressia that he'd slept through the murders, and he's wanted to believe that to be the truth. In reality, that day was the first time he should have died, but far from the last. The fact that he's alive is accidental.

He climbs the stones and walks to the edge of the cliff. It's dark but the moon is bright. He spreads his wings wide and leans into the wind. For a moment, he thinks the wind will go slack, and he'll fall forward and fly.

But he doesn't have wings that will hold him.

Flying. That's not the ending.

The ending is in ash and dust.

He was meant to be a martyr, alongside his parents.

He's borrowed this time with his brothers—El Capitan and Helmud. He was never meant to be in love or to have someone love him—Pressia. When he thinks of her, it's as if his heart has been kicked clean out of his chest. He could have died with her on a frozen forest floor. He could have died bound to his brothers, their blood mixing together. But neither of those was the end.

Here, on the cliff, he sees the end: He's lying on the ground amid the ash and dust of his homeland and his chest is ripped open. The truth lifts from his body like a long white unfurling ribbon, flecked with his blood.

How will it happen? When?

He only knows that it's not far off.

With the wind cutting through his wings, he feels like he's careening toward it—or is the end rushing to meet him? This time he won't hide. This time he'll run toward the cry.

PRESSIA

KEY

THE DOOR TO PRESSIA'S ROOM is locked. The caretakers come and go with rings of keys, jingling—how many rooms are there? Where's Bradwell? Helmud and El Capitan? Where are her things—the vial, the formula?

The caretakers never answer her questions. They tell her to get well. "I'm not sick." They tell her to rest. "I can't sleep." They smile and nod and point out the alarms attached to each of the walls in her room. "Push here if there's an emergency." The caretakers wear necklaces with emergency buttons attached to them too. But she doesn't know what kind of emergency to expect. When she asks, they say, "Just in case..."

"In case of what?"

They won't say.

Each day is the same. Too many days to count; weeks have passed—almost a month now?

The caretakers are all women and golden, each of them, almost glowing. Is it the firelight? Is it that so many of them are pregnant—don't pregnant women glow? Is it some inner radiance? Most of them have bellies that bloom out from their hips. Engorged.

But it's not just the caretakers who are golden. The children out in the field are too. They're sent out at different intervals throughout the day to play. They have sticks and balls and nets on poles dug into the cold ground. Golden, all of them, as if steeped in something slightly metallic, and no fusings or scars or marks. Just skin. The alarms bob on the chests of their coats.

The caretakers bring Pressia trays of food: warm broths, porridges, tall glasses of cold milk—white, white milk, not a dot of ash stirring within it. The ash eaters are everywhere, skittering across spoons, along the edge of the metal bathtub, on the windowpanes, both inside and out. Beetle-backed and lightly iridescent, they seem to work night and day, resistant to cold.

One caretaker told her that they've been bred into existence to use their delicate arms to shovel ash into their tiny mouths, *to clean the slate*—that's how she put it.

They're the reason why the sky outside the window is tinged blue instead of gray.

They're why the sheets, the pillowcases, even the tiny goose feathers that escape the comforter are often bright white. Pressia can't remember ever seeing something so pristine.

Everything in her room is kept clean. Her sheets are changed every day. In the adjoining bathroom, there is always a new bar of soap. Someone even pulls out the tangled strands of loose hair wound through her brush; each morning it's clean.

She traces her finger on the window and then looks beyond it. She can see an ancient stone tower, tilted as if leaning into the wind, strange lumbering beasts—the size of cows but with thick, rubbery, hairless coats, occasional tusks—roaming the misty, downward slope. Beyond the herd, there's the airship, locked to the earth by a mound of greenery; it has been swallowed by vines.

Will they ever get back again? Home. Did it ever exist? And now, after all that's happened, after all she's done, does she deserve a place called home? Bradwell, his massive wings—she did that to him. She wants to go back to the way it was before. But there is no going back.

To clean the slate.

But what do you do when the slate cannot be made clean?

Is anyone working on the airship? Have Bradwell, El Capitan, and Helmud regained enough strength to travel? Will Bradwell ever forgive her?

"This is a waste of time!" She's lost her patience a few times and yelled at the caretakers. "We have to get back home! People need us!"

They smile, nod, point out the alarms on the walls.

At night, when her room grows dark, the alarms glow red and she hears the howling. It comes every night—dogs off in the distance. Wolves, foxes, coyotes? What howling dogs live in this land? Sometimes she wishes the dogs would circle in closer, threaten to devour her. Maybe she wants to be torn to bits, to disappear.

And she wakes up feeling the same way. It's her guilt that she wants to be torn to bits, devoured, to disappear. Bradwell. She thinks of him now, her room filling with morning light. After she injected the serum into the birds in his back, after those wings grew quickly and wildly as his ribs and shoulders also expanded, he said, "What did you do to me?" She knows now that she betrayed him. He didn't want to be saved by the contents of the vial—the medicine that might one day lead to Purifying the survivors of all their scars and fusings. He wanted to die Pure—by his own definition of the word. But she couldn't let him go.

Alone, still feeling dreamy, she lies in her bed and remembers what it was like in the stone underpass on the hard ground with Bradwell, his hands rough and warm, cupping her face. It was like being fully alive for the first time in her life—alive in every cell of her body. And now, something inside of her feels dead. She feels vacant. Bradwell hates her. She hates herself. She isn't sure which one is worse. She would do anything to win back his trust, but she knows the damage can't be undone.

She understands why he hates the idea of being able to reverse his fusings, erase their scars, philosophically; he doesn't want to reverse or erase the past, the sins of the Dome. But she doesn't understand why there isn't even one small part of him—deep down—that desires to be made whole again.

She touches the scar on her inner wrist—a thin, puckered line where the synthetic skin of the doll's head is traced through with her own nerve endings. At thirteen, she tried to cut off the doll head. She remembers the feel of the knife on her skin. It stung sharply. It was something she was in control of—not something that was happening *to* her. She would like to be in control. Did she think a stump would be better? Did she think at all? Not really. She wanted only to be free of it.

She still wants that. The vial and the formula get her one step closer to that possibility, but Bartrand Kelly confiscated these things—what they all risked their lives to unearth. If she can get these things back into the Dome where there are scientists still working in labs, it wouldn't just help her. No. There could be a future where all the survivors are whole again.

She rubs her hidden knuckles locked within the doll's skull and rakes her fingers up her arm. She wants to be whole. After all these years, who wouldn't?

A key rattles the lock. The knob turns. It's a bright morning.

Pressia sits up and scoots to the edge of her bed, waiting.

Fedelma is the only caretaker whose name she knows. She's in charge of the other caretakers and pins her hair like two horned knots on top of her head. She has more power and maybe for this reason she's allowed to do more talking. Pressia is relieved to see her.

Fedelma is pregnant too. Her belly is a taut drum she has to negotiate around, and she's not young. Her hair is graying at the temples. The skin around her eyes crinkles a bit when she smiles. She pushes the heavy door wide open with one hand, holds a tin tray aloft with the other. "Did you sleep?" she asks.

"Barely," Pressia says, and she drives to the point. "I want to see Bartrand Kelly." She hasn't seen him since the first day—a blur of noise, thorns, blood, and wings—when they were all loaded into a cart and taken in. "He has things that belong to me."

"He's good to his word," Fedelma says, setting the tray on the bedside table. "He'll tell you everything when the time is right."

Everything. About her mother and father? About the past? Bartrand Kelly was one of the Seven. He was friends with her parents when they were all young. He knows more about her parents than she ever will. It seems incredible to her now that she ever hoped to find her father here. She misses him even though he's a stranger to her.

"And the airship? Is he just going to let it stay covered by vines out there?"

"The vines are camouflage for now. They'll keep the airship safe from predators and bands of thieves. It's why the vines were bred to be carnivorous. A protection."

Bred to be carnivorous? Pressia thinks. Somewhere there are laboratories, breeding grounds . . .

Fedelma reaches out and gently holds Pressia's wrist—not that of the doll head, no. Fedelma is startled by the doll head, disturbed by the way it's fused to Pressia's fist, though she tries to pretend she isn't fazed by it.

"What are you doing?" Pressia asks.

Fedelma pulls up Pressia's sweater sleeve, revealing her arm. "See? Your skin has started to turn a bit golden," she says. "Your food is laced with a chemical that deters the vines—a scent that emanates from your skin."

Pressia sees it now too. The faintest hue. She pulls down her sleeve. "People don't like to be poisoned," she says.

"People don't like to be choked to death by thorned vines." This is true. Pressia saw how the vines almost killed Bradwell, El Capitan, and Helmud. "Eat," Fedelma says, pushing the tray toward Pressia.

"Why won't anyone tell me about the alarms? What are you afraid of?"

Fedelma rubs her arms as if chilled. "We don't speak of it." She walks to the window.

"I've heard the howling."

"The wild dogs are ours. They help keep us safe."

"Why won't you just talk to me? Tell me the truth."

"We've never had strangers arrive. We don't know how to treat them, except as something foreign, maybe a threat."

"Do I look like a threat?"

Fedelma doesn't answer. "One of yours has started walking the grounds. I don't know how he's gotten permission. He was the one worst off when you arrived. Maybe he hasn't gotten permission at all and yet he's out there. I've seen him two days in a row now."

Pressia gets up and walks quickly to the window. "Bradwell?"

Fedelma nods. "He's a bit unsteady on his feet still since..."

The domesticated beasts have been herded elsewhere, but the children are there—running with balls and sticks. Much of the toys seem new, as do the hats and scarves. Christmas just passed. Did they get them as gifts? They shout and whistle. A few are singing in a small group, making hand gestures in unison.

One little girl in a bright red sweater skirts the edges of the groups. She's holding a doll to her chest. Pressia imagines herself at that age with her own doll—the one that's fused to her fist, forever. It was new once—its eyes shone and clicked in unison. To be new. To *feel* new. She can't imagine...

Another girl walks up to the one with the doll—an identical twin. The two of them link arms and keep walking.

So many children, so few adults. They're repopulating. They have to. Where's Bradwell? "Do you see him now?" Pressia asks.

"No," Fedelma says. "But he's out there somewhere."

"I have to go out too," Pressia says.

Fedelma shakes her head. "You need to eat. You need your sleep. If you're going to get stronger, you need—"

"I need to see him—with my own eyes." Pressia walks to the door, which Fedelma forgot to lock behind her.

"No!" Fedelma says. "Pressia! Stop!"

But Pressia's already through the door and starts running down the hall. She finds a stairwell and pounds down the steps. She can hear Fedelma behind her. "Pressia! Don't!"

Should she be running while pregnant? How old is she anyway?

Pressia finds a heavy door to the outside.

The air is cutting and damp. She walks swiftly through the field of children, all of them golden.

One group is playing a game where some form a loose circle and the others, inside of the circle, spin and spin.

Look in a looking glass.
Look for a match.
Find yourself! Find yourself!
Don't be the last!

The children in the ring shout the song, and then the dizzy children start chasing the others, fanning out across the grass.

But others, not playing the game, stop and stare at Pressia. And now that she's among them, she spots another set of twins. She sees a third who looks identical. She's never seen triplets before. She doesn't want to stare at them, though; she doesn't like being stared at herself.

A boy with jet-black hair says, "Look!" and he points at the doll-head fist. Pressia refuses to hide it.

Fedelma, huffing behind her, shouts, "Quiet, boy! Go on about your play."

Pressia heads toward the stone tower; she needs to get a better view. These kids remind her of what things might be like in the Dome. The breathable air, the lack of deformities, scars, and fusings. She wonders where her half brother, Partridge, is now. He turned himself back in to the Dome. Is he finding people who will help him find a way to take over his father's reign? Will he remember those suffering on the outside? Will he do the right thing? Is Pressia doing the right thing, imprisoned here, wasting precious time? Will Bartrand Kelly be true to his word?

"You shouldn't be out!" Fedelma shouts after her. "You're under strict orders to recuperate! If Bartrand Kelly knew about this, it wouldn't be good. Are you listening? Are you?"

Pressia runs the rest of the way to the tower, her lungs stinging from the cold. She takes the small circular staircase two steps at a time, pulling herself up the handrail with her good hand. She presses the side of the doll's head to her chest, as if it can hear her pounding heart.

The tower is round with a peaked roof. The narrow windows are just casements—no glass. The wind tunnels in. The stone is cold and weathered, with patches of slick moss. She stops at one of the casements and looks out—rolling fog, another view of the airship. The vines rustle and the airship seems to bobble a little. Are the vines digging in so deeply that the ship itself is shaken by them?

Will they ever get out of here? Without the airship, it's not possible.

She moves quickly to the next casement—a few beasts, the kind she can't name, nosing grass near a stony ledge.

She hears Fedelma's boots on the stairs. Pressia turns and there Fedelma is, breathing heavily.

"Should you be running after me in your condition?" Pressia says.

"Should you be out running around in *your* condition?" Fedelma counters. They both left the main house without coats. Fedelma clamps her arms on her chest, atop her belly. The wind whips the fine hairs that have spun loose from the two pointy buns on top of her head.

"Why do you think *I'm* sick?" Pressia asks. "Bradwell, El Capitan, and Helmud—they were the ones who almost died. Not me."

"They're sick from the thorns' puncture wounds, but your case is more serious, in some ways. You're sick of heart."

Pressia's startled. "I don't know what you're talking about." But she does. Her pain is inside of her like a heavy stone that has been laid on her chest. Guilt, loss, betrayal. She moves to the next narrow window and looks out. She sees only sky and earth and distant trees. An ash eater is crawling up between the tightly wedged stones. She nudges it with the tip of her finger.

"You have to heal within," Fedelma says. "It takes time."

Pressia's eyes fill with tears. The weight feels so heavy it's hard to breathe. It brings pressure to her lungs, sharp aches inside of her chest.

"Kelly wants to see you today. All of you."

"Why didn't you tell me earlier?"

"I'm not supposed to have told you." She sighs. "He'll help you, but he'll want something in return."

"What?"

Fedelma dips her head to a window. It's quiet for a moment, except for the children playing in the field and the wind. "There's the one you're looking for," Fedelma says, and she steps back from the window. "Have a look."

Pressia moves quickly.

Bradwell is walking downhill through the tall grass. Three pairs of massive wings are hunched on his back, dovetailing at his boot heels. The tips of the wings drag behind him. He's not used to the weight of the wings, and the harsh shifts of wind push him. The wings make him ungainly, clumsy, and tentative—almost like a colt trying to get used to new legs.

Fignan, ever loyal, follows him, the black box of his body suspended on his spindly legs connected to his wheels, which flatten a narrow swath of grass behind him.

She remembers the syringe in her shaking hand and how she injected each of the three small birds embedded in his back. He wanted to die on his own terms. She robbed him of that. Still, he's alive. Her heart thrums in her chest. She can't apologize for saving him, no matter what. She can't.

And he'll never forgive her for that.

He stops, and for a moment, she wonders if he can feel her eyes on him. But he doesn't turn toward her. He looks up at the sky—birds wheeling overhead. He's still pale from the loss of blood, but his jawline is sharp, his eyes steely. He takes a deep breath, which broadens his chest. As he watches the birds glide, one of his wings twitches, almost imperceptibly.

Turn. Turn and look at me, she urges him. *I'm here.*

But he hunches again and keeps walking into the wind.

PARTRIDGE

GRIEF

IT RISES IN HIS THROAT. *I killed him.* Sometimes he even opens his mouth as if he's really going to tell someone. *I killed my father. The leader you love—Willux, your savior—I murdered him.* But then his throat cinches.

He can't say this to anyone, of course—except Lyda. After he confessed to her, he felt lighter—but only for a short time. He sees her every few days, and he spent the night of Christmas Eve with her, almost a month ago now. Christmas morning they woke up and exchanged small gifts in her beautiful apartment, the one he had set up for her on Upper Two. It was the first thing he did when power was transferred from his father to him. He got Lyda out of the medical center, and now she has people who take care of her—and the baby growing inside of her. *Their* baby.

He's surprised by how loudly a secret can ring in your head. *I killed him.* It's not just a secret, though. He knows this. It's murder. It's the murder of his father.

Partridge is sitting in an anteroom next to the main hall where he can hear the mourners starting to line up. They're muffling their grief, but soon enough they'll let loose. It'll get loud and stuffy with all of the bodies packing in, and Partridge will have to accept their condolences, all of their twisted love for his father.

Partridge isn't surprised when Foresteed walks into the room. He's been the face of the Dome's leadership for some time, and he attends most of these services. Partridge's father had used him as a figurehead ever since the start of his deterioration, and surely Foresteed expected to step in as Willux's replacement upon his death. Naturally, he's not fond of Partridge.

Foresteed isn't alone. He's flanked by Purdy and Hoppes, who work for him. They all say their hellos and sit across from Partridge at the mahogany table. Partridge is wearing one of his black funeral suits. He has seven of them now—one for each day of the week.

"I thought we'd take a minute to talk," Foresteed says.

"Well, I'd like to know how many more memorial services there are going to be," Partridge says. It's like being on tour with his father's urn—a grief tour. The worst part is sitting through the eulogies. Some of the speakers talk about what his father saved them all from—the wretches, those vile blights on humanity, soulless, no longer human. He's had to tell himself that he can turn them around—when the time comes. He's said to Lyda, "When they meet a wretch, like Pressia, everything will change." But the whole thing makes him sick and anxious.

Foresteed cocks his head and says, "This too much for you? I mean, dealing with your personal grief on top of all this adoration? You sure you can handle it?"

Foresteed is a layered conversationalist—Partridge will give him that. Is he being sarcastic about Partridge's *personal grief*? Is he hinting that Partridge isn't grieving enough? Does he suspect that Partridge killed his father? Or is Foresteed simply calling Partridge weak? "I just want to get to the work at hand," Partridge says, "the work my father wanted me to do." Partridge puts his chin to his chest and scratches his forehead, hiding his eyes for a moment because they've gone teary. Fact is, he killed his father, yes, and he doesn't regret it, but he misses his father too. This is the sick part. He loved him. A son's allowed to love his father no matter what, isn't he? Partridge hates how the emotions come upon him so fast—guilt, fear of being exposed, sadness.

Purdy checks a planner on his handheld.

For someone who lives in the Dome, Foresteed is very tan. His teeth are so shiny they look polished. His hair is stiff as if it's been misted with hair spray. He says, "The people are still in need of public mourning."

"How about some *private* mourning?" Partridge says. "Culturally speaking, I think we're pretty good at bottling our emotions."

"Your father wanted a public mourning period," Foresteed says. Sometimes Partridge thinks Foresteed might have hated his father. Always the second in line, he had to be jealous of the power.

"But this service is different," Purdy says.

"How?"

"I mentioned it in my last report," Foresteed says. He gives Partridge reports all the time—fat stacks of papers filled with bureaucratic policy updates written in dense, senseless language ("Heretofore the forewith will be presumed to forbear and withstand the aforementioned duties..."). He can't stand reading them.

"Ah, right," Partridge says. "I must have missed that part. Can someone fill me in?"

Purdy looks at Foresteed. "We've got all the dignitaries and socialites coming in this time," Foresteed says. "It's closed to the public. We'll be broadcasting it, however. Live streaming. We want this one to have the feel of magnitude. The moment when the people truly recognize the leaders of tomorrow, moving into this new phase."

Partridge sits back and sighs. He'll recognize these people from political functions, parties, those who live in the apartment building where he grew up, the parents of his friends from the academy. He shakes his head. "I don't want to sit next to Iralene this time.

Don't get me wrong. I like Iralene. I respect her. But they've got to get used to the idea that we're not going to get married. Every time they see me with her, it's going to be harder to explain that I'm with Lyda." On Christmas Eve, Partridge and Lyda kissed a little. He put his hand on the soft skin of her stomach where the baby is just starting to grow. "I'm going to be a father. Lyda and I are going to get married. We have to introduce this idea and undo my father's lies."

Hoppes shakes his head and his fatty jowls wag. He's taken over managing Partridge's image. "We're working on a story that will set this all right. We've got a plan. But it's just too soon. My staff is working diligently. Trust me."

"How about the truth?" Partridge feels a surge of heat run through him. Lies were how his father operated. He told the people fairy tales so they could sleep at night—tales of a world divided into Pures and wretches. "How about the goddamn truth for once?"

Foresteed sets his fists on the table and stands up, leaning over Partridge. "The truth is that you knocked someone up and you're engaged to someone else. Your concubine's set up in a nice place to keep her quiet—like father, like son."

"I'm not anything like my father." Partridge stares at Foresteed, waiting for him to back down but Foresteed doesn't. He glares at Partridge as if he's begging him to take a swing.

Purdy breaks the silence. Scratching the back of his head, he says, "I just don't get why you wouldn't be interested in a girl like Iralene. She was made for you."

"Literally," Partridge says.

"Well, she's a real catch," Purdy says. "Sometimes you've got to rely on someone else to hold up a mirror. Am I right, fellas?"

Hoppes says, "Yes, of course."

Foresteed nods.

Partridge feels tight pressure in his chest. "I'm in love with Lyda.

I'm not going to be peer pressured into falling out of love, okay? So why don't you keep your goddamn opinions to yourself?"

Purdy raises his hands in the air. "We're going to work this out. It's going to be okay!"

He hates this most of all—defensively chipper smiles that cover up all the lies. He can't take it anymore. His chest feels like it could explode. He leans forward. "I know the truth. And I am going to lead with the truth. My father was the biggest mass murderer in history," Partridge says. This is the truth he's held in for a long time. It feels good to warn them. He feels powerful for once. "The people know this, but they pretend they don't. They've all been handed a lie, and they're living by it. It's got to be eating at them. They have to be ready to acknowledge it. It's the only way to move forward."

"Jesus," Hoppes says. He's taken a handkerchief from his pocket and presses it to his upper lip and forehead.

"To what possible end?" Foresteed asks, his eyes wide with astonishment. "I mean, do you want the wretches and the Pures to walk hand in hand into a beautiful tomorrow?"

"Would it hurt to prepare for the time when we leave the Dome and start making a life for ourselves out there? I mean, how about a little compassion for the survivors?" Partridge and Lyda have been writing out plans, simple things they can start to do to improve lives on the outside—clean water, food, education, and medicine. "We can really impact their lives for the better."

"Isn't that noble," Foresteed says.

Partridge can't bear his condescension.

Purdy says, "Let's slow down a minute."

Partridge is sick of putting things off, avoiding conflict. Now is the time. He shifts his tone, tries to sound as calm as possible. "Look, I've been thinking about this. What would be so wrong with a council, made up of people from the inside and people from the outside?" He, Lyda, and Pressia could all be on that council—plus Bradwell and El Capitan. They could make real progress.

"God." Foresteed walks to the door, checks to see if it's locked, and then sits back down at the table.

"What's wrong with a council? What's wrong with some progress?" Partridge says. There has to be progress. This is why he handed himself over to the Dome in the first place. This is why he killed his father—to push for something hopeful.

"No, no, no," Hoppes says quietly. "These are your people, Partridge, the people of the Dome. They like normalcy, consistency. You can't barge into their lives and start ripping things up."

Partridge feels like flipping over the table. He crosses his arms on his chest to try to contain his pounding heart. "Why not? Maybe it's the only way we're going to be able to rebuild."

Foresteed laughs.

"What's so funny?" Partridge hates Foresteed with a sudden rush. His face flushes with anger. It'd be better if Foresteed punched him or at least argued—but to laugh at him?

Hoppes says, "As a researcher, I'd like to explain to you that the 'lie,' as you call it—"

Purdy interrupts, "A term I deeply disagree with."

"That 'lie,'" Hoppes continues, using air quotes, "has created the framework that allows the people to accept themselves, to be able to look themselves in the eye, to love each other, and to go on. If you take that away, well—"

"Well what?" Partridge says.

Foresteed smiles. "If you rob them of their lie, they'll self-destruct. That's what. How about a little compassion for the people *inside* the Dome? Huh?"

The room goes quiet. These men aren't going to see his side. There are others inside the Dome who are supposed to be on Partridge's side—the Cygnus—those who had a plan to get him into power, a plan his mother had tried to put into action from the outside. Where the hell are they now? Partridge could use some reinforcements. He can't even really tell if Foresteed is telling the truth. Does the lie keep these people together or is he just trying to keep Partridge quiet? "I want to see Glassings," Partridge says.

"Glassings?" Hoppes says.

"My old World History teacher." Glassings is one of the secret leaders of the sleeper cells, part of Cygnus, and the one who got the pill that would kill his father to Partridge. In some ways, Glassings got him into this. He'd like for him to at least show up in his life again.

"Why do you want to see him?" Foresteed asks. Does Glassings' name alarm him?

"I have some questions about world history," Partridge lies quickly. "It would help to know how some other leaders have led. Don't you think?"

"Your father was a great leader. What more could you ask for?" Purdy says, smiling nervously.

He wants to ask Purdy to schedule a meeting with Glassings, but he doesn't like the suspicious look in Foresteed's eyes, so he sighs heavily as if he's bored. "How many more of these services?" he asks again.

Purdy reexamines his planner. He taps dates and counts aloud to seven. "That's it. Seven more memorial services. Not bad."

"And then we can roll out the new story—the break between you and Iralene and the news of your new love, Lyda," Hoppes says. "We'll broach the baby situation about two months after that."

Are they just going to keep putting it off? "The new story about Lyda will go out soon, right? Days, not weeks?"

"Of course," Hoppes says.

Foresteed says, "Just go out there and say your lines, Partridge. Let them show their respects."

"Okay, but no Iralene," Partridge says. "She needs a break anyway. Just send her home, okay?" He worries about Iralene. She's under a lot of pressure, feeling terribly scrutinized, and she knows that her role is going to change. Partridge has assured her that she'll always have a place in his life—as a friend—and a respected role in society, but he just doesn't know what that's going to look like.

"We can't make any promises about Iralene," Hoppes says. "You know that there are a lot of moving pieces here." He means Mimi, his father's widow and Iralene's mother, who can be unpredictable.

"We can't be held hostage by Mimi." Partridge stands up. "I'm in charge," he says, though he feels nervous saying it. "No Iralene this time. Okay? I don't want her sitting next to me on live-streaming feed." Lyda will be watching, won't she? He imagines her as he last saw her. She was wearing a long white cotton nightgown. She was tired—she's not sleeping well—but also restless.

"I feel like a caged tiger," she told him. "I don't know how long I can take it. When are you coming back?"

He kissed her and told her, "As soon as I can. My life isn't really my own right now, but it will be soon. It's coming. I promise."

"This meeting is over," Partridge says. Sometimes it's the little things that feel so good—like calling the end to a meeting. It shouldn't matter, but he likes that he can flex this muscle and no one can contradict him.

Foresteed strides to the door, gets there first, and unlocks it. "Allow me," he says. He opens the door for Partridge. There's the line of mourners, immaculately dressed. Their heads turn, and they stare at Partridge. He hears a few stifled sobs. They gaze at him expectantly.

Foresteed claps Partridge on the shoulder, his grip too sharp. He leans in close and whispers, "You're wrong, you know. Your father wasn't just the biggest mass murderer in history. He was the most successful. There's a difference."

Partridge puts his hand on the door, ready to walk out of the room. "I won't live his lies for him. I'm not his puppet, and I'm sure as hell not yours."

Foresteed smiles at him. His teeth nearly glow they're so white. "As if you don't have lies of your own already, Partridge," he says so softly only Partridge can hear. "If you're going to come clean, why don't you start with yourself?"

EL CAPITAN

ARMOR

EL CAPITAN DOESN'T HAVE A KNIFE. "Don't need one," he explains to Helmud. "We're all dosed up." He first noticed the change of skin color on Helmud's arms—always dangling around his neck. At first he thought it was jaundice, but then, as soon as the caretaker told him it was a chemical that repelled those vines—their thorns as sharp as canines—he asked to have his dosage upped. "Two hearts here, two sets of lungs, two brains—more or less," he said. "We need double the meds. Got to keep that in mind."

And now his skin looks like he's been at the beach for an entire summer. Not red and blistered, but golden brown. It's almost got a metallic shine to it. He remembers getting tan on his arms, face, and the back of his neck as a kid—a farmer's tan, or so it was called. But his tan was always mixed with dirt too. He and Helmud were the kinds of kids who spent a lot of time on dirt bikes, climbing trees, rooting through mud. Maybe he was more like this than Helmud. In fact, as a kid, Helmud had seemed somewhat refined. El Capitan had been the bully, the brute—he'd had no choice. He was the man of the house so young.

His hands wrapped in towels stolen from a cabinet in his room, he uses the vines to climb to the hatch, which, as the airship has rolled to its side, is now on top. But where's the hatch? It's not sticking up, which is how he left it when he went out looking for Bradwell. The vines must have shut it when they wound their way around the airship.

The vines seem to sense the chemicals that are emanating from his and Helmud's skin. They don't recoil but they certainly aren't aggressive and do seem to shift away. El Capitan hears the skritch of their thorns against the airship's exterior. It kills him that they're scratching it up.

The vines spook him—not just because they almost killed him once, but because they're not natural. "There's something not right about this place," he says to Helmud. He means the herd of creatures grazing on the hillside—are they giant boars? And the children—all of them are under the age of nine, or so it seems, which means they were born after the Detonations. Plus, too many of them look alike. It doesn't make sense to him, but he knows it's messed up. "Not right at all. But who am I to talk, right?"

"Who am I?" Helmud says. Is he speaking philosophically? El Capitan's glad that Helmud can only communicate in repetitive ways. If Helmud could really express himself, El Capitan's afraid Helmud would push him to take the conversation one level deeper. El Capitan isn't one for philosophizing.

El Capitan laughs. "Who are you? Let's keep our shit together, Helmud, okay? Let's not go off the deep end. You know what I mean."

"You know what I mean," Helmud repeats, and El Capitan knows to drop it. Helmud's in one of those moods where he wants to assert himself. There's no talking to him.

A knife would help, but he didn't have time to go hunting for one. He wanted out. He wanted to see his airship, and he's finally built up enough strength again to roam. He sneaked out, and now is he being watched from afar? Maybe. Who cares? He's got a ship to get back in order and hopefully up into the air. He has people to get home—Bradwell, Pressia. He thinks of her and remembers the kiss.

Jesus.

He kissed her. Each time he thinks about it, his heart feels like a crooked thing in his chest, all bent, all wrong—a freak heart. His heart will beat for Pressia for the rest of his life. He'll love her forever. Bradwell might have been able to turn away from her, but El Capitan could never do that. He'll just have to take this ache. He'll have to bear it inside of him forever. He's survived this long under the weight of his own brother. He understands the burden. He feels aged by it, and yet he's still young. He was a kid when the Detonations went off, just a little older than Bradwell, but he feels middle-aged—probably because he never had much of a childhood. Without a father and with his mother taken away and dying young, he was rushed right into manhood while still a little boy.

He only hopes that Pressia isn't forever wrecked by what she did to Bradwell—saved him, yes, but killed him in a way too. A death-blow. El Capitan saw her face when she realized what she'd done, and he knew the one she really loved. It was over. Screw it. El Capitan had to simply move on—no matter how sick it made him feel. Homesickness—that he could fix. Matters of the heart? They just build up scar tissue. He'll be thankful, one day, that she toughened his heart. "Scars are good. Right, Helmud? It's the body's way of making armor."

Helmud is quiet. Maybe his silence means he doesn't agree.

El Capitan keeps pushing through the vines, and after feeling around blindly for a few minutes, he finds the outline of the hatch.

He knows what to expect—the rot of their rations, his smeared blood, the chaos of the crash landing. The aft-bucky—one of the tanks that helped keep them aloft, dirigible-like—cracked in flight. It started taking on air and is the reason they went down. The other buckies might have broken on impact. But he won't know these things unless the airship is running and the diagnostics are functional.

He pulls vines, loosening them enough to open the door.

He's here just to see it, just to be in it again. There's no other place on earth where he's felt so powerful, so in control. He looks down into the airship's interior. The vines choke so much of the light that it's just a dark hole. It doesn't smell like rot. Maybe rats worked their way in and ate the rations.

He swings his legs in first and tells Helmud to hold tight. He lowers their doubled weight down. His boots hit, and the airship shifts a little.

He loves this goddamn airship. "Baby," he says, "I'm home."

The airship has an underwater feel to it now. The vines stripe the windows, cutting up the sunlight. He walks past the seats, crawls through the cockpit door, and steps inside. He walks to the console, runs his hands over the toggles and switches and screens. They're weirdly pristine. In fact, they seem freshly polished. The fractured glass of the window has been replaced. He touches it. No—the glass wasn't replaced. It was somehow mended. He can feel the ripples of where the shatters once were, and the glass has a pale cloudiness to it, just in that one spot.

Who's been down here? Some of Kelly's men? If they fixed the glass, did they fix the aft-bucky too?

He feels hopeful. Is the airship operational? Of course he can't get it airborne. It's held in place by the vines, which have enormous collective strength.

"We might just be able to get this baby up in the air again," he says to Helmud. "God, it felt right being up here at the helm. Didn't it?"

"Didn't it?" Helmud says.

"You'll never get it—not like I do," he says to his brother. "You don't understand, Helmud."

Helmud shifts his weight on El Capitan's back. "You don't understand Helmud," he says.

And he's right. El Capitan used to think he understood his brother because he thought his brother was a moron, a grotesque puppet that sat on his back, forever. But over the past few months, Helmud has changed, come into his own somehow—or maybe Helmud has always been more complicated than El Capitan's given him credit for. "Fair enough," he says to his brother. "Fair enough."

He looks down where there was once the spray of food, the dark stains of his own dried blood, an errant tin cup. "I could have died here."

"Could have," Helmud says.

And then El Capitan remembers Pressia's face, hovering over him—her beautiful face—and the way she touched his head and stared into his eyes. She was afraid he was dying. She wanted to save him. He wanted that to be proof that she loved him. Maybe that's why he kissed her and told her that he loved her. He'd confused her tenderness with love. He was too afraid to tell her how he felt before. He'd wasted his time being a coward while Bradwell was moving in, winning her over. But in that moment, he shook off fear and chose to really live.

He wonders now if he should have told her earlier. Maybe he waited too long. But then Helmud starts humming behind his back—an old love song: *I'll stand right here and wait forever 'til I've turned to stone*—and he knows that it wouldn't have mattered. She wasn't going to fall in love with him anyway. He feels his chest well up. He refuses to feel sorry for himself. "Shut up, Helmud!" he says. "Nobody wants to hear that shit!"

"Shut up, shit!" Helmud shouts back.

"Are you calling me a shit?"

"Nobody!"

"Screw you, Helmud. You hear me? If it weren't for you, Pressia might have been able to fall for me. Don't you know that? Do you think anyone's going to ever fall in love with either of us? We're sick. You understand me? We're grotesque. And we always will be."

Helmud pushes his head into El Capitan's shoulder. "If it weren't for you..."

"If it weren't for me, you'd be dead."

"*You'd* be dead."

"I know. I know," he says. "You think I don't know that we need each other now? I'd have killed you a long time ago if it didn't mean killing myself."

"Killing myself!" Helmud says, like he's lobbing a threat.

"Don't talk like that. Don't be so dramatic. Shut up."

"Shut up. Shut up. Shut up," Helmud says. "Shut up."

El Capitan backs sharply against metal. Helmud lets out a huff of air.

"Shut up," Helmud wheezes once more.

El Capitan slides down and sits there, feeling a pang of guilt for shoving his brother so hard. He hates the guilt. They're still relatively new, these pangs. He didn't really have them before he knew Pressia—or he did but didn't know what they were—and he wishes they'd go away.

He looks at all of the windows curtained with greenery. What's the point of going home if he can't be with Pressia—not here, not ever? "You know what the real wreck is, Helmud? Love. Love is what really wrecks us." He lets his chin drop to his chest. "What do you think, Helmud? Don't just repeat me. What do you really think?"

Helmud is silent for a moment, and then finally he says, "Think. Really think."

El Capitan shuts his eyes. What would Helmud have to say about love and its wreckage? "I don't know what you'd say, Helmud." But then it comes to him—as if they are truly wired together in some elemental way. "Maybe you'd say that we're already wrecked, so what's a little more wreckage?"

"What's a little more wreckage?" Helmud says. "We're already wrecked."

And then there's noise—rustling vines, boot scrapes overhead—and voices. Have others come to claim the airship for themselves? Did they follow El Capitan and Helmud here? Are they armed? There's nowhere to go. "We're trapped," El Capitan says to Helmud.

How many are there? Two, maybe three...maybe more.

"Trapped," Helmud whispers.

PARTRIDGE

IN MEMORIAM

IN THE RECEIVING LINE, Partridge's desire to confess to his father's murder is worse. The grief comes at him like an assembly line. Guards stand on either side of him; Beckley, whom he's come to trust, is to his right. Beckley has offered to move the people along, but Partridge wants to be an approachable leader—real, human. And maybe it's part of his punishment. His own sadness is so fraught with anger that it barely counts as grief, so he has to accept theirs. He's a repository for it, a storehouse.

Partridge looks down the long line for Arvin Weed. This memorial service is reserved for dignitaries, and Weed has certainly become one. They were friends at the academy—not all that close, but still. Arvin was the brain of their class. In fact, he's proven to be smarter than anyone ever would have guessed. He was Partridge's father's personal physician, the one who was going to transplant his father's brain into Partridge's body—his father's plan for immortality, requiring Partridge's death. Weed performed his father's autopsy and declared his death to be by natural causes, but Partridge hasn't seen him since. He wonders if Weed knows the truth, if he covered up the murder for Partridge, if he can be trusted. Partridge could use an ally.

Also, Weed might be the only one he can ask about his father's "little relics," the bodies his father suspended—frozen, but still alive—and kept in the building Partridge lived in before his father's death. Weed might know who's trapped down there and how to free them. Pressia's grandfather is down there and Jarv Hollenback, who's just a toddler. Partridge's father pawned Partridge off on Mr. and Mrs. Hollenback—both on the academy faculty—for the holidays, and Partridge has grown fond of them.

Mr. Hartley, an old neighbor, is next in line. Behind Hartley is his wife and then Captain Westing and the Elmsfords—their twin sons are Partridge's age; he knew them in the academy, and they're now in Special Forces. They're teary-eyed—because they're mourning his father or because Partridge reminds them that they have, in a way, lost their sons? He's not sure.

They shake Partridge's hand with both of theirs—smothering it. They slap his shoulders, hug him so close he can smell their powders and colognes. They cry and pull tissues from their pockets and purses, and blow their noses.

Some others bring their children, as this is as close as they might ever get to the new leader. The heir. "Shake his hand," they tell their kids. "Go on."

"We're so sorry."

"It's such a loss."

"You're holding up so well. He'd be proud of you."

He wants to tell them they're right; his father *would* be proud of him. When a murderer is killed by his own son—the one he always pegged as weak and worthless—isn't there a glimmer of pride, just before death?

Partridge still hates his father. Can you hate someone for forcing you to kill him? Forced. That's how it felt. It doesn't seem right and yet it's why he hates his father most right now.

Partridge watches a young mother, holding a toddler, steady

herself by putting one hand on the glass enclosure surrounding his father's urn. Her thin ribs contract under her black dress as she sobs. One of the cameramen in the crew gets a close-up of her tear-streaked face and her child, who seems to know that this is a somber occasion.

His father doesn't deserve this outpouring.

I killed him, Partridge wants to say. *I killed him, and you should thank me for it.*

Then, when he least expects it, there stands Arvin Weed.

Partridge grabs Weed's hand and pulls him into a hug. "I want you to do a favor for me," he whispers. "Those people suspended on ice. You know about them?" That's all he can get out before the hug is over.

Weed nods. "Yes."

Partridge looks at the line of mourners, the guards—and, not too far off, Foresteed's talking to Purdy. How can he get his point across with all these people around? "I miss the academy," he says. "How are Mr. and Mrs. Hollenback?" Mr. Hollenback taught science. Mrs. Hollenback taught domestic arts at the girls' academy. "And their kids?"

Weed nods, like he understands that the suspended people and the Hollenbacks are linked. "Fine, I think."

"Check on them for me. Especially little Jarv. I miss him." He remembers finding Jarv in the row of glass-enclosed egg-shaped beds that held children with tubes in their mouths and ice crystallized on their skin.

Weed says, "I'm sorry for your loss. I imagine it's almost impossible to get over something like this." Does he mean the death of his father or the fact that Partridge killed him?

"It's good to see you, Arvin," and then, as if overcome with emotion, he grabs Weed again and hugs him. "Belze," he whispers. "He's an old man. Get him out of suspension too." And then he lets him go.

Weed nods and starts to leave, but Partridge says, "Wait. Have you heard anything from our old teachers at the academy?"

"What?"

"You know—our teachers. Do you keep up with any of them?" He wants Arvin to bring up Glassings.

Arvin shakes his head. "Like I have time for that," he says. "I know you won't find them here." He's right. The professors at the academy aren't elite enough for this invite-only crowd. Arvin walks away. Partridge wishes they'd had more time, more privacy.

A ten-year-old is next in line. He's wearing a navy blue suit and a striped tie. He doesn't say a word. He simply salutes Partridge.

"Take it easy," Partridge says. "At ease." The boy is frozen like that. Where are his parents? "You can stop," Partridge says.

One of the cameramen senses the moment and edges in for a close-up of the kid.

Now Partridge has to stand there and accept the salute. But it's clear the kid is waiting for a salute in return. Partridge won't do it. He doesn't want to be seen as a military leader. He doesn't want to align himself with world war and annihilation. He reaches out and ruffles the kid's hair. "Go on now," he says gently. "It's almost time for the service, okay?"

The kid raises his hand and touches his head where Partridge touched it as if awed by the personal contact.

The cameraman zooms in on Partridge. He stares straight ahead, refusing to look directly into the camera. *The truth*, he thinks to himself. *It's time for the truth.*

Finally, the line dwindles, and Partridge is escorted to the front row of the hall.

There is Iralene, the shock of her: her upright posture, creamy skin against her black funeral dress (she seems to have an unlimited supply of them), and her perfect features lilting in the soft sadness of her expression. He specifically asked that she not be here, and yet there she is. Iralene was raised to be the perfect wife, one who does as she's told. She's been groomed for her role so thoroughly that she seems always prepared, but that facade clouds her motives. Partridge rarely knows what she really wants. Did they ask her to leave and did she politely refuse? This is absolutely possible. Iralene can talk people into or out of nearly anything with such stealth that they walk away thinking that they'd just convinced her of something and not the other way around.

Her mother sits to her left—Mimi looks barely stitched together. Her eyes, round with fear, dart around the room as if she's lost. The seat to Iralene's right is empty, reserved for Partridge, of course.

He sits down and leans over to her, whispering, "I told them to let you go home. You've been through too many of these. Seriously, you should take off if you want to."

She touches his knee. "You both need me here," she says, indicating Partridge and her mother.

"Actually, I'm fine." He glances around for another seat nearby, but they're all taken.

"Your father would have wanted it this way." She smiles sadly.

This is the part that's confusing. Iralene knows that he killed his father. She was the one who delivered the poisonous pill to him. So why would she think he'd be moved to do things the way his father would have wanted?

"I wish Glassings was invited," he says.

His name startles her. She whispers, "I heard he stopped showing up for classes. His office is cleared out too."

"How do you know that? Who told you?"

"I do have some friends, Partridge. Your father made sure that there's a handful of academy girls who know me well enough. I have to have *someone* to ask to be my bridesmaids!"

"Bridesmaids? Iralene, you know that—"

"I didn't say I was marrying *you*. Did I?" She touches her hair to make sure it's perfectly straight.

He unbuttons his suit jacket. "Sorry. I didn't mean to . . ."

"Glassings will come through when you need him. No matter where he's run off to."

"I hope," Partridge says. But it makes him nervous that Glassings is gone. There's nowhere to run off to inside the Dome. Nowhere at all.

Someone reaches forward from the row behind him and gives his shoulder a squeeze. Partridge turns and sees one of his father's fellow architects of the Dome from ages ago, Walton Egert. Partridge's father and the other architects called him Gertie. He says, "Stand strong, Partridge. You hear? Stand strong, sonny."

Partridge looks over his shoulder and says, "Thanks, Gertie. Thanks so much." He'd never have been allowed to call Walton Egert by his nickname if his father were alive. It's a power play— Partridge's way of saying, *I'm senior to you now. So why don't you back off on the condescension.*

Gertie gets it. He says, "Of course. You're welcome," and sits back in his seat stiffly, looking side to side to see who else heard it. A few people did, and they look away so as not to add to his embarrassment. It dawns on Partridge at this moment that he's going to have to do that same move a thousand times in so many different ways.

Important people walk to the podium and speak about his father's dedication, intelligence, and foresight, but mainly about how indebted they are to him for saving their lives. The speeches made during these services always make Partridge uncomfortable, and tonight is no exception.

One of his father's advisers leans into the mic, saying, "Willux saved each and every one of us from death, from mutilation. We don't have to live among those wretches: murderers, rapists, monsters—all of them! We were chosen. Let us be worthy of that choice forever." And then he raises his hand and points at Partridge. "We have a new leader now. Willux's only surviving son.

Lead us," he says to Partridge. "Lead and protect us. You are here for us in this turbulent time of sadness and grief, during this time of change. Thank you for rising up and taking your father's place."

Everyone in the room turns and looks at Partridge. The cameramen point the cameras at his face. He feels flushed and yet cold inside. His face is frozen. His eyes move from one camera to the next. Iralene elbows him gently. He nods and gestures back at the man at the podium. The cameras pivot away from him again, and only then can he breathe.

Partridge tells himself that all he has to do is get up after Foresteed's talk and say his lines: *I'm here to represent my family. My father is dead. And now is a time for healing. Thank you for coming, and I hope we can all move into the future with confidence and hope.* Those are the only things that he and Hoppes could agree on. It's as far as Partridge could take it. This is almost over, he tells himself. He hears Gertie's voice in his head—*Stand strong, sonny*—which only churns his stomach.

Foresteed takes the mic. He's saying what he always says: "Ellery Willux was the foremost intellectual of his generation. A man of science, of vision, of innovation..." His voice is perfectly modulated. His eyes tear up on cue, but his jaw is bravely jutted. His voice is edged with enough emotion at one point that Partridge wonders if the guy really loved his father. Willux was charismatic—even when he was the mastermind behind the scenes before the Detonations. How else could he have amassed such unchecked power?

He can still hear Foresteed saying, "Your father wasn't just the biggest mass murderer in history. He was the most successful..." Is that what some of these people are worshipping here?

Foresteed's eyes roam the crowd as he speaks and then lock on Partridge. "May we never forget what he's done for us, and may we carry his legacy into the future."

Partridge's back prickles with sweat. He doesn't want his father's legacy carried into the future.

And now it's Partridge's turn at the mic as if he's the man to *carry his legacy into the future*, and supposedly he is.

Partridge stands and walks along the row of blown-up photographs, which start during his father's days as a cadet in the Best and the Brightest, when he founded the Seven, fell in love with Partridge's mother, and might have started to go a little crazy— perhaps showing just the first few signs of mania, narcissism, and maybe some good old-fashioned paranoia. They move on to photos of him as a lead engineer of the Dome, standing beside more than one president, and, more recently, photos of him inside of the Dome, giving speeches, standing in front of the most recent elite corps of Special Forces.

And then there's one photograph of his father with an arm around each of his sons. Partridge looks lanky, small for his age, and is wearing the worried brow of someone middle-aged. Sedge, on the other hand, went through puberty young. He's tall and thick shouldered. He stands straight and smiles at the camera. They're standing in front of a Christmas tree. It might have been the first Christmas after the Detonations. They have the air of survival. They've gotten through something. They're safe now.

Partridge walks up to the podium set up for the broadcast. He looks out across the audience but can barely see through the glare of the bright lights. He spots Mimi, who looks at him, bleary-eyed. Beside her, Iralene gives him a tight-lipped smile and a nod of encouragement. Foresteed stands along one wall next to Purdy and Hoppes.

As if you don't have lies of your own already, Partridge. If you're going to come clean, why don't you start with yourself?

He coughs into his balled fist and then opens his mouth to state his given lines. *I'm here to represent my family. My father is dead. And now is a time for healing…*

But as he starts to speak, the words that are there are simpler: *I killed my father.*

He panics. What's he going to say to these people? The cameras are pointed at him—it's like being surrounded by oversized eyes. Out there, Lyda could be watching. Everyone is watching. This is actually the first time he's addressed all the people of the Dome.

The first time.

The truth.

It doesn't matter what Cygnus wants from him, what Glassings expects. None of them have gotten in touch with him since his father's death anyway. Why? He doesn't know, but he does know that he's in charge now. He's the leader. It's time for him to lead.

He thinks of Bradwell looking at this footage one day. What if it ends up in his footlocker with all of the other old stuff he's kept? He hears Pressia wondering aloud if he's got enough courage and El Capitan shouting at him, "Say it! Tell them! What are you afraid of? The worst has already happened to us."

Damn it. He's going to be a father himself one day—soon. His own child could see a recording of this moment in the distant future.

He looks out and spots Gertie, who seems too old to look so ashamed, but he is and quickly looks down at his knees. Partridge doesn't want to have to send a message to each and every Gertie in the Dome one by one. No. Damn it. Now's the time.

He opens his mouth again. *If you rob them of their lie, they'll self-destruct.* He can't keep the lie going. He has to be able to look himself in the mirror too.

"Thank you all for coming," he says and glances at Hoppes, who looks pleasantly surprised. Hoppes wanted him to be more conversational, but Foresteed's face darkens. He knows this break from the script isn't good. These people like consistency, normalcy...

Partridge takes a deep breath and grips the podium. "Here's the honest truth about my father. He was the mastermind behind the Detonations. He was a mass murderer." Partridge can feel the air in the room tightening, going silent and still. "I've been outside of the Dome. I've met people who know the truth, including my own mother. My father killed her and my brother too. I was a witness." This feels like the most important thing, suddenly. Giving witness. He sees a flash of his mother and Sedge, the explosion. He looks down at the podium and back up again at the sea of blanched faces, staring at him wide-eyed. He sees Iralene. Her eyes are shining with tears. She shakes her head just the tiniest bit, urging him to stop, but he can't stop now. "The only reason you all needed saving was because he blew up the world as we knew it. My father saved you because he wanted to scorch the entire earth and start over."

Foresteed has started pushing past Hoppes and Purdy up the aisle toward the back of the hall—maybe looking for the person in charge of the cameras.

Partridge speeds up. "Why start over alone? In addition to having the lower class of fused and broken wretches as servants, why not have a more or less handpicked population of like-minded sheep to herd into some new version of the planet that my father wanted to rule, solely? You were his sheep." He shakes his head. "No—he was no shepherd. Not like that. You weren't his sheep. You were his audience. We are all complicit. We let the Detonations happen. We have to be honest. How else can we move forward into the future if we can't at least acknowledge the truth of the past?"

Iralene's mother, Mimi, is out of her seat, marching toward the aisle, saying, "I can't take this! I can't take it!"

Iralene scrambles after her.

Others are standing up too, trying to leave, pulling others with them.

Partridge has lost Foresteed in the lights at the back of the hall, but he hears his voice now. "Cut the mic! Cut it!"

Many voices rise up, but Partridge keeps going. "We owe it to the survivors out there—the ones we call wretches—and we owe it to ourselves. We can do better. We can move into the New Eden with all of our losses. We can own up to them now. And we can feel the guilt at last. If we do, that's how we can maybe—just maybe—be forgiven. I want each of you to know—" The mic cuts out. The spotlight dims. Partridge can see more of the audience now. Those still in their seats are stunned. Their faces are slack with shock, their eyes widened with fear. The boy who saluted him earlier is sitting next to his mother, who's covered his ears with her hands.

It's silent. The cameramen shift away from the cameras, now dead.

Partridge says, "I want each of you to know that I'm going to build a bridge between the Pures and the wretches—from inside the Dome and out. I'm going to make it right again so when we move to New Eden, we're not—" Foresteed is rushing toward him. He would call the guards, but he has no control over them. They answer to Partridge alone. "We're not tyrants and oppressors. We have to say the truth so that we can forgive ourselves and one another and hope to be forgiven by the ones we left out there. The ones we left to die."

Foresteed is standing next to him now, breathless from running behind the scenes. He grabs Partridge's arm and shoves him back a little. "It's okay," Partridge says calmly. "I'm done now."

He steps down from the stage, loosens his tie, and marches down the middle aisle. The guards jog to catch up and flank him on either side. He passes the anteroom and pushes open the double doors.

But he's not outside. He's never *outside*.

For a second, he doesn't know where he's going, but of course he does. He wants to know if Lyda saw the broadcast. He wants to see the one person who'll understand, who'll know he did the right thing.

However his future unfolds, he'll build it around her. That's the next truth that has to go out to the people. He'll force Hoppes' hand. One truth at a time... until there's just one truth left—that he killed his father. He'll hold on to that one.

LYDA

ORIGAMI

THE REPAIRMAN IS LONG LIMBED, wiry, and tall. Lyda imagines him outside the Dome—as a hunter, a scavenger. He might actually do well out there, but then he picks up the broken orb—her Christmas gift from Partridge—and she notices how soft and pale his hands are. He holds the orb so delicately that she knows he's afraid—of her? He showed up so fast that her request must have gone through some special channel. Does he know that she's Partridge's . . . what? Lover? Mistress? What is she?

She knows the words people have used for pregnant, unmarried girls like her—ruined, disgraceful, pitiful . . . These girls had supposedly fallen in love, gotten *caught*. Lyda only heard the rumors. Certain girls disappeared from the academy, and if they came back, they wore shiny wigs, as their heads had been shaved, and they looked pale and frightened—like shrunken porcelain-doll versions of their former selves.

They'd been locked up at the rehabilitation center. Lyda remembers it well—her lonesome cell with its fake light, the rows of pills, the specialists with clipboards, including her own mother who worked there and could barely look at her because of her burning shame. What does her mother think of her now? She hasn't come to visit though surely she knows Lyda's here in this apartment that Partridge has set up for her, Partridge with his newfound power.

And Lyda has a strange power too, she realizes now, looking at the shaking hands of the repairman, but she doesn't understand it. Maybe girls who are ruined, as she is, are known to be wild, to have broken from society in a way that can't be fixed, and therefore the rules no longer apply to them. Is there some freedom in her ruination—even though she's locked up here out of the public eye? Or is it simply her connection to Partridge that gives her power? She can't read the repairman's nervousness.

Lyda's hair is growing back. She tucks just a small bit behind each ear. "Thanks for coming so quickly," she says, testing him a little. "Do you respond to all complaints this fast?"

"These orbs are special!" he says holding it up. "Don't get many calls for them. I actually worked on the prototype for these." Boyd is his name. It's printed on a tag pinned to his shirt. "My first job out of the academy."

The orb is a small electronic device that allows Lyda to change the decor of the room—even the images that appear as views from the bank of windows—so that the apartment can suddenly feel like it exists in some version of Cairo, Paris, the Canary Islands, or the Swiss Alps, and on and on—all during the Before. "You know how this thing really works?" Lyda asks.

"Sure. Yeah. The corrections should be pretty simple." He takes the orb to the small glass-top table in the dining room, pulling out a small set of tools. "Mind if I work on it here?"

"It's fine by me," she says. "Do you want something to drink?"

Boyd looks up at her quickly and then away. "No—no thank you. Nice of you to offer, but no thank you." He sits quickly, blushing, and bows his head to the orb.

He's so flustered that Lyda wonders if he thinks she's flirting with him, trying to seduce him. Maybe others think of her not as pitiful so much as dangerous. She prefers that.

She gets herself a glass of water and sits across from him at the table. "Tell me how it works."

"It's really complicated. Maybe you should watch the broadcast of the memorial service. We were all watching it at work, but then I got this urgent call, so..."

"Urgent? I don't know about that."

"It's the only reason I'm missing the broadcast, which is mandatory. It's running live in every home right now. I think you're supposed to—"

"I don't have to do what I'm supposed to do anymore. That's the upside of being a social outcast."

He jerks his head, nodding quickly. "Still, we should probably have it on. They know, you know, what's on and what's not. I'd just feel more comfortable with it on. I mean...you know."

Lyda gets up and walks to the television but doesn't turn it on. She knows what she'll see—Partridge living a lie. He'll be with Iralene, maybe even holding her hand. On Christmas Eve, he promised her that it would end soon, that someone was in charge of handling this so that Lyda and Partridge can emerge, together. Only a few more days, he promised a few days ago, the last time he saw her—a week tops. With the room set on Cairo and a view of moonlit pyramids out the bedroom window, he confessed that he killed his father. He wouldn't tell her details—only that he hadn't wanted to, but he did it. She understands that kind of thing now, having lived among the mothers and coming to understand survival on the most basic level. But still, his confession made her feel a fissure deep inside of herself. It was right, yes. She doesn't doubt that Partridge felt like he had to do it—for survival or to right the wrongs of the past or to make change inside of the Dome possible. But it was also wrong. Even if it was noble, there's no way around this immutable fact. And it changes a person. Partridge is different now. She felt it before he confessed to the murder, but as soon as he did, she knew it was the reason for the change—a change that's almost imperceptible. "And Lyda," he said to her, "something good has to come of it all. It has to." She knew that he meant he wanted to make this wrong thing the source of something right.

And yes, everything was thrown at him when he came back into the Dome—Iralene was part of a package. It wasn't his fault. Lyda believes him but sometimes wonders how hard he fought for her. Iralene is undeniably beautiful in a way that Lyda always wanted to be but fell short of.

"Are you going to turn it on?" Boyd asks again. But she ignores him.

She leans in close to the screen and sees her own reflection. Her face has grown just a little plump, and her lips are fuller—as if her body knows what's coming.

There's the humming of the air filtration system and yet it feels airless in the Dome—she feels like she can barely breathe. And she's still nauseous sometimes. The bookshelves are stocked with books about pregnancy and childbirth. She's not Lyda. She's the vessel carrying a Willux.

"I can turn it on without sound, Boyd. Is that a compromise you can live with?" Partridge told her what's said at these services for his father, and she can't take the outpouring of adoration.

"I really think we should—"

She glares at him. She still carries the fierceness that the mothers taught her—something she'd always had but never tapped into.

"Fine," he says. "Okay."

She turns on the television and there's Partridge, shaking hands, accepting condolences. A broadcaster is giving a narration of who's standing in line, how they've served the Dome or their relationship with Willux. She hits mute. "Can you reprogram the orb?" she asks Boyd.

"What do you mean? Why would you want to do that?" He looks around the room, and she knows he's searching for surveillance cameras. Partridge assured her that all recording devices were forbidden here. Still, Lyda—and surely Boyd—has doubts.

"I want you to add a world. Can you do that?"

"If the algorithms have been invented, yes. There are lots of shortcuts. It's actually been made so that a layperson can choose between different options pretty easily. Willux wanted these to be made affordable and user-friendly for everyone. They're still a little too expensive to just hand out like candy, but they're getting closer. Where do you want it to take you?"

She imagines wind pushing ash, the cool shadows that she felt right at the edge of the stunted forest, and snow. God, yes—gray snow sifting from the sky. "I want out there."

Boyd stops. His hands freeze. "Out there?" he says in a sharp breath.

She narrows her eyes, looking at him. "Yes."

"But why?" He looks down at the orb and then glances at the television as if the faces there can see him in this room, can hear this conversation. Lyda looks too. A little boy is saluting Partridge. His beautiful hand, his perfect face—so clean and sleek, it seems almost unreal. "What's it like out there?" Boyd asks in a hushed voice.

"Hard to explain," Lyda says. "I didn't really remember the Before so I was shocked by the air, how quickly it spins things. The real sun—it's cast-over but amazing. And the moon too—like a bright bulb in the sky. The people, the Beasts and Dusts, the deformities, the grotesque . . . You can't imagine what beauty there is in their lives. Everything's dirty and real. There's nothing fake or sterile. It's . . . life. You know what I mean?"

Boyd has started crying. Two tears streak his cheeks. He doesn't wipe them away. He says, "I remember it. I'm a little older than you so . . . yes. I know what you're talking about. I used to climb trees. I even fell out of one once and snapped a bone in my hand." He clenches his fist. "Sometimes, when I lie down at night, I remember what it was like to fall through the air and land hard on the muddy ground. I couldn't breathe. All the wind had been knocked out of my lungs. But I just stared up at the blue sky. There were clouds—big, fat, white clouds that seemed to be moving really fast across the sky." He shakes his head. "Goddamn it."

Lyda walks over to the table and puts her hand on his. "I want the detonated world. I want the truth of it," she says. "Will you make it for me? Wind, ash, dirt, dark clouds, everything burned and charred and broken."

"I don't know," he says, glancing at Foresteed on the TV screen. He's just finished his address and is stepping off the platform. "I don't think I'm supposed to..."

"I think you're supposed to do what I tell you to do," Lyda says. She's not sure if this will work. Is this repairman above her social standing because she's ruined, or is he below her because the baby is a Willux? The hierarchies of the Dome are strict, but this is uncharted territory for her. She flattens her voice, trying to make it sound more detached, less shaky. "Do you know who I am? Do you know who's in charge?"

Partridge is going to speak now. He's going to give his remarks, which will end as they always do: *I hope we can all move into the future with confidence and hope.* Lyda helped him with those lines. She might have to point this out to Boyd. She walks to the television and turns up the volume.

But Partridge isn't saying what he usually says. He's telling the people that his father's a mass murderer; he's calling them sheep. No—not sheep. Audience members. He's telling them they're complicit. He wants them to acknowledge the truth. *How else can we move forward into the future?* Lyda's heart starts thrumming in her chest. *We owe the survivors...ourselves. We can do better.* He's still talking—about New Eden, being forgiven...The screen goes blank.

Lyda can barely breathe. Partridge did it. He told the truth. She's thrilled and stunned. This is a vindication. She wants to tell the mothers and all of the wretches outside of the Dome. She wants to shout to Bradwell, Pressia, and El Capitan and Helmud, *He did it!*

But, too, she's scared. This means change—huge sweeping change. The future. She spreads one hand on her stomach. She's started into her second month of pregnancy. She feels puffy, the first hint that her body's going to start to swell. The future, the world their child will live in—it just shifted into a new shape.

She walks back to the table and looks at Boyd. "Did you...?" She can't finish the sentence. She just wants to make sure that she has a witness. She hasn't gone crazy.

Boyd says, "Yes."

"Everything's going to change," she tells Boyd, though in the pit of her stomach, she isn't sure if it will change for the better or for the worse. "Can you believe it?"

Boyd stands up. He looks uncomfortable with his height, his lanky arms. He covers his mouth with his hands and shakes his head.

"What is it, Boyd?"

He doesn't move.

"What is it?" He's a stranger, but still she reaches up and grabs his wrists and pulls his hands from his mouth. "Tell me."

He closes his eyes slowly and then opens them. "It was too soon," he whispers. "We weren't ready."

"We?"

He reaches into his pocket with his right hand and then shakes her hand, as if they're just meeting. She feels the pressure of something he's pushed into the center of her palm. She takes it, hiding it in her folded hand, and then sits down in one of the dining room chairs. She hunches over slowly, and through the glass of the table-top, she sees a small piece of paper—an origami swan.

She looks up at Boyd. He's one of them. He's part of the rev-olutionary movement on the inside, the sleeper cells that were aligned with Partridge's mother—those who wanted to take down the Dome. It's as if some silent prayer has been answered. She feels connected to something larger than just her and Partridge, alone.

She closes her hand over the small paper swan. She thinks, *Too soon? We weren't ready?* Has Partridge just made a terrible mistake? She feels shaken.

"But it's good," she says. "He's going to tell them about us too. This is what he was supposed to do. He had to tell the truth."

Boyd looks down at her hand in her pocket.

She's scared of the swan now. She turns it over in her hands, and sees the edge of a word under one wing. She unfolds it. And there's a message. *Glassings needs your help. Save him.*

Isn't Glassings the one who's supposed to be helping Partridge? Partridge has been hoping to get in touch with Glassings. He needs Glassings, but now he's going to have to save Glassings first? The network that, just moments earlier, seemed like it could help them now feels fragile.

Lyda says, "He promised me that he was going to..." tell everyone about her and the baby. He promised that they would be able to be together—publicly. But she knows that everything's changed now. He told the truth—it was *too soon*. But was there ever going to be a good time to say what he had to say? She's angry now and scared. What's happened to the future?

Boyd doesn't ask her to finish her sentence. He knows there's nothing he'd be able to do to help.

Lyda puts the swan in her pocket. She looks at Boyd. "I'll take care of this when I see Partridge again, but you have to do something for me in return."

"Of course."

"Program the orb the way I asked you to," she says to Boyd. "Will you do that for me?"

"Yes, Ms. Mertz," he says, "of course. I'll do what you tell me to do. That's my job."

Partridge

CONTAGION

Partridge feels the change immediately as he steps onto the street. Everything is different. The air is charged in a way he's never felt before. The noise of muffled voices rises behind the windows of all of the apartment buildings. Most windows in the Dome are sealed shut—the buildings are temperature controlled. Why open a window ever? Frankly, it only invites people to jump, and suicide rates in the Dome are high enough.

Still, he can hear yelling and shouting—muted, yes, but it's everywhere at once. And Partridge knows why. He's taken away their lie—the one that allowed them to function in the world around them. *If you rob them of their lie, they'll self-destruct*, Foresteed had warned. Was that true? Or are they angry at him? Surely, there are the sleeper cells, the Cygnus, who've seen the footage and are rejoicing. Some of this noise could be joyful, right?

As he rounds the corner, Beckley and the two other guards are in step, surrounding him. "Where are you going?" Beckley asks.

"I'm going to Lyda's," Partridge says. "I need to see her."

"I think that might be a bad idea."

Partridge pulls his tie through his collar. He balls it up and shoves it in the pocket of his suit jacket. "If I want your opinions, I'll ask for them."

They pass by Smokey's Restaurant. Some people must have gathered there to eat brunch and watch the broadcast together. Someone spots Partridge through the window and shouts, "There he is! He's right there!"

Partridge doesn't like the hostile tone. He and the guards keep a fast pace, but people pour out of Smokey's double doors and start to follow him.

"Why are they coming after me? What do they expect to happen now?"

"You're the one who called them sheep," Beckley says.

One of the younger guards says, "I'm requesting backup." He pulls out his two-way radio and gives the name of the upcoming cross street.

"Backup? We're fine," Partridge says, trying to laugh. "It's just some people who had brunch."

The small crowd has gotten the attention of others stepping out of shops: a tearoom, a gym, a bank. One teller stands behind a caged window, staring at Partridge. Most of them are silent, as if they're waiting for another speech. But a few call his name.

"Just keep walking," Beckley says calmly.

"Really? Just ignore them?" Partridge says.

"Yes," Beckley says firmly.

Partridge stops. He thinks about doing nothing, but that just doesn't feel like a real option. He turns around quickly and raises his hands in the air.

The crowd stops too. Some turn and walk away, but most just freeze. "I'm not sure what you want, but I gave my speech. I'm not giving any more today."

They turn and stare at each other as if each one is hoping someone else will talk first.

Finally, a young mother holding a baby says, "Partridge, what should we do?"

"About what? The truth?" Partridge says. "You can try to accept it."

A man in a dark gray suit says, "Say it's not true!"

"Let's keep moving," Beckley says in a low voice.

Partridge looks at the man in the gray suit. "What I said is the truth. And I'm not taking it back. In fact, I'm going to lead us into the future with that truth."

"But we're Pure," an older woman says, clutching a crocheted pocketbook to her chest. "That's the truth. We are *Pure*. We deserve what we have."

The woman with the baby says, "God loves us. That's why we're here."

"Yes," Partridge says, "but..."

Another man steps forward. He has a thick belly and broad jowls. He's wearing a dark suit with a button of Willux's face on it, as if Partridge's father were running for some kind of reelection. "You called your father a murderer, you little punk." He spits at Partridge, a white splotch landing at Partridge's shoes, and the crowd suddenly looks like it could turn on him.

The guards move swiftly. One pops the man in his thick gut with the butt of his rifle. He falls to the ground on all fours, huffing.

"Stop!" Partridge says.

"Let them do their job," Beckley says.

The other guard cracks his gun over the man's back. Partridge realizes that the guards are likely coded to do this to any aggressor.

Most of the people turn and walk away quickly, back into storefronts, down alleyways. But some stand their ground.

The man on the ground, now on his side, looks up at Partridge defiantly. His lip is cut; he starts to cough, flecking the ground with blood.

One of the guards pulls the man's arms behind his back and cuffs him with plastic ties that cinch tight. Two guards yank the man to his feet. His teeth are smeared red.

Beckley pulls out his gun, two handed, steady, and levels it at those who remain. "We're asking you all to disperse. Please do so now."

The rest spin off.

"Let's go," Beckley says.

Partridge shakes his head. He can't believe what's just happened. "I don't want people to shut up like that," he says. "I want people to be able to speak their minds, even if they disagree with me."

"Not much you can do about that," Beckley says.

A woman in a white jumpsuit with a bucket walks up, kneels, and without a word, scrubs the man's blood from the ground, making a bleached white stain. Partridge thinks of Bradwell. His lessons in Shadow History—how fast the truth is washed clean.

A car pulls up then—not a golf cart like most people use but a navy blue sedan. Its doors open. A new set of guards file out, flank Partridge, and guide him into the car.

"Take me to Lyda's," Partridge says as he sits in the back seat, wedged between two broad-shouldered men.

"You think this is a taxi?" Beckley says from the front seat.

Doors shut. The car rockets forward, bumping a curb and driving through a public park, over soft turf and past fake trees.

"Where are you taking me?"

"We're on lockdown protocol. You're going to the war room."

"The war room?"

"Your father had to have a secured facility in the Dome," Beckley explains. "The war room is it."

"You really think the people are that angry? You think they're dangerous?"

Beckley keeps his eyes straight ahead. "You forget these are the people who elbowed their way into the Dome, sir. Nothing sweet about them, down deep."

One of the guards makes a very soft bleating noise. "Baa, baa, baa." It's so soft that Partridge isn't sure he really heard it. Did he imagine it or is one of them making fun of his speech—how he called them sheep?

"Who has access to this room?" Partridge says gruffly, trying to maintain his dignity.

"Your father held meetings there, but within it there's a chamber that was only for him. The most secure place in the entire Dome. It's been retooled so that only you can enter it now—retinal scans, fingerprints."

"A war room," Partridge says. "My old man had a war room with a chamber just for him?"

"And now *you* have one," Beckley says.

"A real old-fashioned hand-me-down," Partridge says. He sees his father's face just before he died, his eyes widening as he realized Partridge was killing him. "Why didn't I hear about this before? A room *just* for him? If there was an attack, was he going to come to get me or just leave me at the academy?"

Beckley doesn't say anything. He either doesn't know or doesn't want to tell Partridge the truth.

Partridge remembers his winter holidays with the Hollenbacks. If the survivors had risen up and attacked, is that who he'd have died with? "I want Lyda Mertz to be able to enter it too. Retool it again."

"Lyda Mertz? Are you sure, sir?" one of the guards asks.

"Dead sure." She's the only person he can really trust. If anything happened to him, she could still get in. He won't have a room that only he can enter. He won't be that person. "Get someone to bring Lyda to the war room. I have to see her."

"Yes, sir," Beckley says.

They've come out the other side of the park now. People have taken to the streets. Some wander aimlessly. Others charge through the crowds as if looking for someone they've lost. They shout and cry. One woman stands stock-still, tears rolling down her face.

A few fights have broken out. One woman grabs another by her arm, twisting her bare skin. Two young men are on the ground, pummeling each other.

"Hopefully they'll wear themselves out," Beckley says.

Partridge isn't so sure. They've held on to a lot of guilt and anger and blame for a long time. "What if this is just the beginning?" Some guards jog down an alleyway in tight formation. More appear on the other side of the street. "I don't want this to get bloody," Partridge says.

"Did you really think that you could do what you did without bloodshed?" Beckley says.

"I want peace, Beckley. That's what I'm after. In here and out there."

"And that's usually paid for in blood," Beckley says.

Partridge recognizes some of the faces here and there—not anyone he can attach a name to, but there are only so many faces in the Dome. They circulate and become familiar. But maybe it's hard to place them now because they look different—desperate, helpless, lost.

A few people spot the long dark car and assume there's someone important inside of it, so they run after it for a block or two, gesturing wildly and angrily. One boy is fast. He jumps onto the back of the car, pounding it with one fist. "Slow down! There's a kid on the car!" Partridge says.

"You want him to climb inside?" the driver asks.

"I said slow down!"

The driver slows the car but then fishtails enough that the boy jerks backward and then falls to the ground, stunned.

Partridge stares out the back window—the boy is on his back, kicking the ground, while others are running and shouting and brawling. Amid the chaos, there's an older man, wearing a necktie, standing in the middle of the street. Partridge knows this man. Tommy. That's all he has—a first name. Tommy was his father's barber. He got dressed up for the broadcast. His sport coat is folded over his arm. His chin tucked to his chest, he rubs his eyes. Is he crying? He then staggers a little and stares straight up as if expecting to see the sky.

Surrounded by bodyguards, Partridge is ushered from the car and taken to the set of elevators reserved for the Dome's elite. The war room is buried in the core of the Dome on the lowest subterranean level. The elevator doors open, and they step into a building with mazelike halls that echo loudly with the clomp of their bootheels.

One of the guards opens the door to the war room with a series of codes typed into a wall-mounted keypad. The door opens, revealing a long mahogany table surrounded by leather chairs. The walls are covered with black screens, now dark and glassy, almost wet-looking.

The guard ushers Partridge in along with Beckley.

Partridge walks the length of the table and runs his hand over the back of the chair at the head of the table. His father's chair. His father's body was once here. His mind flashes on his father's face again—his skin festered red and, in some spots, already blackened with necrosis, and his hands, curled inward, shaking with a constant palsy. Willux had overdosed for decades on drugs to enhance his mental abilities. It caught up with him, causing Rapid Cell Degeneration. Partridge tries to remind himself that his father had done himself in, but it doesn't mute the guilt. There's no way to let it go. "Has anyone been inside the chamber since my father's death?"

"No, sir," Beckley says. "We were under strict orders only to retool the codes. We weren't allowed to enter—only outfit it so that you could."

Partridge wonders if this room is really meant for his protection—or was it a trap, a way to eliminate him if he didn't perform exactly as the Dome wanted him to? Is this something that his father dreamed up for his successor, or has it been rigged by Foresteed so that he can take over? Partridge feels a cool ridge of sweat across his back, and he thinks about his father, who was a leader for so long. Is this the kind of doubt and suspicion he lived with all the time? Is that why he ruled with such an iron fist?

Partridge looks at the guard who opened the door. Partridge has never been completely sure who he can trust. Even his trust of Beckley has been hard-earned and sometimes feels shaky. But now that he's spoken the truth about his father, Partridge is even less sure who's been rocked by that news and how they might decide to turn on him. These are the Pures—not the types to rise up. But he still has to be careful. He glances at Beckley, trying to gauge his read on this guard. Partridge doesn't want to go into the chamber only to be isolated and get attacked.

Beckley looks back at him calmly. "You okay?" he asks.

"Fine," Partridge says. He has no choice but to trust those around him. They're all he has. "Let's see it."

Beckley nods to the guard, who reaches under the head of the table, perhaps pressing a button hidden there, and one wall breaks into panels and opens, revealing a door.

On the other side of the door could be his father's secrets. He's never understood his father. His father was so absent—even when he was in the same room, his mind was working on something else. Partridge doesn't remember ever having the feeling that his father was actually looking at him. His father was more than aloof. He seemed nearly hollow. But he hadn't always been like that; there was something about his father—once upon a time—that had made Partridge's mother fall in love with him. Hadn't he once been funny? Thoughtful? Maybe even a little vulnerable?

He's also well aware that on the other side of the door there might be proof that he could offer the people here—proof that his father was the mastermind behind it all, that the people on the outside need their help.

He walks up to the door. "How do we do this?"

"You look into this beam of light for the retinal scan," the guard says, "and press your hand on this square to check your fingerprint." The beam is blue and it appears from a small camera-like lens in the wall. The square is made of glass, but it too has a bluish glow.

Partridge leans into the beam. Something inside of the lens clicks. He presses his hand to the glass square, and he hears another series of clicks. Partridge puts his hand on the knob, but the door opens automatically. The room is dark.

Beckley moves forward to usher him in.

"Wait for me outside," Partridge says. "All the way out. In the hall."

"Yes, sir," Beckley says, and he tells the rest of the guards to back out of the room.

Partridge steps just inside the dark room; he can tell that it's relatively small, and it feels cluttered. From the dim light cast by the war room, he can see that the chamber walls are covered in something that seems to shiver. He thinks of wings—the birds on Bradwell's back and how, when they shifted, his shirt would flutter.

Is his father's chamber filled with batting wings? He wants to call this off, back out of the room, but he can't. He's gone too far now. They'd know he's afraid.

It's not logical, but he feels like he's about to move into his father's mind. He always sensed that his father held infinite secrets, that he seemed so absent because there was a version of himself that he refused to share. A secret self.

And Partridge has uncovered so many secrets—destruction,

death, so many layers of lies. He doesn't want to know any more of them.

He shudders then takes a step past the threshold.

Immediately, the lights flicker on. The room fills with light. The door slams shut behind him.

The walls are covered with sheets of paper—hundreds, maybe thousands of them. Some are glossy and thick, others white and papery.

The glossy sheets are photographs, and the papers are covered in his father's handwriting. Partridge walks to a wall. He sees his mother's face, poised over a baby swaddled in a blanket. Sedge is at her side, peering at the baby. It's Partridge, a newborn.

He looks at the paper taped to the wall beside the picture. It's a letter. It reads,

To my beautiful wife,
I remember you in this moment. Was I there? Do I only have a mem-
ory of looking at this photograph? Our lives are layered like this.
I miss you still. I miss you always. You're mine. Don't forget that.
Mine.

Ellery

Partridge moves to the next sheet of paper.

To my beautiful wife...

And the next: *To my beautiful wife...*
And then he finds one that begins,

Dear Sedge,
What happened? Why did you turn away from me? Why...

Did Sedge ever turn away from his father?

Partridge,
Look at how young you once were. You used to shout and sing when
I came in the door, and now you're grown. An Academy Boy . . .

His father's brain was affected by the enhancements. It was deteriorating, and he was willing to sacrifice his own son to be able to live on. Partridge whispers through his dry lips, "My father was insane."

Partridge reaches up and grabs the letter. He balls it in his fist. His father was writing letters to them all this time? He was making a walk-in photo album, a display. And he kept it to himself all these years.

Partridge pulls loose a photograph of himself at five on a bike, of Sedge in his ice hockey gear, of his mother and father dressed for a formal occasion.

His love and hate for his father churns within him. Who was Ellery Willux? Did he love them after all? Is this place proof that he couldn't show it?

Partridge lunges at the wall and tears down as many photographs and letters as he can. They fall to the floor. He drags his hands down the walls, ripping one swatch and then the next. His chest contracts. He feels like his heart is clenched, and his breath is suddenly shallow. He holds his fist to his chest. "Damn it," he says.

And he staggers to the only chair in the chamber, the one behind his father's desk. He sits down heavily and slowly looks around the room. This is everything he ever wanted from his father. Some show of his love. Some gesture of affection. And all along he was building *this*?

He hears a knock on the door.

"I told you to wait in the hall!" he shouts, then tries to catch his breath. Is he having a heart attack? Jesus, is his father trying to kill him with this shit?

"It's me. Lyda."

Lyda. He pushes himself up from the chair and moves to the door. He turns the knob and, as before, the door opens automatically.

There she is. He takes her in for a moment—her face, her lashes, her parted lips.

"You told the truth," she says, astonished.

For a second, he's not sure what she's talking about—saying all those things at the service feels like it happened a long time ago. "I was hoping you were out there, watching." He pulls her in close. He smells the lavender scent of her perfume. "I told them to bring you here. I had to see you," he says. "Come in here with me."

"What is this place?"

He puts his hand on the small of her back and guides her into the chamber. She looks around at the floor littered with photos and letters, and at the walls splotched with tape. "Partridge," she says, "was this your father's room?"

"His secret chamber." He's relieved that she's here. She's like an antidote to his father's lonesome madness. She brings sanity to this room. He can focus on her and let the rest of it all blur behind her.

"Why did he do this to you?"

"To me?" Partridge asks. "What do you mean, *to me?*"

She looks up at him, surprised. He can tell that she's holding back. She doesn't want to say something that will hurt him. She's not good at hiding it.

And then it hits him, and he looks around the room again—this time seeing it the way she sees it. Is this all for show? His father must have worked on this for years—long before he'd planned to use Partridge's body to move on. Is this room some kind of prank? Are all of these photos and stupid letters an attempt to wrench Partridge's heart? Or maybe it was originally designed to mess with Sedge. He was the rightful heir.

Is this all fake? A ploy to garner sympathy? A final power grab at love?

"Do you think he's messing with me still?"

She walks to Willux's desk with its shiny surface. She circles behind it and pulls out his chair.

"Don't," Partridge says.

"Why not?"

"I don't know. It's just . . ."

"What?"

"This room. It feels like it's filled with contagion. Don't you feel him in here? His presence? It's like he's not dead. Not in here, at least. He fills up the room, the air." Partridge wonders if the contagion he feels is his own toxic guilt. He looks at the faces of his family staring up at him accusingly. He was once a baby; now he's a murderer.

"This room is yours now," she says.

"What if I don't want it?"

She walks toward Partridge, kneels down, and picks up another picture of him as a baby. In this one, Partridge is wearing a cap. His face is a bright pink. And it's his father who's holding him. "You were a pretty baby," she says. She stands up and hands it to him. He stares at it for a minute. And in an unexpected rush of longing, he wants to go back. He wants to be that baby again. He wants to do it all over.

But he can't let his father get to him. He was led here, and he'll use this room for his own end. He'll use his father's secrets against him, try to undo what his father's done.

He hands the picture back to Lyda, walks to his father's desk, and says, "What else does he have hidden in here?" He won't sit in his father's chair again. He pushes it back from the desk and then presses his hands flat against the glossy surface. Suddenly the desk lights up.

Before him is a map of the world, dotted with blue lights, each of them pulsing except for one—located on the map where the Dome stands. It glows.

"What the hell?" Partridge whispers.

Lyda walks up and stands beside him. "It's the world and that's us."

"Yeah," he says. "So the question is what do all the blinking lights represent?"

"*What* do they represent, or *who*?" Lyda says quietly.

Partridge's skin feels suddenly chilled. "These could be other places that were spared. Could it mean that there are other survivors out there?"

"Touch one," she says.

Partridge thinks of Pressia's father, Hideki Imanaka. He was one of the Seven. One of the tattoos still pulsing on his mother's chest before she died was proof that he was still alive. Maybe this is one way to find him. One of the flashing lights is on the island of Japan. Partridge reaches out and touches it.

Static rises up from unseen speakers, and then a voice. "Partridge." It's his father's voice, and for a second, he thinks that his father's still alive, that the murder wasn't a success. He looks at the door to the chamber, but it's closed. Lyda reaches out and grabs his hand. Is his father back from the dead? Is he unkillable? "My son," his father says.

"No." Partridge feels dizzy. He grips the edges of the desk and sits in his father's chair.

His father's voice goes on: "Your fingerprint—that tiny swirl that's been there since birth. You found this room, this map, my world. You unlocked my voice with a single touch. And this means only one thing: You're alive and I'm dead."

"Lyda," Partridge whispers. "I can't listen to this."

She grabs his arm. "It's okay," she whispers. "We have to."

"With that touch, a message has now gone out to all the others that I'm gone and you're in charge. Did you really think I was content with just one little Dome to take care of?"

Partridge wants to press the heels of his palms over his ears, but he can't move. He can barely breathe. He killed his father, and his father's still here.

"Open the top desk drawer. There, you'll find a list of my enemies—now they're yours. You'll find out the truth that I've hidden from everyone—even you. You'll find the simple, honest irony of everything I've tried to accomplish. Hopefully you'll understand the fragility of what you've inherited. You might hate me. I understand. I hated my parents too. This is the way of the world. I saw the end, Partridge, and I was trying to save you from it. Believe what you want, but this is what fathers do." His father pauses then. Did Willux see his own end in sight? What end? "One more thing," his father says. Is he going to sign off by telling Partridge he loves him? What does Partridge really want from the dead man?

His father lowers his voice and says, "A question. Is there blood on that fingerprint now?"

There's another brief burst of static and his father's voice is gone.

It's silent. He stares across the map with its blue lights. His breath feels high and tight in his throat. He flips over his hands and looks at his fingertips—the tiny intricate swirls that are his and his alone. His father knew that if Partridge was listening to this recording then he probably killed his father.

Lyda whispers, "He knew you'd do it."

"Don't," Partridge says.

"He's still in power." Her voice is cold, or maybe fearful.

He lifts his head and turns to look at her. "No," Partridge says. "I killed him."

Lyda's face looks pale and stiff. "He's still..." She pulls her hands up to her throat, tightening her fists. He stands up and she backs away. "It's changed you, Partridge. Part of your father knew you'd do it, knew you were capable of killing him, and it's changed you deep down." She backs against a wall, the photographs rattling.

"What else could I do? Let him kill me?"

"No," she says, shaking her head angrily. "It's just…"

"Just what?" He remembers the feeling he had just after he'd done it. His hands went numb. He couldn't feel his legs. He couldn't think. His heart was pounding, though, like it was the only thing left. And he feels that now because Lyda's never been afraid of him like this, and he can read it on her face so clearly. "Lyda," he whispers.

"I don't know," she says. "It's another secret. We grew up with all of these secrets and lies. How can we keep living this life, Partridge? I don't know if I can…" She takes a deep breath, quickly touching her stomach. The baby. The future.

"Without you, I'll be alone in this," he says. "Don't turn your back on me."

"I'm not." She glances around as if adding, *I have nowhere else to go.* But then she reaches into her coat pocket. "We're not completely alone." She pulls out a crumpled piece of paper. He walks to her and she hands it to him. "They're here—the sleeper cells: Cygnus, the swan."

It's an origami swan. "They made contact with you?"

"Read it."

Partridge unfolds a wing and reads *Glassings needs your help. Save him.* "Who gave this to you?"

"The tech who came to fix the orb."

"Save Glassings from what? Where the hell is he?" he says.

"This is all I've got." She sighs and then rubs her eyes. "Are you going to open the drawer?"

"What?"

"I think you should do it."

"I watched my father all my life, you know—how people looked at him and how he was spoken to. I didn't mean to, but I took it all in, and I think, on some level, I must have thought my father's life would one day be mine. I mean, he was my father." He stops abruptly. He draws in a sharp breath. He's worried that he's going to cry. "It's not just that I killed him, Lyda. It's not just that I'm a murderer." He rubs his thumb against his fingertips, thinking of his father talking about blood on his fingerprint. "It's that I'm afraid I'll become him."

"Open the drawer," Lyda says.

Partridge isn't going to argue with her—not now. He puts a finger on the blue lit square on the top desk drawer. It glides open, revealing a stack of folders.

He picks up the top folder and drops it on the desk. Just like his father said, its label reads ENEMIES. He opens it up. It's filled with people's pictures, each with a page of data—suspicious activity, family, friends, affiliations.

Partridge flips through the stack, and Lyda walks over, close enough to see the faces. He stops when he comes to Bradwell. Lyda gasps, and he knows it's because she recognizes the background too—the woods where his mother and brother were killed. The picture is of Bradwell shouting, the cords of his neck taut; he's caught mid-action, and Partridge realizes that this picture was taken from a video stream of one of the Special Forces soldiers who attacked them. This picture was taken minutes before his father killed Sedge and their mother.

"Go on," Lyda urges. "Who else is there?"

He turns to the next photo, and there's a picture of El Capitan and Helmud from that same place on that same day. He closes the folder and shoves it back in the drawer. "These aren't my enemies," Partridge says. It's a relief. His father was wrong.

There's another folder. He reaches in and pulls it out.

NEW EDEN.

He opens it and skims plans—handwritten in his father's loose scrawl—to enslave the wretches as a subhuman class to serve the Pures once the earth is habitable again. "New Slavery for a New Eden," Partridge says, his stomach twisting. He shuts it.

The next folder is called REVERSAL. His father usually goes for more symbolic references, so this practical word makes him nervous. He flips it open so he and Lyda both can read together.

First there's an official report from a team of scientists and doctors. The list of names at the top of the report is lengthy, but the name Arvin Weed pops out at him. He points to it. "Look."

"I saw it too," Lyda says.

From the samples collected and the incubation of those samples in a simulated environment, our specimens did poorly overall. Of the twenty, twelve died within the first ten days. Four contracted cancerous tumors that took root almost immediately and seemed to thrive in their healthy tissues. Two of these four were cured of the cancers but died from more growths within the year. The four survivors—one male and three female—have fared poorly overall. Two are sterile. The male has contracted an eye disease, rendering him blind. He and one female have asthma and compromised lungs. We do not expect them to be able to rejoin the general population within the Dome. The male is in a critical-care unit, and the female suffers mental problems and is currently in solitary confinement in the rehabilitation center. The other two are being studied and evaluated. They have been released back into the public with their memories of this study erased.

In conclusion, we believe that those who survived in the Dome have, by lack of exposure to the outdoors and to disease in general, become more vulnerable over time. If we move into New Eden, we will lose a large number of people within the first year. Those who survive will be far outnumbered by the survivors outside of the Dome. However, the longer we wait to enter New Eden, the more vulnerable our population will be to the elements that will kill us.

Meanwhile, the original survivors of the Detonations have been weeded out, leaving only those with extreme abilities to adapt and survive. The remaining have superior immune systems. Operation Wretch Purification contains the most detailed information about the survivors of any of our observational studies.

Partridge's father circled the word *Wretch* and wrote in the margin two words: *Superior Race.*

Partridge lifts the sheet of paper and studies his father's letters. "My father created a superior race after all, but it happened to be the wrong one." That's the irony. His father knew it before he died. He said that he could see the end and that he was trying to save Partridge from it.

"Did he think we'd have to live here forever?" Lyda asks. "We can't. The resources are limited. Was he just going to let the Pures die out?"

"I don't know." Partridge flips to the back of the report. The final page is just a bunch of scientific equations—nothing he could ever sort out. "What the hell is this?"

She says sarcastically, "Like the academy would think it was worthwhile to teach girls science. Keep it," Lyda tells him. "It could be important." He folds it and puts it in his pocket.

Partridge thumbs through a few more folders and then his back goes rigid.

He pulls out a folder. It's labeled PROTOCOL FOR ANNIHILATION.

"What's that mean?" Lyda asks. "He's already annihilated everything."

"Not everything." Partridge opens the folder.

There is a list of instructions explaining how to engage a voice-activated process. A sketch of the room points to a small metal square on one of the walls. They both look up, and there it is, unassuming, the size of a wall socket. With a set of commands, the metal will retract, revealing a button. If pressed, it will "release an odorless gas outside of the Dome." The gas is "carbon monoxide based," but more potent. It will "induce sleep" and then compromise the lungs and cause silent mass death. The gas would kill all living creatures within a one-hundred-mile radius. Willux has written that the voice activation knows his own voice only, but then this has been scratched out and Partridge's name added.

"He taught the computer to respond to my voice? To kill all living creatures in a one-hundred-mile radius?"

"But they're the super race," Lyda says. "Why would he want to kill them?"

"Maybe it was my father's plan B." Partridge shoves the folder into the drawer and slams it shut.

Lyda turns and stares at the photographs on the floor. "You and your father are different people," she says. "You're not him. You never will be."

"I had to do it," he whispers. "I had to kill him." He hunches forward, rocking a little. He rubs his eyes.

"Come back home with me," Lyda says. "I have a surprise for you." Is this her way of telling him that she's not afraid of him anymore, that he hasn't really changed, that she won't turn her back on him? She turns to him and wraps her arms around him. They hold each other tight, and he wants to freeze this moment. Right here, now.

There's a knock at the door that startles both of them.

Beckley says, "Sir, the situation's gotten worse."

Partridge doesn't let go of Lyda. "Worse how?"

"We need you, sir."

Partridge doesn't feel like a leader. His father's still calling the shots from the grave. "I don't know that there's anything I can do."

"There's a death toll," Beckley says. "It's rising."

Partridge lets go of Lyda, rushes to the door, and opens it.

There's Beckley. He's a little out of breath; his eyes dart between Lyda and Partridge. "People are killing each other?"

"No, sir."

"Then what?"

"They aren't killing each other. They're killing themselves."

PRESSIA

DUTY

Fedelma leads Pressia down a long hall with a stone floor. Each door they pass has a small window. Pressia glimpses labs, people curled to delicate scientific work—test tubes, machinery. "What are they doing?" she asks.

Fedelma stops and looks at her. "You know what they're doing, Pressia."

"No," she says, "I don't." But some part of her wonders if she just doesn't want to know, if the truth is too chilling, and so she's shutting out the obvious.

"Surely you can imagine our greatest challenge and how we might overcome it. You've seen the children. You know what we can do with mere vines. You've seen the boars in the fields, right? Haven't you?" She seems angry suddenly. "And me. You know my lot."

Pressia glances at Fedelma's stomach and now she understands: Fedelma hasn't chosen to be pregnant. It's her duty. How many children has she had? How long will this go on? "I didn't go to school," Pressia tells her. "All I know is what my grandfather told me. He was a flesh-tailor, a mortician. How would I know what's going on in labs?"

"You came here for a formula. You had one of the most potent vials of bionanotechnology known to man. Do you expect me to believe you don't understand what we're doing here? This is child's play compared to what you dug up." She starts marching down the hall again.

Pressia reaches out and grabs Fedelma's arm. "I don't know. I swear."

Fedelma's eyes search Pressia's face. She still doesn't completely believe Pressia, but she says, "Willux saved Newgrange, the holy site. He gave Kelly word that it would be spared. Only thirty of us made it inside of the mound in time."

"But there's all this land, this building, and labs, right? What about all of that?" Pressia wants to know how advanced these people are. Can they repair an airship and get it off the ground?

"Willux spared a three-mile radius. And you must know how the Detonations worked. You can't play dumb on that score." She glances at Pressia's doll-head fist. "You lived through them, didn't you?"

"I barely remember," Pressia says. "But it comes to me in flashes. I know there were massive cyclones of fire that swept through. And the ash blew in and there was black rain. Did anyone outside of Newgrange survive?"

"Another twenty survived that, making fifty, but with disease, we dwindled again."

"And what did Kelly do then?"

"Everything he could."

"This place," Pressia says, "it's not like where we come from. The ash eaters, for one thing. He's invented all kinds of things, hasn't he?" The more information that Pressia can get out of Fedelma, the more she has to share with El Capitan and Bradwell. If she wants Bradwell to forgive her, maybe the first step is making him see that she's valuable, that they still need to rely on each other if they're going to make it back.

"Well, he had a background in the genetic engineering of plants and molecular-level cloning. He created agrifacture, which is why our vines work as a defense team."

"Cloning." She knows what this means, in a general way. Replications. Copies. "How do you do it?"

"We use our DNA to create clones," Fedelma explains. "But each embryo still needs a womb to develop inside of. All of the women do their part. I will carry babies to term until, eventually, I can no longer do it; even if I die in the process, it's worth the risk." And then she adds, defensively, "We can't risk dying out!"

Pressia feels a chill spike up her backbone. *Look in a looking glass. Look for a match. Find yourself! Find yourself! Don't be the last!* The children meant it literally. Find a match; find a copy of yourself. Pressia has slowed her pace. She's thinking of the children's faces— the ones that were nearly mirror images. Finally she stops walking altogether.

Fedelma turns around. "Are you judging us? We all make sacrifices. It's the only way to be of worth!"

"I'm not judging you. I understand sacrifices," Pressia says. She thinks of Bradwell. She wasn't willing to sacrifice him, though that's what he wanted. "The boars..." she says, trying to piece it together.

"Some gene splicing, yes. They're engineered to be domesticated like cattle but vicious too. If need be, they will attack on our behalf."

"Attack who?"

Fedelma walks up close. Though no one is around, she lowers her voice. "You have to be careful. Beyond the three-mile radius, the territory we have marked with the vines, there are those who want in—who'd kill for what we have here."

"Who are they?"

"They're not unlike what you have in your part of the world."

Pressia says, "How do you know what we've got in our part of the world?"

Fedelma whispers, "He spared us. He knows we're here. He keeps tabs on us, and probably others."

"Who? Willux?"

"We're lucky to be alive at all."

"Willux and Bartrand Kelly are still in contact? They're still...friends?" Pressia squeezes her eyes shut and shakes her head. "Willux knows you're here! Alive!"

"Shhh," Fedelma says. She takes Pressia's hand and places it on her stomach. Pressia feels a thump from within. "We have the future to protect. You understand, don't you?" Fedelma says.

Pressia pulls her hand away. "Where's Bartrand Kelly?"

Fedelma sighs. "He wants you to wait for him." She continues down the hall.

Pressia follows her. They turn a corner and stop at the door to a small room. Fedelma says, "Here. You'll wait." She pulls open the door.

Pressia's stomach flips. Will Bradwell be here? Is he going to speak to her? Will he even look at her? She tries to think of something to say to him but can't imagine where she'd even start. She steps inside.

The room is small—just an oversized closet really. No furnishings. El Capitan is there, leaning against the wall with Helmud resting his head on his shoulder. One of El Capitan's eyelids is puffed and red—the early shades of a black eye. El Capitan straightens up and says hello in a formal way. Helmud smiles. "Hello," he says.

She'd been so afraid to see Bradwell she'd forgotten that everything between her and El Capitan is strained. He professed his love for her and kissed her. Where do they go from here? She feels stiff and shy. El Capitan glances at her and then quickly away.

"Hi," she says. She feels flushed. What El Capitan did was so dramatic, so full of emotion. It was brave. This is what she admires about him—and that he's tough and yet has a tender heart. She still remembers the kiss.

"Kelly will be here directly," Fedelma says, and she shuts the door.

"Bradwell isn't here. I don't know where he is," El Capitan says, as if she'd only want to see Bradwell and not him.

"I'm glad to see you two," Pressia says. "You're not bleeding to death. It's a real improvement."

"And we're all golden," El Capitan says, "like movable statues."

"Golden," Helmud says.

"Yeah," Pressia says, looking at her arms.

"It looks good on you," El Capitan says and then looks down at the floor.

"Cap," Pressia says, though she's not sure what she should say next—*I hope it's not strange between us? I hope we can still...*

But then the door opens again. Pressia knows it's Bradwell before she turns. The deep rustling of his wings is noisy. She hears Fignan beeping at his boots.

"I'll wait out here." It's his voice.

She turns and sees his quick dark eyes, his wind-struck cheeks, the gold tinge to his skin too. The wings are long and ragged—but also muscular and beautiful.

"No room for me in there," he says to a caregiver at his side, a nervous young man. "Can't you see that?"

"Sorry, so sorry," the caregiver says. "I'll wait with you out here."

Before the door swings shut, Bradwell looks at Pressia like he wants to say something. She opens her mouth to ask him how he's doing. But he turns before she has the chance. The door closes and he's gone.

EL CAPITAN

BACTERIUM

BOARS!" BARTRAND KELLY SAYS as he walks across the fields. "I'll want to start with the boars!"

Pressia glances at El Capitan who shrugs.

"Boars!" Helmud says.

El Capitan elbows his brother behind his back. "Shut it," he whispers.

Bradwell walks a few paces behind them with Fignan alongside him. He's all shoulders and ribs—bigger and broader than anyone El Capitan's ever seen, aside from Special Forces. The birds in his back must be large, though they're hidden by their thick, broad wings, which are so big they hunch up around his neck and trail behind, frayed like old, worn hems. Every once in a while Bradwell's wings arch from his back, revealing the thick angular overgrown bones and dense feathers of the birds. El Capitan feels for him. He knows what it's like to haul something around on your back forever. Still, Bradwell's got it easier than El Capitan, right? At least his birds don't talk back.

Kelly is the one talking now. He's backtracked from boars and is giving a lecture about Ireland from the Before—its monuments, its fertile earth, its rich history, its poets. El Capitan isn't interested in a tour of the past. He wants to know where Kelly's taking them and the status of the airship. When he and Helmud were found in the cockpit, El Capitan put up a fight. It turns out the guards didn't want to kill him. They just wanted him out of there. They beat him up enough to subdue him and then marched him back to his room. He asked them about the airship—if they'd fixed it, if it could fly—but they refused to answer.

Kelly's out in front of them walking with great energy and purpose, swinging a leather satchel. The green fields are empty. The wind cuts across them. It makes El Capitan's eyes tear—especially the one that's puffed nearly shut.

El Capitan learned to ride a bike in a field like this. His mother rigged a towel under his arms, around his ribs, and ran beside him until he had enough momentum to keep going—wind in his hair, bumping over the grass. When he thinks of it now, he imagines himself as light—not just without the weight of his brother but without the weight of his life.

They're approaching a distant barn on the rise of a hill. Fignan powers through the fallen grass, his lights flashing across the top of his black-box exterior. "So where are you taking us?" El Capitan says, interrupting Kelly. "To the airship?"

Kelly turns around and looks at El Capitan as if noticing him for the first time. "I heard that's where they found you. It's going to take a couple more days to get it ready for the air. You took a little tour of it, did you?"

"It wasn't a tour really. It's my ship," El Capitan clarifies.

"It's *my* ship," Helmud says, which sounds like he's contradicting El Capitan. El Capitan particularly hates when Helmud does this in front of others.

"Really?" Bartrand Kelly stops and thinks about this. "Because I thought you'd stolen the airship." He turns and starts marching again uphill into the wind. El Capitan can hear it gusting against Bradwell's wings.

"It was my airship to steal," El Capitan says. "Willux blackened the whole earth. He owed me one."

"You had other options."

"Did I? Because I'd like to know what those were, exactly."

"How do you know he stole it?" Pressia says, but she seems to know the answer. El Capitan feels out of the loop. He glances at Bradwell to see if he seems to know something El Capitan doesn't, but Bradwell's expression is steely and unreadable.

Kelly doesn't respond, and moments later, they reach the barn. He stops in front of its door, lifts a heavy latch, and swings the door wide. "I know things. I have my connections," Kelly finally says.

The barn has a few high windows. Shafts of light pour in, filling the dusty air with sun. They follow him in, Fignan first. One side of the barn has narrow stalls—twenty or more—all filled with massive boars. Their ribs are as wide as cow ribs. Their backs are arched. Their backbones are almost as big as fists running along a ridge divided by mounds of flesh. They have dark hooves and thick yellowed tusks that curl up from the sides of their large rubbery snouts.

"Connections?" El Capitan says. There's only one person he could be connected to who'd have information about this airship, right? "You're in touch with Willux, aren't you?"

"Well," Kelly says as he brushes his hands off and then crosses his arms on his chest, "I was, but not anymore."

"Why's that?" Bradwell asks. His voice seems rough from disuse.

"Because he's dead."

"Dead?" Pressia says.

The wind sweeps in and then hushes. It's like Willux's ghost—just a breath of him, here then gone. El Capitan's mother believed in ghosts. For the moment, he can't accept that Willux is dead. But then El Capitan has always thought of Willux as death itself. The mothers called all men Deaths, but Willux was the hardened sediment of it. El Capitan knows that it's the truth. Willux is dead. It feels right—deep down. He's gone.

It's quiet as the news settles over them. There's only the noise of what must be the boars' grunting and the light hum of Fignan's engine. El Capitan can feel Helmud holding his breath. El Capitan looks at Pressia and Bradwell, who look like they can't quite believe it.

Pressia says to Kelly, "How do you know? Are you sure?"

Kelly nods emphatically.

"He's really...dead?" Bradwell says. His face looks conflicted.

"That's what I said," Kelly says. "Is it so hard to imagine?"

Bradwell nods. He's breathing a little hard. "It's just...I didn't expect for it to be this quiet. This matter of fact. I was expecting..." He grabs the front of his own shirt. "I wanted..."

"Yes," Pressia says, as if picking up his thought. "It should be bigger. It should feel like more of a..."

"Relief," Bradwell says. "Or ending." But he doesn't look at Pressia. He turns away from all of them. El Capitan wonders if Bradwell's disappointed. The man who ordered his parents' assassinations is dead, and Bradwell didn't get to play a role. There's no justice in it.

And then Pressia says, "Partridge." Did Partridge actually organize a coup? She covers her mouth. She shouldn't have said his name.

Kelly looks at her sharply. "Yes. Willux's youngest son. He's in charge now."

"Partridge?" Bradwell says, scoffing. He turns back to face them. "You sure about that?"

El Capitan is stunned too. "How'd that happen?" He remembers the last time he talked to Partridge. They were in the subway car, locked underground. El Capitan thought he didn't have long to live, and he trusted Partridge. He had to have faith in him. Still, he can't imagine Partridge holding that much power. El Capitan knows firsthand that power can corrupt a soul.

"He did it," Pressia whispers almost to herself. "He's in! Partridge will change things."

"Or," Kelly says, "he could turn out to be just like his father."

"No," Pressia says. "He hated his father."

"Yeah, but how far will he go?" Bradwell asks, a sharp spike of anger in his voice. "How hard will he push for change? Does he really have what it takes? The only way he'll get anything done is if he's willing to risk everything. Can he do that?"

El Capitan doesn't know the answer. No one does. Bradwell is asking about the depth of Partridge's conviction. Partridge himself might not know. El Capitan isn't sure how deep his own runs. Was it a moment of weakness when he told Pressia he loved her? Or was that conviction?

"Sometimes the man makes the power," Kelly says. "And sometimes the power makes the man."

But then Pressia shakes her head and looks at Kelly. "You're in contact with the Dome? How's that?"

"You know that Willux and I go way back." He looks at Pressia. "I knew your mother and father well too. That's no secret."

"So, were you on good terms with Willux before the Detonations?" Bradwell says quietly, as if to disguise the rage just beneath the surface. "Is that how you survived out here? Willux playing favorites?"

Fignan buzzes around the room on his nubby wheels, gathering information about the new place. He noses close to the stalls of boars—but not too close.

"He gave me a heads-up—just enough time to get into the safety of Newgrange. So maybe it helped that we were old friends, but I wasn't just friends with *him*." Kelly says to Pressia, "Your mother died recently. Her tattoo stopped pulsing. It was strong and then it stopped." He takes a deep breath. "I don't know what happened."

"I was with her." The wind whips around Pressia. She crosses her arms to shield herself from the damp chill. "Willux killed her and Sedge together."

Kelly draws in a long breath. His cheeks flush red. He looks stricken but then furious. "How did he find her? I thought she was safe!"

"He used Partridge and me to find her. We were pawns."

Kelly takes a few steps away, trying to gather himself. "I'm sorry," he mutters, but it's not clear what he's sorry for—the fact that Willux used his own child as a pawn or the loss itself.

"You were close friends with my mother back then," Pressia says. El Capitan knows that she craves details from her mother's life. She was so little.

"We were all close once," Kelly says.

"And what about my father?" Pressia asks. "Do you know where he is?" El Capitan can't bear how vulnerable Pressia looks. She's desperate to find her father again. He's barely a dream to her. El Capitan understands. He never knew his father. He lived his whole life in the shadow of a man whose features he could never make out.

Kelly turns back around. "I know there are more of us. Pockets like this. Survivors. And I think Willux was in communication with many. If your father survived, it was because Willux wanted him to survive—for better or for worse."

"What do you mean, for worse?"

"Your father's pulse still beats on my chest—that's all I know."

Pressia curls the doll head to her chest, protects it with her good hand.

"Willux doesn't just give people protection," Bradwell says. "They have to have some value to him. You've been working for him all this time, haven't you?"

"You might have noticed it's smart to stay on Willux's good side," Kelly says angrily, and then he makes a sweeping gesture with both arms. "I was setting up a number of labs in Ireland and the UK just before the Detonations. One of the facilities was funded through Willux's connections and sat within the three-mile radius he would spare. He told me, in no uncertain terms, where I needed to be to survive. I knew him well enough to believe him. I brought only my immediate family with me. That was all he told me I was allowed." The boars grunt and paw the dirt. "It makes me sick to think about it now. Could I have alerted anyone who had the power to change the course of it? I don't know." He rubs his hands through his hair. El Capitan's sure that this is the thought that keeps him up nights. El Capitan knows the signs of festering guilt—intimately, from the inside out.

"There was a tour going on—and I urged as many people as I could into the mound. We were spared, as well as the environs, but many died after the fact from disease, fire, and, to be quite honest, despair—one of my two daughters and my wife among them." He steps into one of the sun shafts, bits of hay spinning around him, all golden. "My daughters died first. My wife died of despair."

"We know despair," Pressia says. "It's something we all have in common." Her eyes cut to Bradwell, but he still won't look at her. El Capitan wants Bradwell to glance at her at least; can't he give her that? It kills El Capitan to see the look in her eyes. Helmud must sense some suffering in El Capitan because El Capitan can feel his brother leaning away from Pressia as if trying to pull El Capitan's focus away from her—for his own good.

"The boars," Kelly says, reminding himself of the matter at hand. Fignan moves toward the animals again. They startle at first but then sniff in his direction. "Boars can be vicious and unpredictable, but when genetically mixed with cows, they can become bigger and more docile. And yet they're tractable too. They can attack on command."

"A word? A sign?" Bradwell asks.

"Either," Kelly says.

El Capitan registers the threat. Kelly's brought them here for a reason. Is he setting them up? "So you get some sympathy for the deaths of your wife and daughters, and then you politely inform us that you can have us skewered at any moment." El Capitan walks up to the edge of a stall and one of the boars lets out a short, high-pitched squeal. "Tell me if I've got this right."

"The term is *gored*, not *skewered*," Kelly tells him calmly.

Fignan reverses from the boars back to Bradwell's boots.

"The boars were a successful experiment." He shakes his head and looks out one of the windows. "There's another that went horribly wrong."

Worse than the boars that attack on command? What's out there? No one has the guts to ask.

El Capitan can see the boar's wiry hairs, the blackened folds of its snout, the sharp curve of its tusks. He imagines the tip of a tusk piercing his rib cage, tearing up through his chest.

Pressia says, with a hint of suspicion in her voice, "You could do this to a man, couldn't you? Splice the genes between species. Why not humans?" She looks at Bartrand Kelly, narrows her eyes. "Did you give your research to Willux?"

Special Forces. El Capitan imagines them as he first saw them, shifting through the trees—some had the muscularity of elk or deer and others seemed to hold the meaty bulk of bears. They lifted their faces to the wind, their nostrils tensing as they were alerted to different scents. Animallike. He thinks of his friend Hastings—is he actually a Beast, one genetically created under Willux's orders with Kelly's research?

Kelly says, "You do what you have to do."

Bradwell's wings arch and broaden. "Some people do what's right."

"Research is research. How Willux chose to use it is his own sin. Not mine."

El Capitan recognizes the rationalization. He's tried it out himself. Sin is sin—individual and collective. His life is full of it.

Bradwell walks up to Kelly. "You knew how he'd use it."

Kelly raises his hand in the air and snaps his fingers. The boars tense. Their heads turn, heavy tusks and all, almost in perfect unison. "How about you take a few steps back?"

Bradwell looks at the boars, their eyes all trained on Kelly's hand. Bradwell walks toward the barn door, looking out at the sky.

El Capitan steels himself. "Why don't you just tell us what you want?"

"I probably want what you want."

"What's that?"

"To be left alone."

"But Willux saved you," Bradwell says, "and you've been playing nice with him."

"He's dead," Pressia says. "And Partridge is in charge now. Everything's about to change."

"You have more faith in human nature than I do," Kelly says.

"Well, we don't want to be left alone," Bradwell says. "We want the truth to come out. We want justice."

Pressia shakes her head ever so slightly. It seems for a moment that's the only contradicting she'll do, but then it's as if she can't stop herself. She says, "No. We want the vial that belonged to my mother and the formula that we found. And we want to bring them back—to save lives."

Bradwell looks at Pressia. For a second, El Capitan thinks Bradwell's going to break through all of the anger and resentment, walk over to her, and kiss her. But he says nothing. He has always simply wanted the truth to be known—to fulfill his parents' mission. Willux arranged for the death of Bradwell's parents before the Detonations and forced Arthur Walrond to end his own life—

Walrond, a family friend who loved Bradwell. All three of them, gone. Pressia's mother, dead.

El Capitan says, "I wouldn't mind a little old-fashioned revenge. I don't think I'm alone."

This gets Kelly's attention. "I gave Willux what he wanted, but I've been working on another agent as well, not unlike the thorned vines—a living but nearly undetectable bacterium that can eat the radiation-resistant material of the Dome."

"How does it work?" El Capitan asks.

"It acts incredibly quickly." He fits his hands in his pockets.

"Are you saying that you have something that can bring down the Dome?" El Capitan says. His heart starts hammering in his chest.

"Bring down the Dome?" Helmud repeats for clarity.

"That's exactly what I'm saying," Kelly says.

"That's not what we want at all," Pressia says. "We need the Dome. If we get the vial back and the formula, we can get them to Partridge. He'll find the right person on the inside who'll help us. We can reverse fusings—with no side effects. We can make everyone equal again."

"Including you. Finally you'll be able to free yourself of the doll head," Bradwell says to Pressia, "so you can be a Pure. What's more selfish? Your desire to make yourself whole or revenge?"

"That's not fair," Pressia says. "I want Wilda and the other children to survive. I want to save people."

"But admit it," Bradwell says. "You'll save yourself in the process."

El Capitan grabs his head with two hands. He feels dizzy. He says, "We can bring down the Dome, Pressia. This is why I survived. This is my mission! Jesus! Once and for all, we can end this."

"That's no ending. That's just more destruction!" Pressia's eyes are angry and yet shining with tears. She looks at the barn's wide floorboards. "Now that Partridge is in charge, we can make a difference. We can cure people of their fusings." She turns to El Capitan and Helmud. "I think there could come a time when you two could be your own people again."

El Capitan hasn't ever thought this was possible. Could he and Helmud be made Pure? Could they be taken apart and made whole? *No*, he thinks. *No—it's not possible.* The idea terrifies him. It's all he's ever really wanted, and yet he refuses to believe it.

Pressia says to Bradwell, "You could have those wings you hate so much taken from you." Bradwell opens his mouth to fire back at her, but she raises her hand. "Look, you don't have to want it for yourself. But think of other people out there. Don't answer for them. Let them have a chance to answer for themselves."

"Pressia," Bradwell whispers, but he doesn't say any more than that. It's a soft whisper, more like he's pleading with her—for what?

"She has a point," Kelly says. "The people in the Dome have survivors' guilt. They hate all who survived on the outside because they hate themselves. But if they have a new role and paternalistically save you all, well, they'll be able to redeem themselves and feel like heroes."

"And maybe the survivors can forgive them because the Pures are finally doing the right thing. See?" Pressia says to Bradwell. "It could work."

"Hell no!" Bradwell says.

"Why not? We could start to rebuild," Pressia says.

"I'm not letting the Pures get out of this," Bradwell says, his voice rough with anger, "and I sure as hell am not letting them come out as heroes. Not after what they've done. Never."

El Capitan understands. His gut agrees with Bradwell, but he knows what Pressia's thinking: What does it matter who comes out a hero if there's a shot at starting over? It's quiet again. Kelly's waiting for the next question, and El Capitan knows what it has to be. He says, "What are you proposing exactly?"

"I'll give you the vial and the formula and get you airborne again, but you have to take the bacterium with you. If you choose not to use it, there's nothing I can do." He looks at Pressia for a moment and then back to El Capitan and Bradwell. "But if you want what's yours, you'll have to take what's mine."

Airborne again. This is what El Capitan really wants right now—to be up in the air.

Pressia turns to Kelly. "If we agree to this, how soon can you get us out?"

He pauses, taking in the volatility of the conversation and then says, "Well, as El Capitan has seen, the airship is nearly repaired. We'll need another few days, and you'll need to time the trip so that you're landing during daylight."

He opens his satchel, reaches in, and pulls out a small metal case. He pops a small clasp and opens the lid. The box is velvet lined and molded to protect a flat square slide—two pieces of glass held together by a thin welded metal border. He holds the square up to the light, illuminating small red flecks. The bacterium.

"So, are you going to take it with you in exchange for your vial and formula and an airship home?" Kelly says. "It's the opportunity of a lifetime—for all of us."

El Capitan reaches forward before he even realizes it.

"Wait," Pressia whispers, but he's already holding it in his cupped palm.

"The opportunity of a lifetime," El Capitan says to Pressia.

"For all of us," Helmud says.

LYDA

SEVENTEEN

W E'RE NOT TAKING A CAR," Beckley says. "That drew more attention than it was worth. It's after curfew now. It should be safer to just walk you there."

Beckley and another guard are on either side of Lyda and Partridge. They're walking down the hall to the elevators.

"How many have we lost?" Lyda asks.

"In the last hour alone, seventeen," Beckley says. "The good news is that some of the other attempts have not been successful."

"Can't we put people on watch?" Partridge asks.

They step into one of the elevators. The doors close, and there are Partridge and Lyda's reflections in a gray blur. She doesn't like how they both look pale, scared. Most of all, she's stunned by how young they look. The idea of the war room made Partridge seem powerful; the reality was something else altogether. Now, he looks scrawny, and she's gripping his hand—not romantically; she's frightened. She doesn't like that feeling. Not too long ago, she was out in the wilderness, a hunter. Has the Dome already made her weaker and more frightened? She lets go of him, crosses her arms as if she's cold.

"Who would we put on watch?" Beckley says, clearly frustrated. "Who's stable? Who isn't? It's impossible to say."

They step out of the elevator and soon they're out on the street again, which is empty except for guards posted every one hundred yards or so.

"Martial law," Beckley says. "For now."

"And you're taking us to Lyda's?"

Beckley sighs. "Just for tonight. Then we'll move you to another location. We have things to talk about."

"How are they doing it?" Lyda asks.

"There are more guns out there than before," Beckley says. "There are caches of arms in certain locations throughout the Dome, in case of an attack from the outside. Some of those have been raided."

Lyda thinks of Sedge. That was supposedly how he'd killed himself—a self-inflicted gunshot wound. But of course she knows that Partridge might be thinking of Sedge's actual death—his head exploding as his mother bent to kiss him. She hasn't been able to shake the stain of the image; she never will. Partridge told her on Christmas Eve how he felt in that moment—the burst of blood and how everything went silent, even the sound of his own screaming. He was furious and dazed.

"Others are cutting their wrists in warm tubs and bleeding out," Beckley says. "A few have managed to get to rooftops. Some of those we've been able to catch in time."

"And where are they now—those who were caught in time?" Lyda asks, even though she fears she knows the answer.

"The rehabilitation center was already packed. It's going to be overwhelmed soon if this keeps escalating," Beckley says.

"That place would only make you want to kill yourself more," Lyda says. The blank walls, the fake sun, the little paper cups of water and the pills. "It's awful. It's a form of punishment."

They take one of the elevators reserved for the elite that move between levels within the Dome. Again, there's their reflection. A grim couple. They look straight ahead. She thinks of some of the portrait pictures of Mr. and Mrs. Willux on the floor of the chamber in the war room—so often regally dressed, staring at the camera with forced smiles. And she feels a well of sadness thinking of all the other photos—a mother, her sons, a family that once was and now no longer is. They were all so painfully beautiful, so young—blowing out candles on birthday cakes, riding on a merry-go-round's painted horses, waving from docks filled with fishing gear. It's a life she and Partridge and her child won't have—not here in the Dome and not on the outside.

"Maybe this is just a first-round reaction," Partridge says. "Hopefully, people will calm down. Maybe they just need time."

"I don't know. Not only have we lost people, their family and friends are angry about the losses," Beckley says. "And the suicides will add to their own underlying anger."

"But an angry rebellion wouldn't be a bad thing," Lyda says. "If they're really processing what happened."

"The people of the Dome aren't rebellious by nature. That's how they got here, Partridge. You said it yourself," Beckley says. "They're sheep."

"What do they want?" Partridge asks.

"They want to restore the status quo."

"They can only revolt against themselves," Lyda says. "In here, suicide is the only socially acceptable form of anger, hatred, and despair."

Beckley says to Partridge, "You've got to shut it down."

"How?" Partridge says. "I told the truth. That has to stand."

"You have to give a little," Beckley says.

"I'm not going back on what I said."

Beckley pulls out his walkie-talkie and asks someone if the monorails have been cleared. The voice on the other end tells him that a few more trains have to get back to the station, but they're close. "Keep them running," Beckley says, "until we give the word."

They step out of the elevator and onto the platform of the monorail. Beckley tells the other guard to stay behind, making sure no stray passengers follow them.

They walk through the echoing tunnel in silence. Overhead, in the distance, they hear the whine of sirens—one overlapping the next, needling the night air.

PARTRIDGE

TRAIN

Beckley looks at the digital sign that tells which trains are arriving at the platform. "This next one isn't ours; it's an express. We'll wait for the one after."

Partridge and Lyda follow Beckley toward the end of the platform that would put them on the first car.

Lyda grabs hold of Partridge's hand. They look ahead into the mouth of the tunnel. Partridge's eyes search the darkness, as if some answer could be found there. The suicides feel unreal. It can't be happening, and yet the guilt washes over him. It's his fault. He's to blame. He squeezes Lyda's hand and she squeezes it back. At least he's not alone.

Just then, a man in a black jacket steps out toward the tracks. The jacket is unzipped, and an untucked white undershirt ruffles underneath.

Beckley half turns and motions for Lyda and Partridge to stop, and they do.

"The station's closed; you'll need to exit the platform and go on up," Beckley says.

The man looks at him blankly. "There's no place to go," he says.

"Why are you down here?" Beckley says. "It's closed, sir."

"You know why I'm here."

Partridge lets go of Lyda's hand, reaches forward and grabs Beckley's arm. Is the man here to jump in front of a train? Beckley looks at Partridge as if asking if he wants to handle this himself. *A leader takes control of a situation like this*, Partridge thinks. Partridge gives Beckley a nod.

Partridge steps toward the man but looks back at Lyda before saying anything. What should he say? She lifts one hand, almost like she's giving him a blessing. "Yes, there's been trouble, but it's going to be okay. Things are going to work out," Partridge says. "You need to give it time."

The man registers for the first time that this is Partridge Willux. His face contorts, as if he's physically pained. "I got my time," the man says. "Time the others didn't!" He stares down at the single rail. "I knew it all along. I knew it, and I didn't do anything about it."

"Partridge," Lyda whispers. Is she warning him? Is she scared of the man? If Partridge gets too close, would the man try to take Partridge down with him?

"You had to carry on. We all did," Partridge says, approaching the man as Beckley and Lyda hold back. "We had to survive."

"My sister killed herself already," the man says almost proudly. "She got the pills down before anyone could catch her."

"You have to be brave," Partridge says, trying to be calm. "This won't be easy, but you have to hang on."

Partridge hears the distant rushing of the monorail at his back. The man hears it too. His head jerks up and he looks into the tunnel then back at Partridge. "No. Brave is what I'm doing now. Brave is ending the lie," he says, and an awful smile cracks at the edge of his mouth. "I've been a coward until now."

"Don't say that. Look, we can get you help," Partridge says, and he's relieved to see the man take a step backward, just as the train is speeding their way.

"Sure, help," the man says, and then, without another word, he jumps forward into the path of the train, the black flap of his jacket curling like burnt paper.

"No!" Partridge yells against the monorail's rush, and the static of adrenaline in his ears, and the sickening thud of the train ending another man's life.

And then the bright train windows glide on, shiny and dark, the train dragging in the air.

Partridge drops to his knees.

The brakes screech, a delayed reaction; the train comes to a stop down in the tunnel.

Lyda rushes to Partridge's side. "You tried to save him. You really tried. You did all you could." She grabs his arm then reaches around his neck, hugging him.

Beckley is shouting into the walkie-talkie—*monorail jumper, presumed dead*.

———

It's not real.

Not the scream they hear overhead as they run through the side streets.

Not the scuffle in the alley.

Not the collective whine of ambulances.

Not the next elevator they take inside of Lyda's apartment building. Not the hallway with its red carpeting. Not the door to Lyda's apartment. Not Beckley or this new guard who stands by the door.

Not the sofa where Partridge sits or the glass-top table where Lyda picks up the orb.

Not the orb itself.

He told the truth. People are killing themselves. He couldn't stop a man from throwing himself in front of a train. Partridge has seen too many people die—his brother, his mother. Their deaths flash in front of his eyes—bright with blood. And his father's death—his fault; it wasn't a death. It was murder. "Too many," Partridge says. "There've been too many."

"Yes," Lyda says, "too many."

Will he ever see Glassings? Partridge needs Glassings, not the other way around. He needs a plan. He needs someone to tell him what to do. Is Glassings just a stand-in for his own father? Is Partridge really just a lost kid, an orphan? Where is Glassings? Partridge can't save him. He can't save anyone. He says, "They need time to process what I said, right?"

"Yes," she says.

"They're going to stop killing themselves. It was just a certain few who were already suffering…"

"You're not taking back what you said. You still did the right thing." She smiles at him, but the smile seems fragile, as if it's already tinged with doubt. She says, "The surprise, remember?"

He barely remembers.

She holds the orb and fiddles with the settings. He remembers the first time he saw it. Iralene held it like an apple—cupped palms. She wanted Partridge to be happy. That's all.

And then the room grows dark. The air is cloudy. Almost silken.

But then he realizes that it's not darkness and clouds and silk.

It's ash.

The walls blacken. The sofa where he sits suddenly seems charred. The windows look as if they've been pounded by fists—dimpled and shattered but not broken.

This is the world outside the Dome.

There's Freedle, flitting through the sooty air.

Lyda curls on his lap. She wraps her arms around his neck and rests her head. He holds her close.

She says, "Remember this?"

"How did you make this? How—"

"I had to have it back."

The room grows cold. It's winter, after all. The wind kicks up the ash and dust, swirling it around them. And finally something feels real.

PRESSIA

TEETH AND HEARTBEATS

IT'S NIGHT. PRESSIA CAN'T SLEEP. The wild dogs are crying out so sharp and forlorn that Pressia pictures the tightening of their ribs with each howl. Are the dogs growing closer?

It's been two days since they made a deal with Kelly. Supposedly, the airship is ready, and they leave tomorrow. Kelly gave El Capitan the bacterium in a locked metal box. He will walk them out to the airship, which is already stocked with provisions. Like the wire that once kept the airship tethered inside of the brittle, crumbling Capitol Building, one of Kelly's men will cut the primary vine and all the rest of the vines will go slack.

They're heading home soon.

But what is home like now? Willux is dead and everything is different. Partridge is in charge of the Dome. He's taken over. Was Partridge in a position to order his father's death, to give some kind of final go-ahead? Or did Willux die in his sleep—a gentle death and one that Pressia can't help but think he didn't deserve?

If Partridge really is in charge, will the boundaries between the two worlds—the boundaries of the Dome itself—be dismantled?

They have to get back to save Wilda and the other children. Hopefully the Dome will now work with them. And Hastings is out there too, being taken care of by the survivors who live in Crazy John-Johns Amusement Park—that is, if he's still alive. He lost a leg and a lot of blood in the process. They have to collect him and bring him with them.

Since the meeting with Kelly, Pressia's door is no longer locked. Maybe it's to establish a sense of trust. And, too, where is there to go? Out into the howling night?

A hall light glows under the crack in the door. Caretakers sometimes pass by—it dims then returns. The red alarm lights the wall. She stares at it as if it's a distant star. The fire in the fireplace is out. There's just ash, a heap of char, like home. The room is cold, but she cocoons in the covers to keep warm.

Bradwell told her she was selfish, and after all they've been through, he wants revenge? She wonders how this change to his body—that massive heavy cloak of wings—has made him foreign to himself. She's seen it happen before. The people who came to her grandfather to have their flesh mended—they'd already suffered some deformity, some fusing, and had adapted to it. But sometimes it was this second injury—a leg mangled in the Rubble Fields, a hand bitten by a Beast, or some other new deformity—that became too much to bear. It's as if the soul can shift its image of the body once, even radically, but a second time? A third?

Is Bradwell still the person she was in love with? Maybe she wants to believe he's changed because it's easier than believing he's still the same but simply can't forgive her—or has fallen out of love with her. There's a difference.

She knows that he'd never go through any process—especially something created in partnership with the Dome—to remove his wings. It was crazy of her to even bring it up in the barn, but she'd meant what she said. He shouldn't decide for other survivors.

She turns to the wall and closes her eyes and tells herself to dream. Her dreams have been filled with shifting cinders, as if some part of her, deep down, is homesick.

But in a few minutes, a distant alarm sounds—a rising whine. She rolls toward the door. Footsteps are running down the hall.

Another alarm sounds. This one is closer—on the same floor.

The dogs are no longer howling. What's happened to the dogs?

Pressia gets out of bed and dresses quickly.

As she pulls on her boots, Fedelma opens the door. "Now!" she says. "There's an attack. You have to leave now!"

"Leave?"

"All the way. To the airship." She's holding a small backpack.

"But maybe we can stay and help." Pressia rushes to the door.

"They've gotten to the children. Three are missing. You can't help us. You need to go." Pressia sees a bright glint at her side—a knife in her other hand. Fedelma lifts it and gives her the handle. "Take it. The vine is marked—red. The one you need to cut."

"How will I see it?"

"Someone has given the brothers a flashlight."

"El Capitan and Helmud?"

"They're waiting at the bottom of the stairwell."

"And Bradwell?"

"He went on alone. It wasn't wise, but there was no stopping him. We have our own troubles."

Fedelma reaches into the small backpack and pulls out a metal box like the one that Kelly had to hold the bacterium, but this one's thinner and longer. She pops it open quickly and shows Pressia the vial—the only remaining sample of Pressia's mother's lifework, the powerful concoction that she injected into the birds on Bradwell's back, the vial rescued from her mother's bunker. It sits in a groove of velvet lining, a small folded piece of paper beside it.

"The vial and formula!" Pressia says.

"Yes," Fedelma says, and she shuts the box, snapping its clasp. "You didn't think we'd keep them, did you?"

Fedelma puts the box into the backpack and hands it to Pressia.

Pressia slips the straps over both shoulders and slides the knife between her belt and pants.

"Thank you," Pressia says, "for everything."

"Be careful out there. Don't wear your fear. They're drawn to it."

"Who?"

"We had so many dead. So many. And Bartrand Kelly thought he could create a force for good, a breed that would go out and kill the violent creatures who came after us again and again. But he built and bred them with a hunger that was too strong. Yes, they killed the others, but now the once-dead have turned on us. Be careful." Fedelma opens her arms and hugs Pressia quickly and roughly and then pulls away. "Especially watch for the fog. Sometimes it has a heartbeat."

A heartbeat. "The once-dead? He used the dead. He built and bred them…"

"They snatch our young. Watch for teeth in the darkness."

"And the fog has a heartbeat…" Pressia's scared and confused.

"I can't explain them any better than that. Go on."

Pressia runs to the stairs and takes them two at a time. At the final landing, she finds El Capitan and Helmud standing by a door, waiting, the flashlight in El Capitan's hand.

"You ready?" El Capitan says.

"Did you hear about what's out there?"

"I heard enough," he says.

"Enough," Helmud says.

"I'm ready," Pressia says.

"I miss my guns," El Capitan says. "I hope they put 'em back in the airship."

"I hope we make it to the airship," Pressia says.

El Capitan pushes out the door.

The fog has a heartbeat.

Watch for teeth in the darkness.

People with flashlights roam the fields, call for the missing children. "Carven! Darmott! Saydley!" Some of the calls ring out from within the woods. Their own flashlight glides across the fields and into the nearby thickets and forests.

"We're not supposed to show fear," Pressia says. "The ones who took the children—they sense it."

"Like dogs."

"Where did the dogs go?" Pressia asks. "They stopped howling."

"I don't want to know, do you?" El Capitan says.

"I don't want to know," Helmud says.

"Bartrand Kelly made these creatures," Pressia says. "The ones that have taken the children."

El Capitan nods. "Then Kelly deserves what he gets."

"Not necessarily," Pressia says.

"Don't we deserve what we get, Helmud?" El Capitan says. "Don't we reap what we sow?"

"We reap," Helmud says. "We sow. We reap. We sow. We reap…" El Capitan doesn't tell Helmud to shut up. He lets him keep going, over and over, which isn't like Cap.

But Pressia doesn't tell him to stop either. *We sow. We reap. We sow. We reap.* It's a singsong enchantment. Maybe it'll keep them safe. At the very least, it gives a rhythm to their steps that keeps them moving at a quick pace.

They head into the woods where the vines start to appear. The vines still scare Pressia. She keeps her distance from the areas where they grow thick and twisted. The shadows on either side of the path are dark. The voices calling Carven and Darmott and Saydley are now farther off. Were they identical—the three of them? What's it like when you're with living, breathing mirror images of yourself—down to your DNA? Are they still alive?

Pressia listens for the children too, just in case they're out here, simply lost.

"Did you hear what they look like?" El Capitan says.

"The children?" Pressia asks.

"The children? What? No. Kelly's creations. His dead and bred."

"We reap. We sow," Helmud keeps on. "We reap. We sow."

"No," Pressia says, tightening the straps on her backpack. "I don't know what they look like. Should've asked." She thinks of telling him that the darkness has teeth and the fog a heartbeat, but she's embarrassed that she knows these stupid things yet didn't get a description, which now seems such a practical and obvious thing to ask.

They walk uphill. The airship isn't far off. In fact, El Capitan raises the beam of the flashlight through the trees, lighting the clearing where he and Helmud and Bradwell almost bled to death in the vines.

"We reap, we sow, we reap, we sow," Helmud says, faster now.

They trudge through the final trees and start across the clearing. The fog has rolled in.

The fog has a heartbeat.

The flashlight's sharp glare strikes the misty air.

On the other side of the clearing, they hear a cry. Human? It's hard to tell. Childlike? Carven and Darmott and Saydley—Pressia imagines finding them out here, wrapped in vines.

El Capitan douses the light, and darkness seems to rush in all around them. Then Pressia feels El Capitan's hand in hers. It's rough and calloused. He says, "This way." She hears Helmud shifting nervously on his back.

There's another cry.

Her eyes slowly adjust to the moonlight.

They step into a stand of trees and stop. El Capitan lets go of her hand, and she misses the feeling of his sure grip.

"They're here," El Capitan says.

"No fear, remember?" Pressia says. "No fear."

"Reap, sow," Helmud whispers.

Pressia nods, but she can't control her own fear. No one can.

"We can slip past them," El Capitan whispers. "The airship is fifty feet away. We can do this."

"What if they have the children?"

"We have more people to save back home than three lost kids."

"But where's Bradwell?"

"Hopefully he's already there."

"And if he isn't?"

El Capitan doesn't answer. "We've got to move quickly," he says.

"Let's go," Pressia says.

El Capitan starts running. Pressia pushes off a tree and follows him. It's hard to navigate the trees with such little light, but soon Pressia—breathless and quick—can just barely see the rounded orb of the airship, pinned down tightly with rooted vines.

She hears another cry and turns.

Nothing but thickening fog and trees.

Then a quick shadow.

She faces forward and keeps running but trips and falls. She looks back and sees a wild dog, dead and mutilated.

El Capitan hoarsely whispers her name. She scrambles to her feet. She can't see him through the fog. In just seconds it's gotten so dense that she's surrounded by white.

Another sharp cry and then another, as if replying.

She starts moving as fast as she can—harder now with such little visibility. She has to hold out her hand and the doll head to feel her way from trunk to trunk.

I'm the prey now, she thinks as she skins her palm on the rough bark. She has to protect the metal box in her backpack. She has to get to the airship.

She hears a footfall behind her. She whips around, but nothing's there. She keeps her eyes wide open, as if this will help her see, but it doesn't. White. All around her. White.

She pushes through the trees, but then something brushes her backpack. She lunges forward—away from it. "Cap!" she calls out. "Cap!" Fear. She's showing fear.

She sees the beam of his flashlight, but in this dense fog, it's only lighting the mist. "Cap!" Maybe he can follow her voice.

An arm—long and thin—reaches out and cuffs her elbow. She screams and tries to pull free. The arm is mottled with scars from thick hurried stitches running along its veins. She pulls away but her arm is wrenched so hard that pain shoots up into her shoulder. Still, she manages to stay on her feet.

She hears strange guttural sounds—a call, a response. A few more ahead of her and then behind. "Cap!" she shouts. "Here!"

The light keeps gliding past her. The cries echo around them in all directions. How many are there? What did they do to the children? Where's Bradwell?

A hand grabs her other arm. This time she yanks the arm toward her and a face suddenly appears—a thick jaw with an underbite, gaunt cheeks covered in thin burnt skin. It widens its mouth, showing its yellowed teeth, and the skin stretches—taut and shiny and damp from the wet air. Its mouth snaps. Its eyes are blind and roving. It wants her in the fog because here she's nearly as blind as it is.

She imagines the teeth gouging her flesh and muscle. She tries to pull her arm free, but others appear out of the thick fog and grab her. Their grips are too strong. How many? Five, six? She can't tell. They force her to the ground. She writhes and kicks, but still they pin her on her back. She can feel the sharp outline of the metal box holding the vial and formula. The ground is cold and wet. She manages to cry out for El Capitan. "Cap! Cap!" Is he here?

"Pressia!" he shouts. She turns in the direction of his voice and sees only his flashlight falling and bouncing, and then it goes out.

She whispers his name as two faces loom above her. There's

darkened blood on their skin, splotches of it—from the thorns or from the wild dogs or… "Where are the children?" Pressia says.

They don't seem to understand her. One reaches out and touches her forehead. It runs its cold, bony hand down her face. She twists away but the hand follows. She clamps her lips, and one secures her head with an incredibly strong grip, pressing one side of her face into the dirt. But the creatures have a strange calm about them. They're moving slowly. She's hoping to find their weakness, or hoping for a distraction.

They start humming now—tuneless and dull. One touches her hair softly. This chills her.

Maybe they don't want to kill her.

Maybe they want her.

And now she starts to fight with everything she's got. She throws her legs in the air and kicks one of the creatures in the chest. She rolls away from the other. Its fingernails claw her arm. Her shoulder is wrenched. She gets to her feet. Not being able to see clearly makes her dizzy, disoriented. Her heart is pounding. The fog has a heartbeat—it's her own, hammering.

She pulls out her knife and holds the blade in front of her. The fog thins when there's a breeze, and she can see them—if only for an instant at a time—shifting around her, four of them. They can't see the knife, of course, but they seem to react to her energy. They're misshapen with uneven limbs and staggered gaits. Their scars are Detonation marks and burns and thick ropy keloids, but also scars from stitches. She knows stitches. Her grandfather, the mortician, the flesh-tailor, was known for his tidy work. These stitches were rushed and messy. The scars run around their shoulders, down some of their arms and chests.

They sniff at her—smelling her fear, the small blade of her confidence. Are more being drawn in? Kelly's *dead and bred*—there's an animalism to them. Were they bred to be vicious carnivores? To be insatiably blood hungry? They're mostly bare but for some mossy kind of homemade coats to keep them warm. She can see now that the one female has turned away from the others as if she's drawn to something far-off.

Pressia takes a few steps backward. The pain in her shoulder intensifies with each step. They know she's moving. They step toward her quickly then stop—do they sense the knife? Is it the fog—is it that the moisture in the air connects them all, like some kind of web?

"Cap! Helmud!" Pressia calls out. "Damn it! Where are you?"

And then she hears a dim echo. "Damn it! Where are you?"

Helmud—at least he's alive, but his voice sounds choked. Was this what the female creature was smelling in the air? More prey?

Pressia lunges at the creatures grunting brutishly, then turns and starts running as quickly as she can without being able to see well. She puts the knife back in her belt and holds her good hand out in front of her. Each time she feels a tree, she grabs it and pulls herself around it. She can hear them behind her. Their panting seems low to the ground. Are they on all fours?

"Helmud! Call to me!"

"Call to me! Call to me!" Helmud says.

She's getting closer. "Keep calling!"

"Calling," Helmud cries.

Then she hears the growling. She takes out the knife again. The fog ripples enough that she can see one of the creatures has El Capitan and Helmud shoved to the ground. His clawed hands are on El Capitan's throat.

But the creature must sense Pressia—the vibration through thickened air? *The fog has a heartbeat.*

This time she moves decisively, running at the creature with her knife. He jumps off of El Capitan and Helmud, and, his eyes glazed over, he has enough of his senses intact to dodge her attack. And then, in one quick snatch, he grabs her wrist with such force she drops the knife. She has nothing.

El Capitan gasps for breath and manages to stand up. Helmud gasps too—though maybe he's only an echo.

The other four creatures have been drawn close and start to circle.

El Capitan says, his voice raw, "Thank you."

"For what?" Pressia says, gripping her arm to her ribs. "We're about to be eaten."

"True."

"Eaten!" Helmud shouts as loudly as he can. "Eaten!"

The creatures shout back at him in yawps and caws. They keep circling, some on all fours, others upright. The curtain of fog sometimes parts, revealing a thick thigh with stitches across it, a bit of moss on a back, the glisten of eye whites.

El Capitan says, "I want you to know something."

"What?"

"I wouldn't do what Bradwell's done. I would have forgiven you right away."

She looks at him, wide-eyed, trying to make out his expression through the fog.

"If you were the person standing there with me," he says, "I'd always, always stay."

This is what Pressia wants to believe in—the kind of love that stays, no matter what. It's a declaration that's come out of the wrong mouth. As if El Capitan knows what she's thinking, he says, "Don't worry. You don't have to feel the same way about me. I just needed to say it."

"I understand, yes," Pressia says. Yes, yes, yes, she wants to say, because he's made it better. He's made her feel a little forgiven.

"I'm glad about the fog," he says. "This way we don't have to see each other get killed."

"Killed?" Helmud whispers.

The creatures start to growl, low and deep. She feels like crying, not because she's afraid—which she is—but because El Capitan deserves to be loved the way he loves her. It's wrong to die without that. Unfair. She wants to tell him that she loves him. Why not? They're going to die, but she can't say it unless it's true. Really true.

"You're good," she says instead. "You really are full of goodness, Cap. Helmud too."

"Ah," he says. "I get it." His voice cracks. She's afraid she's only made it worse.

The creatures dare to move in more closely. They reach out and claw at them. They rip Pressia's pants, her coat. One cuts Helmud's cheek. The blood spills down his neck. El Capitan punches one, but the others howl and snap at the air near his face.

When there's a small break in the fog, Pressia has enough aim to kick one with her boots, but it's up again quickly, unfazed.

Pressia feels an arm around one leg and then the other, and she falls hard. El Capitan is tackled next. They fight and kick and claw back, but it's little use. The creatures' faces cut in and out of the fog—the scars, the teeth, the blind eyes.

"I don't want to die like this!" Pressia shouts, and then she thinks of Bradwell. She doesn't want to die unforgiven.

"I don't want to die!" Helmud cries.

"Pressia!" El Capitan shouts, trying to crawl toward her. "Pressia!"

But it's no use. The creatures were bred to be strong and heartless. Pressia remembers the mutilated wild dog. That's how she'll look—she knows it—in a matter of minutes.

And then she hears Bradwell's voice. "Back off! Get off them!" He's fighting one of the creatures, but then the others jerk their heads toward the noise. They start to run toward the agitation of molecules, the fresh heartbeat. She sees Fignan's row of lights blinking in the fog.

"Run!" Bradwell shouts. "Get to the ship! I'll be there!"

"You won't make it!" Pressia says.

El Capitan starts running. "Trust him!" he shouts, taking off toward the ship. "I'm going to cut it loose so we're ready to take off. Come on!"

"No!" Pressia shouts. Her fear makes some of the creatures turn toward her.

Then she hears Bradwell fighting hard. His wings are wide and beating the air. Fignan lets out a shrill alarm she's never heard before. "Go!" Bradwell shouts. "Pressia, go!"

"I'm not leaving you!"

His pulsing wings are creating a breeze that cuts the fog, creating more curtains that lift and rise. She can see more of the creatures and kicks the nearest one, on all fours, in the stomach. It lets out a moan but then quickly springs to its feet. Bradwell's wings keep pushing the fog—rippling, rippling. And suddenly, the creature seems lost and truly blind. Another one holds out its hands and pats the air.

"Keep beating your wings!" Pressia shouts breathlessly. "They need the constant fog to sense where they are and where we are."

Bradwell beats his wings harder, the fog gusting now all around them. His wings—she's never seen them fully spread, massive and strong. She wants to tell him that this is how he was meant to be— as wrong as it was for her to do this to him, as wrong as it feels, he is this person in this moment, and there's nothing more beautiful.

The creatures run off in search of the fog that makes sense of their world, retreating into the trees.

Bradwell stops beating his wings. They fold in tightly on his back. And then it's just the two of them, staring at each other through the thinning mist.

LYDA

A FAIRY TALE

LYDA AND PARTRIDGE HAVEN'T EATEN or slept well in days—not since the man threw himself in front of the train. The suicide numbers are rising. Partridge pushed for the meeting with Foresteed because he wants clearer data, more statistics, a plan to put an end to what's now, clearly, an epidemic.

They find themselves in Foresteed's office, which is glutted with memorabilia devoted to the past and the Dome.

"I've never been in here before," Partridge whispers. Lyda hasn't either, of course. Foresteed's assistant offered them a seat while they're waiting, but they can't help walking around, taking it all in. Righteous Red Wave recruitment posters are framed on the walls—young men with firmly set jaws stand shoulder to shoulder, a smoldering city in the background: JOIN NOW! BEFORE IT'S TOO LATE... In the mix, there's a framed trifold flyer celebrating the opening of the Righteous Red Wave Museum. Lyda skims the text, remembering dimly her own childhood.

Inside the museum, live actors perform plays set during the troubling times when criminals with dangerous ideas roamed our streets, when feminism didn't properly encourage femininity, when the media regularly sabotaged the government in its great efforts at reformation, when the government didn't have the ability to fully protect good, hardworking citizens from harmful, dangerous citizens, and much, much more! Join us on the lawn for historic reenactments in full surround sound! Cheer on Righteous Red Wave soldiers as they defeat protestors and criminals and other evil elements! Prepare to be awed by our growing prison system, our rehabilitation centers, our asylums for the diseased...Bring your students to this educational opportunity! Families, spend time together bonding over the dark recent past and our hopeful bright future! Shop in our patriotic Righteous Red Wave gift shop. Admission for children under 12 is free.

Lyda is chilled.

Partridge walks up beside her. "I went as a kid. Did you?"

She shakes her head. "My father wouldn't let me. I think he had some hidden ideas of his own about the Righteous Red Wave. It might be why he's no longer with us."

Lyda moves to a glass cabinet protecting leather-bound editions of *The Academy Handbook for Girls*, *The Academy Handbook for Boys*, and *The New Eden: Prepare Your Heart, Mind, and Body*—a book given to every household in the Dome. It details guidelines for the timing of the return to living on the outside, as well as lists of character traits that should be cultivated and praised—loyalty, devotion, purity of heart. Lyda remembers her family's copy, prominently displayed on the mantel for any guest to see.

In another display case, there are old uniforms and newspaper clippings about the plans for the Dome's construction. One includes a picture of Partridge's father at a ribbon-cutting ceremony.

"I wonder if Foresteed was ever married," Lyda says. "Did he have a family? Did they not make it in?"

"I don't know," Partridge says. "I didn't know him back then."

"He misses it," Lyda says. "The asylums, the battles, the prisons. He misses the oppression of the masses."

"He's sick in the head," Partridge adds.

Lyda walks to Foresteed's desk, leans over it. There's a stack of parent authorization forms for enhancements—the signatures of parents scrawled across them as if they have a choice—and then she sees a file with her name on the tab. Suddenly, everything feels more personal, setting her on edge. She lifts the folder ever so slightly. It's her psychological evaluation from the rehabilitation center. "What?" she whispers.

Partridge is on the other side of the room, engrossed in newspaper articles about his father. Lyda picks up the folder quickly.

Reason for referral: Lyda Mertz is believed to have suffered an emotional trauma due to an event in which she participated in a theft and the disappearance of a classmate, Partridge Willux...

Under SOURCES OF INFORMATION, there's a list of all those they interviewed and deposed—her teachers, Miss Pearl and Mr. Glassings; a few of her classmates; her mother; her pediatrician. There are summaries of their accounts and then a list of psychological tests—all waived. Why? Because she would have passed them. She wasn't crazy.

The team who interviewed her when she was brought into the rehab center describe Lyda in her interview.

Ms. Mertz was agitated and nervous...easily distracted by the window image and often rubbed her hands on her knees. She was self-conscious about her shaved head and kept it covered. She did not make consistent eye contact...a reluctant interviewee...She found it painful to talk about her father and his death. She didn't want to discuss the difficulties of being raised by a single mother. She talked only briefly about her life in the academy, saying it was "good" and that she'd been "happy, you know, more or less."

She had been happy, more or less, but only because she didn't know what happiness was. She didn't understand it because she hadn't ever had the freedom to make her own decisions, to choose a life. Freedom and happiness are entwined—one can't truly exist without the other.

She sees herself in her mind's eye—that girl in the rehabilitation center who was scared and quiet, embarrassed and ashamed. She never wants to feel that way again.

Lyda reads some dense medical language about her diagnosis, none of which sounds at all accurate.

And then the conclusions.

Short-Term Prognosis: We believe that due to Ms. Mertz's delusional thinking, willful disobedience, disregard for rules and laws, new history of criminal activity, and deep level of denial, she is a threat to herself and others . . .

She shakes her head. No, not true. Not at all.

Long-Term Prognosis: We believe that Ms. Mertz will likely never be able to transition back into normal society. Her prospects of finding a mate—in light of her psychological deficiencies—are remote. We do not believe she will ever return to the level of a fully participating and contributing member of the community. We will suggest—subject to later review—that she be rendered unfit for partnership. We strongly urge that she not be given the right to procreate, as we see her psychological weaknesses as possibly stemming from a genetic source on her paternal side.

Final Determination: Lifelong institutionalization.

Lyda puts the folder down, steps back from the desk. She feels trapped again, like she did in the rehabilitation center. She remembers the shadows of fake birds flitting across the square of light that was supposed to make patients remember the sun. She wants to call to Partridge, to show him the folder, but she can't. There's some old shame inside of her. Professionals thought these things about her—*unfit for partnership, not be given the right to procreate*...She wants to hide this from Partridge. Why announce that this was once a determination, her deadened future?

Why is this on Foresteed's desk?

She whispers, *"Ms. Mertz will likely never be able to transition back into normal society."* And she wonders if this is the truest thing she's ever read. Now that she's been out in the wilds, could she ever survive here—even with Partridge at her side?

She walks toward Partridge. Does she need him in here in a way she didn't out there? She used to be so fearless, bold, and strong. She misses her spears. She misses the mothers and the smell of the forest and the way the ash spun through the air. "Partridge," she says.

He turns and looks at her, his face both anxious and weary. "What is it?"

And then the door swings open and Foresteed—lean and tan—strides into the room. "Sit down! Make yourselves comfortable."

"Not really possible," Partridge says. "We need the new count on suicides. Still rising?"

Foresteed sits at his desk. He looks at the folder as if he knows that it's not exactly in the same spot he left it. He glances at Lyda.

She looks away, takes a seat in one of the leather chairs.

"The numbers have only gotten worse," Foresteed says. "And we're overloaded in all facilities, trying to care for those who've just botched the whole thing." He almost laughs.

"I'll do anything I can to help the situation," Partridge says. "Except, well, you know where I stand on taking it all back. I can't do that."

"Of course not," Foresteed says. "Damage done. Right?"

Partridge looks down at his hands. He's been racked with guilt. Lyda's tried to tell him that there's no way he could have known that people would start killing themselves, that it's not his fault. But nothing has helped.

Foresteed knocks on the desk, his knuckles like a gavel. "I think there are things we can do."

Partridge sits down and leans forward. "What's the plan?"

"You have to offer them some part of the truth, Partridge. You have to let them feel like there's something that's going to happen that they were promised, something they recognize. And it'd be great if it was also something that could distract them, give them a little something to celebrate." Foresteed picks up the folder holding Lyda's psychological evaluation, tapping it on his desk. "Purdy and Hoppes have a great suggestion, and they want me to ask you to consider—"

"Purdy and Hoppes? They're supposed to be reworking the story so that Lyda and I can be together."

"As you can imagine, all of that's on hold." Foresteed looks at Lyda. "Now is not the time."

Lyda feels a flush of shame. She's the unwed mother again, an embarrassment for her family, her school. She reminds herself quickly that she's proud of who she is and how strong she's become, but shame doesn't listen to logic. Where does it come from? Why is it so uncontrollable and sudden? Foresteed seems to know just what to say to trigger it. "It's okay," Lyda says, trying to sound confident. "We're in no rush. The first priority here is to save lives."

Foresteed barely acknowledges her. "Things are serious, Partridge. Purdy and Hoppes want me to ask you if you'd be willing to reverse course a little. There's much to be gained from a public persona that's more in line with what was promised to the people. Romantically speaking—"

Partridge seems to know exactly what Foresteed is suggesting. "No," he says.

"No to what?" Lyda asks Partridge. It's like he's cutting her out of the conversation. "He hasn't even asked you anything yet."

"I know what he's going to ask and the answer is no."

"Partridge," Lyda says. "People are killing themselves. They're *dying*. Children are finding their parents in blood-filled tubs. If you can do something without going back on the truth, you should. You have to." She grabs his hand.

"Lyda," Partridge says. "Don't you know what he's going to suggest?"

"No, I don't."

"The people were told a fairy tale," Foresteed says. "They want a happily ever after. They want something that seems like things will go back—even if they don't."

"A fairy tale?" Lyda says. "Happily ever after?"

"Purdy and Hoppes told me to ask you. It wasn't my idea," Foresteed says, tapping his fingers across her folder. "But it's not a bad one, considering we don't really have any others. Why not give them a wedding? The one they were promised."

Lyda looks at Partridge. She lets go of his hand. She laces her fingers together and stares down at them. "Iralene." She wants to be sure she understands.

"Iralene," Foresteed says.

"A wedding. Partridge and Iralene," she says, her voice now a whisper. She presses her hand to her forehead. Her skin is cold and damp.

Foresteed speaks quickly. "We can put out a press release within the hour. We feel that it will distract them, at the very least, and put a stop to the explosion of deaths. We have to do something." And then he takes a deep breath and sighs. "Do you want your very own child to be born in a world with this much instability, violence, death?"

Lyda hates that Foresteed has even mentioned her child. She feels suddenly protective. "This isn't about my child," she says.

"Well, think of other people's children, then," Foresteed says. "The ones who will grow up without one of their parents—like you did, losing your father so young."

She knows that Foresteed is trying to manipulate her, and she hates him for it, but she misses her father and wants these unnecessary deaths to end. He smiles at her grotesquely.

"It's just a fairy tale," Lyda says. "They want a fairy tale. A happily ever after. It can be a temporary marriage until things are stable again?"

"Exactly," Foresteed says.

Then why does she feel such a deep well of sadness open up inside of her?

"We don't have to do this," Partridge says to her. "We really don't."

"People have jumped off roofs. There are gunshots going off in bedrooms." She looks at Partridge. There's nothing else. He takes a breath but doesn't say anything. She turns back to Foresteed. "Do it," she says. "Tell them what they want. See if it works."

It's silent and then Lyda whispers to Partridge, "No more blood on your hands. No more."

Pressia

LOOKING GLASS

The air is stagnant, the engines loud. The airship buffets in the wind. The entire trip will take over fifty hours. She's checked the metal box a few times, touching the vial and the formula—both intact, thankfully; it's become a nervous habit. Much of that time has passed, but still the remaining hours—how many exactly?—stretch out before Pressia restlessly. On the one hand, there's only the view out the porthole down at the glinting sea; on the other, the airship is dangerous. El Capitan is a novice pilot, and he was angry when he realized they'd be heading back without his guns. He looked lost and desperate. "How the hell does Kelly expect us to get anywhere without guns?" He settled down enough to take off, and occasionally he sends out a laser-reflecting tracking buoy. The noise is deafening as it blasts from the airship, lighting up the portholes, rattling the airship itself. They could die out here—plummet, crash, and then sink, soundlessly, to the ocean floor. This scares her, but she's been scared of death for so long that it doesn't hold as much power over her as it once did.

Instead, the sinking feeling she has in her chest—relentless and awful—is because of Bradwell. He sits just across the aisle from her, and even though he saved her life, they still haven't spoken.

How does it feel to be trapped in a small space with someone who hates her? It makes her want to be smaller and smaller until she disappears.

She's hoping there will be a moment when Bradwell lets his guard slip a little, when he'll let himself soften, open up some. But even when he sleeps, he looks angry. His brow furrows in dreams, maybe nightmares. He kicks restlessly. It's hard for him to simply sit in the seat. Stiff and awkward, his wings seem to jut his shoulders forward, forcing him to slouch.

El Capitan and Helmud are in the cockpit, Fignan at their side. El Capitan is singing old songs—nothing about love, though. She assumes he's being careful now.

But there's no time to be careful with each other. They have to talk about their next move.

"Bradwell!" Pressia says.

He doesn't stir.

"Bradwell!"

Again, nothing.

She unfastens her seatbelt, crosses the aisle, and shoves his shoulder. "Bradwell, wake up!"

He wakes from a dream the way he used to in the mossy cottage where he recuperated after they almost froze to death on the forest floor—his arms and legs jerk, he gasps for air. "What? What is it?"

"We need to talk."

He looks around, wide-eyed, then out the porthole—most likely startled to find himself on the airship careening over the ocean. "I don't want to talk about us," he says. "I can't."

"Not about us," she says, but she wishes they could talk about what they mean to each other. Will they ever? "We need a plan. We need to talk to El Capitan and Helmud too."

He rubs his eyes and nods. "You're right."

Bradwell follows Pressia to the cockpit. El Capitan is singing, and Helmud seems to be humming harmony. It's beautiful. Fignan appears to be in sleep mode, as if the singing lulled him. She hates to interrupt.

The door is open, but she knocks anyway.

He stops midnote. "I thought you two were asleep."

"I was," Bradwell says. He and Pressia step into the cockpit. He barely fits in the space. His ribs and chest and shoulders have broadened. His wings are bulky and arched on his back.

"We have to check on Hastings," Pressia says, gripping the back of the empty copilot's seat.

"We'd have to touch down at Crazy John-Johns then lift off and land again," El Capitan says nervously.

"We can't leave him there," Bradwell says.

"I wasn't saying I'd abandon him. It's just a risk—that's all. If we crash-land like we did last time, we won't have anyone to help us. We'd have to make it back home on foot through a territory we barely survived the first time."

"We have no choice," Pressia says. "He needs us, and we might need him too."

"Need him for what?" El Capitan asks.

Pressia sighs. "I'm going into the Dome. I've got to talk to Partridge. I've got to get the cure to the right people on the inside." She keeps the backpack on at all times.

"You're assuming there are *right people on the inside*," Bradwell says.

"Right people," Helmud says optimistically.

"They can't all be bad. And now that Partridge is in charge, I'm sure he's—"

"I'm not sure of anything," Bradwell says. "Kelly knew that Willux was dead, that Partridge was in charge, so why hasn't he heard about a new order in the Dome?"

"Maybe Partridge hasn't had time," Pressia says angrily. "Maybe his plan is in the works. Or maybe he has started to make real changes but telling Kelly—an ocean away—isn't a top priority right now!" She turns to El Capitan. "You believe in Partridge, don't you?"

"I always doubt people," El Capitan says. "I've survived by not believing in other human beings."

Pressia understands. She's someone who's let Cap down; she doesn't love him the way he loves her. "What's your plan? You bring down the Dome and there's civil war? More blood, more death?" Pressia asks them.

"If you want to side with her, go ahead," Bradwell says to El Capitan. "How you feel about Pressia isn't a secret anymore. Do what you want."

Pressia's shocked that Bradwell's said this out loud. She glances at El Capitan. His cheeks are flushed. He coughs into his fist and looks out the windshield. They're cutting through a bank of clouds.

"You just want to be proven right after all these years," Pressia says to Bradwell. "You'll take justice over peace, even if it means people are going to die."

"I'm not trying to prove I'm right. I am right. There's a difference. The truth is important," Bradwell says. "History is important."

"El Capitan will do what he thinks is right—justice or peace," Pressia says. "I trust him to make that call."

"Peace," Helmud says, giving his vote.

Pressia's glad that Helmud is on her side. "Good," Pressia says. "Thanks."

"Cap?" Bradwell says.

"No," El Capitan says. "I'm not choosing between you. We've got to be united on this."

Bradwell stares out the windshield, and Pressia can only see his profile, the twin scars running down one cheek. He says, "My mother died gripping my father's shirt. Her eyes were still open, staring at him, like she'd died begging him to stay alive. But they died Pure—on the inside." He jabs his own chest. "They died as they were, fighting to get the truth out." He rubs his knuckles together and says. "And what am I?" His wings twitch on his back. "I'm a fairy tale parents tell their children to scare them into living careful lives. I'm not real."

Pressia imagines him as a little boy running through the house calling for them, his panic growing. Sometimes she forgets the little boy he once was—the one who was sent to his aunt and uncle's to live, who ran through the flock of birds when the Detonations hit, the one who found his way back to his parents' house, to the footlocker in the secured room, who fended for himself for years. She loves that kid. She loves the man he's become—complex and stubborn. "You are real. You're the same person."

He shakes his head. "No. That Bradwell is gone."

"What does that mean?" she asks.

"What's really kept me going all these years is the truth and justice. I could look up at that white Dome, its gleaming cross, anytime, and I had all I needed to survive. They killed my parents. They holed up in their perfect little bubble and destroyed the world. I'm a wretch. That's what made me Pure. And now? With those chemicals pumped into me, what am I?"

"You're still yourself," Pressia says. She wants to say more. She wants to tell him that he's real, that she loves him. But his back is stiff. His eyes are locked on the sky. He's cut off. She says, "You have every reason to hate me."

"I don't hate you. I only wish I could."

"Look," El Capitan says, "someone's got to compromise."

The cockpit is quiet.

"Here's my compromise." Bradwell breaks the silence. "Only over my dead body are the Pures coming out of this as heroes." He looks each of them in the eyes and then turns and walks out.

Pressia stares at the windshield that held his reflection. It's now a black screen shuddering with occasional clouds. He let his guard down. He talked about finding his dead parents. She wishes she'd said something different, but what?

She turns to El Capitan's reflection. He catches her eye and smiles sadly. "Sorry," he says. "For everything. I shouldn't have pushed him to—"

"Don't," she says. "It's okay."

Helmud reaches out and quickly touches her hair then shyly looks away.

She sees her own reflection and thinks of the rhyming game of tag the children were playing in the field.

Look in a looking glass. Look for a match. Find yourself! Find yourself! Don't be the last!

She lifts the doll head. Who would she be without it? More herself or less? She can't imagine what it must be like for Bradwell—his body isn't his own. She thinks of her own DNA, the instructions of how to build her and her alone. Hair, skin, blood.

And then she remembers the hairbrush in her room, how it never had a strand of hair in it the next morning. Did they take her DNA? Will there be replicas of her—out there—one day? The idea terrifies her in ways she doesn't understand. *Find yourself. Find yourself.* She doesn't really even know who she is. Neither does Bradwell. Does anyone?

El Capitan says, "We're over land."

"Land," Helmud says, as if commanding his brother to bring the airship down. "Land!"

Pressia pulls the backpack off and holds it to her chest. She looks out the windshield at the rugged horizon. From here, it looks peaceful and calm. But she knows it's teeming with Beasts and Dusts. The land itself is alive—hatefully alive. Maybe vengefulness is part of all of them.

PARTRIDGE

LUCKY US

Hᴉꜱ ᴍᴏᴛʜᴇʀ'ꜱ ᴠᴏɪᴄᴇ. "Partridge! Your friend is here!"

He opens his eyes.

His mother's voice? No—it can't be. She's dead. And yet she used to call to him like this when his friends showed up at the house. He remembers his childhood home—his bed sheets with small trucks on them, the clock in the shape of a baseball, a set of connectable blocks teetering on the floor.

And his mother, appearing in the doorway—the swing of her hair, her smile.

It's not his mother's voice, and it's not Lyda's either. This is his bedroom in the apartment he grew up in while inside the Dome. He sleeps on the bottom bunk. Sedge used to sleep on the top bunk. He didn't like it when Partridge would cry at night. Sedge would tell him to shut up. Their mother was gone, presumed dead. He should have been allowed to cry anytime he wanted to.

His father's bedroom is empty. He doesn't go in there—ever.

Partridge killed him.

This thought jerks him fully awake.

The door opens and it's Iralene. "Arvin Weed's here," she says.

"Should I make you two something to drink? Refreshments?" She's twising her engagement ring.

"What time is it?" He sits up.

"You slept and slept and slept," she says. "It's tomorrow already!"

After he got home and Iralene hugged him, he told her that he wasn't feeling well and thought it'd be good to talk to Arvin Weed, who's now his doctor. Really, he just wanted to grill Weed again about Glassings and the people who are still suspended, and also to show him the sheet of scientific equations Partridge found in his father's war-room chamber. After Iralene told him she'd set up a meeting with Weed, Partridge walked to this bedroom, lay down, and after days of not sleeping, fell into restless nightmares. He used to dream of finding his mother's dead body everywhere—under bleachers, in the academy science lab—but in this dream, he was going about his day in some mundane way when he came across a pile of bodies. One or two twitched, bleeding but still alive, and they got up and staggered toward him. They spoke with the voice of the man who jumped in front of the train—Eckinger Freund, the authorities confirmed. And these dying people called him a liar, but Partridge couldn't tell whether they hated him because of the truth he told about his father or this new lie—marrying Iralene.

"Are you coming to talk to Arvin?" Iralene says. "Should I chat with him to give you some time?"

He rubs his eyes and lies back in the bed, his hand spread on his heart. He's still fully dressed. He feels sick. "No, that's okay. I'm coming." She starts to leave the room, but he says, "Wait."

She turns back to him, smiling. "I love the way you look when you first wake up."

"Iralene, we're alone," he says. "We promised not to..." He asked her not to be romantic with him except for show, in public.

"Can't a girl practice?"

He sits up. "Did the death toll go up any since the press release went out?"

She takes a deep breath. The suicides scare her. Her face goes stony. "Beckley reported that there were no cases overnight."

"Good." If he's going to give up his freedom like this, and a good measure of the truth, it had better be saving lives. "Tell Arvin I'll be there in a minute, okay?"

"Sure." She smiles and shuts the door.

Partridge changes his clothes. He shouldn't be nervous about seeing Arvin. He was once just some academy nerd, a distant friend who'd sometimes let Partridge copy his notes. But Arvin isn't here as a friend. Arvin helped Partridge regrow his pinky, and he seemed to be in charge of the team that swiped Partridge's memory—both his father's orders. And Arvin most likely would have been the one chosen to perform the brain transplant. Would Arvin have gone through with it?

Partridge will never know. Instead of an operation, Arvin performed his father's autopsy, telling the leadership that his father's death was due to Rapid Cell Degeneration while, publicly, people were told that he'd struggled valiantly against a genetic disorder.

Partridge looks down at his pinky and flexes his hand. The pinky curls and extends right in sync with the others. All in all, it's incredible work. While here, Arvin will probably want to test the nerve endings and the re-formation of Partridge's memory too.

Partridge finds the sheet of scientific information where he hid it and slips it into his pocket.

He goes to the bathroom, splashes water on his face, and dries it with a hand towel. He stares at himself for a moment, and he's not sure who exactly he's supposed to be. He feels like a fraud. He knows he'll give himself over to this lie. He'll do it because Lyda whispered, *No more blood on your hands. No more.* But he knows that the blood has just begun.

And Lyda? And his baby? How long will they have to live this hidden life? After the meeting at Foresteed's office, they asked for a few minutes alone together. They held each other. She said, "Partridge, this is the right thing to do." Then she quickly added, "I'm scared."

He told her that he was scared too. And now he misses the feel of her warm body as they huddled together under his coat with the swirling ash, like black snow. He misses the way she looks at him, which always feels honest. He loves how Lyda seems both fragile and tough. On the one hand, the delicate work of making a human being is going on within her. On the other, she's hardened in a way he can't explain.

The truth about his father. This one truth. How many lies will he have to offer up as a sacrifice to appease the people of the Dome? How many?

He walks out of the bathroom, down the hall, and into the living room. Arvin is looking at Iralene's folder of bridal gowns. "I think that's a really beautiful one," he says, pointing to an open page. "Not that it matters."

"Why wouldn't it matter?" Iralene says, hurt.

"You'd look good in anything," Arvin says. And here's a perfect example of Weed. He might have meant he really doesn't care, but he recovers with a compliment. Or does he mean what he's saying? It's true that Iralene would look good in anything. She's perfect. It's why she's here.

And suddenly it hits him: They have him where they want him. He's playing out the life his father designed for him. Iralene, with her shiny hair and her bright smile, is preparing for their wedding. Partridge is going to walk down the aisle cowed by guilt. He tried to lead, and it was all stripped away.

And then his suspicions start up. Have the suicide numbers really been as dramatic as he's been told? The angry crowd, the noise of sirens, the man who jumped in front of the train—it all felt real. In fact, it felt spontaneous—like the most unplanned thing he's ever witnessed in the Dome. And yet, he can't trust Foresteed, who would see the disruption as an opportunity to guilt Partridge into submission. Foresteed might not possess much of a conscience, but he surely would see it as a weakness in others—one he could exploit to his advantage. How real is any of it? Is it a conspiracy to get Partridge to toe the line? Is Weed in on it?

"Sorry to interrupt," Partridge says.

Arvin and Iralene look up. Arvin sticks out his hand and shakes Partridge's. "How are you feeling?"

"I've been better."

Iralene scoops up her bridal packets and says, "I'll let you two talk." Partridge imagines training sessions that Iralene has been put through—lessons on when to be visible and when to politely disappear.

"Let's talk over here." Partridge leads Arvin to the sofas. They sit down across from each other.

"So, the pinky," Weed says. "Any heat, numbness, itching?"

"Nope."

Weed reaches across the coffee table between them, pokes Partridge's finger and bends it. "You feel all this pretty well?"

"Yep. Although sometimes, I still imagine it's gone. And then I look down and it surprises me."

"People who lose a leg say they can still feel it; their nerve endings continue to send messages to the brain that it exists. It's called a phantom limb."

"So I'm feeling the phantom of the phantom?"

"Regrowing parts of the body is all new science. Maybe this will become a commonplace observation."

Partridge wonders if Arvin is talking about Wilda, the girl who was kidnapped, taken into the Dome, and Purified. She no longer has scars or marks or fusing or even a belly button, and she could only say what she was programmed to say—a threat from Partridge's father. "You expecting to regrow a lot of limbs, Dr. Weed?"

"I'm one of the good guys, Partridge," Arvin says. "You know that." His eyes shift away from Partridge and glide around the room.

"Do I?" Partridge says.

Arvin laughs and leans back in the sofa.

"What's so funny?"

"I remember one time you told me that I lived too much in my head. You said, 'Don't you have a gut instinct, Weed? Have you ever just gone with your gut?' Do you remember that?"

Partridge has no recollection of it at all. "Must be the memory loss," Partridge says.

"No," Weed says. "You don't remember it because you said it without even thinking about it. You poked me in the gut with one finger, and everyone laughed."

"Sorry, Weed. I'm sure I didn't mean anything by it."

"Everything you said meant something. You were Willux's son. It was your free pass to do whatever you wanted."

"Really?" Partridge says defensively. "Because I remember people offering to beat my ass, and did you jump in and help me? No. You just kept your nose to your studies. And you know what? I was right. You do live in your head too much."

"And *you*," Weed says, "should try relying on your gut a little less and your head a little more. If you did, maybe we wouldn't be in this mess."

He's blaming Partridge for the suicides, and Weed's right. There's no denying that Partridge sparked it all. Partridge raises one hand in the air. Weed's gone too far. Partridge can no longer allow people to talk to him like this—not even an old friend.

Weed coughs, straightens his shirt. It's quiet a moment before Weed finally returns to his role as doctor. "What about your memory?"

"It's still patchy sometimes—you know, my time on the outside." He remembers most of it—Pressia, Bradwell, El Capitan, and Helmud, and the mothers fused to their children. He remembers the *thunk* of his pinky being chopped off and how it lay there, disconnected. And there are things that still come to him in splotches of color—mainly his mother and Sedge dying on the forest floor. He remembers being with Lyda in the empty brass four-poster bed frame, bundled under his coat, the heat of their bodies. "You know how it is. Some things you want to remember," he says. "Some things you want to forget."

"I bet," Arvin says, a slight smirk on his face.

Does Weed know he's a murderer? If so, Partridge almost wishes he'd come right out and say it. "You bet?"

Arvin leans forward, elbows on his knees, and lowers his voice. "Tell me why I'm really here."

"First off, where's Glassings?"

"Durand Glassings? Our World History teacher? This was what you were trying to get at when we were at the memorial service. Still on that?"

"Yes."

"How the hell should I know?"

"Foresteed's telling me the same thing. But someone knows."

"Not me." Weed looks at him stone-faced.

"I want to know if you've started to successfully take people out of suspension," Partridge says, "like I told you to."

"Look, this isn't easy. Belze is very old. He was very weak when he was put into suspension, postoperative actually. And did you know he only has one leg? The stump ends in a clot of wires. We can't just yank him from suspension. I mean, if you're doing this in some way for your sister's sake, it's not going to do any good if he dies in the process."

"How do you know he's connected to Pressia?"

"I've got the highest level clearance possible. In fact, some of us are curious about what really happened in your mother's bunker. Did you ever come across those vials and maybe some other stuff?"

"I thought you'd only want that for my dad, for a last-ditch effort to cure him, and since he didn't get them in time to do him any good…"

"I could do a lot with them—trust me." Arvin stands up and paces.

"Really? Are you sure about that, Weed?"

"Jesus, Partridge! I've got all the stuff I need to Purify someone, but then they fall apart."

"I've seen your handiwork," Partridge says a little sarcastically.

"You mean the wretches we brought in?" Weed says, walking to the window, looking down at the street. "Those were just experiments."

"No, they were *people*."

He turns to Partridge quickly and says, "And their sacrifices will not be in vain if I have the formula and that one last ingredient. I'd be able to fix all of the wretches without any of the side effects that killed your father. You think the guys in Special Forces are going to come out of it clean? There are friends of ours from the academy in there, Partridge."

"I just didn't know you had this altruistic bent. I mean, Arvin Weed, humanitarian. I had no idea when you were, you know, overseeing my torture."

"Orders are orders. Some would say I was more dutiful than Willux's own son. Say what you want about him; he was a genius, your father was. You'll never even begin to imagine what his brain was capable of. You should show some respect."

"Weed, in your head and in your gut, you know my father was a mass murderer; you've *got* to know that."

Weed nods. He lightly scratches his forehead. He says in an eerily calm voice, "I can make something good happen. I can save people. I can make good where your father failed."

Partridge shakes his head.

"You think you can take over where my father left off somehow?" Partridge stands up, turns his back on Weed, crosses his arms on his chest. "I know you were the one who developed the pill," Partridge says softly. He's unable to look Weed in the eye. In this sentence, he's acknowledging the fact that Partridge used the pill to kill his father, as well as the real possibility that Weed was an accomplice to this murder. It could be that Partridge and Weed are not as different as they seem, bound as they are in a moment in history—in an assassination.

"Without you," Partridge says, "I couldn't have done it." He turns and glances at Weed, then looks down at the floor.

"I'm sure I don't know what you're talking about," Weed says.

Partridge can't stand the lies and denials anymore. He walks over to Weed, pushes him and grabs him by the shoulder. "Goddamn it! If you admired my old man so much, why'd you do it?"

Weed glares at Partridge, full of hate. He pulls his shoulder free of Partridge's grasp.

"I said I don't know what you're talking about."

And then Partridge knows the answer. Arvin already said it: *I can make good where your father failed.* Weed wanted to take over.

Weed walks to the couch and sits down heavily. "You don't know anything, Partridge. It's the same old shit. You're strolling along, being Willux's son, and you haven't done any homework."

Partridge sits down across from Weed again too. He presses his palms together. "That's not entirely true. I've been to my father's secret chamber in his war room. I learned a lot there. In fact, your name appeared in a document there."

"Of course it did! I'm in the thick of it, Partridge, and I have been for a long time. Even when we were both in the academy, I was already being brought into inner circles."

"If I don't know anything, Weed, how about you enlighten me? Go ahead. Lay it on me."

"Well," Weed says, "for one, your sister and her friends stole one of our airships. It was tagged, of course. We know its route. We know who they likely contacted—how they figured out where to find these other survivors is a mystery—but *they* actually do their homework, turns out."

Partridge ignores the dig. "What the hell are you talking about? A route?"

"Across the Atlantic Ocean, and they're on their way back."

Partridge laughs. It's ridiculous. "The Atlantic? In an airship? Not possible."

"They took it to Newgrange, one of your father's special locales. If you've been in his inner chamber, then you know he's spared a few holy places and the people lucky enough to be there at the time."

Newgrange. Partridge thinks back to all of Glassings' lectures on ancient burial mounds and Partridge's father's obsession since childhood with domes. "But Pressia, Bradwell, El Capitan and Helmud—they went all the way there and back again?"

Arvin nods.

"Foresteed should have told me all this!"

"I'm sure it's in the reports."

"I don't read those reports!" Partridge says to himself more than to Weed.

"And there. You've proven my point."

"Newgrange," Partridge says. "In an airship." The world seems to open up. Pressia, Bradwell, El Capitan and Helmud—they've been across an ocean. "My God," he whispers. "But they're not back yet? It sounds dangerous."

"Well, they got there and they're in the air again. The question is why. What did they think they'd find there? And were they successful?"

"Is Foresteed on this, tracking their progress?"

"Foresteed doesn't care much about your sister and her friends. He's got other interests."

"Like what?"

Arvin smiles. "You can ask him that yourself."

"Arvin, listen. I think we could get a council together—people from the outside and the inside sitting down to talk. We can help each side to understand the other. That's where my father really failed. These people are killing themselves, but if they knew some of the people out there, if they met Pressia—"

Weed cuts him off. "That's nice, Partridge. But it won't work."

"Why not?"

"As long as the wretches wear our shared history on their skin, there will be no peace. Guilt, Partridge. You can't live with all of that guilt without wanting to blame the victims and exonerate yourself. Human nature."

"But…"

Weed wags his head, smiling. "Here's an example. You want me to bring these people out of suspension. What the hell are we going to do with all these people? Huh? Some of them are deformed. Some are even wretches. What are you going to do? Get them jobs? Send them into grocery stores?"

"Why not?"

"I've spent the last few days stitching up slit wrists, staring into big, gaping gunshot wounds, pumping people's stomachs. Because of you."

"Wait, now," Partridge says. This is the second time Weed's pinned the deaths on him. It's not completely fair. "My father shouldn't have shoved lies down their throats."

"So while I was cleaning up the mess, you were busy rationalizing it all away? Is that how you've spent your time?"

"No, I told you I went into my father's secret chamber, and I know that my father knew he'd made a mistake. He knew the end was coming."

"And that's where you saw my name, huh?" Weed smooths his hair, rubs his temple. "Yeah, I remember that report. Pretty sobering. So we're not the superior race after all. Imagine how your father felt when he caught on to that one." Weed laughs, but there's no lingering smile.

"I don't know what made him think we were superior to begin with. I'll never understand him."

"Is that what you want from me? A psychoanalysis of your father?"

"I wouldn't ask that of my worst enemy," Partridge says. "But I do know that if my father didn't like a truth, he found a way to change it." Partridge reaches into his pocket and pulls out the sheet of scientific information that he took from his father's files. He doesn't want to show it to Weed, but who else is there? "Explain this to me."

Weed takes the sheet, glances at it, and hands it back. "It's a recipe."

"To make what?"

"People."

"I don't get it. People?"

"Why would you? You're making a person the old-fashioned way, right? Knocking someone up."

"You know her name. She's not just *someone*. Just explain the science, okay?"

Weed smiles, happy to get a rise out of Partridge, and leans back again. "This was his recipe to make them from scratch. A little DNA from Pures, a little from the tougher breed, the wretches. Some cloning, some breeding."

"Did you give this recipe to him?"

Weed laughs. "That stuff is very advanced. Who knows where he got it? But not from us. No. It's high art."

"So he was going to start to build his own super race from scratch."

"He wasn't *going to start* to do it. It's under way. In fact, I was with you when you saw them."

"Saw *them*? Who?"

"Maybe it's one of the patches that hasn't yet come clear. Plus, you were a little drugged up. We were taking you in for cleansing."

"You mean when you almost drowned me?"

"Your father preferred the term *baptism*."

"Who did I see? Where?"

"The babies—rows and rows of tiny babies."

And then Partridge remembers it—clearly. The bank of windows like in a giant maternity ward, but all of the babies were premature, tiny, writhing, some squalling, some placid and still. Babies. He was lying down—no, strapped down—rolling...being rolled on a gurney.

"New Eden deserved its own Adams and Eves," Weed says. "Willux gave up on the people of the Dome too—we're weak and vulnerable with delicate lungs and testy hearts. He started to hate us near the end, Partridge. And when you went out and survived, he was proud of you. You didn't even have any of the things that had been built into your brother's coding. You were just out there, raw and alone and surviving. You should have heard him talk about you." Weed looks sickened by the memory. And Partridge finds it hard to believe. His father was always so disappointed in Partridge. But then he thinks of the war room, all of those pictures from his childhood, all of those love letters. Maybe his father hid his love and pride well.

Still, Partridge isn't sure what to think. His father's feelings for him are so twisted and impossible to pin down. "He never told me he was proud of me. Not ever." Except at the end, just before he died—knowing Partridge had poisoned him—he told Partridge, "You are my son. You are mine"—which made Partridge feel like his father, for the first time, saw something in Partridge that was a reflection of himself. When Partridge thinks of it now, it's as if his father were telling him that he and Partridge were alike, maybe even that Partridge was bound to become his father, which his father would have meant as a great compliment. "He only loved himself."

"Well, the new Adams and Eves became his people, his hope. They were the future." Weed stands up. "You should see for yourself."

"What about little Jarv Hollenback? Did you get him out of suspension? Is he with his parents?"

Weed nods.

"Were the Hollenbacks happy to have him home again?" It's a stupid question, but Partridge wants one good thing—some positive effect of his being here, even if it's small.

"Well, Mrs. Hollenback…"

"What?"

"She's in the hospital."

"Did she try—"

"Nearly succeeded too."

He remembers the last time he saw her—in the kitchen, her hands dusted with flour, the panic in her voice. *Lucky us*, she said. *Lucky us*. And she wanted so desperately to mean it. Mrs. Hollenback, who taught the History of Domesticity as an Art Form—he remembers her singing about a snowman. How did she try to do it? He doesn't want to imagine it. She'd gotten Jarv back. Why would she do this now? Where did her resilience go, her will to live? "I want to see Mrs. Hollenback—first, before anything else." He rubs his hands together, thinking of guilt and blood. "And I want to see the wards. I don't want any more escalation talk from Foresteed, no more data. I want to see the people."

"Are you sure?"

"Yes."

Weed seems to appreciate this. "Okay."

"Do you think the wedding will help—at all? I mean, do they really just need a distraction?"

"You ripped everything away from them. The wedding gives them something to orient themselves around again." Partridge nods. He was hoping that Weed would have given him reason to back out. "Anyway, who wouldn't want to marry Iralene?"

Partridge looks at him. He feels numb suddenly. "You know where my heart's at."

Weed scratches his head and shrugs. "To each his own."

"I want you to bring me to the wards, now," Partridge says. "I need to see things with my own eyes."

Weed tilts his head. "And I want to talk to your sister, Partridge. If they don't crash that ship, I want to know what she knows."

"Do you think they'll crash?"

"Who knows if they've got any real pilot aboard? Chances are slim, right?"

But Partridge isn't so sure. He immediately thinks of El Capitan and how much he loved his car. He'd go crazy for an airship. No way he wouldn't be at the controls. Would he be any good at it? Partridge doesn't really know, but he feels a surge of confidence in El Capitan just based on the power of El Capitan's will alone. "I can't tell you what my sister might or might not know."

"Trust me," Arvin says. "She knows something!"

El Capitan

Crazy John-Johns

EL CAPITAN SITS IN THE PILOT'S SEAT, hunched forward because of Helmud on his back. Fignan is in the copilot's seat, projecting bright maps of the surrounding territory. El Capitan's scanning the horizon for Crazy John-Johns Amusement Park. He wishes he didn't have to go back; they almost died there. In his mind's eye, he can still see Helmud over his shoulder, stabbing each of the Dusts' eyes as they blinked up from the earth, the big hulk of the ones that pulled themselves up from the dirt, and Hastings' leg bitten by the teeth of a trap, how he ripped it free—his leg half gone. And his car—he loved that damn car; it's stuck out there too.

Hastings? Did he survive surgery on his leg? Lots of things could have gone wrong—a clumsy surgeon accidentally snipping a main artery, a loss of blood, a lack of hygiene causing infection.

What if he's dead?

Shit.

The landscape is still dusty and barren. Last time, he crash-landed. He'd like to do it right, but he's already distracted. He's thinking about what Pressia said—that one day, it might be possible for him and Helmud to be severed from each other. The vial has properties to regrow cells. These could be used on Helmud from the place where his ribs lock a little with El Capitan's ribs and where his legs are melted into El Capitan. He imagines a procedure where Helmud is regrown bit by bit as they're slowly, surgery after surgery, separated. Could it be possible?

Helmud has been a part of El Capitan for so long. What would it feel like to be alone again? He tells himself it would feel damn good. He wants to be that man—his own man. But there's an ache in his chest every time he thinks of it, as if Helmud's heart—which rides forever just behind El Capitan's own heart—feels the betrayal and applies sharp pressure, heart to heart.

If it could work, would it allow Pressia to see him as a real person, a man who stands alone—someone she could fall in love with?

She and Bradwell are back in their seats. El Capitan wishes he could feel a twinge of hope that they'll never get back together. But he also knows that he's got no shot with Pressia—with Bradwell around or not.

Pressia's got what she wants—the vial and the formula—and El Capitan has the bacterium. Back in his room, he asked one of the caretakers for strong tape, and he adhered the box holding the bacterium, flat and square, behind his back—right in front of Helmud's chest. He says, "Check it, Helmud."

And he can feel Helmud's fingers pushing against the box. "Check!" Helmud says.

El Capitan doesn't have his guns, but he's the most armed he's ever been in his life.

Crazy John-Johns starts to take shape through the ash. As he allows the buckies to take on air, the airship dips lower. He can see the elongated neck of one of the roller coasters jutting into the sooty clouds and the tilted merry-go-round, but the ash is too thick to see the giant cracked head of Crazy John-Johns himself—his permanent smiling clown face, bulbous nose, and bald head. The dust on the ground is too thick.

"Something's wrong!" he shouts to Pressia and Bradwell.

"Something," Helmud whispers.

Fignan lets out a series of nervous beeps.

"What is it?" Pressia calls to him.

He passes over the amusement park and then starts to circle back. A high fence surrounds the park, but the earth around it is shifting as Dusts tunnel up, pulling themselves from the dirt. Some are loping toward the fence while others claw at it. "The Dusts are rising up!"

The survivors are defending the park with beebees and darts. The Dusts' weakness is their eyes—the spot where they're most human. When struck in the eyes, they buckle and fall, and the other Dusts devour them quickly. "They can't kill them fast enough. There are too many Dusts. Hundreds of them!"

El Capitan doesn't see Hastings. He starts to feel a gnawing in his gut. Pressia has convinced him that they need Hastings. He's a Dome insider—one of their own creations, Special Forces elite. But, of course, he's been debugged and therefore compromised, but he could claim that all of that was done against his will. He can drag himself back to the Dome as the embattled messenger. He's also an old friend of Partridge. He'll take Hastings back in, right?

"I see Fandra!" Pressia shouts.

"And Hastings!" Bradwell calls out.

There they are—climbing up using the roller coaster's rails as a ladder. Hastings is stooped and pale, but still tall and muscular. He's wearing some kind of prosthetic hidden by his pant leg except for a wedge of metal—what's now his foot. Weaponry embedded in his arms, he stops—wind-whipped, hooking his arm to the roller coaster—and fires at the Dusts. He's a good shot and takes a few out. Their bodies spin and fall. But there are too many. Fandra is climbing up behind him. Her hair is as bright as a golden flag. She has it tied back, but thin wisps still bat around her face.

"You can't land," Bradwell says, "not down there with all the Dusts, so they're coming up to meet us!"

He's right. Hastings and Fandra are climbing to them.

"Do they want to airlift everyone out?" El Capitan shouts.

"Too many of them now!" Bradwell shouts.

Through the ash and dust, El Capitan sees darting bodies running through the amusement park. Bradwell's right. There are more survivors than when they were last here. Fignan has extended his legs and is trying to gather data. He states an approximate count—seventy-two—male-to-female ratio, approximate ages.

"Not now, Fignan!" El Capitan says.

"Not now!" Helmud shouts.

It means more people have risked their lives to get away from the city—a bad sign. Something's happened to the city. *What now?* El Capitan thinks. *What now?* He feels sick, a familiar wrenching dread in his chest.

"We need Hastings!" El Capitan shouts.

"Why are they attacking?" Pressia says. "The music was a deterrent. Where's the music?"

"Can't hear it over the engine," El Capitan says. The music kept the Dusts at bay. It was only the stupid plinking notes of an amusement park theme song. Dinky dinks and diddly dinks...But the survivors used it as a deterrent, broadcasting it on old speakers before opening fire. The Dusts had come to fear it.

"We can't hear the music," Bradwell says. "We're locked up in here."

El Capitan touches a button and the seal of a small side window breaks and the window lowers a few inches. He hears movement, probably Pressia and Bradwell rushing toward the open window.

At first there's only the rush of air. But then they hear a scream. Then another. "There's no music," she says.

"Without the music..." El Capitan shouts, and then he whispers what they all know: "They'll die."

He passes over Crazy John-Johns, this time so low he can see the twisted, melted faces of the horses on the merry-go-round. And now he can make out some Dusts ramming their heavy bodies into the chain link, pounding amid the beebee gunfire, small dirt clods spraying from their chests and shoulders. A dozen of them lean into the fence, which bows under their weight.

Then the fence gives, popping up from its posts and folding over on itself. The Dusts crawl over it into the park itself.

The survivors start screaming and pouring from one side of the park to the other.

"Goddamn it!" El Capitan says.

"God!" Helmud shouts.

He hears Pressia shouting, "What the hell are you doing?"

Bradwell bolts in through the cockpit doorway. "They're in," he says.

"I know," El Capitan says.

"God!" Helmud says.

"We've got to get in close to the roller coaster," Bradwell says. "And we need a way to pull Hastings in."

"And Fandra," El Capitan says.

Pressia walks into the cockpit too. "She won't come with us. She won't leave the others. I know her. She's climbing up for a reason, but it's not to run away."

Bradwell is looking out the windshield. "You better hurry."

"I'm going to get in as close as I can," El Capitan says.

"Close," Helmud says.

El Capitan lets more air into the buckies. The airship lists momentarily to one side—Pressia and Bradwell stagger and then hold on to the walls. The wind is strong, coming in from the west. He banks into it. "If I lower the landing prongs, he can grab hold."

Hastings has reached the top of the roller coaster; Fandra is beside him. They're both holding tight. The ashen wind roils around them.

"In this wind," El Capitan mutters, "it's just going to be harder to get in tight."

"You can do it, Cap," Bradwell says.

"I crashed it last time. I crashed!" Jesus! He crashed. They could have died. He remembers the ground running close below them. He braced for the landing, and things went black.

"Bradwell's right," Pressia says. "You can. We know it."

"We know it," Helmud says.

El Capitan tightens his grip on the wheel and leans forward. He circles again. The Dusts are roaming the park. A few are hunched over a body—a survivor? Another Dust? They're feasting.

Up ahead, Hastings and Fandra are waiting at the top of the roller coaster, their clothes rippling.

And then they wobble. They look at one another and then below.

"What's wrong?" Pressia says.

"The Dusts," Bradwell says.

El Capitan sees that they've gathered at the base of the roller coaster. They're bashing it with their shoulders.

"We can't leave Fandra," Pressia says. "We can't abandon them."

"What other options do we have?" El Capitan says.

"It's too terrible to imagine how they'll all die. Too terrible." Pressia's eyes well up, and she covers her face with her one hand and tucks the doll head under her chin. El Capitan wants to comfort her, but he can't; even if he could take his hands off the controls, he wouldn't touch her in front of Bradwell.

But just as the horror of it all starts to wash over El Capitan— these Dusts devouring survivors in the bombed-out amusement park—a few tinny notes fill the air. Fignan. He's playing back a recording that he must have captured the last time they were here.

They all turn and look at Fignan, who detects the sudden attention and quiets down.

"Fignan!" Pressia cries. "You've got it!"

Fignan flashes his row of lights proudly.

"And he can blast it louder too," El Capitan says to Bradwell. "Can't he?"

"Blast it," Helmud says.

"Yes," Bradwell says, "but—"

"We'll have to hand him over," Pressia says.

"Wait," Bradwell says. "There has to be another way."

"But Fignan can save them!" Pressia says. "Who knows what happened to their system."

"But we can't hand him over," Bradwell says. "He's got important information. He's one of a kind."

"We have to. They're going to die. They need him."

And then Fignan's lights pulse and again the little tune rises up from him—light and soft and quick.

"Get to the door in the cabin," El Capitan says. "Be ready to pull Hastings in and lower Fignan down. I'll find a way to hold this thing steady."

"Keep playing, Fignan," Pressia says, picking him up and carrying him out of the cockpit. "As loud as you can."

"Careful with him," Bradwell says, following her out. Fignan has become his loyal companion, an old friend.

Fignan gets louder and louder until the notes are shrill and piercing, even over the growling engines. El Capitan releases the four long legs that steady the ship on the ground. Hastings is still coded for strength, agility, speed. Hopefully he's strong enough—after his loss of blood, his loss of a limb—to grab hold. The landing legs buzz loudly and then lock into place.

El Capitan feels a gust of wind whipping in through the cabin. Pressia and Bradwell have gotten the cabin door open. El Capitan allows the buckies to take on more air. The airship lilts and sways and glides toward Hastings, who's locked his legs—one real, one prosthetic—on the final rung of the roller coaster, now swaying from the frantic Dusts beating it below. El Capitan won't be able to see if he slows the airship enough for Hastings to grab hold. It will happen under the hull.

In his final glimpse of them, Fandra is looking at the Dusts below, and Hastings stretches out both arms, reaching up.

PARTRIDGE

COAL

Arvin Weed is leading Partridge and Beckley through a wing of the medical center. Arvin is explaining that Mrs. Hollenback is sharing a room that should only be a single. "Nothing we could do at the time. Of course, the other two patients have been temporarily moved—to give you privacy. It's been a mad house," Weed tells him. "At one point, we had beds lining the halls."

This makes Partridge's chest tighten. He'd like to have his dead father keep shouldering the blame, but how long can he keep that up? *Rationalizing*—that's what Weed called it, and he was right.

There are only a few medical personnel, talking over a stack of charts. All of the doors they pass by are shut. He feels guilty for thinking that Foresteed was exaggerating the epidemic of suicides. Maybe Partridge just wanted a reason not to believe it and accept the guilt.

"Does Mrs. Hollenback know I'm coming?" Partridge asks.

"I asked to have her prepped for the visit. I asked a lot of the people on staff if she's ready for this," Arvin says. "They thought it might actually be really good for her. She loved you like her own, you know."

Partridge knows that she accepted him into her home and was kind about it, but he'd always felt like a burden on some level. "She was good to me," he says.

Now they walk up to Mrs. Hollenback's door. Her name is on her chart, sitting in a holder attached to the wall: HOLLENBACK, HELENIA. FEMALE. AGE 35.

Only thirty-five? She'd always seemed old.

Weed hovers a few feet from the door. It's strange to Partridge suddenly how grown-up Arvin is—a doctor, a scientist, a genius. Weed hates him and has for a while—that's what Partridge figured out from their heated conversation. Still, he can't help but be impressed by Weed; he seems like an adult already and Partridge feels like he's only faking.

"Your parents must be proud of you," Partridge says, maybe stalling—he's scared of the condition he might find Mrs. Hollenback in. "How are they?" Partridge might not be sure exactly where Arvin stands, but his parents were both on his mother's list—the Cygnus, the good guys.

"They caught colds, actually."

"Colds? Nothing serious, I hope."

"Nothing serious," Arvin says, and then he claps Partridge on the shoulder. "Good luck in there."

"I'll stand guard," Beckley says.

Partridge nods, takes a breath, and knocks.

"You'll have to just open the door," Weed says. "Her voice isn't strong enough to tell you to come in. I'll be down at the nurse's station."

"Wait," Partridge says. "Are you going to tell me how she tried to do it?"

Weed shakes his head. "She'll tell you if she wants to."

Partridge puts his hand on the knob, turns it slowly, and walks into the room. It's clean and white, brightly lit. He walks past two empty beds. The beds of the patients taken away for Partridge's visit are fitted with straps loosely dangling by the bed rails, which chills him.

He hears Mrs. Hollenback's voice, a hoarse whisper. "Is it you?"

He walks to the curtain pulled around her bed, reaches up—and thinks of his own mother, the hazy memory of the small room where he and Pressia found her again, the glass-covered capsule, her serene face, her eyes opening…He pulls back the curtain and says, "Yes. It's me."

She's thin and pale. Her eyes are hollowed. She wears a hospital gown that's too big for her and gapes around her neck so much that she holds it down with one hand, as if pledging allegiance. But the most disturbing part of her appearance is her mouth. It's blackened—her lips look ashen, and when she smiles, even her teeth are dark as if she's chewed a piece of coal, like her mouth is a dark pit.

She reaches out her hand.

Partridge walks quickly to her and takes it in his. Her hand feels bony and cold, like a child's hand in winter.

She says, "Oh, Partridge." Her voice is raw.

He's not sure if it's said in tenderness or if it's edged with scolding. She's been a kind of mother to him. Over the last few years, she was the one who set his presents out under the Christmas tree, who gave him a warm bed and fed him from their Sunday food rations. Julby and Jarv treated him like an older brother. "How are you doing?" he asks.

"I'm fine," she says. "I'm alive, right?" Her face tightens into a painful smile. "When you get better, we'll have dinner together. Your family and me and Iralene," he says, wanting to do anything to make things right. "I owe you so many dinners!"

She shakes her head. "Oh, Partridge."

"You're like family to me," he says.

She turns her head to the pillow. "What do we know about family here?" she whispers.

"You taught me about family," he says. "And Jarv is home, right? Don't you want to go home to Julby and Jarv?"

"Jarv." She clenches her fist on the hospital gown, twisting it tightly, and closes her eyes. "Don't you know why he's not right? Don't you know?"

"No," Partridge says softly.

"He comes from me," she says, opening her eyes and turning back to him. "I'm sick inside. Diseased. If you cut me open, Partridge, there would be nothing but rot. Do you understand? I've been dying ever since I got into the Dome. Rotting from within."

"That's not true. You're such a good mother and teacher. Everyone loves you."

She shakes her head. "They don't know me."

"I know you," Partridge says. "I know you, and I love you."

"Do you know what I did to get in this hospital bed?"

He's not sure he wants to know. "It's personal. You don't have to tell me if you don't want to."

"I took all the pills. The ones for Jarv, the ones for my headaches, the ones for Ilvander's back, even the ones to calm Julby when she gets into one of her fits. I took them all. I wanted to die. I needed to die. But they didn't let me. They pumped my stomach and gave me charcoal tablets and tried to cleanse me. There is no way to cleanse me—not really. Not ever."

"Mrs. Hollenback," Partridge says. "Don't..."

She reaches up and grips his shirtsleeve. "You spoke the truth," she says. "It woke me up."

He doesn't want to start crying, but he can feel his chest tightening with guilt. "I didn't mean what I said. Not the way you heard it. I didn't mean it, Mrs. Hollenback. If I'd known anyone would do this, I wouldn't have—"

"Do you know who I left to die out there beyond the Dome? My father was friends with someone who had spots reserved for himself, his wife, his two daughters. One of his daughters was a revolutionary, though. She told him she refused to go. I overheard my father and her father talking. He said, 'If it goes bad suddenly, we'll take one of your girls with us. She'll take my daughter's place. I wish I could offer more.' I had two sisters. Which one would my parents choose? I had an advantage. I was the only one who knew we were competing. I didn't want to let on that I knew, and so instead, Ilvander, who already had a spot, made a plan with me. I told my parents I was pregnant. I knew that this would never be exposed as a ploy to be chosen. There was so much shame in it, and yet I also knew that my parents would choose to send me if I was pregnant, a child inside of me. And then things happened more quickly than anyone thought they would. I was taken in. My sisters weren't. They stayed behind with my parents and likely died. You said it—we are all complicit. I'm a murderer too, Partridge, like your father. I let them die. I should have died with them."

The story stuns Partridge. He's only able to mutter, "Don't say that. Suicide is never the answer."

"This wasn't suicide. It was a death that I was owed a long time ago."

He's panicking. How can he make this right? "My wedding is something to look forward to. I want you to be there—your whole family—in the front row."

"You spoke the truth."

"What if I was lying?"

"You weren't."

"What if I told you..." And for a few seconds, he stops breathing. Can he tell her the truth? Can he accept some of her guilt to spare her? "I'm a murderer too."

"You were too young. You didn't understand what was happening—not like we did. No."

"You don't understand," he says. "I killed him. I'm a murderer."

Mrs. Hollenback searches his face. "You killed *him*?" she says, but he's sure she knows who he's talking about.

"I had to stop my father." Now that he's said these words aloud, he wants to tell her everything. "I had no choice. He was planning to—"

With one hand, she presses her fingers to his mouth and with the other brings her fingertips to her own blackened lips. Her eyes quiver with tears. She shakes her head and then lets her hands fall to her bed. She stares up at the ceiling.

"Forgive us," she whispers. "Forgive us all."

Pressia

FRESH SMOKE

Pressia is leaning out of the airship. She's going to lower Fignan to Hastings, who will then give him to Fandra. Then they'll have to drag Hastings up into the airship. The wind whips Pressia's hair into her mouth, across her cheeks, stinging her eyes. She holds Fignan tightly and leans deeper toward Hastings, trusting Bradwell's grip on her waist, familiar and yet foreign. His wings are rustling, buffeted by the gusts.

"It's okay," Bradwell reassures her. "I've got you. I do."

Fignan is blaring out the Crazy John-Johns theme park music so loud it's already caused a few Dusts to start to retreat. But still, some Dusts are slamming at the foundation of the ruined roller coaster. Hastings has his arms held high, and Fandra crouches beside him, flinching each time the Dusts thump the base.

"Slower! Tell him to go slower!" Pressia yells into the wind at Bradwell. It feels good to scream at him after their argument and all the distance between them.

"He's doing what he can!" Bradwell says at her back. She knows his face so well—the long scars, his eyebrows, his lashes—that she can imagine the face he's making right now, grimacing to hold on to her, furrowing his brow with effort. She's so close she can see the wrinkles on Hastings' knuckles, the fine sand blowing against his cheek, the shine of the guns on his arms.

Suddenly the wind lifts the front end of the airship. It's as if Hastings is falling beneath her. She wants to drop Fignan to Fandra, hoping she'll catch him, but can't risk it.

"We missed!" she yells.

The heavier drone means that El Capitan knows and is pulling up to circle around for another try. They were so close.

Bradwell pulls her back into the hull, and they sit breathing heavily.

"Maybe he can reapproach facing the wind," Bradwell says without looking at her. "He almost had it."

"We were really close," Pressia says. And as she hears herself say these words to Bradwell, she wants to say them to him about them. They were so close. They were in love. Now this: the long silence, the tension, the disappointment. She wants back that tingle when he walked near her, not the thud of dread. Sitting this close to Bradwell should make her feel confident, happy, even as she's about to lean out of the airship hundreds of feet off the ground.

"We'll get it this time," Bradwell says.

Pressia nods. But there's no hope for the two of them, is there? She looks back toward the amusement park, the roller coaster like a giant sliced serpent, the gray horizon. This has been Fandra's home, and Pressia is going to help her save it. Pressia misses her own home. As dirty and wrecked as it is, she's almost back, which is a strange comfort.

The airship moves in, closing on Hastings' outstretched hands.

Pressia faces the opening again and leans to Hastings, Bradwell's strong hands on her hips. The airship lurches up briefly and then into almost a complete halt that allows Pressia to drop Fignan just a couple of inches into Hastings' grip.

"He's got it!" she yells.

Hastings turns quickly with the little black box playing its haunting melody and gives it to Fandra. He says something to Fandra, who looks up at Hastings through her wind-crazed hair, through the pelting sand and dust and ash. She smiles. And Hastings turns away and leaps at one of the airship's legs. He balances there for a few moments, and then makes eye contact with Pressia, readying himself to swing up to her.

"When I count to three," Bradwell says.

She nods.

Bradwell tightens his grip. "One, two, three!"

Hastings swings off the leg of the airship and clasps Pressia's hand. She pulls with all her strength; Bradwell's arms flex, pull her to his chest. The ground below is a blur. The wind fills her lungs, the airship noise roars in her ears—overwhelming. Hastings' eyes are shot through with confident determination, and she feels the depth of her own strength as she and Bradwell pull Hastings toward the safety of the airship. Pressia is a link, saving Hastings from the sky and then the ground. Bradwell reels them all the way in, falling backward on his enormous wings, pulling Pressia with him.

Hastings tumbles in, his metal prosthetic rattling on the floor.

"Go, Cap! We've got him!" Bradwell yells. "Go!"

Hastings rights himself and moves quickly back to the open cabin door. He holds up his hand, and then he lets it fall. He sits on the floor of the airship and leans against the wall, propping his good leg.

Bradwell shuts the cabin door, locks it, and sits on the edge of his chair.

Pressia moves quickly to the porthole. The Dusts are lumbering away from Fignan's music, lugging their heavy bodies back over the broken fence. She sees Fandra. They lock eyes. Pressia spreads her hand on the small circular pane of glass. Fandra nods and smiles. She mouths, "Thank you!" Pressia wants to stop time, wants to confide in Fandra, to tell her everything, but the airship speeds up, banks left.

El Capitan shouts, "Everybody okay?"

"Okay?" Helmud cries.

"We're all good!" Bradwell says, relieved.

"So glad you made it," Pressia says, turning to Hastings.

She sees some of Hastings' prosthetic. Pressia specialized in making prosthetics while at OSR headquarters, and she can tell that the joints aren't very flexible, but it's sturdy workmanship. The lower leg is made of two bowed pieces of metal. She figures that they'd have a lot of parts to choose from in a fallen amusement park.

"I made it, yes," Hastings says, still breathing hard. "But we're not okay. We're not all good."

Bradwell leans forward. "Why are there more survivors at the amusement park now?"

"They had to leave the city," Hastings says. "It was no longer safe."

"It's never been safe," Pressia reminds him.

"It's worse now. Attacks—new ones."

"What kind of attacks?" Bradwell asks.

"Special Forces attacks, and not even really coded troops. The wretches say the Dome is sending out troops that are still just boys, just a little bulked up. The fusings with their weapons are still so raw the skin puckers around them." Hastings swallows hard. "I'm worried about what's going on in the Dome."

"But Partridge is in charge now!" Pressia says. "Things are supposed to be better!"

"Partridge is in charge?" Hastings asks. "Is Willux...?"

"Dead," Bradwell says. "I don't like this. What kind of attacks are we talking about?"

"Bloody ones," Hastings says. "The boy soldiers are killing those in the city—a blood bath—but the mothers have moved in and are picking them off. Bloodshed on all sides."

Pressia feels sucker punched. *Partridge*, she thinks, *how is this happening?* "What else?" Pressia asks, sitting in her seat. "Tell us everything."

"I only know what I've told you. I haven't seen it myself."

She doesn't want to look at Bradwell. Will he blame Partridge?

Bradwell says, "We have the means to take down the Dome, Hastings."

Hastings is lost. "How? It's not possible."

Bradwell explains the bacterium given to them by Bartrand Kelly. "It's ours now." The threat lingers in the air.

Pressia sits back and stares up at the curved ceiling. The engines are noise, and the airship bobbles and lifts.

She looks out the porthole again. They're passing over the terrain quickly—rocks, rusted hulls of trucks, traces of roads, charred rubble. They soon come to Washington, DC, and glide over the fallen tower, the Capitol Building with its crumbled dome, and what was once the White House, reduced to hunks of mossy pale rocks—all that marble and limestone. And then a zebra bounds through tall grass that gives way to marshland and woodland. The airship rises over a hill.

Her heart starts beating more quickly. She takes a deep breath and blows it out. They're getting close now, and what will she see? Bloodshed.

She closes her eyes. Maybe Hastings is wrong. Maybe this is a miscommunication. Not bloodshed. There's been enough loss.

But then she hears Bradwell say, "Look at that."

She doesn't want to open her eyes, but she does. And there is the darkened horizon—blotted with the rise of fresh smoke. Their city is on fire.

Partridge

SQUALL

He walks out into the hall—into the shine of the tiles, the glare of fluorescent lights. He blows past Beckley.

"Are you okay?" Beckley asks as he catches up to him.

He doesn't stop to answer.

Forgive us. Forgive us all.

Weed is there. He touches Beckley's shoulder and says, "Give me a minute with him." Weed walks up to him and says, "What's wrong?"

Partridge shakes his head to try to clear it. "I'm fine."

"No, you're not."

Partridge walks to the wall and stretches his hand on it; it's cool to the touch. "I thought I could push it off on everyone else by telling the truth. I thought that made me better or exempt or something." He sees his father's eyes widening just as he realized that Partridge had poisoned him. "I'm one of us. No," he says, and he feels short of breath. "I'm worse."

Arvin grabs his arm. "Shut up!" he says in a hoarse whisper.

"I know what I am now," Partridge says. "I haven't processed my father's lies, what we were all complicit in—the guilt."

Arvin leans in close and whispers in Partridge's ear, "Shut the hell up!" His face is rigid with anger. "Did you let her get to you? Jesus."

Partridge swings around to Weed, confused by his sudden anger. "I'm just realizing that I'm—"

"You want to go home? Is this too much for your delicate constitution?"

"Back off, Weed." But actually, Weed's nailed it. Partridge doesn't want to see his father's next generation: rows of clones. He can't stomach it.

"I'll call you a car so you can go. That what you want?"

"No."

"You have to want to know. I can only take you where you demand to be taken," Weed whispers. "You know what I'm saying?"

Partridge isn't sure. Is Weed under someone else's command—a command that only Partridge's demands can override? "Okay," Partridge says. "Let's keep going. Take me to the babies."

Arvin calls to Beckley, and together without talking, they make their way down corridors and then to an elevator to another floor.

They step into a hallway that's lined with guards—one every fifty feet. Partridge remembers the smell—sweet, and like bleach. "Why are there all these guards?"

Beckley eyes the guards and stays close to Partridge's side.

Weed says, "This floor is reserved for special cases."

"Special how?"

"People who deserve a second chance!" Weed's voice sounds forced. Does he think he's being recorded? Weed stops then and says, "Do you want to turn back, Partridge? It can be arranged."

Partridge feels like this is staged. He says what Weed's told him to say. "I demand to see the babies."

Weed nods without any hint of emotion.

They walk down a corridor lined on one side with windows. Partridge walks up to the glass, and there he sees the rows of tiny incubators. The babies are so small they'd fit in a man's palm.

Some are sleeping; others kick. Some of their mouths are open, squalling, but the windows must be soundproof, because he hears nothing. Inside of the babies' incubators and above them, there are screens showing human faces. The faces stare at the babies intently. They smile and blink. Their mouths are moving too—as if they're singing.

A nurse walks down one row and up the next.

Partridge touches the glass and it's warm. "What's going to happen to them?"

"They'll be raised in a perfectly structured environment where they'll receive the best education and physical fitness and affection."

"And parents who love them?"

Weed doesn't answer. He glances over his shoulder as if someone else is with them. "Are you ready to be escorted out?"

Partridge thinks of Lyda—their baby. He feels like he's on a train barreling away from them—an engagement, a wedding...How's he going to get off the train?

And then from far away, a scream echoes down the hall.

"What was that?" Partridge says.

"What was what?" Arvin says. "I can have someone escort you out," he says again.

Partridge ignores him and starts walking quickly toward the sound. Beckley keeps up with him. The guards stiffen and put their hands on their guns, but they don't draw them.

As Partridge rounds a corner, a guard reaches out and grabs his arm. A few others block the hall, side by side.

"Hands off him," Beckley says to the guard.

"Sir?" one of the other guards says to Weed. "Should we bar him?"

"His word overrides all of ours," Weed says. "If he demands to go forward, he can go forward."

There's another scream.

"Goddamn it!" Partridge says. "I demand to go forward!"

The guard loosens his grip. The other guards part.

Partridge turns to Weed. "You're still torturing people? Is that what you meant by giving people a shot at a second chance?"

"Your father's protocols are still in place. We can't stop everything now that you're in charge—just have the Dome come to a screeching halt?"

"Goddamn it, Weed! No more torture."

"Your father's enemies could become your own."

"I don't care. This is over. Shut it down. Does Foresteed know about this?"

Weed nods. "He's overseeing the day-to-day until you get through your"—he pauses, looking for the right word—"grieving process, not to mention your upcoming wedding. You're busy."

"I'm not a figurehead to be propped up for weddings and memorial services, Weed. I'm in charge, okay? I'm in charge of everything! Tell Foresteed I want another meeting."

There's more screaming up ahead. Partridge starts running toward it. He passes large empty rooms, their shelves filled with Tasers and small, strange implements he doesn't recognize. Some of the rooms have cameras; others are bare. Some have syringes lined up on metal trays and cuffs attached to the wall.

"You're making more changes," Weed says. "Don't you know these people can't handle change?"

Partridge turns on Weed. "Who are you, Arvin Weed? Who the hell are you? You want all of this to keep going? Why? Out of respect?"

There's a man's guttural cry—not far off. Partridge runs to a door. It's locked. "Open this door. Now."

Weed walks to a panel on the door. He enters a code. As the door opens, he shouts, "Incoming!"

There are three people wearing surgical gear lightly splattered in blood. Cuffed to the wall is a man. Partridge can see his arms streaked with blood, covered in precise incisions. On the table in front of him there's a Taser, a metal rod, and surgical implements.

"Step away!" Partridge shouts.

They all step back.

And now Partridge sees the man in his entirety; his body has been cut open and stitched back up. He's been beaten so badly that his skin is blackened with bruises. His face is so swollen that it's unrecognizable—almost.

Partridge's heart is beating so loudly in his ears it's deafening. He walks up and says, "Mr.—"

The man's eyes open, and yes—it's him. Glassings. His World History teacher, the man who lectured on beautiful barbarism.

"Partridge," he says through his swollen, split lips.

"Teacher," Partridge says, and then he spins around and says, "Get him down. Now! I want him taken to my apartment. Nowhere else. I want him given round-the-clock care. You hear me? Now!"

"He's your enemy," Weed says.

Partridge clenches his fist, swings, and punches Weed in the jaw so hard Weed staggers into the wall and slides down it. Weed looks up at him, dazed. Partridge is stunned too. He forgets that he has some coding in him—strength, speed, agility. Not a lot—not like Special Forces—but more than Weed, who was brought in for brain enhancements, not those of the body.

Partridge faces the others. "Get a doctor," he says. "Move!" He walks back to Glassings. "It's going to be okay," he says, but Glassings has lost consciousness. His face is slack.

Partridge can't stand to be in this room anymore. He looks at all the instruments, the remaining torturers' blank faces. He says to Beckley, "Make sure they do it right."

Partridge heads for the door, passing Weed, who's rubbing his jaw.

"Where are you going?" Beckley asks.

"Just stay," Partridge says. "Make sure they treat him respectfully. Make sure..." But he can't even finish the sentence. He glances at Weed and is sure that he's smirking at him. He'd like to punch him again.

But he turns and walks out. Glassings. He loves him. When Partridge was sure his father didn't care about him, he thought of Glassings as a father figure—and he can't bear what they've done to him.

He hears Beckley's voice—"Careful now! Careful!"—and then he starts running down the hall. His knuckles are ringing with pain, but it felt good to punch Weed. He doesn't know where he's going, but he keeps running until he is back at the bank of windows.

He rests his fists and his forehead against the glass and looks at all of the swaddled bodies, the small buds of the faces. He says, "I'm going to be a father." And he's scared—of what Mrs. Hollenback did to herself and what's been done to Glassings and of the future, but mostly in this moment he's afraid of the infants' delicate skin, the tiny fingers, the eyes that barely open. He takes his fists from the window and puts them in his pockets. He's not allowed to be scared anymore.

Partridge

Lovebird

T HEY'RE IN THE ACADEMY GARDENS, surrounded by fake shrubs, fake flower beds, fake birdcalls in the fake trees. It's winter, but they keep the garden looking like spring. Partridge hates the dishonesty. He's still shaken by what he saw in the medical center. The shine of this garden—the cheery polish of buds and waxy leaves—only reminds him of the ugliness that's hidden under the surface of things in the Dome.

Partridge and Beckley are waiting for Iralene and the photographers who are supposed to catch them on this date, as if it's not all staged. He's restless. She's late. He doesn't want to be here anyway.

"I want to see Glassings set up right. Make sure he has nurses coming in shifts and everything he needs, okay?"

Beckley nods.

"And when I say we're done here, we're done." Partridge feels guilty. Even though Lyda urged him to go through with this charade, it feels like a betrayal. But he can't bail. What if there were another surge in suicides? He'd only have himself to blame. And he can't take on any more guilt. He feels like his chest is leaden with it all.

It's quiet except for the birdcalls. Partridge looks at the dimpled center of a sunflower and wonders if it could be a small speaker. He trusts nothing.

Beckley says, "I can't believe how you laid into Arvin Weed." He smiles broadly.

Partridge rubs his knuckles. "I didn't think about it. I just did it." He looks at Beckley's broad shoulders. "You've got some coding in you, right? There's a mummy mold in the medical center with your name on it, I bet."

"Actually, I was given just some raw stuff. Nothing high-end. No molds."

"What do you mean?"

"Well, there's a way to do coding right with all the built-in protections to make it as safe and specific as possible. And then, for a lot cheaper, you can do it fast. I don't think it was as good for my overall health, but I'm not an academy boy, right? I'm expendable, in the long run."

Partridge remembers Wilda—just a nine-year-old girl—who was made Pure inside the Dome, and how she started to break down so quickly because it was all too potent and she was so young. What's going to happen to Beckley ten years from now? Five? Partridge stands up and looks at the boys' dormitory. "I don't think you're expendable. Not at all." He glances at Beckley, who gives a curt nod and looks away.

And then he hears Iralene's voice, set on edge, giving instructions of some sort. He turns and there she is, wearing a canary-yellow dress that floats around her legs silkily. The dress is low-cut and looks like an evening gown. Partridge is underdressed. She's surrounded by a small clutch of young women with fixed smiles. Her mother, Mimi, is with her, looking cold and angry. A half dozen photographers file in behind them, their cameras pointed at Partridge like they're armed.

"Hey, Iralene," Partridge says. "Ready?" He wants to get this going.

Her mouth becomes a perfect *O* of surprise. She smiles and then, oddly, she takes off her canary-yellow heels, hooking them in her fingers, and runs to him. She opens her arms, and if he doesn't open his, she's going to run right into him. And so he has to open them, and as he does, she jumps a little so that he has to catch her and set her back down on the ground.

"You've been working so hard we've had no time together! None at all!" She tilts her head and gazes at him.

The cameras erupt with clicking and flashes.

"Don't look at them," she says. "We're not supposed to know they're here."

Iralene's friends—though he doesn't recognize any of them and wonders if they've been assigned the job—are cooing and awing like they're watching kittens. Partridge hates it. "Do they have to make those noises?"

"We're all alone now! At last! Let's walk to the wooden swing near the trellis."

"Fine."

They hold hands and walk. "How are you doing?" she says. "Tell me everything I've missed!"

"Mrs. Hollenback tried to off herself taking pills. There are these premature babies...I can't talk about them. They've been torturing people. Glassings among them. He looked almost dead. I punched Arvin Weed."

"Stop it!" she says suddenly, flushed with anger. "Just stop it!"

"You asked."

They're at the swing. She puts her high heels back on, which is as inexplicable as her having taken them off. She sits on the swing and freezes, looking up at him, smiling lovingly.

He can't smile back. He feels sick. He looks at the dormitories again. The freshman wing is all lit up. The other floors, though, are dark and quiet. Did the older three grades go on one of those dismal field trips to the zoo? He misses it all suddenly.

He wants to be a kid again. He'd like to know nothing. Is that wrong?

"Push me! Push me!" Iralene says, sounding more like little Julby Hollenback than herself.

Her friends call out, "Yes, yes! Push her!"

Mimi looks on with disgust.

He feels so deeply manipulated that for a second, he can't move. He refuses to do what they're telling him.

But he's already here. He's signed on. *No more blood on your hands*, he hears Lyda whispering. He reminds himself that he's not going through this little fairy tale for Iralene's entourage. He's doing it to save lives.

He steps behind Iralene, grabs the ropes over her head, pulls the swing back, and lets it go. A few pushes later, she's really gliding, and now he understands the dress. It was made to ripple perfectly along her legs while swinging on a wooden swing.

"Aren't you happy?" she calls to him, and by this she probably means, *Smile, okay? At least try to smile!*

He forces the smile onto his face. It's painful—worse, maybe, because Beckley's there. The young women clap their hands lightly.

"Talk about something!" Iralene says. "Something pleasant."

Partridge can't think of anything pleasant except Lyda. He misses her. He wishes he were here with her instead. But he pushes himself to make idle conversation. If he says the right things, maybe this will end faster. "I wonder where they took the academy boys. The freshmen are here, but that's it."

"Oh, who knows?" Iralene says. "I'm sure it's educational!"

"Right," Partridge says, but then he glances at Beckley, who's turned away. Why? "Beckley, you know where the older boys are?"

Beckley doesn't answer.

"Beckley! What is it?"

"A bird!" Iralene cries out then. Is she trying to distract him? "A real live bird!" She points up into the branches of the tree.

Partridge glances up. She's right. It's a real bird. Sometimes they escape the aviary. They even try to nest in the trees. But without anything to eat, they die quickly.

"It's so pretty! Catch it for me, Partridge! Catch it!"

"People catch butterflies, Iralene. They don't catch birds."

"But you can! For me!"

"No, I can't actually catch a bird." He walks away from the swing and over to Beckley. "Tell me what's going on with the older academy boys."

Beckley won't look at him. "I'm not allowed."

"Do I have to make it an order?"

Beckley nods. "Yep, you do."

"Then tell me, damn it—that's an order."

"I only overheard this, so I don't know if it's true or not."

"What?"

"Foresteed's attacking. He's taken all the boys sixteen and up and started massive coding. Some are already out there, having joined Special Forces on the outside. Others are being geared up."

"Who's he attacking?"

"Wretches."

Partridge feels like his head could explode. He presses the heel of his hand against his temple. "Why? For the love of God..."

Beckley shrugs. "There's an airship that was stolen, and he had to start to neutralize the situation before a serious threat could be..." The airship that Pressia, Bradwell, and El Capitan and Helmud stole—but still, an attack makes no sense!

They crossed the Atlantic. Weed told Partridge that Foresteed didn't care about Pressia and the airship.

"He can't attack! He doesn't have the authority!"

"He leads the military, and since you've been preoccupied..."

"I'm not preoccupied! Damn it. You think I want to be at memorial services and photo shoots?" He thinks of Pressia, Bradwell, and El Capitan and Helmud. They can't come back to an attack from the Dome. He needs them—in one piece, alive.

"Radio ahead. I want a meeting with Foresteed ASAP."

"Partridge!" Iralene calls out. "I need another push." The swing is still. Her dress, no longer gusting, looks like a wilted flower.

"They got enough pictures. I've got to go, Iralene. Sorry." He walks off quickly. Beckley is at his side.

Iralene calls out, "No, Partridge! The bird! Come and catch the bird for me! It's a lovebird!"

Was the lovebird planted there? Did someone actually expect him to catch it for her and give it as a gift?

"It's going to die out here," Partridge says. "It needs to be taken back to the aviary."

Iralene cries out, "Oh no!"

He glances back and sees the bird flapping into what would be the sky.

LYDA

SECOND SKIN

Lyda SET THE ORB so that the living room looks like part of a suburban ranch house, pre-Detonations—she would never share her ashen world with anyone but Partridge. She hasn't seen him since their meeting with Foresteed where she gave Partridge permission to marry Iralene—or did she urge him? And if she'd said no, would it have actually mattered to a man like Foresteed? Looking back, she thinks they were meant to wander the room, and she was meant to find her psychological evaluation. In retrospect, it was a silent threat—lifelong institutionalization.

Now she's in the care of a woman named Chandry, who is unloading a tote full of yarn balls and knitting needles. "So what would you like to start with? Booties? A baby hat? A blankie?"

"Can I ask who sent you?" Lyda says, trying to sound sweet.

"Oh, it's my duty! I'm in charge of preparing you for your little bundle's arrival." She pats Lyda's knee. "Plus, it's soothing to knit. Knit your troubles away!" she chirps. "I have friends who are truly shattered by the recent events, but not me! Not with knitting on my side!"

She either means Partridge's speech about the truth or the suicides or both. "Recent events?" Lyda says, playing dumb.

"You know," Chandry says. "You of all people..."

Lyda, *of all people*. She wonders if Chandry blames her somehow.

Chandry starts to knit while giving a play-by-play of her quick work. Lyda interrupts, "What's wrong with shattered? Sometimes it's the right way to feel."

This flusters Chandry, but she keeps stitching. She wouldn't want to undermine her own arguments about the soothing powers of knitting. "Not for me!" she says, and she continues on, telling Lyda how to hold the needles. She gives her a little practice piece Chandry started for her at home. She seems oblivious to the fact that Lyda learned how to knit at the academy. All the girls did. But Lyda doesn't tell Chandry. She pretends to be a terrible student. It's not that she's against swaddling her baby in handmade blankets; it's that she doesn't want to be soothed—not by anything.

"I'm also giving you a *Baby's Own* baby book. You can start writing in it to log the joys of your baby—starting from the womb!"

"The joys."

"Yes! The joys! Cute stories. You know...maybe you crave strawberry milkshakes! You could write that down in the journal. These are things your child will one day want to know about their fetal experience!"

Lyda craves ash on her skin. She craves hunting in the woods at dusk. She craves the unknown rumble of a Dust—the earth trembling underfoot. She says nothing. If she raises her child in the Dome, would she ever be able to tell her child these things?

The TV screen is blank. She's watched too much of the news, which is feverishly whipping up excitement over Partridge and Iralene's engagement while reporting that all else is well. They don't mention the fights in the streets, the suicides. Instead there are pictures of Partridge and Iralene wandering the academy gardens, holding hands, smiling.

Chandry catches her gaze at the TV. "Oh, honey," she says. "You

don't want to see what's on that old chatterbox. You know that."
And she smiles at Lyda with deep cloying sympathy.

Lyda wants to slap her. She doesn't want her sympathy. She folds
her little strip of knitting, takes the needles and the ball of yarn and
hands them back to Chandry. "I don't want to do this anymore."

"Do you feel sick? Are you craving strawberry milkshakes?" she
smiles.

"I'm going to my bedroom."

"Yes!" Chandry says. "You must get off your feet some and lie
down."

Lyda grabs the orb and walks to her bedroom, shuts the door,
and sets it to ash. She lies on the bed and stares up at the ceiling.

She couldn't tell Partridge not to fake the engagement. The
stupid photo shoots might actually save lives. But still, she feels
fragile, as if made of fine glass. She could shatter. She remembers
feeling this way when she was a student at the academy, but not
outside the Dome—not among the mothers, hunting in the woods.
Is all of her toughness going to erode? Is she bound to be the person
she used to be in the Dome? Does the Dome, once she steps foot in
it, define her?

When she hears Chandry talking to the guard and the door
to the apartment shutting again, Lyda walks around her room,
looking for something. What? At first she wants to make art—not
something sweet like her old bird made of wire. No. She wants to
make something tough that will endure.

When she opens her closet, she finds wire hangers. She pulls
them out and drops them on the floor—which looks sooty and
streaked.

She remembers the idiotic sitting mats they had her weaving
with colored strips when she was locked up in the medical center,
how she wove and rewove hers back in solitary. She sits amid the
hangers and unwinds them so that each springs loose. She straightens each one and then begins weaving.

What is she weaving? She's not sure. She just weaves and weaves until the metal forms a large rectangle. It doesn't soothe her, which is good. It makes her feel vital, in control. She can still see Partridge in his father's chamber, the pictures of his lost family strewn around him. She still loves him—murderer and all. But after seeing her psychological evaluation, her desire to get out has grown. She wants to be out there in the world—whatever it looks like, no matter how wild and untamed. Even if everything gets worked out and Iralene disappears and Lyda can move into that role—Partridge has promised her—she can't stay here and be Partridge's happy wife, wearing pearls, knitting booties, writing in baby books. That night when she and Partridge lay together under his coat in the brass bed frame in a house with no roof, only the gray sky overhead, he wanted her to come with him. She refused. This time, though, she'll talk him into coming with her. This time, they'll stick together. The baby will keep them together, right? That's what babies do. They make families.

His father saw the end. Did he see how there will eventually be too little to live on? People will hoard and stand guard and then steal and fight and kill for what's left. They're all animals. She doesn't want to be a caged one.

She keeps pulling the wires, tightening the weave until her fingers are too stiff to go on. She holds up what looks like a woven shield—beautiful, strong, but also bendable. She stands up and walks to a mirror—darkened by the image of ash. She can see her dim reflection. She presses the woven metal to her body. Her belly is going to swell, but the metal is malleable. It could be molded around a belly—however big.

And then she knows what she's made.

Armor.

A second skin of metal.

It's art, if anyone asks. But to her, it's also protection and control. This is who she is—not someone who knits booties to soothe her nerves. She might feel a little shattered, but she's also strong. She can't rely solely on Partridge. She has to be able to defend herself. This is her protection.

She hides it in the back of her closet, behind fluffy maternity dresses.

El Capitan

FLUTTER

It's not just the city. From up high and circling, he can see that everything's been newly torched. The Deadlands didn't have much to burn, but El Capitan takes the airship in low enough to see a few blackened Dusts arch from the ground like dead fish rising to the surface of a pond, sucking air. The other Dusts are quiet, as if they're afraid to lift their heads.

He cuts across the Meltlands, which are vacant. The plastic jungle gyms were already melted to blobs, but some of the houses that had been partially rebuilt have been ravaged again by fires. Tarps flutter in the battering winds. OSR headquarters and the surrounding woods where he and Helmud have hunted for years are still smoking, lost in great billowing gray clouds.

The outpost that was once a boarding school might be the worst off—the survivors' tents are blackened and have collapsed in on themselves like clenched fists. The buildings' stone still stands, but the fires have gutted the buildings themselves. He gets close enough to see that there are some people still there, dazed and searching for those they've lost. Only a few of them look up when they hear the droning engine. But they don't take cover. They only stop and raise their faces to the noise. The little cottage where Pressia helped Bradwell regain his strength is still there, but its roof has caved in and the trees around it that had limbs that tethered them to the ground like roots are only charred stalks.

Here and there, even the smallest structures have burned or are still smoking—the huts of shepherds and pickers, lean-tos, the wood roofs of hand-built altars, the posts around graveyards. Smoke shivers to the sky, gusts, and swirls across the terrain in gray billowing sheets.

Shortly after they picked up Hastings, he walked into the cockpit to tell El Capitan to prepare for devastation. He told him the stories of the survivors who'd made it to Crazy John-Johns. El Capitan nodded. "One thing I know is devastation, Hastings. Don't worry."

"Worry," Helmud had said, and he was right. Nothing could have prepared him for this. His homeland has always been burnt and charred but fighting its way back. And now it's as if all of the life and energy and strength that it took to rebuild have been wiped away.

He sees a sloping field where the Dome worshippers, once upon a time, built a pyre of their own. Gone. All of it. That's where he'll bring down the airship.

He takes them lower and lower and finally shouts to the others, "Brace for landing!"

"Brace, brace!" Helmud shouts and grabs hold of El Capitan so hard that El Capitan has to pop his elbows out to have enough mobility to work the instruments.

"Ease up, Helmud."

The airship glides then bobbles as it starts to descend. The ground is coming at El Capitan too quickly.

"Ease up!" Helmud shouts. "Ease up!"

El Capitan slows a little, but the engines sound weak. He doesn't want to stall out. So he lets the buckies take on more air—too much. The airship drops. One landing prong hits, drags, gouging the earth, sending up a black plume of ash. The airship pops to its other leg and also skids. The airship tips forward on its two front legs, teetering for a moment with the nose hovering just above the ground before it rocks back onto all four prongs solidly.

El Capitan whistles a sigh. Helmud echoes it.

El Capitan hears the cabin door open. He'll let the others hop out. He's in no rush to see more. He takes his time shutting the engines down. He doesn't know when he'll fly again. He pats the wall of the cockpit.

"We'll miss it, won't we, Helmud?"

"Miss it," Helmud says, as if he's ready to move on. They follow the others out onto the ground, which is stiff with the cold. They don't talk. What the hell could any of them say? The smoke is so thick that it rolls around them as dark as the fog of Ireland was white. His eyes burn and tear. He covers his mouth with his sleeve.

Pressia turns a circle, trying to take in the destruction through the waves of smoke. "Where are Wilda and the others? How are we ever going to find them now?"

Bradwell extends his broad wings and then wraps himself in them—only his face shows, his jaw jutting out. El Capitan's legs feel like they might buckle, and Helmud feels suddenly so heavy on his back that he rests on one knee.

Hastings stands in a wide-legged stance, balancing his weight between his real leg and the prosthetic. Finally he says, "This summer, I bought books for the whole school year."

At first, El Capitan doesn't know why he'd say something like that now, but then Bradwell says, "I remember giving those lessons in Shadow History. I had it all down. I knew what I was doing and why." And El Capitan gets it. Hastings and Bradwell are wondering what the hell happened to everything they once knew to be true.

Pressia says, "I made windup toys. Sometimes they'd flutter, but I could never get them to fly."

El Capitan says, "I had this journal. I'd test berries on the recruits to see which ones were poisonous. I had a system. I drew pictures in it. I was good at that."

"I was good," Helmud says, as if that sums it up. Once, long ago, before the Detonations, they were all good. El Capitan feels a surge of anger like he's never felt before. He punches the cold ground with his fists. He feels the desire for revenge pulsing through him.

Bradwell's the first to say it. "Let's take 'em down."

El Capitan says, "The bacterium is a gift. We were given a *gift*." He can feel the twinge of the thick tape holding in place the box protecting the bacterium.

"A gift," Helmud says.

"No," Pressia says. "We have to talk to Partridge. Something's gone wrong. He wouldn't do this. I know it."

This time she has someone to back her up without hesitation. "Partridge wouldn't ever let this happen," Hastings says. "I know him. We were friends. Trust me."

"You *were* friends," El Capitan says. "I know power firsthand. I know what it can do to your head. You come out on the other side of it twisted."

"Twisted," Helmud says. He knows what El Capitan's talking about. He bore the brunt of it.

Pressia says, "We have to try to get inside. Let's stick to the plan."

"That was never my plan," Bradwell says.

"Well, it was mine," Pressia says.

Bradwell walks to her. "Do you smell that in the air? Do you know what that smell is?"

She looks at El Capitan and Helmud, then Hastings. "Smoke."

"No," Bradwell says. "What's riding in that smoke?"

"Don't," El Capitan says.

"Hair and flesh. That's what's burning, Pressia. How many

times are you going to forgive? How many times are you going to fall into the trap of thinking we can reason with them? They're murderers. Partridge is either too weak to stop them or he's one of them. Either way..."

"You are your father's son too, Bradwell," Pressia tells him. "And your mother's. They weren't trying to kill Willux. They believed in the truth. It was their religion, right? You said that. They believed it would set people free. Don't you believe?"

Bradwell closes his eyes and lets his wings catch in the wind and open a little on his back. "No," he says. "I don't know what I believe anymore."

Pressia tucks the doll head under her chin, covers her mouth with her hand. She says, "I can go it alone."

"Let's stick together for now," El Capitan says. "At least until we know what we're up against, until we get our bearings again."

"What we're up against," Helmud says fearfully.

Pressia doesn't look convinced.

El Capitan tries another angle. "There are people who need us here, Pressia. You want to help them, right? You want to find Wilda and the other kids. Don't you?"

She looks at the face of the doll head. She tilts it so its eyes close. Is she afraid they're dead? Is she afraid that it's too late to get the cure to the Dome, find the children, save them?

"I can't let you go into the Dome," Bradwell says. "I can't let you go."

El Capitan looks at Pressia. He can tell that she's surprised. She looks at Bradwell, then El Capitan and Hastings, then quickly away from all of them. Is Bradwell confessing something here—about love? El Capitan feels sick.

"Before we left," Pressia says, "word had traveled that Cap had set up medical tents in the city. Once the outpost was burned, that would have been the most logical place to take the children."

The medical tents are gone. That's the truth, but El Capitan doesn't say it. Maybe Pressia knows that or maybe she's living on hope. "Okay," he says. "Let's start there." But he knows he's probably only bought a little time before she leaves them all to make her own way.

PRESSIA

CALLING, CALLING

PRESSIA'S ALREADY DECIDED to leave them. When the time is right, she'll slip off. It's easier this way. No arguments. No fighting. She has to find Partridge. She has to know the truth.

When Bradwell asked her if she knew what that smell in the wind was, she wanted to spin around and slap him. She remembers the smell of burnt flesh and hair from the days the OSR was in power as well as from her early childhood—from the Detonations. She'd blotted the memories out for so long, but now she remembers the fires, worse than these because they were fueled by radiation—or was it that the blasts made everything susceptible to becoming tinder? The fire cyclones tore through everything, drove people to water—people half-dead already. Her grandfather held her to his chest and, one legged, he crawled through the wreckage. He helped her climb across a river clogged with the dead.

They passed over that river as they flew in. It was edged with ice, a white rim. Pressia remembered what it was like to almost drown in it—the cold darkness all around her, that feeling of being saved, lifted by unseen hands. Did Bradwell see the river outside of his own window—the place where they almost froze to death? Does he remember the feel of their skin touching? She does. She'll never forget it. The flash of it still makes her skin hot.

And then Bradwell said that he couldn't let her go? He only means that he won't let her go. He's telling her what she can and cannot do. He looked her way once, then later again. But she pretended not to notice. If he can't forgive her, she has to harden her heart, doesn't she? She has to steel herself. Meanwhile, she's making her plan.

Of course, she can't shake the question that pounds through her head—*Did Partridge do this?* It echoes with each step. She has to believe in Partridge. What else does she have to hope for? Pressia sees a stand of twisted, burnt trees in the distance. Has she ever seen them before? She knows she has. But now, they have been whittled to spokes of char. She feels older now. The dead trees, like monuments to the destruction, stand out to her as individual. Each has suffered on its own. Each has been stunned into being something it never was intended to be. Each is now part of the greater loss.

They walk through the trees toward the city, using what's left for cover. The trees look like cacti. Stark. Isolated. The silt climbs up their trunks on the side of the prevailing wind. Spider-root systems turned vertical catch what the wind drags in—mostly junk and rot that's wandered across these wastelands wanting rest, some place to stop, an end to it all. She stares through the low limbs, looking for any shift of a figure or flash of color. "Hastings," she says every few minutes or so, "anything?"

His senses have been coded, but the smoke riding on the air limits his vision and sense of smell. "We have to keep moving," he says.

"Are we being followed?" she asks.

"They're weak," he says, "and there aren't many. We just need to keep going."

More than once, they hear footsteps, the rattle of brush. Is it Special Forces? Are they being tracked? If it is soldiers, they don't open fire.

And then, once in the open again, Pressia sees the swaths of blood in the dusty dirt. It's the scene of a battle—the bloody tracks of bodies being dragged away. But whose bodies were dragged— mothers and their children or Special Forces? They pass a mound of debris caught against a berm. Maybe there was a highway here, maybe a holding pond for water. But the berm caught everything that didn't blow over it. They pass a pickup truck with vacant headlights, a grocery cart, busted concrete slabs, iron rods, and dirt and ash and stuff so blown it's beyond recognition. Somebody made the truck. Somebody drove it. Somebody pushed the cart and somebody laid the concrete. And there, under a slur of dried mud, a flattened ball. She can almost hear the child kicking it. It crushes her.

After a while, they come across another bloody mess—this time, the bodies of the survivors that haven't been taken away. The dead litter the ground, their limbs akimbo, the gunshot wounds gaping and dark with dried blood.

They keep going.

Once in the city, Pressia glimpses the distant cross on top of the Dome. Somewhere in these alleys and rubbled streets, she'll leave the others behind. But it's hard to stay focused on the Dome. El Capitan was right; she's growing desperate to find Wilda and the children. She can't leave until she knows they're safe. Closing in on the area where the medical tents once stood, they start calling for Wilda as they make their way.

The rain seems like a miracle at first, clearing the smoke, cooling the rubble, dousing anything that still smolders, but it doesn't let up. It only gets worse, driving down on them as they search for Wilda and the children, calling and calling through the vacant streets. Their clothes and boots are soaked. Pressia's hair sticks to her face. Bradwell fares better—his wings bead water.

The pyre to dispose of the dead has gone out, and even if it stops raining, it will be a long time before they can get the wood dry enough to start it up again.

They find a group of survivors digging a mass grave, bodies piled nearby. At least now the ground is no longer frozen and gives a little.

Deeper into the city, they start to hear the cries of new orphans and parents calling for their children. The fresh burns and welts and blisters cover the old scars—a layer of fresh pain on old pain. Pressia is more protective of what's in her backpack than ever. The vial and the formula can make them whole again, can't it?

"Wilda!" Pressia keeps shouting, her voice joining the chorus of voices calling for the lost. "Wilda!"

Hastings stays close to them so that it's clear he's not a threat— maybe even a prisoner. Pressia asks survivors if they've seen the children. "They might have looked like they were shaking. They might have been carried in on people's backs."

The survivors give only blank stares and shrugs.

But then Pressia sees a man she recognizes from the outpost. He has a spray of metal on his arms and a gear lodged in his jaw.

"Excuse me," she says.

He looks up.

"We're looking for children who were being taken care of in the main building at the outpost. They were sickly. They shook and would have probably been with nurses. You were at the outpost. You know who I mean."

"Gone," the man says, the gear in his jaw clicking.

"What do you mean—gone?" Pressia steps closer. "Are they dead?" She feels a swell of dread.

"They carried children out on their backs and kept going. Who knows where? Who cares where? There's nowhere to go. They were everywhere. They wanted to kill us all. I beat one to death with a rock." The man looks down at his hands, crusted with metal, his fingers curled like he's holding the rock at this moment. His eyes flash wide. "And it was a kid. It was just this kid. A dead boy. A bloody, dead boy." He looks up at Pressia. "Like my own son. That was the thing. He looked like my own son—if my son had been born right and lived."

Did Partridge do this?

"I'm sorry," Pressia says. "I'm so sorry."

The man looks at her clearly, as if he's just woken up. "They were going to take them to the city—those shaking children on their backs, those pale shaking children. The city. For help. But I saw the smoke coming up from the city too, so who knows where they went? Who knows?" He shuffles on.

Hastings, with his enhanced hearing, is good at locating people moaning from the remains of fallen lean-tos and searching for people trapped inside. They stop and dig, finding bodies—some living, some dead from smoke inhalation. El Capitan works with survivors, tending wounds, making splints. As Pressia digs, pulling up the stones and rocks, she still calls for Wilda. It's become a song, a prayer. Her voice is rough and worn.

Wilda. She shouts it so many times that it doesn't sound like a name anymore—just two sounds locked together and echoed again and again.

They keep going, passing people who are barely hanging on. She sees a Groupie sitting on rubble—three women she vaguely recognizes. One is so badly burned she won't make it. What will happen to the others she's fused to? They won't survive the death. One holds a wet rag to the victim's lips. The third stares off.

Pressia, Bradwell, El Capitan, and Hastings help carry the dead to the mass grave. They lean into the cold wind, sweating from the work, hands starting to go numb. Sometimes one of them will walk to the edges just to recover. They breathe heavily. Sometimes they cry. But then they come back. Ready to keep going.

The Dome worshippers are broken. It's not that they no longer believe in the Dome. It's that the grief has swept through them. They're vacant.

One man with a crooked leg and a face tainted with coppery flecks tells them that the dead include Special Forces. "Them bodies over there—we stripped the weapons from their ligaments. Got some of 'em to work even. But we keep the bodies covered. Can't bear the sight."

There are three lumps wrapped in a single dark sheet, splotched with dried blood. Pressia understands why they wouldn't want to look at the enemy's dead eyes staring at them.

"Young ones they're sending down now," the man goes on to say, "like they run out of the ones old enough to be soldiers and sent in their little brothers."

Pressia imagines arms bulked with weapons too big for their thin frames to hold.

"Careful," the man says. "Some still out there. Not many, but they got good eyes too."

Pressia keeps calling for Wilda as they move through the Black Market stalls that have all been burned to nothing, the tarps, carts, and lean-tos. All the wares are charred past recognition, heaped in piles. Survivors pick through them.

Pressia hears whimpering. She walks to a pile of rocks—what used to be a homemade house—and starts digging.

"Someone's alive here!" she shouts, and the others gather. They don't step on the pile of rubble—too much weight. But they take the rocks from her as she lifts them up. "I hear a voice!" she says.

El Capitan and Helmud's faces are smeared with ash. Bradwell's face is flushed by the cold. Hastings hasn't cried—maybe he's programmed not to—but his face looks lost and broken.

She's dug closer to the moan. Is she going to pull a final stone away and see Wilda? She wraps her hand around a rock, jimmies it until it gives and she can pull it loose.

And there's a woman's face, pale with blue lips—she gasps and then her eyes go glassy. She's dead, but then there's whimpering. Could this woman be one of the children's nurses?

Pressia says, "Wilda! Wilda!" even though she knows it can't be Wilda—can it?

El Capitan says, "Pressia," like a warning. Maybe he knows that her heart is set on finding the girl.

And then she pulls away enough stones to see a small gray dog—it looks up at her wide-eyed, shaking. The woman protected the dog, pulling it in tight to her body. Pressia reaches down and grips the dog under its bony ribs.

She lifts the dog, rubs its ears, and as soon as she's climbed down the rubble, the dog twists from her arms and jumps to the ground, darting off.

Her arms are empty. Her heart feels like it might heave from her chest. She sits down on the dirt.

Bradwell walks over to her. "Are you ready now?"

"What?"

"Have you seen enough?"

She feels dizzy and sick. "If I go in and find Partridge and try to figure out what's going on in there, and I can get to the labs and start them working on the cure while you all keep looking...You just keep...looking...for Wilda and..." She feels breathless, like her throat is starting to constrict. She puts her hand on her chest.

Bradwell holds his head with both hands. "Pressia, after all we've seen, after all these dead bodies and destruction, you want to go in *and try to figure out what's going on?* I think we know what's going on! Partridge needs to be stopped. He's worse than his father—whether he's too weak to keep this from happening or ordered it himself."

She shakes her head. "We have to try to talk to him. We have to try to help the children."

"Goddamn it, Pressia!" Bradwell says. "Wilda and the other children are dead!"

The air seems to snap all around her. She blinks and it feels like an electrical pulse in her head.

Bradwell whispers, "Wilda's dead."

"You don't know that," Pressia says, but her voice is small. She looks at El Capitan. "Cap, tell him."

El Capitan looks at the ground, and she knows he thinks they're dead too.

She stands up and grabs El Capitan, gripping his coatsleeves. "How long have you…How long have you kept it from me? Cap, tell me. How long?"

"I never thought the chances were very good," he says. "But when there were only more and more dead—"

"Shut up," she says quietly.

"Pressia," El Capitan says, "we should hear Bradwell out. He's—"

"Shut up," Helmud tells him.

Wilda and the children can't be dead. They're lost—that's all. Pressia starts to cry and walks away from them toward an over-turned market stall. Wilda is a survivor, like Pressia. If she's dead, then some part of Pressia will die with her. "No," she says, turning back toward the group. "You don't know that they're dead. You can't give up on people."

Bradwell shakes his head.

"Let's just keep moving," she says.

And they do, but soon enough there are only more dead to tend to. Bradwell, El Capitan, and Hastings haul a dead Groupie—two broad men—out of the rubble. They're engrossed in the effort—even Helmud.

Pressia knows the only way she can truly help her people is to get the vial and the formula into the Dome. She takes one last look—El Capitan with Helmud clinging to his neck, the sooty shine of Bradwell's wings, and Hastings hefting the bulk of the Groupie's weight—and turns down an alley and starts walking quickly. She won't run. It's too much like running away. She turns down one street and then another.

The voices of men and women calling for children ring through the streets, overlapping. And children too. Lost children. Their calls not matching. The voices seem to only have grown louder, more insistent. *Wilda, Wilda, Wilda!* She can't open her mouth and call her name. She'll break down. Instead, the girl's name rings in her head.

She sees a boy about twelve years old or so. It's hard to say. Survivors are often stunted. He's walking quickly too, though one of his legs seems fused to a knot, as if his knee joint is part metal and it has rusted up on him, locked shut. One side of his face looks freshly scalded. He doesn't look up. When he passes, she says, "Excuse me. Can you do me a favor?"

"World doesn't work on favors," he says. "What you got?"

She has precious things—the vial, the formula—but they'd mean nothing to him. She reaches into her pocket, rummages. She pulls out a tin of meat. "I need a messenger."

He eyes the tin hungrily. "What's the message? Who's it for?"

PARTRIDGE

PILL

PARTRIDGE STORMS DOWN THE HALL of his apartment building, shot through with adrenaline. He'd like to punch Foresteed the same way he laid into Arvin Weed, but that wouldn't do much good. He has to be rational with Foresteed—steady, steely, calm.

And who the hell is Arvin Weed anyway? Weed helped make the assassination possible, and yet he's still carrying out the dead man's wishes? But then Partridge thinks of his time in his father's secret chamber: Is he just carrying out his dead father's wishes too?

Beckley jogs to keep up with him. They aren't speaking. Partridge shouts down the hall to the guard at his door. "Foresteed here?"

"Not yet," the guard says as he fumbles to open the door for him.

Partridge and Beckley walk into the living room, where a doctor is giving a nurse instructions.

"Is Glassings here?" Partridge asks.

"Hello, Partridge," the doctor says.

"Where is he?" Partridge says, blowing by them and walking down the hall to the bedrooms.

He hears Beckley ordering the doctor to stay put.

Partridge isn't sure why, but he expects Glassings to have been put up in Partridge's own bed. Then he hears a ragged cough coming from his father's old bedroom, the door to which he's kept closed since he arrived here after his father's death.

He walks up to the door, puts his hand on the knob, but he doesn't turn it. He's frozen there, worrying for a moment if his father's on the other side. His father still seems so alive it wouldn't surprise Partridge to find him sitting in bed, pillows plumped behind his back, reading reports.

"Stop it," Partridge says aloud. "He's dead. He's dead already."

He turns the knob and opens the door. The room is lit by a single bedside-table lamp. Glassings jerks as if he's expecting strangers, torture. Partridge says, "It's just me."

Glassings' face is battered, his arms blackened with bruises. Both legs have now been set with casts, propped up on pillows to keep them elevated above his heart. The room smells of ointments and alcohol swabs. His breaths are shallow and sharp. He tilts his head so he can see through the puffed slits of his eyelids.

Partridge walks over to the bed and sits on the edge. It's bizarre to see Glassings' broken and battered body in his father's bed, his head on his father's pillows. "You're going to stay with me here until you're completely recovered."

Glassings opens his lips and whispers, "I won't recover."

"Of course you will." But Glassings doesn't just look beaten. He looks small and sick. Partridge is worried now that Glassings is right.

"We weren't secret," Glassings says. "He knew who we were all along."

"My father knew about Cygnus? About you?"

Glassings shakes his head. He coughs again, wincing with the pain in his ribs.

"Take it easy," Partridge says. "We can talk later. You have to get feeling better."

"No," Glassings says, his face stricken with pain. "Now. You have to know this now." His voice is hoarse, nearly gone.

"Okay," Partridge says. "Who knew?"

Glassings draws in a wheezy breath. "Foresteed."

"Foresteed knew about Cygnus?"

"He let us work. He protected us without us knowing it."

Partridge thinks of that pill in his pocket just before he killed his father, remembers touching it with the tips of his fingers. "The pill."

"We thought we stole it."

"But it was easier to steal than you thought," Partridge says, "because Foresteed wanted you to steal it, wanted you to get it to me. He wanted me to kill my father." Partridge gets up and looks at his father's bedroom. He feels breathless and sick. "Foresteed wanted me to kill my father. He wanted my father to die, and I did it for him." He hears Beckley's voice in the living room and then Foresteed's voice too. He's here for their meeting. A streak of heat burns across Partridge's chest. "He had a shot at being put in charge. And then, at the last minute, my father switched the power to me."

"He wants to take you out too," Glassings says, reaching and grabbing Partridge's arm, gripping it tightly for a moment before his hand sags.

"How do you know?"

"He told me himself. He didn't think I'd make it out alive. He thinks," Glassings says, trying to steady his breath, "you'll be easier to take down than your father."

Glassings is right. Willux was a powerhouse, insulated on all sides. Partridge feels completely vulnerable. He clenches his fists and then rubs his temples. God. What the hell is he going to do?

"I failed you," Glassings says.

"No, you didn't." Glassings has been a father figure for Partridge for a long time. He remembers him in a bow tie, a chaperone at the dance, and when they met under the stage in the academy's auditorium. Partridge never had the father he wanted. "What would you do if you were me?" Partridge says. "Tell me."

Glassings shakes his head. "My advice isn't any good."

"Just tell me something—anything."

"Don't let him know you know. Take him down when he least expects it. Play dumb."

Partridge nods. "Considering the grades I got in World History, that shouldn't be too hard."

Glassings tries to smile, but his face is too constricted by swelling.

"Get some rest." Partridge walks to the door.

"You can do this," Glassings says.

Partridge leans his forehead against the edge of the open door for a second, trying to calm his nerves. He hears Foresteed's booming laugh. Did the doctor say something funny? Is Foresteed laughing at his own joke? Glassings believes in Partridge. He has to remember this, hold on to it. He doesn't have much else.

Partridge is about to walk out the door, but first he has a question. "The pill—it was designed to be time released, the poison untraceable," Partridge says. "Someone stole it for you?"

"Yes," Glassings says. "Someone on our side."

"Who?"

"Arvin Weed."

"No, you're wrong."

Glassings closes his eyes and shakes his head.

Was Weed helping because he's really on the side of Cygnus or was he a mole for Foresteed? After all, someone had to have been feeding Foresteed information, and how convenient that Weed was the one to steal the pill for them. In either case, Partridge punched Weed in the face. He remembers his stupid smirk before Partridge stormed off. Was Weed leading Partridge to Glassings—to save him?—while trying to give the impression of remaining loyal to Foresteed? "Weed?" Partridge says. "Are you sure?"

"Weed," Glassings says.

Pressia

MIGRATORY BIRDS

THE SMOKE HAS THINNED, but the air is, as always, sooty. Pressia hears a sharp zing and a pop near her boots—Special Forces? Sniper rifles?

She runs and crouches behind an oil drum.

A groan echoes down a nearby alleyway.

She moves to the far side of the oil drum, sees a figure limping along the alley, dragging a hand along the stone wall. It lets out another groan. She presses her back to the oil drum, aware that an oil drum is how all this started. She saw a stranger being attacked by a Groupie and distracted them by throwing her clog at an oil drum. That stranger ended up being Partridge, her half brother, which wasn't a coincidence. They were being set up, herded toward each other, used. She can't regret that meeting—even after all they've been through, even after the losses. It all feels inevitable, looking back.

As the figure comes closer to the end of the darkened alley, it pauses—afraid of the light? It moves like a wretch—an uneven gait caused by carrying some foreign weight lodged in the body, which is sometimes another body. Is it a survivor?

She looks behind her, searching the rubble around a fallen building for signs of Special Forces, who must have shot at her.

Maybe the sniper has heard the groans and now lies in wait for the Groupie or Beast to emerge. Which will attack her—the figure in the alley or Special Forces, hidden somewhere out there? A little of both?

Whatever is in the alley lifts its head as if catching her scent. It jerks toward her and leans forward into the light. She hides again behind the oil drum, wishing she had her knife.

Then she hears a strange noise—chirrups, sad and mournful. She looks again carefully, and the figure has walked into the light—fully. It's not a Beast or a Groupie or a survivor at all.

It's a soldier, but not a Pure—no. It's small and, yes, young, reminding her of her conversation with the man who said these soldiers were like the little brothers of the others who'd come before. He isn't sleek or agile. His musculature has been pumped up, but the muscles are bulky and hardened—almost calcified—making him stiff, and the strangest part is that the soldier has burns on his face. She remembers that once, not long ago, she saw a snowman in the city—it was warped and covered in the detritus of the street. It looked like a wretch. This is a Special Forces soldier, but he's also a wretch. How is it possible? And moreover, why would they make a soldier who wasn't Pure? Why make a soldier burdened by the deformities of the enemy?

He makes noises that are soft and almost sweet. He lifts his hands in the air, and she's expecting to see his metallic guns, the ones fused into his arms.

But now she sees that one of his arms is a bloody stump. The other has been gutted, and the gun is gone. Has someone stripped him of his guns while he was still alive?

He chirps at her. "Help me. Help me."

He reaches out, his arm barely there, and staggers toward her. She grips her backpack, guarding it above all else.

But just before he falls, a shot is fired by someone unseen. It strikes him squarely in the chest, and he falls hard to the ground, inches from her.

He lies there, blood pooling from his body, mixing with the dark rain puddles. His body twitches twice.

She moves closer to him while still under cover. She looks into his eyes. She wants to give him peace. "It won't hurt for long." He reaches, one last great effort, and grips the meat of her upper arm—pinching her skin.

He makes the strange chirping noise a few more times, and then his hold loosens. His hand falls. He's dead.

She knows that most likely survivors stripped his weapons and that somehow he got free of them and ran off, but they've hunted him down and have just shot him, probably with his own rifle. They'll approach as soon as they're sure he's dead.

And so she sprints to the alley to a jagged pile of bricks and hides again.

Sure enough, within moments, survivors are picking over him— they take some knifelike weapons lodged in the boots, something razor sharp from his shoulders. They work quickly and quietly. They're experts at this now.

She rubs the sore spot where he pinched her arm, finds a small rip in her jacket and a bit of blood.

She looks up again. The survivors are gone, leaving the body behind.

Pressia can't help but look at what's left. The body is slumped to its side. She can see the boy's face scarred by burns, an upper arm that's lightly furred as if he were part Beast, and the hump on his shoulder isn't a hump at all. It was some kind of animal that existed beneath the skin. Why beneath the skin?

This isn't a Pure. This is a wretch. But not like any wretch she's ever known. He's been enhanced, and yet it's as if, with the enhancements, he was also bred to be a wretch. Why would anyone do this? Why? Pressia remembers the awful creatures in Ireland—the fog's heartbeat, the night baring teeth, the idea of that stitched-up skin, the blind roving eyes. How many like this one are already dead? How many are still out there?

She gets up and runs. The rain starts pounding. She hunches her shoulders, pumps her arms and legs, and pounds against the ground. Her breath burns her lungs.

She's trying to find the shortest route to the Dome. Soon she recognizes the streets around her, this air, this smell.

These are the streets that she ran as a little girl, and finally she finds herself standing in front of the blasted husk of what was once a barbershop. Her grandfather told her about migratory birds. They know home. They always come back to it. Here she is.

Home.

LYDA

NURSERY

THERE AREN'T MANY USES for matches in the Dome. Fires, large and small, are frowned upon. Lyda remembers many conversations between her mother and her mother's friends on the subject. They missed having pumpkin-scented candles in the fall. "How else will we know it's autumn?" her mother said once. And the men missed their grills. Fireworks on the Fourth of July were replaced by an electric light show.

But Lyda wants matches. So she tells one of the guards that she wants to make a special dinner for Partridge. "I want to do it with candles and everything—to make it romantic! Can you get me candles and matches? And keep it a secret. I want to surprise him."

The guard gives them to her, secretly, bundled in brown wrapping paper.

She winks at him.

She doesn't care about the candles. She hides the matches in a pocket, takes them into the bathroom. She also brings a metal bowl and one of the books Chandry brought her, *How to Decorate the Perfect Nursery*. The nursery already has a crib and mattress, a rocking chair, a changing table, and a small chest of drawers, but she's supposed to be picking out her color schemes, her motif—starfish, elephants, balloons? The book is supposed to help.

She shuts the door.

The soot here in the simulated world isn't real. Lyda can't feel it. She needs to feel it.

She closes the toilet lid, stands on it, disengages the smoke detector—just a little knot of wires—and turns on the fan. She sits on the tiled floor, starts ripping out the book's pages. She pulls the matches from her pocket and burns the pages, one after the other, in the bowl.

The flames remind her of the mothers. They often cooked over open flames. They gathered around fire pits and talked in small groups, their children fused to their hips and shoulders, heads bobbing.

Her own mother? She imagines her face—stern, shut off. Her mother loved her—she's sure of it. But it was a locked-up love, a buried-down love, a love to be ashamed of because…because that kind of love makes you vulnerable? Makes you weak? Why hasn't her mother come to visit? Is she too ashamed of her daughter now?

Lyda misses the mothers and their fierce love.

She misses the cold, the wind, the fire.

She touches some of the ash, rubs it together until her fingertips are smudged black.

She knows what she misses most of all. Her spear—the weight of it in her hand as she ran through the woods.

She wants a spear.

It's impossible. Where would she find something that she could make into a spear? Not here. She'd need a stick, long and straight.

But then, wait.

She stands, walks out of the bathroom, shutting the door behind her, and into the nursery.

The crib—with all of its spindles.

A row of spears—if she could get them loose and whittle them with a kitchen knife. How to get them free?

She needs a hammer.

She walks into the living room, turns a circle, sees a lamp with a marble base. She picks it up and weighs it in her hand—heavy enough.

Tonight she will pull her *Baby's Own* baby book from her bedside table and write in it:

I crave.

I crave.

I crave.

PARTRIDGE

A BEAUT

Partridge runs his hand down the hallway wall as he makes his way to the living room. He hears Glassings' raspy voice in his head: *Don't let him know you know. Take him down when he least expects it. Play dumb.*

Partridge was never the smart one. Sedge won all the awards in school—athletics and academics both. Partridge was the scrawny little brother with average grades. The comment section of his report card was full of euphemisms for Partridge's disappointing efforts: *If he applied himself a little more . . .* How do you tell Willux that his son is inadequate?

Arvin Weed, on the other hand, was a boy genius. He wanted Partridge's father dead? He's on their side? Partridge isn't sure he can trust Arvin Weed. He's not sure who he can trust anymore.

He walks into the living room. Beckley is standing by the front door. The doctor has left, but the nurse is at the dining room table, organizing all of Glassings' medical papers into a folder. Beckley says something to the nurse and she responds, "I'll go check on him now," and disappears.

Partridge finds Foresteed sitting in Willux's favorite armchair—

the one no one was ever allowed to sit in. He must have pulled it from the corner of the room, closer to the coffee table.

"That was my father's favorite chair," Partridge says. "It's a beaut, isn't it?"

Foresteed starts to get up.

"No, no," Partridge says, "don't get up."

Foresteed rubs the leather on the arms. "Your father had good taste."

Partridge sits in a less regal chair a few feet away. "How are things?" he asks.

"You called the meeting. I assumed there were issues you wanted to discuss."

"I've heard about the attacks on the survivors."

"We had reason to believe that the wretches needed to be subdued."

"I want that to stop."

"What?" Foresteed says, as if he's hard of hearing.

"I want the *subduing* to end," Partridge says slowly.

Foresteed twists in his chair and props a heel on a knee. "I'm in charge of the defense."

"And I'm in charge of you."

"Or so it seems." Foresteed smiles.

"What's that supposed to mean?"

Foresteed pulls a small handheld out of his pocket. He points the screen at Partridge. Partridge's face is on the screen. He's at the medical center at Mrs. Hollenback's bedside. Partridge knows what comes next. Foresteed hits play, and Partridge sees a quick clip of his confession.

"What if I told you . . ." And there's the pause—the moment Partridge could have chosen to stay silent, but then he says, "I'm a murderer too."

"You were too young. You didn't understand what was happening—not like we did. No," Mrs. Hollenback says.

"You don't understand," he says. "I killed him. I'm a murderer."

Mrs. Hollenback is in the frame too—her gaunt face, her charcoal-blackened mouth. "You killed *him*?"

And then he says the words that damn him. "I had to stop my father. I had no choice. He was planning to—"

"Turn it off!" Partridge says. He doesn't want to hear what Mrs. Hollenback says next, but Foresteed is too slow. "Forgive us. Forgive us all," he hears her say.

"It's called patricide," Foresteed says, "and people don't care for it. Do you think the Dome wants to be ruled by a murderer?"

Partridge feels sick with anger and shame. "You knew, though. You facilitated the whole thing, didn't you?"

"How could I have predicted that you'd actually go through with it? I mean, killing one's own father—that requires a deep corruption of the soul. I didn't know you had it in you."

"Maybe you underestimated me."

"No. You underestimated me, Partridge. If I show this recording to the people, they'll call for your execution."

"Is that your plan?"

Foresteed shakes his head and laughs. "If there's one thing I've learned from working for your father, it's the advantages of being the puppeteer, not the puppet."

Partridge rubs his knuckles. He'd love to punch Foresteed, rip the handheld from his hand, destroy the clip. But he knows that the clip exists in multiple locations. Foresteed is not an idiot. Partridge is powerless now.

"So let's pretend this meeting went well," Foresteed says. "I will stop subduing the wretches—as if following orders—and I will even stop the torture program that you interrupted. And you will go along with the wedding. You will concentrate on cake tasting and registering for blenders. I hope you're taking this all in, Partridge. Because if you don't do what I say . . ."

Partridge feels the blood pounding in his face. "What?"

"You know your father's collection of enemies, all locked up in their frozen chambers? His 'little relics'?"

Partridge turns his head. He can't look at Foresteed's tan face and gleaming teeth.

"You know why your father kept his greatest enemies alive?"

Partridge shakes his head. He doesn't want to know.

"He'd bring them out every once in a while to torture them, for old times' sake. Sometimes the mood just struck him. I believe in people being punished for their crimes. And if the crime is truly abhorrent, I believe the punishment should be painful." Foresteed leans forward. "Who knows? Maybe one day I'll have a collection of 'little relics' of my own."

"Sounds like something to look forward to."

Foresteed rubs the leather on the arms of the chair once more and then stands up. "Well, this was pleasant. Let's do it again soon."

"Yep," Partridge says. "Real soon."

EL CAPITAN

BOY

A<small>T</small> FIRST, EL CAPITAN THINKS the kid is following them because he's lost and dazed and has nowhere else to go. He ignores
the boy—a gimp with one stiff leg and his face half-burned. They're
looking for orphans as it is, though he knows they're likely dead.
Still, they don't need any more lost souls hanging on to them.

He also doesn't have the heart to tell the kid to shove off,
though—not yet.

But then Bradwell says, "Where's Pressia? I haven't seen her in a
while."

El Capitan and Helmud both look around. It's still raining hard,
the wind pushing it across the streets. Hastings freezes and sniffs
the air.

"Hastings," Bradwell says, nervous suddenly. "Where'd she go?"

Hastings climbs onto some rubble to get a better view.

"Hastings!" Bradwell says impatiently.

And the boy walks closer. He tugs on El Capitan's sleeve.

"Not now," El Capitan says.

The boy cowers but then says, "I got a message from her."

"Who?" Bradwell says, walking to the boy, who's afraid of Bradwell's hulking frame and large wings. He takes a few steps away,

and El Capitan has to step in, talking in a quiet voice and getting down on one knee.

"Tell us," he says.

"Tell us," Helmud repeats in a soft singsong.

"The one you're looking for. Pressia Belze."

He's got her full name, which means a lot out here. Hastings clambers down from the rubble, and they all gather a little closer.

"What's the message?" El Capitan says.

"She had to go. She had to head out."

"Where?" El Capitan shouts.

"We know where!" Bradwell yells.

"Where? Where?" Helmud says to the boy, again using his singsong.

"She didn't say. She said you'd know."

"We know," Hastings says.

"She said she'd send you a message once she got there," the boy says. "She said she'd find her brother, and he'd help her send it."

"What kind of message?"

"She said she'd tell you to take it down or not. She said you'd know what she meant and that she'd draw a picture on the message."

"A picture of what?" El Capitan asks.

"She wouldn't tell me, but she said you'd know by the picture that it was a message from her."

"See what you did!" El Capitan shouts at Bradwell, who runs his hands through his wet hair and backs away from the kid.

"See what *you* did?" Helmud says, shifting blame back to El Capitan.

"Listen to your brother for once," Bradwell says, shaking rain from his wings.

"You told her she couldn't go. You acted like you owned her," El Capitan shouts, standing back up. "She left the way she did so she wouldn't have to fight you!"

The boy takes a limp backward and crouches behind some rocks, one straight leg propped to the side, watching.

"You were willing to let her go," Bradwell says. "You'd let her do whatever she wants because you want her to be in love with you."

"You want her to be in love with you," Helmud says to Bradwell coldly.

"What did you say, Helmud?" Bradwell says.

"Helmud means that you want her to still love you so you can punish her with it. At least I told her how I feel," El Capitan says. "If you weren't so scared, maybe you would."

Bradwell charges him, driving his shoulder into El Capitan's sternum. They hit a brick wall, ramming Helmud into it. El Capitan feels his brother's ribs contract, airless.

Hastings moves in to break them up, but El Capitan rolls away from him, grabbing Bradwell by the throat. Bradwell rips loose and gets El Capitan in a headlock. Helmud punches Bradwell in the back of the head while El Capitan drives his elbow into Bradwell's gut. Bradwell loses his grip and falls to one knee.

"Don't ever shove Helmud around!" El Capitan says, reaching up and supporting the back of his brother's head. "You hear me? I'll protect him with every drop of blood in my body. You got that?" He turns his face to his brother's. "You okay?" he whispers.

Helmud's breath is ragged. "Okay," he mutters.

Bradwell and El Capitan are breathless too.

"Did you even think about the bacterium?" El Capitan shouts. "You idiot!" And then he shouts at Helmud. "Check it!"

He feels Helmud's nimble fingers touch its outline. "Check," Helmud says weakly.

"Sorry," Bradwell says, pushing on his head with both hands. "I wasn't thinking."

"She's unprotected," Hastings says.

"She wouldn't have it any other way," El Capitan says.

"She told us she'd send us a message," Hastings says. "Let's give her time to assess the situation."

Bradwell looks at El Capitan sharply.

El Capitan lets his eyes rove the rubble around them, the distant pile of bodies. "She could die before she even gets there."

Bradwell draws a deep breath. "Why didn't she at least let us help escort her in?"

"If she dies, it'll be on her own terms," El Capitan says. "That's what you wanted, right? To die on your own terms?"

Bradwell rubs his eyes. Maybe he's crying. El Capitan can't tell.

The boy says, "There was something else."

El Capitan had forgotten about the kid, who steps out from behind the rocks. This time he talks as fast as he can. "She said don't give up on the kids. Wilda and them. Don't give up on them. Keep looking." And before they have a chance to ask him any questions or get in another fight, he turns and runs away.

They're all silent for a moment.

And then Hastings stands tall. "She might get mad, but I have to at least try to find her and protect her. I still have some loyalty coding, and it's fixed on her. I have an excuse." And that's it. He jerks his head as if flipping his hair out of his eyes and moves off into the rain, swinging his prosthetic in front of him and hopping over it with quick agility.

"I've got somewhere I need to go too. Somewhere I can think straight," Bradwell says. He looks at El Capitan almost pleadingly and then down at the ground. "Will you come with me?"

"Depends. Where?"

"I didn't say it was someplace I *wanted* to go. I said I *need* to go there. Just say yes. We'll stay together."

"Together," Helmud says.

"Okay," El Capitan says. "We'll stick together."

PRESSIA

HOME

PRESSIA STEPS IN THROUGH what was once the doorway, her boots crunching the broken glass. Its roof is gone, like a gaping maw over her head. The floor shines with dark puddles of rain. There's the old striped pole, lying on its side, the row of blasted mirrors, and tucked in way back, up against the solid wall, the one remaining barbershop chair, the counter, the combs upright in an old glass Barbasol container. The fire made its way here. The walls are even more blackened, the remaining shards of the mirrors fogged gray as if sealed shut. Pressia reminds herself that it hasn't been that long since she was here. But that doesn't help. Everything is different.

There could be snipers near, but she doesn't care. *Kill me*, she thinks. Wilda and the children are dead. If she'd gotten here faster, if she'd never left them so unprotected… It's her fault.

She sees the fake panel that her grandfather built along the back wall—her escape hatch—fitted back into place. It leads to the barbershop's back room, her childhood home. She walks up to the panel, wedges it loose.

And there is the cabinet where she once slept. She rubs her hand on the wood, the fine grit of ash. This was where she drew the lopsided grin of the smiley face. She promised her grandfather she'd come back, and now here she is, finally. Even though he's dead, she should be true to that promise—to herself if no one else.

The cabinet door is slightly ajar, and she can see the old storage room—the table legs, her grandfather's chair. She crawls into the cabinet and fits the panel back into place. Once inside the small space, she tightens the cabinet door from within. It's dark, and she feels small again. She tucks the doll head under her chin. She tries to remember what it was like to be here that first time—the cramped space, the fine motes of dust and ash spinning in the air, and how some part of her hoped she could survive just by being good and quiet and small. She remembers her grandfather sitting in his usual spot by the door, his stump knotted with the veins of wires, the brick on his lap, the fan in his throat whirring one way and then the other with each of his ragged breaths.

She misses him. She misses who she once was in this cabinet. She was his granddaughter. He's dead, and it turns out she wasn't even his granddaughter. She was just a lost little girl surrounded by dead people in an airport. He saved her.

She wants to be saved again.

She thinks of the shoes her grandfather gave her for her six-teenth birthday—that pair of clogs—as if he knew she was leaving soon and wanted her to have sturdy shoes at least so that she could make it in the world. And what kind of world was it?

Nothing she could have ever imagined.

As awful and bloody and filled with suffering and death as it is, she fell in love in that world. Love. Who would ever have guessed that it could still exist—after everything—but it does.

She touches her fingers to the cabinet door lightly. It creaks open. The room is more or less intact. The table is singed but not gone. Her grandfather's old pallet went up in smoke. It's small and blackened—mostly soot. But the brick is there. It sits by the back door.

She can tell that someone else lived here since her grandfather was taken. There was a sack hanging on a hook in the wall. The sack is mostly gone, but the handle still rests on the hook. The table is covered in bits of what looks like an attempt to rebuild something electronic—a radio, a computer, a simple toaster? Impossible to say.

This is no longer her home. Her grandfather is gone. It's as if he never existed.

She closes the door and climbs back out through the fake panel into the barbershop and brushes herself off. She's wasted time. She feels guilty about it but then angry. Would Bradwell go back if he could to a time when he had parents to watch over him? Wouldn't El Capitan take Helmud back to the place in the woods where they lived with their mother before she was taken away?

Is that why she wants to get the vial and the formula to the Dome laboratories? Because she thinks that if enough people can return to the way they once were, it won't just feel like they've been cured but that they've been able to erase this awfulness and return to a time when... what? When they felt safe? Has she ever felt truly safe? By safe, maybe she just means not alone in the world.

What if Bradwell and El Capitan are right? Maybe the world doesn't need more intervention from science and medicine. Maybe they just need to even the playing field and take down the Dome.

She has to see Partridge first, though. She can't be a part of that unless she knows what's happened. She still has faith in him. She has to. If she loses faith in him, her faith in everyone slips. And she can't afford to lose any more faith. It's too precious.

She walks to the gutted door, back out on the street. Again, she runs—head down, breathless. She knows the way now. She runs until she can see the bright spot of the Dome, far-off, its cross shining against the dark silk of the clouds.

EL CAPITAN

SAINT

BRADWELL STOPS ON TOP OF SOME RUBBLE. He lifts a piece of cast-iron gate. "This way." He goes in first, down a small set of stone steps. El Capitan knows this part of town—or thought he did. He used to make rounds back when he drove the truck, picking up unwilling recruits, but he's never seen this hole before.

El Capitan says to Helmud, "Where's he taking us?"

"Us?" Helmud whispers, as if he'd rather stay behind alone.

El Capitan follows Bradwell down the stairs, pulling the gate back into place overhead, covering them.

The room is small, but not just because it's caved in. No, it was built to be small. "Is this near where the old church used to be?" El Capitan says, trying to get his bearings.

"We're in it."

"The church?"

"It's a crypt."

Bradwell looks too big for the space. His massive wings rub the walls. He hunches down and keeps his head bowed—because he's too tall or is he being respectful? He walks to a wall and kneels.

But Bradwell has folded his hands together. He's whispering into them. Why? El Capitan's never understood religions.

"I didn't know you were churchgoing," El Capitan says, more to himself than Bradwell. At first it looks like Bradwell is praying to a Plexiglas wall, a little shattered but still holding up. Then he sees that the Plexiglas is covering a recess in the wall, and through the splintered plastic, he sees a girl. Her face is slightly lifted; her hands are in her lap. She's sitting there, wearing a long old-fashioned dress, her hair pulled back from her face—a beautiful face, simple and yet profoundly sad. She's patient. She's waiting for something or someone. Maybe she was waiting for Bradwell. Maybe she's waiting for God.

"Who is she?" El Capitan says, but he knows Bradwell won't answer. He's praying. His eyes are clenched, his hands locked together. Dome worshippers used to kneel and pray like this. He's seen them lined up in the Deadlands before, all pointing toward the Dome.

"Who?" Helmud says. "Who?"

A row of candles on a ledge have melted, covering it in wax. Offerings. Many people have been here. El Capitan spots a placard. He steps up to it closely. Half the words are gone. It's all banged up. The statue is of a saint whose name started with Wi. He knows that she was a patron saint of something. He sees the word *abbess* but doesn't know what it means. There's more about small children and miracles and the word *tuberculosis*, which he knows well. It's likely how the saint died. A disease of the lungs. His mother died young of a disease. She was like a saint—to him at least.

El Capitan moves to the back wall and sits down, leaning against Helmud. Helmud lets his head rest on El Capitan's shoulder.

El Capitan wonders how long Bradwell is going to take. He seems pained. His whispers—El Capitan can't make out the words—sound urgent. Is he praying to the saint to keep Pressia safe? Is he praying to be forgiven? That's something that always comes up with religions, isn't it?

El Capitan props his forearms up on his knees and clasps his hands together. He sits that way for a while before he realizes that his hands are linked almost like someone who's praying. He closes his eyes, wondering if in a place like this, something might come to him.

He whispers, "Saint Wi." He tries to imagine who she was. Did she help children? What were her miracles? He thinks of her face. He doesn't have to look at her. Her face is locked in his mind—her way of gazing. She's waiting patiently. For El Capitan? For him to say what he needs to say?

Say it, he hears the words in his head whisper. *Say it.*

He sees the face of someone he killed. And then another. He remembers driving that truck, making rounds, picking up kids he knew wouldn't ever be soldiers—too sick, too weak, too fused and deformed. *Say it.* He sees a mangled arm. A festered leg. He sees the cage where he kept the ones who would never make it. He remembers the smell of death in that cage. *Say it.*

There was the time he took Pressia, just a fresh recruit herself then, out into the woods to play The Game—hunting down a sickly recruit. Ingership gave the order to have Pressia play The Game, but would Ingership have ever really known if El Capitan hadn't gone through with it? No. He could've faked it. And then the boy, crawling through underbrush, got caught in one of El Capitan's traps. The metal spokes drove into his ribs, punctured his chest. He begged for them to shoot him. Pressia couldn't, but El Capitan could and did. It was easy.

So why does he see the boy's face now, begging him to pull the trigger? Why does the pain of it dog him still?

He takes a breath. He feels sick. *Say it.* He gulps air.

He knows he should ask for forgiveness. The thought is there in his head.

Say it. Say it.

He opens his mouth, but instead of saying *I'm sorry*, he says, "We got to go."

Bradwell lifts his head, turns, stares at him. "Give me a minute."

"Okay, but that's all—just a minute." El Capitan gets to his feet, but his head doesn't feel right. He lurches toward the statue of the saint, dizzy now. He presses his pale, scarred hands to the splintered Plexiglas, and lowers his head so that it touches the plastic too.

"You okay?" Bradwell asks.

El Capitan straightens up, rubs his face. "Fine," he says. "We're fine. Right, Helmud?"

"Right?" Helmud says.

And El Capitan turns and runs up the stone stairs, moves aside the piece of cast-iron gate, and steps into the dusty air. He breathes deeply. He looks up and down the streets. He remembers running through these streets—in Death Sprees. He leans over and spits on the ground.

"Right?" Helmud asks again.

"Not right," El Capitan says. "Not right at all." He imagines Pressia making her way to the Dome. She's the one who has hope, who still believes in Partridge. He's glad she's free of them. "She's out there trying to make something right. And you and me, Helmud? What should we do? What's the point of the two of us on this earth? You tell me that."

"You tell me," Helmud says.

Bradwell climbs up the steps, covers the opening again, and says, "I'm going after her."

El Capitan feels a spike of jealousy. He wants to tackle Bradwell and beat his head with a rock. That's how he would have handled something like this—before he met Pressia. "Let her go."

"No. I have to find her—not to protect her. I have to tell her something."

El Capitan knows that he loves her, that he's figured that this might be his last chance to tell her the truth. Bringing down the Dome will likely lead to something like war. God, it would feel good to grind Bradwell's face into the ground, but this is beyond El Capitan. He has to bow out. He's got no shot at love. He says, "You'll go this one alone."

"I know the ending, Cap."

"What ending?"

"My own."

"How does it turn out?"

"It could be better, but I have to see it through."

"I guess that's all we can do—see it through."

"See it through," Helmud says.

"Will we meet up?" El Capitan says.

"We can meet at the old vault. Should be safe and dry there."

"The bank?"

"What's left of it." Bradwell is about to go, but then he turns back. "What happened to you in there?"

"In there?" Helmud says, reaching around and tapping El Capitan's chest.

El Capitan doesn't know, so he doesn't answer. "Promise me you'll *really* tell her." His chest burns. "Tell her the whole truth. Whatever it is. She deserves that much."

Partridge

PROMISE

THE WEDDING PLANS COME AT HIM nonstop. Iralene insists that he be involved. "You have to be emotionally invested in this," she whispers, "or they'll be able to tell. They'll know! The whole thing could backfire!"

She holds out swatches of fabric for bridesmaid dresses, tablecloths, napkins. She makes him choose silverware patterns and dishes, candlesticks and gravy boats for their registry. A pastry chef brings in cake samples. A cook brings in meal choices and wine—more samples. He tastes and sips and points. "That one."

"Really?" Iralene says.

"Okay, fine. That one."

"I want you to love it!"

"What do you want me to say? Which one is the right choice?"

Iralene tears up whenever he gets frustrated. "This is supposed to be a blessed occasion!"

"No," he says. "The wedding is an event to distract people and raise morale and stop people from killing themselves. It's not a blessed occasion; it's not even a marriage. There's a difference."

She sighs, as if realizing that she's pulled out the big guns too soon, then leans toward him and whispers, "Pick the salmon."

And he picks the salmon. As a concession, he adds, "I like the hollandaise sauce very much." He looks at Iralene as if to say, *See? I'm trying.*

"If you just focus a little," she says.

He can't focus. There's one thing that Foresteed said that's stuck with him—his father's little relics, a collection of his greatest enemies. Partridge remembers the chamber that was different from all the rest—the one Iralene showed him once while they were walking those long halls. It was unmarked and heavily secured. Partridge didn't know how to break into it. But if his father's little relics are truly his greatest enemies—ones he kept around so he could pull them out and torture them when the mood struck— then who's in *that* chamber? Could his father's greatest enemy be Partridge's greatest ally?

He wants to get to that chamber somehow and try to open it. He keeps wondering if it's possible that one of the Seven is kept there. His father's greatest enemy was a personal one: Hideki Imanaka, the man Partridge's mother fell in love with, had an affair—with Pressia's father.

Also, Pressia's grandfather is still in one of those suspension chambers. Is Weed on Partridge's side or not? Is he even trying to bring Belze out of suspension? Now that he's punched Weed, he'll either be more compliant or refuse to help.

How will Partridge get down there? He's faced with relentless wedding plans—being fitted for a tux and shiny shoes, picking flower arrangements, talking about seating the guests in a very strict social hierarchy that he doesn't understand or care about.

Partridge feels light-headed. He hasn't been eating much— not with this gnawing in his stomach all the time. He's started taking some indigestion pills—chalky and bitter—but they don't help. He feels like one of the big cats at the zoo—like the pads of his feet are worn raw from pacing the hard cement. He feels locked up.

And then, while it's just the two of them and Iralene is asking him about ribbon trim on centerpieces, she grabs his hand and gives it a squeeze. "Which is your favorite?"

Her hand is so cold it shocks him, and he remembers that Iralene spent most of her life in suspension. She's told him that she thinks of those halls of chambers as her childhood home. Iralene is his suspension specialist. She was the one who first showed them to him.

He puts his hand on hers. She looks up, startled. "Iralene," he whispers, "I want you to do something for me."

"What?" Her eyes are bright and wide. It scares him sometimes how desperate she is to please him.

"I want to go to the chambers again."

She shakes her head. "That part of my life is over," she says with a quivering smile.

"I need your help. I wouldn't ask this otherwise."

"Don't make me go back." She bites her lower lip.

"I need a guide. I need you to explain all of it to me. I need you to take me to the unmarked high-security chamber." He can't just announce his plans. He's no longer his own person now that Foresteed has wielded his power over him. He wants to keep this visit quiet, and he doesn't know who to trust. Iralene is trustworthy, and she knows that building.

She shakes her head, closes her eyes.

"I need you. I can return the favor somehow. I promise."

She crosses her arms on her chest and stares at him coolly. "Without any conditions. A favor. At any time in the future. You'll owe me."

He's a little scared; he's not sure what he's gotten himself into. "Yes. I mean, I don't want to have to—"

"No conditions."

"Okay," he says. "Fine. Can you get us there undetected?"

She thinks about it. "With Beckley's help, yes."

"I want to see if Odwald Belze has been taken out of suspension too."

"Up for air," she says. "That's what we call it."

Up for air. Partridge wants to come up for air.

All the while, he misses Lyda. It's worse at night when there aren't as many awful distractions. Foresteed has sent word that Partridge can't see Lyda until after the wedding, after the scrutiny dies down. It would be too dangerous if word got out to the public.

Later, Partridge sets up his bed on the sofa. Now that Iralene sleeps in Partridge's old bedroom and Glassings in his father's bedroom, Partridge has started sleeping in the living room. But he has trouble sleeping. He writes Lyda letters and passes them to Beckley, like Partridge is just a school kid passing notes in class. His letters at first were short—*I love you. I miss you*...He doesn't tell her that he's under Foresteed's thumb. He knows he should, but he can't. He's too embarrassed. The writing does help him clear his thoughts, though, so he's started to try to carve out some kind of future. Tonight he writes,

> *I haven't given up on the idea of a council. Pressia should be the head of it. Bradwell needs to be in charge of writing the new history, the truth, so we can start to get that information out to everyone. And we need someone like El Capitan to take over the military. We'll still need to be able to keep the peace...*
>
> *I'll be able to get away soon. I promise... When we're together again, everything will be all right.*

He knows Lyda's scared about the future. She has to be. Everything is so unknown. He imagines the people out there who've tried to kill themselves and the attack on the wretches and the babies lined up in incubators awaiting his father's New Eden, the people in suspension, and all of those survivors out there—scattered around the globe.

It all weighs on him until he feels incredibly small.

Tonight he sneaks the newest letter to Beckley as usual. Beckley stands guard near the front door, and Partridge asks if she's written anything back.

The answer's the same as always.

Beckley shakes his head. "Not yet." He tucks the letter into his breast pocket.

"And how's she doing?" Partridge asks.

"She stays in the nursery most of her days. She's decorating it to surprise you. She won't let anyone in."

Partridge imagines her painting the walls, decorating the crib, keeping herself busy. That seems like it should be a good thing, but he knows Lyda well enough to assume she's feeling caged too.

Another guard shows up, and Partridge goes back to the couch. He grips his hands together so hard that they start shaking. This isn't what he wanted. This isn't his life. Power—he has all this supposed power, and yet he's powerless.

He remembers asking his father once if God was real. His father told him that it didn't really matter, in the end, if God was real or not. "Religion holds us together. Church is important. It gives us order and structure. It's the best place to legislate policy—from on high. It teaches the masses the difference between good and evil."

There were so many policies—whom you should and shouldn't fall in love with, how and when you should marry, what you should and shouldn't discuss or question in the home, how to raise your children so they never break any policies, and entire books on how to be a good wife and mother.

No, Partridge thinks now. Policies are man-made. God is important. People know the difference between good and evil in their hearts—if they search them. Religions twist good and evil. Their differences are the kind that need to be taught because they aren't natural. Why else would people think his father was a good man and mourn his death unless someone had shoved the idea of his goodness down their throats? Religion was one of his father's many tools. He used it well.

Partridge whispers, "God." It's all he has. Just one word.

Pressia

RUSTLING

By NIGHTFALL, SHE'S MADE IT to the woods that lead to the barren terrain surrounding the Dome—what was once home to shepherds and pickers of berries, morels, tubers. There were farmers too, but so little grew—and never quite the way they expected—that it was hard to think of them as farmers. Some called them tinkerers. They've all been flushed out by fire. Pressia feels the trunk of a burned tree, its wet bark peeling like a charred layer of skin. The light rain is ticking against the ashen forest floor.

It's quiet out here now, and she wishes it were still light. She needs to find a place to sleep before she heads toward the Dome in the morning. She knows how hard it was for Partridge to escape. Will it be that hard to enter? She intends to walk to the door by the loading dock where Lyda was escorted out. She remembers the maps that Partridge and Lyda made. She knows where to look for the Dome's seams.

It also crosses her mind that she won't make it to the door at all. There's a good chance she'll be devoured by a Dust or a Beast hoping to slaughter fresh prey, or she could get shot as she approaches. It's strange how used to this idea she's gotten.

Will someone answer the door? She plans on telling them that she's Partridge's half sister, and she has no idea how they'll react to that. Things could be volatile in the Dome now, in the aftermath of Willux's death. People might be resistant to let Partridge take over. They should be. He only happens to be Willux's son. Why should that grant him automatic authority?

The air smells of burned-pine smoke and metal. She finally comes to a stretch of woods that, surprisingly, doesn't look like it caught fire. Most of the limbs are bare because it's winter. But she looks closely at a scrubby pine with its twisted branches, spiked limbs, and bulbous roots shouldering up from the ground like buried knees. Its needles are sticky to the touch. She picks up a leaf from the ground; it's dusty with rust as if the tree has been tinged with iron. New hybrid species keep popping up. Could it possibly be seen as a good thing—a land and its creatures trying to adapt?

She stops and checks the vial and formula again, opening her backpack, popping open the metal box, touching them. They're fine, and this gives her a little courage. They remind her of her mission here.

She walks deeper through the trees, hoping to find a clump of brush to hide in, a rock or fallen log to block the wind.

But then there's a rustling.

Birds or rodents? A fox? She remembers the stitched arms of the blind creatures that Kelly set loose—their roving eyes, the way they touched her hair. She shivers. It's not them. She knows that, but she can't shake the feeling of them touching her. What would they have done if she hadn't gotten away? She draws her arms in across her chest and stares into the darkness, hoping for something small and harmless to reveal itself. *Please be a bunny*, she thinks. *A little bunny. I could really use a bunny.* The last bunny she saw was years ago, and instead of fur it had thick scarred skin, dark and wrinkled, its ribs poking through in warped slats. But it was still a bunny, with long ears and sharp front teeth, and it scampered off, afraid of her. *Scamper off*, she pleads with the bunny that's probably not a bunny at all. *Please scamper off.*

The cold night sky shifts with dark clouds, thick with smoke. She wants to get out of the wind and sleep. That's all. She's tired—deep in her bones and joints. It's a fatigue that seems to have crashed down on her.

More rustling. She crouches. Her adrenaline starts to kick in, but it's not enough. She doesn't have the strength to fight. She doesn't want to be eaten here, mauled to death—not now. She pulls the backpack off and holds it to her chest. She looks down at the doll head, its glassy eyes glinting in the dull light, as if pleading with her for protection. She failed Wilda and the others—the doll head seems to know, and it's as if it has lost some faith in her.

More rustling, footsteps. She grips the doll head and backpack and freezes.

And then she hears her name. The rough voice of Bradwell. She sees him, between two thin trees. He opens his wings, streaked dark with rain. "Pressia," he says.

She stands up slowly. He came after her. She's angry that he doesn't have enough faith in her, but then she's relieved to see him. Her heart kicks up.

"Look at me," he says.

And she does: the meat of his shoulders, the long spokes of his collarbones, the twin scars on his cheek, and his eyes, his lips—all wet with rain. His skin, like hers, has lost the golden tinge from their time in Ireland. But the wings—that's what he wants her to look at. Some of the feathers shine. Others are tattered. The quills are thick and strong. She says, "I see you."

"All of me."

"I see all of you." He's like a dream. He's staring at her as if really seeing her for the first time in so long.

"I had to try to find you." How did he track her down?

"I had to go," she says.

"I know, but I didn't get to say what I needed to."

"And what's that?"

He runs his hands through his wet hair. "You think I don't imagine being inside that Dome, inside those academy classrooms, in the dance halls with you? I do. But not the way you do. You see yourself fitting in."

"No, I don't."

"You think it's possible. You can imagine what it'd be like to have your hand back, to have your scars gone. Me? I don't have that kind of imagination. I can only see myself as I am. And every time I imagine myself there, I see how they would look at me. To them, I'm sick. I'm diseased. I'm a perversion of a human being."

"You're not any of those things to me."

He rubs his knuckles together. She knows this is hard for him—excruciating. "We were born to die, Pressia. We're the ones no one really expected to survive. So my life is a mistake; it's only something that was given to me by accident. It's not mine. It's borrowed." He walks up close to Pressia. He whispers, "Sometimes I think I'd go back if I could. I would bleed to death, bound to my brothers. But then I know I'd rather go back further than that. If I could, I would die with you on the frozen forest floor. We were wet and cold and naked. That's how we came into this world. We could have gone out like that together." He touches his forehead to hers. He closes his eyes. "I know why you did what you did. But now I've got that stuff in my blood, and I'm no longer who I am. You can't love me."

"But I do."

He says, "Don't."

She says, "I'm trying not to."

She reaches up over his shoulder and lets her hand run down one of his soft, wet wings. It feels silken. He touches the crescent-shaped burn curved around one of her eyes then cups the head of the doll in his hands.

"I can't let you go," he says.

She leans in toward him, close, the rain beading on her eyelashes. She puts one hand on his heart and can feel it pounding. "I have to."

"I know."

"How long will you give me before you use the bacterium?"

"Not long. Anything could happen to you in there. Cap was right about that too."

"It'll take me a day to get there at least. So how long will you give me?"

"I don't know."

"If I get to Partridge, I can get a message to you."

"Within three days?"

"I can try." She wants to kiss his wet lips. She misses him so much her chest aches. *Tell me you love me*, she wants to say. *Tell me you love me like you used to.*

And then he dips toward her and kisses her on the mouth, the rain still coming down. When he pulls back, she's breathless.

"Three days," he says. "Okay?"

"Okay," she says and then, even though her legs feel numb, she takes a step back.

"Hastings has come after you too," he says. "I'm surprised he hasn't found you already. He only wants to help."

She nods.

"Pressia, what if we don't see each other again? What if this is the last time?" He's scared. She's not sure she's ever seen him look this way.

"I'll be fine," she says.

"I know you will," he says. "It's just…"

"What?"

"In case there's a heaven…"

"Don't talk like that," Pressia says.

"In case there's a heaven, I want us to be together there. Joined.

Forever." His eyes search hers. "I've never seen a wedding," he says.

Is he asking her to marry him? She whispers, "I've heard they were held in churches or under white tents."

"What if the forest is our church?"

"Are you asking me to marry you—*here*? *Now*?"

"I've loved you since the beginning—since the first time I saw you. Why not get married—yes, here and now?" He lifts her hand up and places it on her heart. He then slips his hand between her arm and chest and puts his hand over his own heart. He leans down and puts his cheek to hers. He says, "Will you be my wife forever? Here and now and beyond all of this?"

She closes her eyes. She feels her arm entwined with his, his cheek against hers—both rain-wet and cold. She nods. "I will. Will you be my husband forever?"

He says, "I will." And he bows his head, kisses her neck, her jaw, her lips.

"This isn't the end," Pressia says. "We're just starting, Bradwell."

He tips her up off the ground and kisses her again—she feels his lips, his tongue, his teeth.

And she feels so alive that she can barely breathe. She's happy. This is what happy feels like—it doesn't have to be about this moment. Happiness can be a promise.

When he sets her back down, she feels heavy.

He turns then and heads back through the woods; the rainy wind gusts his wings a little. She's going to keep going. But now she knows what she wants: to make it back to Bradwell, to find a beginning.

She walks quickly now, shaking with relief and joy, marching with purpose. She has to find that safe place. She walks for a while, and then a whirring sound zips through the air—a taut *zing* that ends in a *thunk* just over her head. She looks up at the tree behind her, and there, lodged deep in its bark, is a thick blade, sharp on all sides.

There are mothers out here. That's probably why this part of the woods hasn't burned. It's been heavily guarded.

Pressia stays low but calls out, "I'm just a girl! I'm friends with Lyda! My name is Pressia, and I've met Our Good Mother! I'm alone! No Deaths with me!" But she's not just a girl—she's a wife. She's not alone, even if it seems that way. She has Bradwell, forever.

The forest is silent. She moves behind a tree. Another blade whirs through the air, pinning her coat to the tree behind her. She wants to rip her coat loose and make a run for it, but the mothers aren't to be messed with. If you defy them, they can retaliate brutally.

She puts the doll head in the air. "What do you want?" she calls into the woods. "I surrender! Okay?" She hopes Bradwell is long gone, that he can't even hear the echo of her voice. "I surrender," she says again, and as she says those two words, they seem like the truest thing she's said in so long. *I surrender. I'm tired. Take me in.*

Finally, there's a woman's voice, sharp and clear. "Get her," the woman says. "She's ours now."

LYDA

BECOMING

LYDA IS HIDDEN IN HER OTHER WORLD. The orb—which is set on the outside world—exists in the nursery now. It's where she keeps the ash of the burned baby books and the row of cylindrical slats from the baby crib that she's sharpening into spears. The door stays locked. If anyone asks, she says, "It's a surprise! For Partridge!"

Partridge has ordered more guards to stand watch at her door. A small army is collected there now. Is he afraid someone is going to attack her? Or is he making sure she can never leave?

She's worked hard in that small room, and now she lies in bed, clean and sweet smelling, her hair damp from a midday shower. She writes Partridge another letter. She's written so many she can't keep track. She gives them to Beckley whenever she sees him—every few days he takes a shift—but he never has any for her.

"What does he say when you give them to him?" she's asked.

"He smiles and slips them in his pocket—to read later, I guess."

"I don't understand why he doesn't write back."

"He's busy. You know—plans."

Wedding plans. Yes, she knows.

Partridge,
When are you coming back? I am becoming

What is she becoming? She doesn't know. It seems most honest to just say that *she's becoming*. The becoming is what matters maybe more than the result.

She thinks of writing him that she's nesting—a term she learned in the girls' academy in an infant-care class, one that Chandry uses often when she comes for knitting lessons. Lyda likes the word because when she was in the girls' academy, she loved walking through the aviary and watching the birds fortify their nests. Her nesting instincts might not be what Partridge expects, but she does feel like she's building a place for herself and this child—just for them. She feels safe in the nursery. But lying here, in her own room, on her fresh sheets, having combed her hair smooth, she's vulnerable.

Something's coming. Things are unstable. It's not just that Willux has died. It's as if the air is agitated, combustible. And while Partridge is out there, busy with his wedding plans, he doesn't even notice. No one seems to. The guards stand stiffly outside of her door. Chandry comes and goes. Sometimes Lyda looks out the window and sees people on the street, bustling with packages, walking miniature dogs, pushing strollers.

It's almost completely back to normal—like the truth was never spoken.

Sometimes, she writes Partridge,

I feel like the fire is inside of me. I don't know what I'm becoming. But I think it's to help me meet some future I can't imagine, but a future that's coming all the same.
When will I see you again? Ever?

Love,
Lyda

Pressia

MOTHERS

THE MOTHERS EMERGE FROM THE WOODS one at a time. A bush becomes a body. A woman jumps from the thin limbs of a tree. It's dark, and their bodies—alive with the restlessness of their children—are hard to make out. One of the mothers says, "Take her to camp. Guard her closely. We'll send word to Our Good Mother of her presence." Pressia, still staked to the tree by the dart through her coat, isn't sure what Our Good Mother might think of her being one of their prisoners.

Two mothers walk up to her, one in a woolen cap and the other with white hair.

Pressia hopes that they don't confiscate her backpack. That's what matters most.

The one with white hair pulls the blade from the tree—leaving a fresh rip in Pressia's coat—and tucks the dart back into a small bag strapped over her shoulder. "This way," she says. "Hands on your head."

Pressia walks between the two mothers. Her arms start to ache. She can see their children now—one on his mother's shoulder, another curved across her mother's chest.

"You've kept these woods from getting burned," Pressia whispers.

They nod, walking her past a small camouflaged lean-to. Inside, Pressia glimpses strange contraptions—catapults on wheels?—and baskets of what look like grenades. "I made some of those from the robotic spiders sent down from the Dome."

"And we continued the effort," the woman with white hair says. "We're the first line of defense. We take out the new Special Forces when they step out and descend, when they're still disoriented." The mother stops at a large barrel filled with guns—freshly polished. "We gut them for their guns, clean them off. The stockpile is growing."

Pressia remembers the Special Forces boy—not Pure, a wretch. "Aren't some of them young?"

"They send their boys off to die. We comply." The mother with white hair squints at Pressia. "Why are you here?"

Pressia doesn't want to tell them. The mothers are erratic—calm and then murderous, capable of most anything. "I was looking for someone," she says.

"Who?" the mother with white hair says, and Pressia wonders if the woman in the wool cap has a voice at all. Is she mute?

"The children who were Purified in the Dome, especially one named Wilda."

The mother in the wool cap makes a clucking noise with her tongue as if Pressia's said the wrong thing and the mother is rebuking her.

"Stop looking. It's a waste of time," the mother with white hair says.

"Because they're dead or because they're hidden away somewhere?"

"Some questions are better left unanswered," the mother says. "Plus, you're lying."

"I'm not lying."

"You're not telling the whole truth, which is lying."

The mother in the wool cap clucks her tongue again.

The mother with the white hair reaches up and pulls one of the few remaining leaves from a branch overhead. She says, "This is a season of death. We are not sure there will be another spring."

"What do you mean?" Pressia says. "The earth has endured this much. Of course there will be spring." She thinks of Bradwell saying, *If we don't see each other again...*

"After they took Lyda, we decided we would never back down. Some say it's a death wish. We don't wish for death. We're already dead."

"Took Lyda? She was going into the Dome with Partridge. She wasn't taken. She went on her own..."

"She was taken!" the mother with the white hair says.

"Mmmhmm," the mother in the wool cap purrs from the back of her throat.

Pressia isn't sure what to believe. The mothers sometimes tell themselves the stories they want to believe. Pressia can't blame them. But right now, she wishes she understood. "What happened? Tell me."

The mother in the wool cap shakes her head and glares at the other mother.

"You can't be trusted," the mother with the white hair says.

"But I need to know. Lyda's my friend. She's like a sister to me. You understand?" The mothers have built their lives around the notion of sisterhood. They exchange a glance.

"No," the mother with the white hair says. "We will tell you nothing."

They walk through the forest, deeper and deeper, until it's almost completely dark. They come to a small camp of lean-tos. The mothers lead Pressia to one of the tiny tents.

The mother with the white hair says, "You can drop your hands now."

Pressia rubs her arms, tingling from the lack of blood. The

mother in the wool cap sees the doll head, reaches out and cups it in her pale, raw hands.

The mother with the white hair nods and says, "It's like she's one of us."

The mother in the wool cap purrs again.

"One of you? Why do you say that?" Pressia says. She's nothing like the mothers. She isn't a woman who's been deserted, and she never will be. She has Bradwell—here, now, and beyond. The mothers scare her. They always have. Their underlying strength is shot through with something vicious. It's how they've stayed alive. "It's just a doll."

"It's part of you, isn't it?" the mother with the white hair says. "It defines you completely, and then again it doesn't define you at all—like motherhood. You'll be one of us. It's a matter of time."

Pressia pulls the doll head to her chest but doesn't know what to say. She doesn't want to be part of this tribe of women. She wants to get through this and build a life with Bradwell. *If we don't see each other again*—the thought alone scares her.

The mother with the white hair says, "We will be standing guard. Don't try to leave, or the next time we shoot, we will aim at your heart."

PARTRIDGE

STRAWBERRY

JUST A COUPLE OF DAYS LATER, Partridge and Iralene are at a picnic surrounded by a low gate. Where did the gate come from? Was it put up overnight? It's the kind of gate that was used to enclose people's front yards during the Before inside of the larger gated communities—gates within gates. It's in place now so people know not to get too close. This picnic—though unannounced—has a growing audience.

"Act natural," says one of the women in Iralene's entourage as she fixes the collar of Iralene's dress.

"Act natural?" Partridge says. "Isn't that an oxymoron? I'm acting and so it's not natural."

The woman sniffs and walks off.

These women were the first to gather at the gate, but soon there are over a hundred people. "Who knew anyone would want to spend their time watching me eat a triangulated sandwich and sip lemonade?" Partridge only picks at his food, shoves it around on the paper plate.

"Not *you*," Iralene corrects. "*Us*."

"Us," he says. "Sorry." He thinks of Lyda—that's the *us* he's supposed to be a part of.

"Now I know how fish feel at the aquarium," Partridge says.

"Don't tap the glass!" Iralene says.

He looks at the upscale apartment buildings surrounding the park. One of them is where he stayed when he was first brought back into the Dome—where, on one of the lower floors, there are people suspended in time, each in their own dark, icy capsule. "You know we're not far from *them*," he says.

"I know," she says so quickly and unemotionally that he's not sure if she really knows what he's talking about. She lifts a strawberry. "It looks real. Doesn't it?"

"Isn't it real?"

"I think it's edible."

"That's different from real," he says.

She bites and the crowd—people who mainly survive on soytex pills and supplements—seems to lean in. She smiles and says, "Mmmmm." Then she lifts the strawberry and holds it to Partridge's lips. "Eat it." He wants to ask her if she's still on board as a guide among the capsules.

He opens his mouth. She pulls the strawberry away, and then as he starts to protest, she fits it into his mouth so his teeth bite into the cool sweetness. The crowd murmurs happily.

"You know that if I tapped your nose right now, they'd erupt in *awww*s," she says. "We have a lot of power."

"I've never had less power in my life."

Partridge glances at the crowd. He catches the eye of the young woman who told him to act natural. She waves a cautionary finger at him; he's not supposed to acknowledge the crowd because it makes them uncomfortable. And they do, in fact, shift their feet and look away.

He turns back to Iralene.

"We do have a lot of power, Partridge." She taps him on the nose, and the crowd *awww*s—maybe led by the entourage, but the awing is considerable. It makes him nervous—the immediacy of it.

He lies back, as if he's at a real picnic, arms crossed under his head, staring up at the false sky—all the better to pretend the audience isn't there, surrounding them.

Iralene lies back too. She rests her head on his chest, nuzzling under his chin.

"Your friends hate me," he whispers. "Aren't I supposed to be the good guy?"

She whispers back, "They think you're spoiled and shallow and cruel."

"Wow. *I'm* spoiled and shallow? I could say the same of them."

"They think you've had everything handed to you on a silver platter."

"Not the first time I've heard the complaint." The academy kids always thought he had it better than they did—Willux's son. Weed was just accusing him of this, in so many words, too. And then when he escaped the Dome and was on the outside, he looked incredibly spoiled to Pressia and Bradwell and, well, everyone he met.

"And cruel," she whispers. "You didn't react to that."

"I *am* cruel. They're right about that," he says, keeping his voice low.

Iralene lifts her head and gazes at him. "You're not cruel. They don't know you like I know you."

"I'm failing everyone I know, everyone I care about."

"Even me?"

"Yes, you. I care about you, Iralene. You know that."

"I haven't forgotten my promise," she whispers. "The favor for a favor."

"You have a plan?" Now he knows why she picked this spot. She's very well aware of how close it is to the building with the capsules.

"I brought a radio. You'll have to dance with me to make this work."

"That's part of the plan? I have to dance in front of all these people?"

She nods. "You have to dance and pick me up and spin me around. Beckley is going to help. And I have someone on the inside—an expert—waiting."

Damn. "Dancing? Can we do this any other way?"

She shakes her head and smiles. "Nope. It's part of the plan."

She sits up, reaches into the oversized canvas bag, and pulls out a small radio. The crowd whispers among themselves restlessly, as if this is just what they've been waiting for. She turns it on and fiddles with the dial. A song comes in clear. It sounds like the dreamy plinking music of the old amusement park he went to as a kid. What was it called? Crazy John-Johns. He remembers the merry-go-round, the roller coaster, the sweet candy swirled airily on a paper stick.

And then there are drums.

He knows what he's supposed to do. The dancing has to be his idea. He stands up and extends his hand. She takes it, and he pulls her to her feet. They step into the grass. He lifts one hand and puts the other on the small of her back. The song is happy and sad at the same time. The singer wants to be older, wants to live with his girlfriend, wants to be able to say goodnight to her and then sleep with her. The last time Partridge danced was with Lyda. They were in the academy cafeteria, which had been transformed for the dance with star decals pasted on the ceiling. He remembers the way she smelled—like honey—and the feel of the silk of her dress and beneath it, her ribs. That was when they first kissed.

But here's Iralene. *Wouldn't it be nice, wouldn't it be nice, wouldn't it be nice*... The singer keeps singing that same phrase. He wants to live in a kind of world that they both belong in. *This isn't it*, Partridge thinks, with the crowd swaying around them. *This isn't it at all.*

Iralene's hand fits perfectly in his. She reaches up and touches the back of his hair that brushes the collar of his shirt. She whispers into his ear, "Pick me up and spin me now. Pick me up."

He lifts her as the singer says he wants to talk about it even though it makes it worse, but still he wants to talk about it. And while spinning Iralene, Partridge thinks of Lyda, which makes it worse, but he can't stop himself. He feels that longing. He closes his eyes. Iralene is light. He spins her around and around. He looks up at her face, backlit by the fake sunlight, and she's smiling, yet her eyes are wet with tears. *Wouldn't it be nice . . .* He sees this song for a second the way Iralene must see it—*Wouldn't it be nice if this were true . . . Wouldn't it be nice if he really loved her . . . Wouldn't it be nice if they could get married and stay together forever . . .* Did she choose the song? Is this what it means to her? The singer wants to get married so that the two of them can be happy. Partridge feels like crying then, spinning and spinning her.

The crowd is clapping now because they know the song is dying down.

If things were different—if he hadn't already fallen in love with Lyda, maybe he and Iralene could be together. Maybe they could even be happy. Maybe he'd love her the way she wants him to. He even wishes—for a moment—that things could be the way Iralene envisions them; it would be so much simpler. Then he feels guilty for the thought. No, he loves Lyda, and he's going to be the father of her baby.

The singer tells her good night, tells her to sleep tight, calls her baby.

As Partridge sets Iralene down, the crowd seems to keep spinning around them. And while still holding her waist, she puts her hand to her forehead and says, "Partridge! I'm so . . . dizzy." And as her knees give out beneath her, he holds her closer—so close he sees her lids flutter.

The crowd gasps, and Beckley is there, quickly. He says to Partridge, "Pick her up."

Partridge lifts her to his chest.

"Stand back, people," Beckley says. "Let's get her somewhere cool." He shouts to the other guards. "Stay here. Crowd control. We're moving her indoors. Make sure no one follows."

Beckley leads Partridge away from the crowd, down the sloping lawn toward the building that Iralene promised she'd get him into and lead him through—the place she's known all her life and never wanted to go back to.

Her eyes flit open. "See, Partridge? I'm good to my word. And you will be too, when the time comes to return the favor, right?"

"Of course, Iralene," he says hesitantly. "Of course."

PARTRIDGE

RISKS

SOMEONE'S BEEN HERE BEFORE THEM. The fake living room flickers over the cement walls. Iralene is holding Partridge's hand, Beckley beside her. This is the home she's known. He can tell that it scares her now. Partridge recognizes the fluffy white rug, the little panting dog, the massive sofas and armchairs and modern art hung on the walls, and the shiny kitchen where the image of Mimi once made muffins, over and over, telling Iralene—sitting at the piano across the room—to start the song again.

But this loop isn't the one Partridge saw before. The image of Iralene walks into the room wearing a robe and slippers, then into the kitchen where she pours herself a glass of milk and grabs a plate of cookies.

"I hate this one," the real Iralene says, gripping Partridge's hand tighter. "Your father made it for my mother. A Mother's Day gift."

Her mother arrives from the image of a door that Partridge doesn't remember being a real door. She too is wearing a robe, tightly cinched.

Mimi says, "How about some girl talk to go with your milk and cookies?"

The fake Iralene says brightly, "Okay!"

Partridge keeps walking. "The hallway is in that corner, right? The one that leads to the capsules?"

Iralene's hand slips away from his. She walks to the image of her and her mother. "Sometimes I think he actually wanted us to be happy," she says.

Partridge glances at Beckley, who says, "We don't have much time here. If we stay too long, people will think you're actually sick, and they'll start to panic."

Iralene steps inside of her own image. She knows her part and her lines. She lifts her hand in perfect sync with the image and twists a strand of hair. She and her image both say in unison, "There is this one boy at school. I think he's really special."

"Oh really!" Mimi says. "And does he think you're special too?"

The image of Iralene dips her head down shyly. But the real Iralene reaches out to touch her mother's face. Of course, it's not there. Her hand slips through the air. "There are ones of me when I was even younger. My mother teaching me to sew. Her reading storybooks to me on the sofa."

Partridge is chilled by the idea of watching your life instead of living it. "Did my father watch these?"

"He couldn't just take us in and out of suspension every time he missed us. He had to have these little moments of us now and then. And my mother and I watched them, of course. They were fairy tale versions of our lives. We loved ourselves in them. Each time he'd bring a new one to us, we'd savor it together."

This was happening when Partridge's father was ignoring him and Sedge, when he'd sent them off to the academy, when, after Sedge was supposedly dead, his father didn't even bother to let Partridge come home for the holidays. He's weirdly jealous but also sickened. This was no way to love a family.

Iralene laughs at her mother's image, which is saying how wonderful Iralene is, how any boy would be lucky to win her heart. "My mother would have never said that in real life. She'd have said,

You have to make him fall in love with you. You have to be perfect, Iralene! If he's a worthwhile man, you'll have to trick him into loving you." She turns to Partridge and Beckley as the images of her and her mother keep talking. "I'm not the kind of girl a boy would naturally fall in love with."

Partridge isn't sure what to say. She's lovable—just the way she is—but he can't love her.

Beckley's the one who speaks up first. "Do you know how many men are in love with you? Your image has been plastered on every screen."

"They love my image, then," she says flatly.

Partridge shakes his head. "No, I don't buy that. One real look at you and—"

"And what?" Iralene says, so eager that she cuts him off.

"They see through the image to you," Partridge says. "The real you." She walks to Partridge, grabs his arm, and pulls him close. He feels guilty every time he's kind to her. He's only giving her false hope, and he's betraying Lyda. But what should he do? Be cruel instead?

"Let's go," she says. "This way."

She leads him and Beckley down a hall. The doors on either side are marked with placards—numbered specimens and names. The air buzzes with electricity. Iralene pauses when she comes to the door where her name used to be. Her mother's name is still there beneath the now-empty space—MIMI WILLUX.

"Does your mother still come here?"

"She can't afford to age, especially now that she's single again," Iralene says matter-of-factly. "But she's been out for all of the memorial services and our date." She puts her hand on the door. "I won't go back, though. I made her promise that I could be free now." She tilts her head. "Well, as free as I can get."

They move on down the hall.

This place is hauntingly dark and cold and dismal. Bodies exist behind every humming door. Bodies held in time—for how long? Damn it. Weed was right. If he can get them free, *up for air*, what the hell is he going to do with all of them?

"Dr. Peekins!" Iralene calls down the hall.

They hear the scuffle of shoes. Peekins turns a corner and stands with his hands on his wide hips. He's a short, duckfooted man of Partridge's father's generation. "Iralene," he says.

"Hi," she says warmly.

The two hug.

Iralene says, "Dr. Peekins was the first face I saw each time I came up for air."

"And I had to put you down sometimes too, which was unpleasant when you were little, before you fully understood." *Unpleasant*—it's the kind of euphemism that people in the Dome use when something is awful, unconscionable...Partridge can only imagine what it was like to put Iralene under as a child.

Iralene tilts her head and says, "You told me bedtime stories, remember? The baby in a basket in the woods who grew up to be strong and beautiful."

Peekins' eyes are wet. Was he a father figure for Iralene? "Of course I remember." Then Peekins turns to Partridge. "And this must be the young man himself!" Peekins holds out his hand. Partridge shakes it. "We've never had the pleasure of meeting, but of course, I know who you are." For good measure, he shakes Beckley's hand too, which Partridge likes. A lot of people ignore Beckley.

"Partridge needs your help," Iralene tells Peekins.

Peekins' eyes dart up and down the hall. He takes a step closer, lowering his voice. He seems to know that helping Partridge might be dangerous. Has Foresteed told Peekins that he's in charge? "Does this have to do with Weed?"

"Has he been here?" Partridge asks.

"He's sent word. The Hollenback baby," Peekins says softly. "And now Belze."

"Yes," Partridge says. "Odwald Belze. Can you help?"

Peekins rubs his eyebrow. "I'm not supposed to..."

"It's important," Partridge says.

"Yes, but there are conflicts, you know." He scratches his chin. "Things beyond my control. I can only do so much."

Iralene touches his shoulder. "Please. Can you try?"

His face softens. "This way." They follow Peekins down one hall and then another. "Belze is an older man and a wretch, and he's been kept under for a long time. The deep freezes are much more complex than the short ones, as Iralene would know—kind of the way it works with anesthesia."

"Can you bring him up carefully?" Partridge asks.

"I'm always careful," Peekins says, and he stops in front of a door marked ODWALD BELZE. "But there are risks."

"The other alternative is to never bring him up for air—never even try it?" Partridge asks. "What's the difference between permanent suspension and death?"

Iralene nods. "Every time I went under, I wondered if I'd be forgotten."

"I'd never have forgotten you," Peekins says. "You know that."

Peekins opens the door. Iralene and Partridge follow him into the small room. Beckley stays in the hall, standing guard.

And there's a six-foot capsule, its glass foggy and iced gray. Partridge feels a chill—from deep inside of him to the surface of his skin. Peekins wipes the glass, revealing an old man's frozen face. His expression is stiff and pained. He has a long dark pink scar running down his neck, bisected a third of the way down like a cross. Pressia's grandfather.

"Where's his leg?" Iralene asks.

"He came in that way," Peekins says. "It's a kind of fusing actually. Something from the Detonations. There's a clump of wires at the stump. From what exactly, who knows?"

Partridge remembers being with his half sister when their

mother died—the murderous blood filling the air. They've both lost so much. And yet, here's this man who took care of her all her life, the only father figure she ever knew and whom she thinks is dead, and Partridge can return him to her. It's the greatest gift he can think of. Love, returned. "I want him treated very carefully," Partridge says.

"Of course," Peekins says. "I can only try. No promises!"

"Don't tell Foresteed or Weed or anyone else in power." Even though Glassings vouched for Weed, Partridge isn't sure. "I'm asking you directly. Okay?"

Peekins nods. "Yes, yes."

"There's something else he's here to see," Iralene says.

"I think I know what's brought you," Peekins says.

"What's that?" Partridge asks.

"You're not the first person to come down and ask about it. Anything that's locked up that tight must have been of incredible value to your father, right?" So he knows that Partridge wants to be let into the chamber. Who's come before him? Probably Foresteed. Maybe Weed. Did members of Cygnus try to get access?

"Do you know what's in there?" Partridge asks bluntly.

"What's in the room isn't meant for you." Partridge isn't sure what this is supposed to mean. Was it meant for his father? For someone else?

"I wasn't expecting to find my inheritance, Peekins."

This comment startles Peekins. His head jerks a little, and then he looks away.

"Do you know what's in the room? Or should I say *who*?"

Peekins doesn't answer.

"You have to tell me."

"No," Peekins says. "I don't."

"I'm in charge now. Didn't you hear?" It's a lie, but Peekins might not know the truth.

Peekins looks at him and blinks.

"Dr. Peekins, I thought you knew how to follow orders," Beckley says, standing in the door, one hand on his gun.

"I am following orders."

"Whose?"

He looks at Partridge. "Your father's."

His father's alive? Is this what Peekins is saying? "Jesus, Peekins," Partridge says, trying to laugh. "He's dead!"

Peekins doesn't move, doesn't say a word. He looks as frozen as one of the suspended bodies. Why would Peekins be following his father's orders? "Unless he's not dead. Is that who's in the chamber, Peekins? My *father*? Did he somehow get resuscitated?" Partridge leans his shoulder against the wall to steady himself. "Is that urn that's supposedly filled with his ashes and that was put on display at every goddamn memorial service just a hoax?" Partridge's ears start ringing. *I killed him*, he reminds himself. *I killed him. I wanted him to die, and he's dead.*

Peekins still doesn't answer. Partridge wants to punch him in the head. Maybe Weed's right and a little act of violence is needed every once in a while. "Tell me the truth, Peekins—right now. Tell me what you know."

"Or what?"

Partridge rears back. *Torture.* "Or I'll send you in."

"Where?" Peekins says. "I heard you put an end to all that."

Partridge's jaws knot. He looks at Iralene and Beckley for help, but what can they say? Peekins is stating the obvious. "Take us to the high-security chamber, Peekins. Can you manage that?"

Peekins walks them through the halls to one that ends in front of a large metal door. It's locked and barred, with a blue-lit alarm system mounted on the wall and a keypad to one side of the door. Partridge places his hand on the blue screen, hoping it will work like some of the fingerprint systems in his father's war room and inner chamber, but as Peekins predicted, nothing happens. He leans down, looking for a retinal scan, but nothing flashes across his eyes.

He stares at the keypad. Is this the only thing keeping him from the suspended body of his own supposedly dead father? Or is it Hideki?

He starts typing in all of the key words that he associates with his father:

Swan. No response.

Cygnus. No response.

Phoenix, Operation Phoenix. Nothing.

"Peekins, am I close? Is this how it works?"

Peekins is silent. Partridge hates him for this. "Damn it," Partridge mutters. He's so frustrated that he starts missing letters, misspelling—he hits CLEAR, CLEAR, CLEAR and starts over. *Seven, the seven*. He starts to type each of the names of the Seven—his mother's, his father's, Hideki Imanaka, Bartrand Kelly . . .

Then Beckley gets a message through his earpiece. "The other guards say that the crowd is beginning to worry. They want someone to call an ambulance. A doctor has identified himself and has asked if he can help. We have to go."

"Not yet," Partridge says.

"We have to go!" Iralene says, pulling on his arm, making him mess up again.

"Iralene! Let go!" He starts over. *Eden, New Eden* . . . Nothing works.

Peekins walks up close and whispers, "You're not really supposed to be here. I know the truth." That Foresteed has all the real power? That Foresteed is blackmailing him? Or is Peekins saying that he knows Partridge killed his father?

"The truth is that my father is dead. You can't be following his orders," Partridge shouts at Peekins. "I know he's dead!" The more he says his father's dead, the less true it feels. The words seem to peel away from their meaning and are just sounds. "You're just trying to get into my head, aren't you? Who are you really working for? Foresteed? Weed?"

Peekins lifts his chin and doesn't say a word.

"I'm going to get into this chamber, Peekins. With or without your help. You might as well be on the right side when the time comes."

"I know the right side from the wrong side," Peekins says very slowly. "Do you?"

Partridge leans in and puts his face an inch from Peekins'. "Don't push me. Are you listening? Don't push me."

For the first time, Peekins looks a little scared. He nods slowly. *Is this what a bully feels like?* Partridge wonders. If it is, then it feels good.

Beckley says, "Come on."

"We have to go," Iralene says. "Follow me."

And they start running down the halls, passing nameplate after nameplate—so many bodies, frozen, stuck, but still alive.

El Capitan

BETTER OFF

Dusk is coming on, but how many days have passed? Where's Bradwell? The broken, smoldering city is losing its edges. The shadows fill in like tidal pools. The Rubble Fields are quiet. Have all the Dusts been burned alive? The streets are nearly silent. El Capitan passes a pile of bodies covered with a tarp, but he can see a folded burned hand, a stiffened foot embedded with metal.

Bradwell's gone to tell Pressia that he loves her. Has he found her already? Will he ever show up at the meeting place? El Capitan knows she loves Bradwell and that she'll never love El Capitan. "Better off," he whispers, and it's an old thought—one he used to rely on when he killed wretches, used them as live targets, counted the bodies after the Death Sprees. Better off dead than living this life, which is just a long death.

Helmud is quiet. He must remember El Capitan's dark moods. He shrinks on his brother's back, doesn't twitch, doesn't hum.

El Capitan is making his way to the old bank vault. There's a good chance survivors are already huddled down there. He'll tell them to get the hell out. He wants to be alone. He wants to be completely alone. He never will be.

He pulls his collar up around his neck and walks next to a wall that used to be a building. At this very moment, Pressia and Bradwell might be falling in love again. He remembers finding them in the stone underpass, kissing. And he has the sudden desire to ram his brother into the wall, to find a stick and beat Helmud with it. All the old habits, comforts—that's what he's drawn to: the power he once knew, the power that once knew him.

He stops walking, clenches his fists, and stares up at the sky, smoke scudding across it.

It used to be that beating his brother made him feel a little more alive. He doesn't know how or why. Maybe because it was the closest thing to beating himself.

"We've got nothing," El Capitan whispers. "Nothing." He grips the front of his coat, twists it, and then screams. He can't remember the last time he screamed like this.

Helmud tightens to a knot on his back.

"Get off me!" El Capitan shouts. And he throws his elbows into his brother's ribs. He reaches over his shoulders and grabs Helmud's arms and yanks him forward so hard that El Capitan falls to his knees. "Get off me!" he shouts, clawing at Helmud.

"Get off me!" Helmud shouts, jerking backward as hard as he can, twisting across the wet ground. "Get off me! Get off! Me! Me! Me!"

"No, me!" El Capitan shouts. He reaches wildly for his brother, who arches and weaves. "Me!" He doesn't care about the bacterium. Nothing matters. He can feel the tape ripping up from his skin.

Then Helmud punches El Capitan hard across the jaw. El Capitan is stunned. He freezes on all fours. Helmud cocks his fist and punches him again. El Capitan rolls over and piledrives his brother into the ground. Helmud gets a choke hold around El Capitan's neck and keeps punching El Capitan in the head.

"I've got nothing," El Capitan shouts at his brother. "I've got nothing!" Helmud keeps beating on him.

And then El Capitan stops fighting. He covers his head with his arms, curls up, and lets Helmud punch him. Helmud is breathless. His knuckles are sharp, and his jabs come at El Capitan hard and fast. "I've got nothing," El Capitan says over and over.

And then Helmud says, "Me, me, me." But he keeps pounding his brother, keeps beating him until he grows weak, until finally he gives out and lies down, holding El Capitan's shoulders. They lie there in the wet dirt, muttering—*nothing* and *me* and *nothing*—until El Capitan isn't even sure which of them is saying what.

Nothing.

Me.

Nothing.

Partridge

Knowing

I𝐓'𝐒 𝐇𝐈𝐒 𝐖𝐄𝐃𝐃𝐈𝐍𝐆 𝐃𝐀𝐘. Foresteed pushed it up without telling Partridge and Iralene why, and maybe there's no other reason than Foresteed exerting his power. But the thought—*wedding day, my wedding day*—keeps jolting Partridge like a sharp electrical shock. It hits him now as he stands in front of a tall mirror rolled into the apartment by the tailor who made his tuxedo. Partridge is wearing black pants and socks and is buttoning up his dress shirt as the tailor, a small and quiet man, unzips a hanging bag that holds the tux's jacket, cummerbund, and bow tie. And Partridge just stares at it. It's all wrong. Everything has gone so horribly wrong—one small step at a time. He whispers, "A wedding. My wedding."

"Sir?" the tailor says.

"Nothing," Partridge says.

No way to get to Lyda. No response to his letters. No way to go back to the high-security chamber. No way to know if Peekins has brought Belze up from suspension or not. No way to return to his father's war room without rousing suspicion, and part of him wishes he'd never see that room again. The thought of it turns his stomach. Those pictures of the past, those love notes from his loveless father. No way to find out what's really going on outside of the Dome.

Where are Pressia, Bradwell, El Capitan and Helmud? Weed sent word that the airship landed safely, but beyond that he knows nothing and has no means of communication.

And Glassings has gotten worse. He said he wouldn't recover, and maybe he won't. Partridge has been staying up late, sitting in the chair pulled to his bedside. He waits for the moment when Glassings will wake up and be conscious enough to talk to him, but it hasn't happened. And since his visit to the high-security chamber, Partridge has been keeping busy writing a growing list of possible passwords to unlock it. Is he crazy to pin his hopes on the idea of one of his father's greatest enemies being not only alive but able to help him? He's not sure when or if he'll get another shot at unlocking the chamber. After Partridge's time in the suspension chambers, security has gotten tighter. Foresteed has to have gotten wind of something. For now, Partridge has to maintain the facade that he has power so that he can quietly take Foresteed down. How? He's not sure.

For now, he feels alone, cut off.

Caged up.

As the tailor is bustling around him, Beckley walks in. "Getting all gussied up, I see."

"I'm pretty sure I'm getting married," he says to Beckley, half statement, half question.

"Does Iralene know?" Beckley says, joking. But the joke falls flat. He's marrying the wrong girl, after all.

Partridge steps away from the tailor and says to Beckley, "Anything?" knowing Beckley will understand that he's asking about Lyda. It's always the first thing he asks.

"No," Beckley says. "You've got to cut her some slack, right? It can't be easy."

"She was the one who pushed it," Partridge says, his voice

hushed. He hasn't heard from her in so long now that he can't help but think she's punishing him—or is she having doubts? Then it hits him. "You don't think she talked me into this because she wanted to get rid of me, do you? I mean, maybe even subconsciously?" Partridge refuses to whisper in front of the tailor, sick of all the secrecy.

"I don't know how my own subconscious works, much less hers."

The tailor coughs politely to get Partridge's attention. He's holding the jacket on its wooden hanger. Partridge lifts his hand, telling him to hold on.

"So you think it's possible? She didn't come back with me into the Dome. I wanted her to. I begged her. But then she said she surrendered herself to get back in, so I thought...well, I thought she changed her mind. But now maybe she's changed it back."

"You two are having a child together. That's a bond that lasts forever."

"It makes us parents, Beckley. It doesn't mean we're in love." His own parents fell out of love. He figures it happens to most couples. His parents had stayed married even though his father knew that his wife had fallen in love with Imanaka and had his child. Partridge steps over to the tailor, pulls the jacket from the hanger, and shrugs it on. "Love doesn't last. It's not permanent." He feels sick, yanks the jacket a little to make it feel less confining. "And now it's my goddamn wedding day."

"You should try to enjoy it," Beckley says.

Partridge looks at his reflection. He's a fake, an imposter. "How am I supposed to enjoy it? If Lyda still loves me, this will hurt. If she doesn't, then what's worse than that?"

"Do you mean that?" Beckley says.

The tailor flips up the collar of his shirt and starts tying the bow tie. Partridge nods. "Of course I mean it."

"What if you let Lyda talk you into marrying Iralene because it's what you wanted—you know, subconsciously, as you put it."

"Don't tell me about my subconscious!" Partridge is suddenly furious. Now that he's caged up, his anger flares quickly.

Beckley shrugs. "Sorry. Didn't mean to throw your own logic back at you."

Partridge stares at Beckley a moment. There's something about him that's different from other people in the Dome. Beckley has these moments when he just has to be honest—as if he can't help it.

"What?" Beckley says.

The tailor is cinching the cummerbund around Partridge's waist.

"I refused to pick a best man," Partridge says. In fact, Purdy and Hoppes handed him a binder of appropriate best men, and he slammed the binder shut and told them to shove off. "But maybe I was wrong."

"You're not thinking..."

"No one gives me shit the way you do, Beckley. And that's what friends do." He thinks of Hastings back when they were roommates. They always shot back and forth at each other. And then there was Bradwell, who always put Partridge in his place, and El Capitan, who wasn't always the nicest guy, but he spoke his mind. "Will you do it?"

"I think you're supposed to pick someone from your...well, your own social class."

"Here's the added benefit. Choosing you will piss off a few people from that class."

"I don't know..."

"Look, you have to stand next to me as my guard anyway. You might as well have something real to do while you're up there. You just have to hand me a ring, I think. You can handle that, right?"

"I think there's a toast too. I have to get up and say something."

"Just say, *To the lovely couple! Raise your glasses! Cheers!* That's all it takes."

"Why not someone else?"

"Like who? Weed? You think his jaw has healed up? Is he able to chew solid food again?"

"I guess that wouldn't be the best pick."

"It's you, Beckley. So let's get you suited up, okay? If anyone asks, you can say you're just following orders." He holds out his hand and Beckley shakes it. As he lets go of Beckley's hand, he says, "This is still good for the people, right? I'd just like to hear someone say it."

"It's good for the people," Beckley says. "They need this."

"I know." He feels nervous all of a sudden. It's his wedding— sham and all. He's got to do this right. His father's not here—he killed his father. Killed him. But now he needs someone to give him advice. Isn't that what a young man needs on his wedding day? He puts on his shoes. "I need to see Glassings."

"But sir!" The tailor's not finished.

"Good enough," Partridge says.

He walks down the hall and slowly pushes open Glassings' door. The room is well lit. Glassings has pillows propped behind his back, but as the swelling has gone down some, he looks sallow and gaunt.

Partridge knows that Glassings probably won't wake up, and even if he does, he won't be lucid enough to give him any advice. But still, he pulls the chair close to the bedside and sits down. "I'm getting married," he whispers. "What do you think of that?"

Glassings' eyelids flutter.

Partridge puts his hand on top of Glassings', which is cold and dry. "Tell me what to do," he says. "I'm scared." Cygnus was supposed to stand with him. Glassings promised him that. "Cygnus is a bunch of cowards, aren't they? Where are they now? Sitting in their apartments staring out at the streets?" Partridge pushes back in his chair. He rubs his new pinky.

Glassings starts to cough, his chest heaving, and it's as if the pain of his broken ribs wakes him up. His eyes are just watery slits. Partridge says, "I'm here. I'm right here."

Glassings' eyes lock on Partridge's. He nods to Partridge, as if wanting him to come closer. Partridge leans forward. "What am I supposed to do?" he says.

"The next good thing," Glassings whispers, "and the next good thing after that. If each is a good step, you'll move forward."

"I'm marrying Iralene. It feels like the wrong step." He's desperate. He needs Glassings to tell him what to do. He feels like he's been careening out of control toward a cliff and that Glassings could tell him how to hit the brakes.

Glassings stares at Partridge. He's quiet for a moment. "You don't love her?"

"I'm supposed to be marrying Lyda."

Glassings narrows his gaze. "Answer the question."

Maybe Glassings is telling him that he should love Iralene. Would that make things better, safer, clearer? He was so sure of himself at that mic telling the truth, and now he's drowning in doubt. Most of all, he no longer trusts his own judgment. Partridge wants to tell him he doesn't love Iralene, but he thinks of holding her up and spinning her around, the fake sun shining on her hair. "It doesn't matter who I love. My life isn't mine."

"Again," Glassings says, "you didn't answer the question."

"What if I don't know?"

"There are things you should simply know."

PRESSIA

HOLLOW REED

Before pressia even opens her eyes in the morning, she thinks of Bradwell's kiss. This is how it's been every morning since she last saw him. She remembers the feel of his wet lips against hers, his skin, the hardness of his muscles against her chest as he lifted her off the ground and the silkiness of his wings. She wants to stay in that reverie, but she hears a small cough, and when she opens her eyes, she's startled by a child's face staring at her. She grips the backpack, which she sleeps with. She's on the pallet the mothers offered her on the cold ground inside of a small tent. The light is hazy. It's early morning. The mothers have told her they'll help, but they haven't said how or when. A hand ruffles the child's hair. Pressia looks up and sees a woman looking at her. There are words burned into one cheek, backward, but she can still read them: THE DOGS BARKED LOUDLY. IT WAS ALMOST DARK.

"Mother Hestra?" She recognizes her from the last time she saw Partridge and Lyda—in the subway car locked underground.

Mother Hestra nods. "I'm here to take you in."

"In where?" For a moment, she thinks that Mother Hestra is going to bring her to the Dome, but that makes no sense.

"To Our Good Mother," Mother Hestra says. "Now. No time to waste."

In a few minutes, Pressia has the backpack on again and is following Mother Hestra through the woods. Mother Hestra limps, weighted on one side by her child, but she's oddly agile. Pressia is eating a small hotcake that was cooked over a fire back at the camp. The air is still smoky. The rain has stopped. Pressia knows she has to try to convince Mother Hestra to let her go, but how? She starts with common ground. "Was Lyda taken? One of the mothers told me she was *taken* into the Dome."

"You've heard no word from her?" Mother Hestra says.

"How could I hear from her?"

"She's on the inside with Partridge. He's your brother. He has ways. Doesn't he?"

"I don't even know if she went in on her own or was taken. Last I heard, she was going in with Partridge." They cross a small brook, jumping from rock to rock.

"She has her own life. She made her own decision. She wanted to stay."

"And then they took her? Against her will?"

Mother Hestra stops. She breaks off a hollow reed and whistles into it—a low, sad note—and then she hands it to her son, who fiddles with it joyfully.

"It was during battle. We attacked the Dome. Didn't you hear?" Mother Hestra says as they begin moving again through the trees.

Is this why the Dome has fired back? "Is the Dome getting retribution, then? Is that what these killings and fires are about?"

Mother Hestra uses the trees to push herself along, and Pressia starts to do the same, falling into a quick rhythm.

"There was a lull, and then their attacks started. We can only guess."

"But Willux is dead. Partridge is in charge. How can this be happening?"

Mother Hestra stops and turns. "Willux is dead?"

Pressia shouldn't have said this. She feels the sick twist of a dagger in her gut. This is bad. Very bad. But there's no taking it back. Mother Hestra's face is frozen in an intense gaze. Pressia nods.

"And Partridge is the one who's sending these Deaths to kill us? Partridge?"

"I don't think it's him. It can't be!"

"But he's in charge," Mother Hestra says. "You said so."

"Don't tell Our Good Mother," Pressia pleads.

"How could I keep this from her? How could I keep it from my fellow sisters?"

Our Good Mother will be enraged. There's no telling what she might unleash. She despises all the Deaths but seemed to dislike Partridge with a special vengeance.

"I just need time. Please, if you—"

"Hush!" Mother Hestra stiffens. "Follow," she says, picking up her pace.

"Please don't bring me in to Our Good Mother," Pressia says. "Please. This is important, Mother Hestra. This is life and death."

Mother Hestra stops and crouches. She motions for Pressia to do the same. Pressia sits down, her back against a tree. She looks up at the sky—gray, always gray, with dark limbs cutting it up like a fractured piece of glass. She's a prisoner. She's failed. "Please, Mother Hestra," she says again.

Mother Hestra raises her hands to her mouth and lets out a strange birdcall—a long, soft cooing.

Pressia feels like crying. She thinks of making a run for it, but she knows that the mothers are well trained. She wouldn't get far.

And then there's a coo in return. It ripples through the woods.

Pressia grips Mother Hestra's coat. "Please," she says again.

"Shut up," Mother Hestra says. "I know why you're in these woods. You're not looking for dead children, are you? You want in. Into the Dome. I'm going to get you there."

"But Our Good Mother . . ."

"I will disobey her. I will pay the price. When I heard you were here, I volunteered to be the prison guard to bring you in. As Partridge's sister, you are the only one who can go in and expect any protection, though that could also make you a target. It must be you."

"How did you know I wanted to go in?"

"You're going in for Lyda," Mother Hestra says. "She can't have her baby inside the Dome. It wouldn't be safe. It wouldn't be right. She belongs with us."

"Her baby?" Pressia blurts out. She's stunned. There must be some mistake.

"Lyda's baby," Mother Hestra says, confused that Pressia doesn't know. "Partridge is the father."

"What?"

"She's pregnant. With child. Not too far along."

Partridge and Lyda are going to have a baby? "I didn't know." Is Lyda scared? Is she alone? Pressia wants to see her and tell her . . . what? That everything is going to be okay? Will it be? She can't lie to her. The voices throughout the city, calling for their lost children—Lyda and Partridge will have a child of their own to fear for, to fight for, to call out for . . .

"How could you not know?" Mother Hestra says. "Isn't that why you're going in—to save her?"

"I'm going in because I have what's needed to cure us. If I can get it to scientists in the Dome, we can undo fusings without side effects. We can make the survivors whole again. All of us." She looks at the child on Mother Hestra's leg. He's watching Pressia, listening, gripping the reed with tears quivering in his eyes.

Mother Hestra's cheeks flush. She clenches her jaw. "There is no cure for this. None!"

"But there is!"

"I thought you were in these woods because you were preparing to save a sister, a sister with child. Do you know how long it's been since we've held a baby from one of our own? Do you know? This child is our new beginning!"

"You were going to bring me in. Do it. Now that I know, I'll do my best to get Lyda out. I promise."

The coo comes again—closer this time. Mother Hestra looks up in the direction it came from. "If Our Good Mother knows that Willux is dead, she will sense weakness. And if she knows Partridge is in charge, she will want to kill him all the more."

"And if she attacks," Pressia whispers, "it will only cause more deaths, and Lyda's in there. If you give me time, I can go in and try to get her out before you attack." She doesn't dare tell Mother Hestra about the bacterium that can take down the Dome. She needs Mother Hestra to be calm, focused.

Mother Hestra grabs hold of Pressia's arm. "You promise you'll get her out."

"I promise to try."

Mother Hestra presses her fists against her forehead, clenches her eyes. "Twelve mothers have died at that post where you slept— just that one post alone. Seven of them had children—they're also dead. The mass grave is full. They've started another. Partridge's father hadn't brutalized us enough?"

"We don't know that Partridge did this. We don't."

"Kill him," Mother Hestra says. "Get inside and kill him."

Pressia shakes her head. "He didn't orchestrate this new attack. He wouldn't. He knows us. He cares about us."

"He's in charge. This is what happened. These are facts."

"I have to have faith in him."

"Deaths only squander faith. They don't deserve our trust."

The cooing comes again, louder, more urgent.

"I can't kill my brother. I won't. But I will try to get Lyda out." She remembers the last glimpse she had of Lyda, when they were in the Deadlands about to be executed. Is this where she belongs?

In the wilds? If she wants out, Pressia will help her in every way she can. "Have faith in me."

Mother Hestra's son wraps his arms around his mother's waist, holding tightly. She kisses the top of his head. "We will pay," she says. "When Our Good Mother knows all, we will pay."

Pressia feels a pulse of anger banging inside of her. "That's not fair." She looks at the child. "I can't ask you to do this."

The cooing echoes again.

"We will survive. It's how we were built." Mother Hestra grabs Pressia's hand, entwines her fingers. "When you see Lyda, tell her that we worry. She was like one of my own to me. My very own." Her son looks up at her, and she cups his chin lightly, as if to say, *Don't worry. I love you most.*

And then Mother Hestra lifts her hands to her mouth again, and her coo floats into the morning air, reverberating through the woods.

LYDA

GLOWING

LYDA'S DRESSED AS IF SHE'S A WEDDING GUEST. Her dress is royal blue taffeta, hemmed to the middle of her shins. She's wearing high heels that have been stained to match the dress and her blue pocketbook, which only has one thing in it—Freedle, swaddled loosely in a hand towel. She wanted one piece of the outside world with her. Freedle's a comfort. She knows she'll need it.

She sits on the sofa, stiffly, next to Chandry Culp, the woman in charge of teaching her to knit. She arranged for all of this and is here with her husband, Axel Culp, and their daughter, Vienna—as if they're old family friends gathered together for some important public address.

Vienna doesn't like the dip. "It's too spicy!" She doesn't like the carrots. "The texture isn't realistic!" She doesn't like the way her mother did her hair. "It's too fluffy!"

Lyda wants to find the right moment to claim she feels weak and nauseous and politely retire to her bedroom. Honestly, she is tired. She hasn't been sleeping much. Every time she dozes off, she wakes up minutes later, gasping for breath as if there isn't enough oxygen in the air, as if she's suffocating.

Why do they think she wants to watch Partridge marry Iralene?

Is this a test? Is she supposed to prove that her relationship with Partridge is over, that all will be as they expect it to be? She feels bullied by the dress and the dip, even by Mr. Culp who walks around saying, "Nice place you got here. Isn't this nice, Chandry?"

The television is showing the people as they arrive, couples with various titles walking into the church in gowns and tuxedos. There are guards here and there, lining the church. But otherwise, it's all beautiful—flowers draped everywhere, ribbon, red carpets. Lyda cradles her pocketbook in her lap, Freedle nestled within it.

She feels sick. Yes, she wants to be the one to marry Partridge, of course. But not this way. Not with all of this pomp and grandeur, while knowing how the people on the outside scrape for basic survival. It turns her stomach. She says, "I think I'm going to have to go lie down for a bit."

"What?" Chandry says. "No, no. She isn't here yet!"

"Are we expecting someone else?"

Vienna says, "It's supposed to be a surprise." She rolls her eyes.

Lyda becomes alarmed. "Who are we expecting?"

"Let me check on her progress." Chandry rushes to the front door to talk to the guards.

Mr. Culp picks up an empty candlestick holder. "I like this!" he says. "Quite nice!"

Lyda walks over to Vienna. "Tell me who's coming."

"I can't."

"Please."

"Don't you get how surprises work?" Vienna says.

"I don't like surprises," Lyda whispers.

"She's coming!" Chandry says. "She's coming right now!"

The door is wide open, and the guards stand on either side of it. Chandry steps back and opens one hand dramatically as Lyda's mother appears in the doorframe.

"Mrs. Mertz!" Chandry says, half-proud and half-relieved.

Lyda's mother looks small and disoriented. She stands there and blinks. At first, she glances around the room, unable to look at Lyda. This is how it was at the rehabilitation center too. In fact, that was the last place she saw her mother. She was so cold to Lyda, hiding behind her official role as a clinician. But she isn't in that role now. She's also wearing a dress—one of the dresses she's worn to church for years.

"Mom?" Lyda says.

Lyda's mother steps forward. She lifts her gaze until finally she meets Lyda's eyes, crimping her lips and drawing in her breath as if bracing for something—what does she expect? What has she been told? Does she know Lyda's pregnant?

Lyda doesn't know if she's supposed to hug her mother or not. And her mother seems equally unsure. "Lyda, dear," she says softly.

And Lyda feels a rush of love that seems to buoy her. She's missed her mother more deeply than she let herself admit. She sets her pocketbook down carefully on an end table, keeping Freedle safe and sound, and walks to her mother quickly, wrapping her arms around her neck. Her mother stiffens but then pats her back. "I didn't think you'd come to see me. I wasn't sure you even knew I was here."

"I know everything," her mother says. But Lyda isn't sure what version of *everything* she's been fed.

Lyda squeezes her mother's hands. "Let's go talk—just the two of us," Lyda says and then turns to Chandry, Mr. Culp, and Vienna. "Do you mind if we have some privacy?"

"No, no!" Lyda's mother says. "It's okay. There's no need to disrupt the get-together." She walks to the television. "It's going to be a lovely event for all of us to share"—she looks at Lyda—"and *accept.*"

Lyda feels like she's been slapped. Her ears are ringing. The nursery. She wants to retreat to the nursery, feel the weight of a spear, the ash on her skin. Those things are real. Her mother's retribution is always made of air. She can't ever pin it down. She can't ever accuse her of anything concretely. But now Lyda knows why she's here: to tell Lyda that her relationship with Partridge is over. This wedding isn't a fake. It's going to stand. There's no reversing it—only accepting it. Her mother is here to help her accept this ending.

Lyda wants this to be a dream. She wants to wake up—gasping for air. But it isn't a dream.

She can't speak. She reaches out and grips the back of a chair.

"Are you going to be okay?" Vienna says. "You don't look good."

"It's starting!" Chandry shouts and turns to the TV. She pulls a tissue from her purse and presses it to her cheek. "Here she comes! Oh my!"

"Doesn't she look nice!" Mr. Culp says.

The whole little Culp family huddles together in front of the glowing screen, with Lyda's mother standing in front of Mr. Culp. There's orchestral music blaring from the television. Lyda imagines Iralene in a long white gown, the audience rising up.

They're all gaping at the television except Lyda's mother, who's looking at Lyda now, gazing at her. "Come and watch," she says.

Lyda shakes her head.

Her mother says with no anger in her voice—just resignation— "Lyda, don't be stubborn. This is what you must do."

Lyda says, "No, thank you."

Her mother walks over to her. "Lyda," she says softly, "It's going to be okay. You and the baby. All of it. I will be here for you now. This is my new role."

"Is it a paying gig? How much did they offer you?" Lyda says sharply.

"What? Lyda, you know that I want to be here. Where else on earth would I more want to be than at your side?" She reaches out for Lyda's hand, but Lyda pulls it from her.

"I have mothers," Lyda says. "I have so many mothers out there I don't need you. Do you hear me? I don't need you at all." Lyda turns, scoops up her pocketbook—Freedle safely within it—and walks down the hall.

"Lyda! Don't do this!" her mother shouts, running after her.

Lyda opens the nursery door, but before she can shut it, her mother jams her body into the frame. She sees the wrecked crib, the pile of spears, the wood shavings, the knife, the stack of ripped baby books, the bowl of ash—all of it lost in the swirling cinders projected by the small orb sitting in the center of the room. "My God. Lyda."

"Get out. This is for me. It's mine alone."

Mrs. Mertz locks her eyes on Lyda. "What have you become?" Her mother stumbles backward, catching herself on the wall, leaning against it, breathing heavily.

Lyda shuts the door and locks it. She slides down, presses her back to the door, and sits on the floor. *What have I become?* She opens her pocketbook and pulls out the swirled nest of the hand towel where Freedle is sleeping.

"Freedle," she whispers. "How did we get here?"

Freedle's eyes blink open. He stretches his frail wings. She wants to dig through her maternity dresses and pull out the armor. She wants to feel encased, protected.

"How do we get back out?" she says.

And then suddenly she feels like her chest is filled with rage. She finds a seam in the side of her dress, grips the dress in her fists, and rips its skirt all the way to her waist. She takes more fabric and rips it, rips more and more, until it's shredded.

"My mothers," she whispers. "I miss my mothers."

Pressia

DOORS

MOTHER HESTRA WALKS PRESSIA to the periphery of the woods. There, a few mothers work quickly. They've pulled out cat-apult machinery and baskets of robotic spider grenades.

"They'll lay down cover for you," Mother Hestra says. "It's the best we can do."

"Did you give her warning? Special Forces are different out there now," one of the mothers says to Mother Hestra.

"I know," Pressia says. "I've seen 'em."

"The ones like Dusts?" Mother Hestra asks.

Pressia shakes her head. "What? Like Dusts? How?"

"No time to explain. You'll see," one of the mothers says, load-ing a catapult with a grenade.

The other mothers move in around her. They explain what's go-ing to happen.

"We'll attack from here."

"You walk the woods' edge that way."

"And we'll distract."

"Okay," Pressia says.

Mother Hestra hands her a knife. "I don't think it'll be of much use, but at least you'll have it."

Pressia thanks her and slips it between her belt and the waist of her pants.

Mother Hestra backs away from her, gives a wave, and then turns to go.

"Wait," Pressia says.

But Mother Hestra starts running into the woods. And in a few quick strides, she and her son are lost in the trees and the brush. Gone. Pressia wanted another moment—one more good-bye. But she realizes nothing would have made this easier. She squints at the Dome and then starts walking the edge of the woods. She just has to manage not getting shot on the way to the Dome, and then hopefully she'll have a chance to say who she is, her connection to Partridge, and be brought in—as a prisoner? Her goal is to be taken in alive.

She hears something in the woods—the crunch of leaves. Are the mothers following her? Do they not trust her? They could decide at any moment to pull their offer and attack her. She starts walking faster. It could be a Beast or Special Forces. It could be anyone, anything. She shouldn't run, because she needs to pace herself, but she sees something—a shape darting between distant trees. She starts running, just inside the tree line. She can't expose herself—not until the mothers fire their first shot.

Through the limbs of passing trees, she sees the motion of a gray shape, then a twisted horn. Finally, she sees a clearing and a sheep, standing stock-still, staring at her with engorged eyes. The sheep has gray wool and a long twisted horn that curls over his skull. He's lost from his herd, maybe the only one still alive. He bleats at her with a voice as sad and desperate as the boy—the soldier—with the stumped arm in the city, shot dead. The sheep paws the wet ground as if making a demand. One back hoof is gnarled, nearly useless. He's gaunt and his ribs protrude. Starving.

She walks toward him. His teeth jut out; his jaw is crooked. He bleats again, showing a bluish tongue. She reaches out her hand.

The sheep inches closer to sniff it. She reaches up and touches the tuft under his chin. "It's okay," she whispers. He nuzzles her fingers.

Beautiful, alone, starving. She can't help him. She couldn't save Wilda either. She isn't sure that she can save herself.

And then there's an explosion. The sheep jerks its head up and then darts off, bounding deep into the woods.

It's time. The mothers have started their barrage. Pressia walks toward the barren land she has to cross and stands behind a tree. She sees the smoke and the rising dust and ash from the first grenade. The clouded air will help provide cover.

She looks at the incline standing before her—at the top of it, the Dome itself.

And then the hill starts to shift. Bodies emerge, covered in dust and ash. Where did they come from? How long have they been there? They're lean boys, lumbering toward the explosion, and then just as quickly as they appeared, some disappear again, becoming one with the ground—fully camouflaged. The mothers send out another grenade. It hits the wet ground and then, after a few seconds, explodes. The boys start firing into the woods, but she can't even see any of them. Occasionally, the dirt seems to move, but then nothing.

She has to start running. The mothers have already wasted two grenades. She scans the ground and takes off sprinting. Like the sheep, she thinks. Like the sheep who's lost the herd.

The grenades, though far off to her right, are deafening. They send up gusts of smoke and ash. One explodes and she's sure it's hit nothing, but then from the ground there's a spray of blood and flesh. Her grandfather once explained land mines to her, and it's as if the boys themselves are living land mines—ever shifting invisible land mines.

She keeps running as fast as she can, hoping that if she gets to the Dome, she'll have enough breath in her lungs to explain who she is. *I'm Partridge Willux's sister. Tell him Pressia is here.*

But then the ground disappears under her feet, and she falls into a shallow pit.

The dirt dents and gives and crumbles around her as she tries to get up.

An elbow.

An arm.

A gun lodged in the arm and pointed at her.

A face freshly punctured and embedded with glass—so new that there are fresh scabs crystallized around each piece. It's a boy's face. He has a crooked nose and dark red lips, and when he smiles—why is he smiling?—she sees the worst part. He's still wearing braces—though crusted with dirt.

I'm Partridge Willux's sister. Tell him Pressia is here. She thinks these words but realizes she isn't saying them. The wind is harsh. The air is thick. The boy's face—his smile—appears between swaths of smoke.

"I got one. I got one," he says in a low whisper. "I got one." It's as if he's so proud of himself in this moment he wants to enjoy it. Killing her would end it all too quickly. He glances around and says more loudly, "I got one!" He's looking for a witness. What's the point of killing her if no one sees it?

She coughs and finally sputters, "I'm Partridge Willux's sister."

His face contorts. He doesn't understand.

"Don't kill me. Take me in. Take me to Partridge. I'm his sister."

He shakes his head. "No sister," he says. "No daughter."

And he's right, of course. No one in the Dome knows that Willux's wife had a child out of wedlock, much less a girl named Pressia.

"I'm his half sister," she says, trying again. "Please. Take me in as a prisoner."

"Take no prisoners," he says. "Take no prisoners!" He shoves the muzzle of the gun under her chin.

"This is a mistake," she says, swallowing hard. "Don't do this."

He softens for just a minute, taking in her face. But then his eyes glance over the doll head and he knows she's a wretch like all the rest—and isn't he part wretch too? He smiles again. He's going to enjoy killing her. She clenches her eyes, waits for the bang.

But then the boy is gone, his body slammed into the ground by someone much bigger and broader.

She sees the bent metal prosthetic first, and then Hastings' face comes into view.

He came after her! She didn't want him to, but damn—she's glad he did.

He pounds the soldier into the ground with his prosthetic—so hard this time she's sure the leg will snap. But it doesn't. He grabs her hand and says, "Let me take you in."

"They know you've crossed over, though, don't they? You'll be seen as a traitor."

"I'm taking you in," he says, and he grabs her arm and sweeps her up to his chest. He holds her so tightly she can barely breathe.

He runs jaggedly but fast. The ground keeps exploding. The air is choked with dirt and death.

And finally she sees the white of the Dome before them. How does it stay so white in all of this dark soot? She tells him to stop. "Let me down. I'll go the rest of the way!"

He doesn't listen.

She wriggles loose her doll-head fist and punches as hard as she can. He doesn't flinch. She tries a few more times. Nothing.

Finally, she finds the meat of his bicep and then the finer skin of the inner arm and she bites it as hard as she can. She tastes blood.

He arches and lets her go.

"Thank you," she says breathlessly.

He rubs his inner bicep. His hand comes away bloody.

She turns toward the Dome.

"Stay straight," he says, "and you'll meet the first in a series of doors."

She nods and looks back at him. "Tell El Capitan and Helmud, tell Bradwell..." She chokes up on Bradwell's name.

"What?"

"Tell them that I made it this far." She turns and starts running. The ground hisses with wind. Sometimes whirls of dirt rise then scatter and disappear.

She can see the door straight ahead, just as Hastings told her. She speeds up, but then her foot catches on the ground and she falls. She turns back to see what tripped her. Matted hair—a head crowning from the ground. A hand reaches out and snatches her ankle. She kicks it with the heel of her boot while fumbling for her knife. She reaches forward, jabs the knife into the wrist. Its fingers flex. She pulls her knee to her chest. The head raises itself up and there's a face. Two bright eyes. A row of teeth.

She gets to her feet and runs to the door as the soldier tugs his bloody wrist loose. She raises both fists and bangs on the door. She wants in. "Help!" she cries. "Help me! Let me in!" Her knuckles ache, but she keeps knocking—sharp and quick.

The soldier is on his feet, and he's lumbering toward her. She's breathless. She tries to flatten herself against the door.

And then she hears a clicking noise—a pop like a seal has broken. The door gives. The air inside is cool and clean.

A uniform. A guard.

She says over the wind, "I'm Partridge Willux's half sister."

A man's voice says, "We know who you are." He grips her wrist, pulls her in against the current of the wind.

She glimpses the soldier one last time, his hand bloody and limp.

The guard closes the door. He's armed and has one hand on the handle of his gun—not yet drawn, but ready.

She's in a chamber, quiet and still, locked between two doors—one to the outside and the other leading into the Dome.

For the first time in Pressia's life, she's on the inside.

PARTRIDGE

IMPERSONATION

PARTRIDGE IS IN ONE OF THE GREENROOMS of what they call the cathedral-gym-atorium. It's the site for the wedding, and moments after it will be quickly transformed into a banquet hall. It's been used for every major event in the Dome that Partridge can remember—politics, religion, entertainment. He listened to his dad's speeches here—Foresteed's too. He's seen the Nativity performed here as well as entertainers dressed in strange costumes lip-syncing the words to pop songs on the sanctioned list. The crowd screamed like they were real and not impersonating anyone at all.

Partridge reminds himself that he's impersonating himself.

Beckley says, "You ready or what?"

Partridge looks at himself in the full-length mirror—a mirror his father looked into many times. He thinks of his father just before he died, how he grabbed Partridge's shirt with one claw-like hand and told him that he was his son. *You are mine.* Murder was the thing that finally bound them together. Partridge looks at himself standing there in his tuxedo, and he knows he's a killer about to become a father too—and now a husband.

"Is anyone ever ready for something like this?" he asks Beckley.

"Yeah," Beckley says, wearing a tux of his own, his gun wedged in the back of his pants. "I think it's something people are compelled to do, actually."

"You sound like someone who's been in love." Partridge realizes he doesn't know much of anything about Beckley.

"I was in love once," he says.

"With who?"

"It doesn't really matter anymore," Beckley says. And Partridge is sure that this means the one he once loved is dead.

"How old are you?"

"Twenty-seven."

And there it is. Beckley was old enough to have fallen in love before the Detonations.

"You think you'll fall in love again one day?"

He straightens Partridge's bow tie. "I sure as hell hope not."

There's a light knock at the door.

"It's time," Beckley says. "This is it."

Beckley opens the door that leads to the stage or the altar or the trophy platform—depending on how someone sees it. Partridge can hear all of the voices talking at once.

He pulls Beckley back. "Tell me I should do it."

"I can't do that."

"But would you do it, Beckley?"

"I'm not you."

"But if you were..."

"I can't even imagine what it's like to be you, Partridge."

Partridge wonders if Beckley hates him. Does he resent him for everything he's been given or is it something else? It's the kind of thing Partridge has gotten good at picking up on, but he can't quite read Beckley. "Still, you understand me on some level, Beckley."

"Do you think that's really possible? Don't you know the trade-offs by now?"

"What? I can't ever expect anyone to understand me—just because of who my father was and the life I was born into?" He thinks of Bradwell and El Capitan. Were they ever his friends? Probably not. They hated Partridge on some level too.

"Do you want people to like you just for being you? I'd have guessed you'd have outgrown that by now."

Partridge feels sucker punched. He likes Beckley because he's honest—but that honesty's a double-edged sword.

Beckley opens the door wide and holds it open.

Partridge has no choice. He steps through it, and the large hall is filled with shushing. It reaches all the way to the back, and suddenly it's quiet. Partridge moves to his spot in the middle of the altar and then turns to face the audience.

My God, Partridge thinks. Everyone is here. He sees a few rows of academy boys, his neighbors from Betton West, Purdy and Hoppes with their families, Foresteed, Mimi wearing a large jeweled hat and staring at the altar, and even Arvin Weed, who gives a nod. Maybe he's forgiven him for the punch.

Partridge scans the sea of eyes staring back at him. People are gazing, smiling, already pressing tissues to their damp cheeks. They love him again. He glances at Beckley, who's standing a few feet away, stiff and tough jawed. He wants Beckley to admit there's something about this outpouring that isn't just about who his father was. There's something personal about it. How else could you explain these faces, these tears, this gazing?

He keeps searching the crowd, realizing that he's looking for Lyda. Is she out there somewhere? Would she actually come to this event? She approved of it. In fact, she pushed him to do it. But would she even be allowed to be here? If Lyda isn't here, is she at home? The cameras are poised on him. The bright lights are hot overhead. He looks into one of the cameras. He wants to tell her something. He wants her to know this isn't real. *I'm an impersonator impersonating myself*, he wants to say. But he can't. So he gives a wink and a small wave. Will she know that it's meant for her?

The crowd notices the wave and they collectively sigh.

Beckley reaches forward and claps Partridge on the back. An apology or a consolation? Partridge isn't sure.

And then with little warning, the faint background music that he hasn't even really noticed fades, and for a few seconds, all is silent.

Then organ music pours triumphantly from the ceiling. The audience stands in unison and turns.

At first Partridge only sees the camera flashes bursting madly, and then Iralene comes into view, emerging from all the popping lights at the end of a long white carpet that leads to the altar—to him. Her face is lost behind a white veil.

For a minute, he thinks it could be Lyda under that veil.

But he can tell by the poised way that she walks, the lift of her chin, and the measured steps that this is Iralene. This is the moment she's been groomed for.

As she steps up to the altar, attendants perfecting her train, Partridge can see her face behind the white veil. She's beautiful. There's never been any denying it, but today she looks even more beautiful, if that's possible.

The minister starts to talk, and Partridge is surprised by him. He must have stepped onto the stage while Iralene walked down the aisle.

Partridge knows he won't remember what the minister's saying. The lights are suddenly overbearingly hot. Partridge curls his shoulders forward and then rolls them back, as if he's hoping to stretch the cloth of his jacket a little. His bow tie and cummerbund are both too tight. Why did the tailor have to cinch everything up?

He glances at Iralene, but she's gazing at the minister, a middle-aged man with a gray-tinged moustache and crowded teeth.

How the hell did I get here? Partridge wonders. He can smell all of the flowers now. They're overpowering. He glances at Beckley. Doesn't he notice how hot it is? How strong the flowers smell?

Beckley looks at him, concerned. He whispers, "Bend your knees a little. You look like you're going to pass out."

"I'm fine," Partridge whispers. But he does as Beckley says because he does, in fact, feel light-headed.

Jesus, don't pass out in front of all of these people, he tells himself. *Don't pass out.*

And then it's time for them to exchange vows.

Luckily, the minister feeds Partridge his lines, which are traditional vows—the ones his parents probably said to each other and then broke.

I'm an impersonator, he reminds himself, *impersonating myself.*

"To have and to hold," he says, repeating the minister, concentrating on each word so he doesn't mess up and the words blur until he gets to the end. "Till death do us part." *Death do us part. Death do us part.* This echoes in his head.

Iralene says her vows too. Her lips are red, her teeth perfect and white. She looks at Partridge. "For richer, for poorer, in sickness and in health..." And Partridge realizes that Iralene is the one who got him here. Without her, he'd be lost. Without her, his father would have killed him. He hears Beckley in his head. *Do you want people to like you just for being you? I'd have guessed you'd have outgrown that by now.*

What Beckley doesn't understand is that people never outgrow wanting to be liked for being who they truly are, especially when they've grown up in the limelight or its shadowy edge. It's all Partridge has ever wanted. Iralene wouldn't be here if he weren't Willux's son, but Iralene loves him. There isn't anything he's more sure of in this moment than that. Glassings asked him if he loved her, and he couldn't answer. People have died because of him—innocent people, ones who could have helped make real changes for good. Gone. What if there's love between him and Iralene, and love can save them? Isn't that what's happening?

But now the minister tells him he can kiss the bride, and as he lifts Iralene's veil, his heart swells at the clear sight of her face—her beautiful face and the way she's looking at him in this moment. The music starts up again, and he kisses her and she kisses him back. He then touches her cheek for a moment, and then weirdly, everything seems to stop—all the people, the noise, the lights, the music—and he says, "Thank you."

"For what?" she says.

"You got me here," he says. "Where would I be without you?" It's the truth. Lyda didn't want to follow him into the Dome, but Iralene's been by his side every step of the way. She is lovable and deserves to be loved. Is this the next good thing to do after all? Is this what Glassings meant?

Iralene's eyes fill with tears, and she grabs his hand. "Should we wave to the people now?"

He says, "Let's wave to the people."

And together they turn and wave. The crowd is on its feet, shouting and cheering so loudly Partridge feels his ribs vibrating. In this moment, he knows it's no longer an impersonation. This is real. Undeniably real.

PRESSIA

WEAK

Y OU'VE GOT GOOD TIMING," the guard says, "but we've got to
go fast."

A series of doors gust open; the guard shuttles Pressia through
each one, and they glide closed behind them. She grips the straps
of her backpack—the vial, the formula—so close now. Everything
is shiny and polished. The air smells of some strange chemical
mixed with something acrid and sweet. "How did you know I was
coming?"

"We saw you in the eyes of a dead soldier. He planted a tag." She
reaches up and feels the spot where she'd felt the strange pinch and
noticed the rip. He was tagging her? "We've been watching your
approach while scrambling your whereabouts as they get reported
to Foresteed."

"Foresteed?"

"He oversees military operations."

"So Partridge didn't order the attacks. Foresteed did?"

He nods.

Pressia is flooded with relief. She was right. Partridge would
never do that.

"We need you in here," the guard says. "We want you to talk to
Partridge."

"What do you want me to say to him?"

"Tell him he has to do this the hard way."

"Do what?"

"Start over."

"And he's doing it the easy way?"

"There is no easy way. This will be bloody. He has to let it be bloody."

He leads her into a small room filled with nozzles, as if she's going to be sprayed to death.

"Clothes stacked for you. Change fast."

"Wait. Who are you?"

"We're Cygnus. We can get you to your brother." He shuts the door.

Cygnus? Like the constellation? The swan. This all ties back to her mother. She feels, strongly, for just a brief moment, that her mother is with her.

And she is on the inside. This is it. The Dome. She's stunned. She touches the white tile, leaving a smear of ash.

She looks at the nozzles, bracing for water—or poisonous gas?

Nothing comes.

She lifts the clothes from the stack—a guard's uniform, including a holster. She remembers the first time she wore the OSR uniform, how much she loved the puff of the warm regulation jacket even though she hated herself for it. She feels that same twinge here. She shouldn't be excited to be on the inside. Bradwell would be seething. El Capitan would want to bash the guard's head in—here to help him or not, the bastard got in. The end. But she's hopeful. They'll take her to her brother, who's innocent. Pressia wants to see the boys' and girls' academies with ball fields, the apartment buildings with tidy rooms and bunk beds, the fields and food and fake sun and light and no cold, no suffering, no absolute darkness. But she's been warned: This will be bloody.

There's a small basin in one corner with a bar of soap and a towel. They want her to wash up. Good thing her skin is no longer a gold hue. She dresses quickly, nervously cinching the holster around her waist. She won't be able to wear the backpack. It will stand out too much. She opens it up, reaches in and pulls out the box. She pops the latch and checks that the vial is intact, the formula in place. She closes the box, slips it under her fitted shirt and tight jacket, and lodges it over one hip, as the clothes are tight enough to hold it in place. She moves to the basin, scrubs her face, her neck, and then she stares and stares at the doll head. In the joy of being inside the Dome, making it all the way here, she'd forgotten this—the doll head's ash-smeared skin, its small pursed lips, its clicking eyes. She washes its face, rubs the row of plastic lashes and then the doll's skull, where Pressia's knuckles are fused beneath the surface. She pats it dry with the hand towel, and the doll head looks fresh and clean, pink cheeked. Could it be removed? Could she be cured here? She steps out of the room, leaving the empty backpack behind.

The guard hands her a gun like his. She slips it in the holster and raises the doll head.

"What about this?" she says. But he's already prepared. He pulls out a bandage roll.

She lifts her arm, and he winds the bandage around the doll head, obviously disturbed by it. He covers it so tightly that for a second, she imagines that the doll won't be able to breathe. Ridiculous, she knows. He clips the bandage in place.

"If anyone asks, tell them you were in an accident."

She nods, but she feels sick. It was no accident. That's the whole reason she's here. This was done to her on purpose. All of the losses, murders, deaths were on purpose. Bradwell would say, *Look how fast they've hidden the truth.*

The guard taps the side of his face, the same spot of her crescent-shaped burn. "Cover that up," he says. "Pull some hair forward." He hands her a cap. "And keep this on."

It's a betrayal. All of it. She's sickened by it.

He leads her down hallways. She hears distant rumbling and thinks about the Dusts surrounding Crazy John-Johns. She feels the same vibrations up through the soles of her boots. She's scared and has no idea what to expect.

But soon they're standing by a tunnel, and a train pulls up. It's a sleek, beautiful machine—so shiny she can see her own reflection. She's a guard now.

The doors open. They step inside. The car is empty.

"Everyone's in front of their televisions today," the guard says.

"Why's that?"

He looks at her and then away. "Wedding. Partridge is getting married."

"He's getting married?"

"Yep."

She thinks of Lyda and the baby. Are Partridge and Lyda getting married because it's mandatory in the Dome if someone gets pregnant? She'd ask, but she's not sure if the pregnancy is common knowledge. She thinks of her wedding in the woods. Real but not real. Intimate. A secret. The only way it seems like it could exist in her ashen, desolate homeland. But love inside the Dome must be different. Here, falling in love can be an event, a proclamation without acknowledging that everyone you love could die an awful death, that loving someone is an acceptance of impending loss.

She feels a little dizzy. She grabs the train's shiny pole, so clean it squeaks when her hand slips. *This is my brother's wedding day,* she thinks, and despite everything, she feels happy, maybe even hopeful.

But at the same time, the train car reminds her of the buried one that the mothers had tunneled down to, its jacked floor and punched windows. Here she smells the lingering perfumes of the Pures' shampoos, aftershaves, hairspray—a sweetness she remembers from her childhood in the barbershop with its small bottles of tonics and gels. Most of all, there's the absence of rot and death, smoke and char. It makes her feel giddy and yet also like she might cry.

She straightens up and says, "Are you taking me to the wedding ceremony?"

The guard checks his watch. "The reception. The place will be packed with guards. High security. You'll fit in."

"Are you sure?" She holds up her bandaged fist.

"Injury, remember? Just say that."

"Accident," she says. "You told me to say it was an accident."

"Same difference."

"Only because neither is the truth."

The guard looks at her. "What?"

"It was no accident. I'm not just *injured*."

"Let's not get into it."

"It?"

"You know."

She feels hot anger coil in her chest. "The Detonations deformed us," she says. "Mutilated and fused us. Altered us on the most basic level. Even the babies born after the Detonations are mutated. Is that the *it* you don't want to get into?"

"I'm one of the good guys," the guard says defensively.

"Does that help you sleep at night?"

"I don't sleep at night." He leans toward the window, his face reflecting darkly in the glass. The train slows. "This is it." He looks at her. "Are you ready?"

She can't imagine what she's about to walk into, much less if she's ready. "I'm not used to having a choice," she says.

The doors open.

"From here on out, we walk shoulder to shoulder. Okay?"

"Okay," she says. "What's your name?"

"Vendler Prescott," he says. "Friends call me Ven."

This is who she's got on her side. Ven. Shoulder to shoulder. "Let's go."

Pressia walks with Ven through some more barren halls. They nod as they walk by an occasional guard. She hears distant music, loud voices. They reach a set of double doors. Ven pauses, glances at Pressia. She nods.

He opens the doors, and there is a huge, beautiful room filled with skirted tables and people in gowns and tuxedos. Waiters whisk around with little cakes on plates. Some of the women seem to be wearing elaborate wigs, with the way the curls are piled on top of their heads. The men have sleek hair, slicked back.

Skin, skin, skin—all flawless.

The children dip under the tables, pick off people's abandoned cake plates. The floor is covered in silken flower petals.

No one is lurching under the uneven weight of another person. There are no animals, no glass or metal or plastic embedded in their bodies. No amputations, no deep ruddy scars, no roped burns.

No thick coating of soot.

Everything is clean and bright.

And the music is glorious. She's never heard music like this—so grand and loud and beautiful. She looks up at the high, airy ceiling. Balloons are trapped in the vaults.

This is a wedding—not two people whispering in a forest. No matter how much she and Bradwell love each other, this feels real in a way their wedding never will be.

Ven grabs her arm, and Pressia remembers she's supposed to be fitting in, not gaping at everything.

They walk along one wall, away from the throngs.

On the dance floor, couples holding hands sway and spin. What's most astonishing is that it's *better* than she ever imagined, and she thought she'd built it up too high, that it would never be able to live up to her imagination.

They pass a cake tiered with columns as if it's a cathedral. Chandeliers—the crystals twinkle overhead. She remembers the farmhouse dining room and how after the fire, the chandelier crashed into the table, looking like a fallen queen. Where is the proof that these people have been ruled by someone as awful as Willux? She wants Bradwell to see this. A wedding! They still exist! Pures can believe in love so deeply that they can openly celebrate it. Could she and Bradwell ever shake being jaded enough to celebrate love? Of course, weddings are probably common inside the Dome, but to Pressia, it feels like such a bold act of hope.

Why in the world had Lyda wanted to stay with the mothers? This is heaven. Pressia drinks in the music; the sweet, clean air; the children squealing happily. *Bradwell*, she thinks, *see? They're not all bad. There's beauty here. There's innocence and joy.* She feels vindicated.

And then she sees Partridge. He's being congratulated by a bunch of guys his own age. They've raised their fluted glasses—is it champagne?—to toast him. She draws in a breath, wanting to call to him, but stops herself. She's a guard, not a sister.

One of his friends taps his empty glass with his fork. Others join in. Ven stops and waits. A clinking chorus rises up all around them. Partridge seems to be looking for someone—Lyda? Where is she?

"What's going on?" Pressia asks Ven.

"They're supposed to kiss. It's a tradition."

A kissing tradition? Pressia thinks of the traditions she was raised with. Death Sprees come to mind.

From a flurry of women, a white gown emerges—puffed and lacy, tiered like the cathedral of cake. Pressia's surprised Lyda would pick such an elaborate and enormous dress, but then she sees the bride's face.

It's not Lyda.

It's a woman Pressia's never seen before.

The clinking grows louder and louder and shriller.

There must be a mistake.

But then Partridge reaches out for the woman's hand, and he pulls her in close and kisses her. It's a quick kiss, but a kiss nonetheless. People stop clinking and suddenly erupt into cheers. Pressia stops breathing.

Partridge and this woman, this stranger, wave and then whisper to each other, smiling.

Pressia grabs Ven's jacket. "What happened? Who is she?"

"Iralene," Ven says. "Willux chose her for Partridge."

"But…Lyda…and…"

Ven shakes his head, and she knows that it's not just the pregnancy that's a secret, but Lyda too.

"I want to talk to Partridge. I want to talk to him now." Pressia's furious. What the hell is he doing? Lyda's pregnant! It's his child, and he's still doing what his daddy's told him to do?

"I'm trying to get you in close; then you two can maybe find a quiet place—"

"I don't care about finding a quiet place," Pressia says, and she heads into the crowd. She hears Ven telling her to wait, but she keeps going—around tables, cutting across the dance floor, and making a direct line for Partridge.

The bride has been pulled away by some other guests. Partridge is talking to an older man with a lean, tan face. *How do you get tan in a place with no sun?*

Pressia stops in front of them.

It takes a few seconds for Partridge to notice her, but when he does, his face lights up. "Pressia!" he says, as if this is a happy surprise.

And for some reason, it's his joy that infuriates her the most. He hands his drink off to a man nearby, leans forward, open armed, ready to give her a hug, and before she even thinks about it, she lifts her hand to slap him, but her wrist is caught.

The tan-faced man has a firm grip on her, pulling her in close.

"Who the hell are you?" Pressia says. "Let go of me."

"I'm Foresteed. Nice to meet you, Pressia."

"How do you know who I am?"

"It's not hard to recognize a well-known wretch like you. You think those bandages are fooling me?"

"Ease up, Foresteed," Partridge says, and his grip loosens, and he lets go. "How did you get here? Let's go somewhere and talk."

"I'm not going anywhere."

His cheeks have flushed a deep red, as if she had slapped him. He rubs his hands together. "We need to talk."

She then notices that all of his fingers are there. She reaches out and grabs both hands, wondering for a second if she's misremembered which pinky Our Good Mother cut off. But both of his hands are intact. His pinkies are both perfectly formed. "How? Why?" She can barely speak.

He pulls his hands from her and looks around the enormous hall, and she can see it dawning on him—how this must look to her. "I can explain," he says. "I'm doing the right things here. It's just...It just doesn't..."

"You make me sick." Her voice is so choked with anger that it comes out as a whisper.

"We've got to get her locked down," Foresteed says. "For Christ's sake, she's contaminated. How the hell did she get in here?" Foresteed looks around the crowded banquet hall.

"They're still killing us out there. And you don't even care. Look at you," Pressia says.

The bride, as if sensing the tension, walks over quickly. "What's going on?"

"It's okay, Iralene," Partridge says. "Just give us a minute." He turns back to Pressia. "Look, I had to marry Iralene! You don't understand what was happening here!"

Iralene looks at Partridge, hurt by this comment. She says, "I want to know who this is!"

"I'm Pressia. Where's Lyda?"

"Lyda couldn't come," Iralene says. "Why would she even want to?"

"Screw you!" Pressia says to Iralene, whose face instantly stiffens. "And you too, Partridge. You're worse than your father. You know that? At least he had real ambition."

Foresteed whispers. "Let me escort her out."

A young man around Partridge's age pushes his way into the tight knot. "Is this Pressia?" he says.

"Not now, Arvin," Partridge says.

"I want to talk to you," Arvin says to Pressia. "I can help—"

Partridge raises his hands. "Just everyone wait..."

"I want to see Lyda," Pressia says. "Where is she?"

Partridge turns around and calls, "Beckley!" A guy in a tux shows up. He's tall and broad with close-cropped hair. "Take Pressia to Lyda's place." He looks at Pressia. "I trust Beckley. You're in good hands."

"Good hands? Who the hell are you, Partridge?"

"I'm still the same person. Have faith in me."

Pressia shakes her head.

"I'll find you at Lyda's. We'll talk then. I can explain, Pressia. I can."

Iralene wraps her arm in his. "Beckley has to give the toast," she says.

Beckley raises his eyebrows.

"Just go," Partridge says.

Beckley starts to escort Pressia away, but Iralene says, "Wait! Beckley's supposed to deliver the toast!"

Pressia walks on a few more paces but then whips around. She can't help it. She's furious. "I stood up for you," Pressia says, her voice shaking. "But they were right all along. You're weak."

"Don't say that." Partridge rushes toward her now. He says in a low voice, "Your grandfather, Pressia—I found him. I'm bringing him back."

"What are you talking about?"

The crowd is pressing in. Iralene has his arm. "Don't make a scene."

"No, no. We wouldn't want a scene, would we?" Pressia says.

"I can explain," he says, but she can tell he's not sure. In fact, his eyes are wide, and she knows he's terrified.

EL CAPITAN

NAME

BEYOND THE STRIP MALL, El Capitan sees a row of toppled columns, lying in front of a large pile of rubble.

He begins to climb it. With each step, he feels the bruises from Helmud's jabs. His brother kicked his ass. So what? He deserved the beating. Plus, it feels right to be a little battered—it matches how he feels inside: punched, worn out, done.

"Check it," he says to Helmud halfheartedly.

Helmud runs his hands over the tape, the square box. "Check?" Helmud says, more question than answer.

El Capitan knows the tape's coming loose—too much fighting, too much sweat—but the bacterium's in place, more or less. "Good enough."

He sees a hole at the top of the rubble. He shouts, "Come out! Come out! Whoever you are!" He wishes he had a rifle to shoot off the air. He'd like to give whoever might be down there the impression that he's trigger-happy. His guns are defining, and to be honest, he needs them back. He feels like he's lost all sense of himself—direction and purpose. He's just here—with Helmud.

His brother can't leave him alone. He hates him and he needs him and he hates himself for needing him.

El Capitan calls again, but still no response. He steps back and waits a little while.

Just when he thinks it's empty, there are some scuffling noises. A man's head appears from a hole not far away. "El Capitan?" he says, blinking into the pale light. He spots Helmud over El Capitan's shoulder. They must look pretty beaten up, but this guy looks a little banged up too—and blanched. He seems scared of El Capitan. His fear feeds El Capitan, who sometimes misses being feared.

"Who are you?"

"Name's Gorse," he says.

"I know that name," El Capitan says. "Fandra's brother?"

He hesitates then nods and looks past El Capitan and to either side of him. Gorse's fusings must lie beneath his coat, which bunches on one shoulder. His hands have a sheen to them as if he had reached into a fire to pull something out. "I heard you were in the city—with Bradwell." Evidently he'd feel a little safer if Bradwell were here.

"He's meeting me. He picked this place. Thought it'd be safe and good to get out of the weather. How many down there?"

Gorse raises his eyebrows. "Just two of us."

"Mind if we wait for Bradwell with you?"

Gorse isn't sure. He glances below and then back at El Capitan.

"I've got good news for you, Gorse," El Capitan says.

"Yeah? What's that?"

"Fandra."

"What about her?" He squints at El Capitan suspiciously.

"She's alive. She survived out there, barely, and she got picked up by survivors out at Crazy John-Johns. She's okay."

"You wouldn't lie to me, would you?"

"I saw her myself," El Capitan says. "Long blond hair. She saved our asses out there."

"Saved our asses," Helmud says.

"You don't have to take our word for it." El Capitan says. "Bradwell's coming, like I said. You can ask him yourself."

Gorse glances at El Capitan and Helmud, and then something behind them seems to catch his eye. "Don't have to wait," he says.

El Capitan turns. Bradwell is climbing the rubble. Bradwell sees Gorse and shouts. "Hey, Gorse! Did you hear the news?"

El Capitan looks back at Gorse. "See? I told you he'd confirm."

Gorse must want to hear it for himself. He plays dumb. "The news? What news?"

"Your sister. We saw her out by the amusement park. She's fine, Gorse. She made it after all."

Gorse goes still. His eyes shine with tears. He clears his throat, excuses himself, and disappears down the hole.

"And?" El Capitan says to Bradwell.

"I found Pressia. I said what I had to say. I let her go."

El Capitan isn't sure what this means. He told her that he loved her? What did she say? He decides he doesn't want to know. Why punish himself with details?

"What the hell happened to you two? You look like hell," Bradwell says.

"We fell."

"Down a flight of stairs?" Bradwell says.

"Yeah," El Capitan says, "something like that."

"Something," Helmud says, "*like* that."

Gorse reappears, his eyes red rimmed. He's been crying. He rubs his face roughly. "Fandra. Alive? You sure of it?"

"Sure of it," Bradwell says.

Gorse lets out a loud shout of joy. "Well, we've got to celebrate, then! We've got some top-notch stuff down here, from before the still exploded."

"Yes," El Capitan says. When was the last time he had something to drink? He'd love to get drunk. Ripsnorting drunk.

"I don't know," Bradwell says.

"Don't," Helmud says. He doesn't like it when El Capitan drinks.

"What don't you know?" El Capitan says to Bradwell. "There's nothing we can do now—not for ourselves, not for Pressia. We can't do anything until we hear from her. We may as well celebrate something while there's still something to celebrate." El Capitan turns to Gorse and says, "Let me make this simple: Hell yes!"

"Hell," Helmud says nervously. "Yes."

"To the mothers," El Capitan shouts, raising the bottle, "who scare the hell out of me!" He's already toasted the Dusts, the Beasts, the dead, the living, the boars, the creatures in the fog…He takes a long swig. It burns his throat, warms his chest. He and Helmud are sitting on the floor of the bank vault with Bradwell and Gorse and one other guy who's passed out and curled up in the corner. The two-foot-thick circular vault door is permanently open, pinched by the buckled ceiling. The metal walls are lined with small rectangular drawers—all of which have been broken into and cleaned out. Most of the drawers themselves are gone. It's cozy in here. Feels safe, secure. Smells like metal. El Capitan likes it.

As he passes the bottle on to Bradwell, Helmud reaches out and tries to grab it. "You're getting your share," El Capitan says. "It's in the blood." He laughs loudly. He knows Helmud doesn't want a drink. He wants to take the bottle away from El Capitan. He doesn't like to get drunk—and they both surely are now. El Capitan forgot how much he missed liquor—the way it softens the world, mutes noise, sets the world to blur. Old Ingership used to give him booze from time to time. He's glad the man's dead, but he misses the liquor.

"Your share, your share, your share," Helmud mutters, arms slumped and head bobbing over one shoulder. He's scolding El Capitan for taking too much.

"Shut up, Helmud!" El Capitan says. "We're celebrating here. Right, Bradwell? Tell him. Right?"

"Right," Bradwell says, handing the bottle to Gorse.

"Right!" Gorse shouts, taking a drink. El Capitan keeps a close watch over the bottle, trying to gauge if he'll get the last swig or not.

He wishes Pressia were here, though he doesn't want to bring up her name—not in front of Bradwell. He doesn't want to know what happened between them when Bradwell ran after her in the rain. El Capitan likes to think of her now—with this nice drunk on. All of the pain is blunted. He can imagine a future with her—the two of them, or even the three of them, counting Helmud. And it's good.

And then, like a switch got flipped, El Capitan thinks of the dead boy caught in the trap. Why now? He rubs his forehead. "Don't. Don't," he mutters, but then there are more faces of the dead, flashing through his mind. Their faces are a blur. What happened to him in that crypt? That's when it started. Why does he feel so sick about it all now? Jesus. He almost prayed to God or that statue of the saint for forgiveness. If he had done that, what would have happened to him? He'd have to admit it was wrong. It wasn't wrong. Look—he's alive! Helmud's alive on his back!

"Why do they scare you?" Bradwell asks El Capitan.

"God and that saint?" El Capitan asks.

"What? No," Bradwell says. "The mothers. You said the mothers scare the hell out of you."

"You're not scared of them?" El Capitan shoots back.

"I didn't say that. I was just wondering why they scare you."

El Capitan leans into the middle of the circle. "They seem good and nice and, well, they're mothers. They used to organize potlucks and talk about curtains, and now they'll kill you as soon as they look at you."

"You're one to talk," Gorse says.

"Yeah, but I never prided myself on nurturing the young minds of tomorrow by picking out the best private school and driving to it in the best minivan."

"We were all innocent once upon a time, though," Bradwell says. "You were technically once a kid, right, El Capitan? I mean, shit—didn't you once have a name other than El Capitan, or is that on your baptismal record?"

"Don't remember it," El Capitan says. Walden. Walden was his name.

"You don't *remember* it?" Gorse says. "Your own name?"

"Helmud!" Bradwell says. "What was your brother's name before it was El Capitan?"

"He doesn't know," El Capitan says. "Don't make fun of him!"

El Capitan can feel his brother's head jerk up behind him. "Don't make fun," Helmud says.

"I'm not making fun, Helmud. I'm just saying you might remember El Capitan's name from your childhood together. I mean, it's in there, deep down. Your mother used to call you into the house when you were little, right? She called, 'Helmud!' and then she said another name. What was it?"

Helmud bobbles some more. Is he remembering? Is there some pinprick of light illuminating the dark corner of his memory?

"Don't bother him with this shit. He doesn't remember and neither do I. My old name's dead. I'm El Capitan."

"What about your last name?" Gorse asks.

"Croll," El Capitan says quietly. "My father was Sergeant Warret B. Croll. Croll."

Bradwell scoots closer to El Capitan. He reaches out and holds Helmud's cheeks in his hands. "When your mother was angry, maybe she called you all by your full names. Moms do that. What did she call El Capitan when she was mad at him?"

"Leave him alone!" El Capitan shouts, pulling backward so his brother's face slips from Bradwell's hands. El Capitan stands up. Helmud feels incredibly heavy on his back and sends El Capitan crashing into the wall of empty safety deposit boxes. El Capitan's head knocks into the metal—a sharp knock. He lets himself slide down to the floor again. He touches his head—no blood.

"What the hell, Cap!" Bradwell says. "We were just messing around!"

"You shouldn't have let Pressia go in by herself," El Capitan shouts. "If she dies, it's your fault. You know that!"

Helmud is propping him up. "Your fault!" he shouts at his brother.

"What?" Bradwell shouts. "You let her go as much as I did!"

"Easy now," Gorse says, hands in the air.

El Capitan can barely see Bradwell and Gorse. They're dim and flickering images in his eyes. He glances at the guy in the corner and hates him—suddenly and for no apparent reason. "You shouldn't have let her go at all."

"Cap," Bradwell says, "you know I didn't have a choice. You know that..."

El Capitan closes his eyes and the ground beneath him feels like it's loose and spinning. "If she dies," he says, opening his eyes again, blinking, "the blood is on your hands."

"Who the hell do you think you are?" Bradwell shouts, his huge wings flaring at his back.

El Capitan doesn't even brace for a blow. In fact, he hopes Bradwell attacks him. "We should tear each other up!" he shouts. "Kill each other. Get it all over with already!"

"You sure about that?" Bradwell says.

But then El Capitan hears scuffling and Gorse's voice. "Let him sleep it off."

Bradwell's voice is rough. "I'm not afraid she's going to die. She's too tough for that. You know what you're not thinking of yet, Cap? You're not worried that she'll like it—that she'll choose the Dome over either of us."

Bradwell's words sink in slowly, and El Capitan realizes he's right. Bradwell could always see all the possibilities before El Capitan could. What if she loves it in the Dome? What if she's gone... not dead, but gone all the same? He can't think of anything to say— nothing at all. He feels like he's going to start crying. Damn it. Tears slip from his eyes.

Then he feels a hand on his head. It pushes the hair from his forehead gently, softly. The hand pets his head like he's a little kid, sweaty from playing in the woods. A voice says, "Waldy. Waldy, Waldy, Waldy." This is what his mother called him when he was little. Waldy. Short for Walden. "Waldy, Waldy." Helmud remembers. Helmud pets his head the way their mother did once upon a time when they were innocent, once upon a time when El Capitan was Waldy.

"I couldn't save her," he says to Helmud. He means not only their mother but Pressia too.

Helmud wraps his arms around El Capitan, holds him tight. El Capitan draws in air and pushes it out. Helmud keeps holding him. El Capitan covers his eyes with his hands. He's crying. "I'm sorry." He whispers, "Forgive me. Forgive me." He's sorry not just for his mother's death, but for all of them. "Forgive me." The boy in the trap, the Death Sprees, the pens of kids out in the cold. He killed people. He was the cause of death and suffering...

He's sorry for all of the pain. Everything.

"Forgive me." It's what he couldn't say in the crypt.

But here, now, with Helmud, El Capitan is asking for forgiveness from Saint Wi or God or whatever force might exist beyond them. "Forgive me," El Capitan keeps saying.

He means, *Take this from me.*

Take this.

And then he feels it—something breaking open in his chest. And being lifted out.

And it's gone.

PARTRIDGE

CONFETTI

D<small>ANCE WITH ME</small>," Iralene shouts over the music. "Come on."

Partridge feels dazed. Pressia was going to slap him. His eyes stutter through the crowd, across the banquet tables, shimmering dresses, shining hair, the glinting silverware, the gilded arches in the ceiling. *This* was Pressia's first look at the Dome? And he's at the center of it all, drinking champagne in a hand-tailored tux, next to his bride, his *wife*? "I can't," he says quietly.

And just then, someone somewhere lets loose some pink confetti. It's blown in from an unseen machine and flits around them. It takes him back to the beginning of it all—running through the massive air filtration system, the giant fan blades, cutting through the pink filters, all the fibers spinning around him. It reminds him of the way ash floats on the air—out there—and of Lyda and what she said about being locked within a snow globe.

Iralene tugs at his jacket. "Don't let Pressia ruin it! She'll get to know me, and she'll like me. You didn't like me at first either," she says.

Iralene starts to pull him toward the dance floor. He stops her and looks into her eyes. He remembers what it was like when he first met her. She was stiff and awkward—almost like a foreigner. And she was a foreigner. She'd lived so long suspended. "I've messed everything up."

She wraps her arms around him, holds him tightly. "No, you haven't. You've done the right thing. I saw you do it. I know it's the truth. You'll explain it all to her. She'll understand."

"I don't think she'll ever understand."

"I know what you'll do, Mr. Partridge Willux."

"What?"

"You have the greatest gift in the world to give her, and once you do, she'll forgive everything." Iralene smiles at him. "Right?"

Partridge has her grandfather. Alive. The fan lodged in his throat was taken out, and he was stitched up, suspended. He might even have her father, though he can't access that chamber—not yet at least. For now, he can give her grandfather back. He can try. But he feels like he's drowning. He's failed. Pressia knows it. She probably doesn't even know the worst of it.

"In the end, you'll look back and it will all make sense."

Will it ever make sense? Will anyone ever look at this series of events and know that he tried so hard to do the right thing—while it all crumbled down around him? "What else can I do?" he says.

"You could dance with Mrs. Partridge Willux."

Still dazed, he lets Iralene lead him to the dance floor, confetti filling the air, dusting the floor like pink snow.

PRESSIA

JUMPERS

I'M USUALLY THE ONE DRESSED AS A GUARD," Beckley says. "Mind if I take off the tie?"

"What do I care?" Pressia says. She's furious. It's like two fists pounding together in her chest. Bradwell was right—about the Pures, about Partridge. She's ashamed that she bought into the joy, love, and emboldened hope of a wedding—even if for a second. She misses Bradwell more than ever. He says what he means—even if he knows she's not going to like it. He's screwed up—all human beings are—but at least he's real. El Capitan and Helmud too. She wonders if she should have come at all. But she can feel the metal box cutting into her hip. She has to try to save people. She has to give it a shot—even if Partridge is a lost cause.

They're walking down the empty street. The storefronts are pasted with pictures of Partridge and Iralene in various poses. She stops at one of Partridge pushing Iralene on a wooden swing. "Look at him."

Beckley stuffs the bow tie in his pocket and stops. "I was there," he says. "He didn't want to pose for the pictures."

"Maybe he didn't want to pose for them, but the fact is that he did. He let someone take that picture." She stares up at Beckley's face. He's older than she is by a good bit, looks a little hardened. "What's it like?" she says. "To live in this place?"

"What do I know? It's been so long I don't have anything to compare it to anymore."

"You don't remember the Before? I don't believe you."

"Maybe that's your first lesson. You shouldn't believe anyone in here." He starts walking again.

She walks after him quickly. "Is it always as awful as it is beautiful like that?"

"It's not usually so brightly lit, but yeah."

"Partridge says he's bringing my grandfather back. My grandfather's dead, Beckley. Does Partridge think he's God?"

Beckley shrugs.

It was cruel of him to say that—to promise Pressia her grandfather. Partridge knows what it would mean to have her grandfather back. He was the only real parent she ever knew. He wasn't her real grandfather, but that only made what he did all the more remarkable. He saved her life.

"Tell me—whose side are you on?" she asks.

"There are no sides."

"And is that the second lesson?"

"I guess it could be."

"I think that there is a good side," Pressia says. "And you're on it or you're not."

He glances at Pressia then up into the stale air. "What's it like out there now anyway?"

How can she describe the world outside the Dome? It's impossible. "I don't know," Pressia says. "Real."

Beckley stares at a spot on the narrow sidewalk that's splotched whiter than the rest.

"What's this?" Pressia asks.

He stops, looks up at a building, and points out one of the windows that's been capped with thick plastic. "Jumper."

"Jumper?"

He nods.

"You mean someone jumped out of that window?"

"Yep."

"And the sidewalk is white because . . ."

"They cleaned up the blood and bleached it." Beckley stuffs his hands in his pockets and walks on.

Pressia looks up and down the sidewalks on either side of the narrow street. She sees another white bleach stain. Then another. All of them look fresh.

"Why are there jumpers, Beckley?" she asks.

"It's as awful as it is beautiful, right? And sometimes it's real here too." He walks up to an apartment building's front door, hits the buzzer. The door opens. They step into a lobby with plush velvet furniture and a long gold-framed mirror. Orchids bloom in ornate vases. They can't be real. Beckley nods to a man sitting behind a desk. He's watching a miniature TV. Pressia hasn't seen a television since the Before. It's grainy but colorful—and then she recognizes the setting. The man's watching Partridge and Iralene's wedding reception.

"It's the big day," the man says, rubbing his belly. "I thought you were there?"

"Another day, another dollar," Beckley says.

The man looks at Pressia but doesn't ask any questions.

Beckley leads her to an elevator. Its doors glide open. Pressia's nervous to step inside of the box, but she refuses to show it. She stands behind Beckley, who hits a lit-up circular button, and presses her back to a wall. The elevator jerks and rides up. Pressia's stomach lurches.

Just as the elevator comes to a stop, Beckley reaches out and holds a button. He says, "Lyda isn't doing so well in here."

Pressia steps forward. "What do you mean?"

"Would you do well in here?"

Pressia shakes her head. "Today might not be easy, for obvious reasons."

Beckley covers his mouth with his fist and coughs. Then, with his fist still raised, he says, "Once she has the baby, they'll put her back in."

"Back in?"

Beckley releases the button and the doors open. He looks up and down a long hallway. "Sorry," he says, taking the gun from her holster. "Protocol." And then he whispers, so softly she barely makes it out. "She'll go back to the rehabilitation center. For crazy people. She'll never get out."

"But the baby..."

"The baby will be fine," he whispers. "The baby's a Willux."

PRESSIA

MOTHER AND DAUGHTER

THE APARTMENT IS PRISTINE, SPACIOUS: white furniture, white drapes, white walls with framed prints of flowers in vases that nearly match the flowers sitting in vases on tables here and there. And seated on the two sofas are two women, one man, and one girl, all perfectly poised around a glowing television tuned to the reception, of course. There's no escaping it.

Lyda isn't among them. Pressia is disgusted by the idle perfection of it all. Someone is going to let Lyda be sent back into a rehab center after they take her baby from her? Do people know the secret?

She thought she knew what hell was. She thought she knew it intimately—a Beast grabbing her in a rubble field, OSR's Death Sprees, the Dusts around Crazy John-Johns, the creatures held by the mist in Ireland, disease, clogged lungs, slow death.

But no. This is a hell she'd never imagined before—a mannered, vicious hell.

"Where's Lyda?" Pressia asks them.

They stare at Pressia, each set of their eyes gliding to her wrapped-up doll-head fist. She can't stand the way they're gawking. She rips the bandage off. She should have done this at the reception—shown them all the truth of who she is. She drops the bandage to the floor. She feels free again—as if the doll head can now breathe.

One of the women grabs the girl and hugs her to her chest.

"Who is this, Beckley?" asks the other woman. She stands up, and her dress ripples like it's underwater.

Beckley steps forward. "Partridge's half sister," he says.

Pressia takes off the hat and throws it on a table so they can see the burns curved around one of her eyes. "Where's Lyda?"

The man says to the woman clutching the girl, "Take her into the kitchen! For God's sake!"

"No!" the girl says. "I want to see this!"

But the girl's mother says, "Hush it, Vienna! Move! Now!"

The man wrenches the girl's arm, and pulls her into the kitchen, the woman following close behind.

The woman in the floaty dress is standing her ground. She says to Beckley, ignoring Pressia, "I don't want my daughter talking to this wretch! Do you hear me? This situation is delicate enough!"

"You're Lyda's mother?"

The woman won't look at Pressia. She simply nods curtly. "I won't have this!" she hisses at Beckley. "I will not have this! Tell her she must leave!"

Beckley shrugs. In fact, he looks kind of amused by the situation. "You can tell her yourself. I'm a guard, not a messenger."

"Excuse me? You can't use that tone with me," Lyda's mother says. "You wait until I report this. You just wait!"

Beckley smirks. He's not afraid of Lyda's mother. It could be that women inside the Dome are never much of a threat as she's heard it was during the Before, at the height of feminine feminism.

Lyda's mother looks like she might cry, as if she's well aware she has no real power. She says, "I want what's best for my daughter. My only daughter."

"Is that right?" Maybe she has power and Beckley is challenging it, for Lyda's sake or hers.

Lyda's mother turns; her skirt flares around her. She grabs her pocketbook, and says, "I can't work under these conditions! I'm a professional."

She's here working? She's a professional mother? Pressia doesn't understand.

Lyda's mother walks to the door. "I want the nursery dismantled. I want it all hauled away and everything replaced. Every last thing. You hear me?" Her voice is cold and distant.

Beckley doesn't answer. He unlocks the door and holds it open wide. As she steps through it, she glances back at Pressia. She doesn't look angry now; it's as if that emotion has suddenly faded and what's surfaced in its place is fear.

Pressia likes it. She thinks of El Capitan—fear is power. No wonder he liked it all those years. It made him feel protected and safe.

Beckley closes the door behind Lyda's mother and turns to Pressia. "I'll get the Culp family out of here," he says. "You can go down that hall. Lyda's probably in the nursery. The door on the right. It'll be locked."

"Thanks, Beckley," she says.

"For what?" he says.

"You know." He stuck up for her.

He nods and walks to the kitchen.

As Pressia walks down the hall, she smells something familiar—smoke.

LYDA

PROOF

N<small>O</small>.

Partridge will come for her. They'll start a new life. He loves her. She remembers walking with Partridge to the subway car, the dusty wind kicking up her cape. He kissed her, quickly, before Mother Hestra could catch them. After they lay with each other in the warden's house, Partridge was the one who wanted her to come with him. The way he looked at her, the way he touched her, the way it felt when they were near each other—that was love, wasn't it? Can love just disappear?

She was the one to tell Partridge to marry Iralene—to stop people from killing themselves. Wasn't it the right thing to do? Was it a setup? Did Partridge want permission to betray her?

She looks around the nursery—the dismantled crib, the small mattress tilted against a wall next to a stack of ripped-up baby books and the bowl of ash where she burned page after page, the pile of spears she whittled from the slats, the shavings littering the floor, and the bags of yarn and knitting needles brought in by Chandry.

She looks down at her torn dress, the tightness of it around her waist where her belly will continue to widen...This is the room of a crazy person, and she's the crazy person within it. Has she just been so sleep deprived that she couldn't see it clearly for what it is?

She picks up the scraps of her dress. She'll throw away the dress, and no one will see what she's done to it. "I can change back," she whispers. "I can be my old self again." She picks up the bag of knitting supplies. "I can do this." She walks to the stack of ripped-up baby books, wanting to hide them, but accidentally kicks the bowl of ashes, which scatter across the floor. She kneels down and tries to brush the ashes back into the bowl, but she streaks the floor with blackened soot. The more she rubs it, the darker the stain seems to become.

There's a knock at the door.

No, no. "Who is it?" It's her mother. She knows it. Her mother is coming back to tell her how ashamed she is, how wrong Lyda's been, what a terrible child she's raised. She'll tell Partridge all about the insane nursery.

"Lyda."

It's not her mother. It's a voice she recognizes but can't place.

Lyda stands up and quietly walks to the door. She touches the wood with her fingertips, lightly, like a water spider on the surface of a pond. She remembers seeing them as a child—pushing and gliding, light as air. "Who is it?"

"It's me. It's Pressia."

No, it can't be. It's a trick. She shakes her head. "I don't believe you."

"Lyda, it's me. We have to talk."

How long has it been since she really slept through the night? Maybe the sleeplessness has made her paranoid, or maybe she should be paranoid. "I don't trust you!" She stares up at the corners of the room where she's covered the cameras. "Just leave me alone. Just tell Partridge…" But she can't finish the sentence. What would she want someone to tell Partridge?

"I can prove it's me," the voice says. "Ask me something only I would know."

She thinks back to the times when they were together. "The farmhouse," she says. "Tell me."

"We were all there. Illia too. She killed her husband." Illia. Lyda remembers her in the tub, her glistening fists shaking in the air.

"She's dead," Lyda says. Maybe people in the Dome know that already. She needs something more specific. "The wallpaper," Lyda says. "Tell me about the wallpaper in the operating room."

"Boats," Pressia says. "The wallpaper was covered in little boats because it wasn't always an operating room. It was once a nursery."

Lyda looks around her own baby's nursery. Is that why she asked? The wallpaper was proof that Illia had once thought she would have a baby and then for whatever reasons there was no baby.

This is what Lyda's most afraid of now. If Partridge is truly married to someone else, what will happen to Lyda and the baby? She's suddenly exhausted. She leans against the wall, resting her cheek against the coolness of it, flattening her palms. She looks at the knob. Is Pressia on the other side? Is it a lie? Can she trust anything anyone says to her inside of the Dome?

She looks at the light ashen print her hand made. She pinches the lock on the knob, turns it, and opens the door a small crack.

She can't look. She wants to see Pressia's face so badly that she starts to cry.

"Lyda."

She looks up.

Pressia. How is it possible?

Pressia steps inside the nursery, shuts the door, locks it again, and the two hug each other.

They hold on tight.

PRESSIA

CYGNUS

LYDA IS SHAKING FROM DEEP INSIDE. She's barely able to stand. Pressia holds her up. "We have to get you out. They're going to put you away and take the baby once it's born."

Lyda nods. Does she already know this is true? If she didn't already know, it doesn't surprise her. "I want to go back to the mothers. This place—it can't be saved."

"Listen, we have the means to take down the Dome," Pressia whispers.

"Are you really going to? Can you?"

"If Partridge has turned on us, we might have to," Pressia says. "Bradwell and El Capitan are on the outside, waiting for word from me."

"Awaiting word to take down the Dome? How would you send the message?"

"I don't know. I thought I'd have help once I was here."

"Cygnus," Lyda says softly. "They're here. They're your mother's followers. They can help us, I think."

"Someone from Cygnus met me when I first got inside the Dome."

"We can try to get them to help. I know we can," Lyda says. "What will the message say?"

"Well, I'm not ready to send it. I have the cure with me," Pressia says. "I need to get it to someone who knows what to do with it. We can still save people—the survivors. We can make them whole. We can't take down the Dome until I try to give this to someone we can trust."

"Yes, but what kind of message would you send? What would it say?" Lyda asks.

"It would be a message that could only be from me." They keep their voices low.

"A coded message?"

Pressia nods. "I would tell Bradwell that our lives aren't accidents. This is the beginning, not an end. I'd tell him to do what he has to do. He would know it's from me and that it was time to bring it all down. Maybe a picture." She thinks of Cygnus, the constellation, her mother's followers—her mother is still with her, in some way. "Maybe of a swan."

"I think I can find someone who can help send it," Lyda says.

"I'm not sure if it will ever be the right thing to do. It's just that Partridge seems gone. Just gone…"

"He is gone," Lyda says. "He is."

"Partridge told me he has my grandfather, that he's bringing him back—from the dead. Is that possible, Lyda? Is it?" Pressia's afraid that Lyda will say yes, and she's also afraid she'll say no.

"Is that why you're really waiting to tell them to bring it down? Your grandfather?" Lyda draws in a shaky breath.

"Is it possible he's still alive? Please tell me."

"They can do things here that seem good, but they're horrible, Pressia. Do you understand me? Horrible." She starts crying again, harder this time, her ribs convulsing. "Send the message! Send it!"

Pressia hugs her, sways gently. "Not yet. Give me time."

"Then do me a small favor," Lyda whispers, her voice shaking.

"What is it?"

"Tell the guard that the orb is broken."

"The orb?"

"The orbs keep the images in the rooms spinning. I can't explain it. Just promise me."

"Lyda, right now we have to concentrate on—"

"Just tell him!" Lyda shouts.

"Okay," Pressia says as gently as she can. "I'll tell him. It's okay. It's going to be okay."

"I'm so tired," Lyda whispers. "I can't sleep."

"I'm here," Pressia says. "You'll be able to sleep now. I'm here."

Partridge

BRASS BEDS

Partridge lifts Iralene up, carries her over the threshold into a penthouse suite. This is a honeymoon. He shouldn't be surprised by the luxury of it all, but he is. The suite is lush—even after all of the luxuries of the day. He sets Iralene on her high heels and together they walk through a living room of leather furniture and a formal dining room, past a baby grand piano and a claw-foot tub in a bathroom as big as a bedroom.

Partridge can't stop thinking about Pressia. Ever since he saw her, he can't help but see everything doubly: his perspective and then hers—all the arrogance, wasteful opulence, and cruelty of so much luxury when they both know what's outside the Dome. He feels choked with guilt.

Iralene drank too much champagne, and he did too—more than he should have because he wanted to drown that guilt. But now he wishes he hadn't. He'd like to be able to think. He's got to get to Pressia and Lyda as soon as possible. How?

Iralene runs ahead of him and opens the door to the bedroom. She calls to him, "You have to see this! The bed is as big as a swimming pool!" She disappears into the room.

He walks to the hall but doesn't go to the bedroom. This isn't a real honeymoon.

She peeks her head out of the bedroom door and looks at him. "Let's dive in!" She takes off her shoes.

"Iralene," he says, "you know it's all fake."

"What?" she says. "I can't hear you."

He walks to the bedroom door and leans against the frame.

Iralene has climbed onto the canopy bed, its white blanket covered in petals. She turns and falls backward, arms spread wide, the petals bouncing around her. "I can't hear you! I can't hear you!" she sings.

Partridge walks up to the bed and holds on to one of its posts, like someone on a boat trying to steady himself.

It is, in fact, a huge canopy bed—with a shiny brass frame.

Like the ruined one on the third floor of the warden's house where he and Lyda cocooned themselves and had sex—where he told her he loved her.

A brass bed.

"I can't sleep here, Iralene."

She lifts her head. "What?"

"You know I can't. You know why."

"I thought you meant it. What you said today. What you promised me. I felt it."

"I think I did mean it."

"Really?"

"I don't know."

"You know what I'm good at, Partridge? You know what my most perfected trait is?"

She props herself up on her elbows. She looks beautiful on the bed surrounded by flower petals. "I have no idea."

"Patience."

She's right. She grew up in-waiting, suspended. She means that she's going to wait for him to really fall in love with her—her and her alone.

"I'm going to get on the phone and talk to Weed," Partridge

says. "I want him to help Peekins with Pressia's grandfather. I want him to try to help me break into the locked, unmarked chamber down there. I've got to—"

"Do what you have to do, but remember—you still owe me."

"I know," he says, but Iralene's voice is charged in a way that's unsettling. He heads for the door.

"Partridge," she whispers.

He stops.

"You might not have meant what you said today, but I did," Iralene says. "Just so you know. Sometimes I don't. Sometimes I have to say what people want me to say or what I need to say to survive. Today, though, I meant it. Every word."

Partridge nods. He closes the door gently and stands there for a moment. Why didn't Lyda ever return his letters? How does she feel about him now? Does he really want to know the answer to that question?

He walks down the hall into the suite's living room. He just got married, but for some reason, he feels incredibly lonely. Maybe it's because he is alone. His mother, his brother, his father—they're all gone.

Right now he misses Sedge most of all. Sedge would have been his best man. He would have maybe even had some advice for him. Partridge doesn't even have a memento of his brother.

Then Partridge remembers the field trip that Glassings took his World History class to—the Personal Loss Archives. All of the academy boys walked the aisles lined with alphabetized boxes, each containing the personal effects of someone who'd died.

He opened his mother's box, where he found some important clues to her existence—clues that had been planted for him. But he never opened his brother's box. He hadn't had the courage. He wishes now that he'd seen what was inside.

And then he realizes that he doesn't need permission to go to the Personal Loss Archives. He's in charge.

He wants to go. Now. He misses his brother and wants to see what's in that box.

He realizes that he seems crazy and maybe drunk, but who cares?

He walks to the door of the suite and pulls it open. There, standing at attention, is a guard. Not Beckley. He's still with Pressia and probably now Lyda. This is a guard he doesn't know well at all—Albertson.

"Sir?" Albertson says.

"I want you to escort me somewhere."

"I can't just do that, sir. I'd have to get clearance. I'd have to make calls."

"To Foresteed?"

Albertson looks away.

"It's my wedding day, Albertson. How about as a wedding gift, you don't make any calls. Okay?"

"I don't know," Albertson says. "I'm just not sure."

"C'mon, Albertson. You know it's the right thing to do. Just a little trip. You and me."

"Now, sir?"

"Yes."

"Where?"

"I want to visit my brother."

EL CAPITAN

HELL YES

EL CAPITAN FEELS GREAT PRESSURE on his chest. He's on the ground in the bank vault, the safety deposit boxes a blur along the wall. It's dark, except for a few flickering lanterns. Helmud's panting breathlessly on his back. "What's this?" El Capitan says. His head is pounding. The air is filled with the smell of bio-diesel.

A hand grips one of his wrists and then the other, and as he feels them getting tied behind his back, he bucks and jerks. "What the hell is going on?"

But now someone is pinning them to the floor.

A man's voice says, "We're ready to haul them up, Frost."

The man on his back, Frost, mutters, "Okay."

Where's the bacterium? Helmud's pushing against him, and he can't feel the sharp edges of the box. "Check it," he grunts at Helmud.

Helmud doesn't answer.

"Check!" El Capitan shouts again. "Check!"

Still nothing. And El Capitan knows it's gone. He's a failure. He's lost the one thing that could bring down the Dome. It's over.

"Bradwell?" El Capitan shouts. "You here?" He lifts his chin, scraping it across the floor, and turns his head. God, he doesn't want Bradwell to know it's gone.

Bradwell's sitting on the floor, already gagged with a cloth, his arms bound behind his back. Two men are standing next to him, one on either side. Bradwell must have fought pretty hard. He has a gash on his head, blood curving down his temple. He jerks his head and cuts his eyes to the wall of boxes behind him. El Capitan can't read the gesture.

He spots the can of fuel near the bank vault's two-foot-thick circular door. What the hell are they doing with that down here? Can't be good.

Gorse's face suddenly appears as he bends on one knee. He's holding an old OSR rifle. "You thought I could forgive and forget all of that business with the OSR, huh? You thought all of us would see some shiny new version handing out food and warm coats, and everything else would just fade away?"

"Why did you tie up Bradwell? He's on your side."

"Is he? Seems he's lost his way, taking up with you."

El Capitan glances at Bradwell. He feels bad for getting him roped in. Bradwell shrugs his heavy wings—a kind of forgiveness. "But I've really changed," El Capitan says.

"Have you ever paid for what you did?" Gorse says. "Have you?"

He doesn't have to think about this long. The answer is no. He hasn't really paid. He's doled out a lot of death and is still alive. "What are you going to do with me?"

"With me?" Helmud whispers.

"Justice will be served," Gorse says, and then he looks up at Frost, who has El Capitan and Helmud muscled to the floor. "Go ahead and gag both of 'em."

"Gorse, wait!" El Capitan shouts. "I thought we were friends!"

"Now you know better."

"But we found your sister!"

Gorse stands and points the rifle at El Capitan's head. "Don't ever talk about my sister again. Maybe she's dead. Maybe she's alive. But the fact is I thought she was dead all these years because of you. How many did you let die in Death Sprees? How many froze to death in your cages? How many did you hunt down and use for target practice? Did you keep count? Huh?"

El Capitan tries to fight the ropes again. If he can't get loose, he's a dead man. He and Helmud both. Gorse kicks El Capitan in the ribs. He folds in half. He wheezes on the ground, crunching around the pain, while Frost wraps a rag around his mouth, making it even harder to breathe.

Justice, El Capitan thinks. That's right. "Kick me again," he grunts into the rag. "Do it!" This is what he deserves. But he can hear Helmud's squeals of protest suddenly muffled. El Capitan won't let Helmud pay. He'll fight for Helmud, for himself. It's who he is. He'll fight all the way.

"Blindfold?" Frost asks.

"No," Gorse says. "I'd like him to see this."

Frost yanks El Capitan to his feet. The two men, both with twisted faces and metal pocking their arms, as if they'd been at the same place during the Detonations and are lucky not to have been fused together, lift Bradwell up too. They walk back through the dented bank vault door into the crumbled remains of the bank lobby and up through a hole dug in the rubble—not easy to do with his hands tied behind his back, under his brother's weight.

Above ground, the wind is cold and sharp. He drank too much; he feels sick. His head's killing him, and he feels a little dizzy. He's almost happy that Frost has such a strong hold on his upper arm; otherwise, he might fall over.

They're surrounded by a dozen people or so, including a few clumps of Groupies. He tries to make out all of the faces to see if there are any friends among them.

Then he hears a voice he remembers well. "Greetings, El Capitan!" He sees the Dome worshipper who found Wilda out in a field when she was first delivered back from the Dome, Purified, as it were. He remembers the bulbous, braided scar running down one side of her face. Margit. She hates him.

Margit walks up close, fits her fingers under his gag, pulling it to the dip in his chin. "What say you?"

"Shit," El Capitan says, shaking his head.

"Not happy to see the likes of me?"

"Last time I saw you you'd been hit by a spider, locked in. So, you didn't blow up?"

"I was spared. By God."

"A gift from the Dome, I'm guessing, to be spared like that."

"And they're not happy with us, El Capitan. They are not happy at all."

"But they wanted their son to be returned to them and he was! What could they possibly want now?"

"They must want another sacrifice," she says.

El Capitan nods slowly. "I'm guessing that it won't be a self-sacrifice."

"Me? No. I want to be here when we are called to join them in the heaven of the Dome. Not to be ash in the wind."

"I see." El Capitan knows what the biodiesel's going to be used for now. Burning to death—not his preferred way to go. "But I'm asking you a kindness."

"What's that?"

"Spare my brother," El Capitan says. "He's an angel. He's good. Spare my poor brother." He can't help the fact that there's an ironic edge to his voice.

"Now how would we spare him and not you, foul man?"

"I guess you'd have to go light on me." El Capitan raises his eyebrows. "You can't let another good soul die, could you?"

Margit lifts her clenched fist and knuckle punches El Capitan in the head. It reminds him of his grandmother who would rap him on the head when he got underfoot. "Maybe that'll be the best part—you knowing your sins caused your brother's death." Margit turns and says to Gorse, "We should beat them good and solid first then set the brother on his back afire so El Capitan gets to hear his cries."

Gorse likes the idea. "Hell yes!" he says, mocking El Capitan from the night before. "Hell yes!"

And before El Capitan can spit out something else, Margit shoves the gag back into his mouth.

Partridge

GUNSHOT WOUND

WITHIN A HALF HOUR, Partridge is standing next to Albertson at the entrance of the Personal Loss Archives. They knock and wait. It's the middle of the night. Will anyone be on duty?

A woman's pale face appears in the small rectangular window beside the door. She's startled to see Partridge. He waves. She freezes for a moment and then holds up a ring of keys. She disappears. The locks are clicking open.

She opens the door wide. "Can I help you?" She's a small woman with a sharp bob.

"I was hoping for a few minutes. There's someone I want to look up," Partridge says.

She glances behind her and then says, "It's after hours. We don't usually have visitors, but in *your* case," she says, flustered. "Come in."

"Thank you."

"You know your father doesn't have a box yet."

"I'm not here for my father."

Albertson says, "I'll give you your privacy." He looks at the clerk who nods quickly.

She locks the door. "Perhaps you know your way."

"I do."

"Okay then. I'll check on you in a few minutes."

As Partridge heads down the aisle, he feels a strange sense of calm. The last time he was here, he was a thief. He stole the contents of his mother's box. His father knew he would. He was played.

This time, he's aware of his father. In fact, at this moment, he feels closer to his father than at any of the memorial services—or is it that his father is closer to him? Closing in?

He finds the alphabetically correct aisle at the end of the room and heads down it. His heels hit the tile floor—quick, sharp knocks as if there's someone at a front door in the cold, waiting to be let in. He's afraid for a second that he won't have the nerve to open his brother's box—just like last time. But the feeling is fleeting. He will open the box, but he'll never know if what's inside of it is what his brother actually left behind or if it's something his father planted in the box for Partridge to find. That's the thought that slows his footsteps. He doesn't want to have anything more to unravel about his father. *Leave me alone*, he wants to say to the old man.

He runs his eyes over the names on the fronts of the boxes as quickly as he can. Under the names, there are the lists of causes of death. He's looking for Willux—Sedge Watson Willux. He walks past the Vs and into the Ws, and then he stops.

Weed.

Marta Weed. Victoro Weed. Arvin's parents' names. They were on his mother's list. Partridge asked Arvin about his parents. He said they were fine, that they had colds, but that was it. They're dead?

Their causes of death read, simply, CONTAGION.

And then there are two more names: Berta Weed, whose death is listed as HEART ATTACK, and Allesandra Weed, who has only one word written under her name: INFANT.

Partridge remembers the day of the field trip with Glassings' World History class. It was Arvin who asked if they could open the boxes. He'd found an aunt—maybe Aunt Berta. His parents weren't dead. Had his mother gotten pregnant again?

Partridge has the strange desire to open Arvin's parents' boxes. No one's here. He's alone.

No. These boxes are sacred.

He walks on a few steps and finds SEDGE WATSON WILLUX and next to it ARIBELLE CORDING WILLUX. He presses his fingertips to his mother's name. His mind replays the moment of his brother and mother's death—together—the kiss, the explosion, the blood spraying finely all around them.

He shakes his head. "No. Alive. I want to see her alive." He closes his eyes and thinks of her on the beach, ankle-deep in the ocean foam lining the shore. Her hair is windblown. She's looking out at the horizon. He whispers, "Look at me." And she turns her head, and he can see her face. She brushes her hair back and looks at him with love. Real love. His throat aches.

He opens his eyes. His brother's cause of death is still the same as it was the last time Partridge was here, the lie that he used to believe: GUNSHOT WOUND, SELF-INFLICTED. He hates his father for killing off his brother—twice. Once with a lie. Once by flipping a switch.

The last time he was here, he couldn't bear to see his brother's life reduced to the contents of a box. But now, he'll take what he can get.

He pulls the small box from its slot, holds his breath, and opens it.

It's empty.

He fits his hand inside and presses it to the bottom of the box— the way Sedge once taught him to dive to the bottom of the deep end of a swimming pool and press his hand flat. A quick sharp memory. Sedge taught him to swim.

He pushes the box back into its slot then quickly pulls the handle on his mother's metal box.

Nothing, of course. It holds nothing at all. Was he expecting something? Does he still want something from his mother?

Yes, he does. He misses her with a sharp pang.

"Not much to steal this time, is there?"

He turns around and there's the clerk. She pulls her cardigan in tight around her ribs and crosses her arms. Partridge must look guilty. He doesn't know what to say.

"I was on duty the last time you were here. In fact," she says, dipping toward him so that her bob swings forward, cupping her cheeks, "I was the one manning the cameras when you took your mother's things."

"You reported it to my father, I guess?"

"Oh, the chain of command is long and byzantine. I didn't know why you were supposed to steal the things. I just knew that it was good if you did and that we should then let you go."

"It was a pretty elaborate setup," Partridge says. "I'll give my old man that much."

The clerk nods. "He tried it with Sedge too. A very similar plan. A few years before you showed up here."

"What do you mean he tried it with Sedge?"

"Oh, Sedge was sent here on a field trip too—not with that teacher of yours. This was someone else. And he went to his mother's box. And inside of it, there were bits and pieces, knick-knacks, like the ones you found. But he didn't steal them. He couldn't. He looked around, and we were watching by way of surveillance cameras—me and another clerk in charge of reporting it but not stopping him. No, no. We knew he wanted to steal her things. We made sure he was quite alone. But there was something in him that wouldn't let him take them." The clerk smiles at the memory. "Not as much of a thief as you!"

So his father tested Sedge. But did his refusal to steal count as passing or failing?

"Sedge took a lot of time, though," the clerk says. "He read a little birthday card—that one was for him, of course, with his name in it. He looked at the necklace with the bobble attached to it, and something else."

"A music box?" Partridge says.

"Yes. It *was* a music box. And if you ask me, he realized something when he held those items. He felt something deeply. He was shaken by what he found. He knew something that he hadn't known before."

"Maybe he knew our mother might not be dead after all."

"Is that it?"

Partridge nods.

"He went into Special Forces afterward. I heard that he was the first to volunteer to leave the Dome. He wanted to be *out there*." The clerk runs her hand down a few of the handles. They each click, metal against metal. "Maybe he went looking for her. Not the way you did, but in his own way."

He handed his body over to Special Forces. He became a fighting machine, a nearly speechless animal. He somehow maintained some part of himself, and in the end, he never turned on Partridge. He fought for him.

Partridge puts a hand over his eyes, bows his head. He starts crying. He imagines Sedge the moments after knowing what was in his mother's personal archives box. Did his father also leave the hint that his mother might still be alive beyond the Dome? Had he felt like he wanted to scour the earth for her, the way Partridge had? "I miss him," Partridge says.

"You think a person only exists in a body? No, no," the clerk says. "Not any more than a person's life can fit in a small metal box. He's here," the clerk says, and she waves her hand in the air as if it's suddenly charged with electricity. "All of 'em," she says. "They're all around us! Everywhere!"

LYDA

WHEELS

LYDA DOESN'T HAVE MUCH TIME. Pressia, still dressed as a guard, is asleep on the far side of Lyda's bed but could wake any moment.

Lyda gently opens her bedside table and pulls out her *Baby's Own* baby book. She sees her writing. *I crave. I crave. I crave.* The words cover page after page. It's all she's ever written inside of it.

The margins are bare. She turns the book sideways and writes along the edge of the outer margin just what Pressia told her she'd write to Bradwell—a coded message: *Our lives aren't accidents. This is the beginning, not an end. Do what you have to do.* And she draws a rough picture of a swan floating on a ripple. She may have sounded like she'd lost it last night, but she was still thinking clearly—about the next step and how to get there. She was wildly heartbroken, but there's no wildness to it anymore. Now she feels a sharp relentless ache. She knows what must happen. Pressia might not be sure it's time to take down the Dome, but Lyda is.

She rips the edge of the paper that she's just written on. She let Freedle loose last night, and now she clicks her tongue softly, calling for him. She hears ticking and then a whir of his wings, and moments later he alights on her open palm. Lyda whispers, "Once upon a time, Pressia's mother set you loose to find her daughter. And you did. This time, hopefully Cygnus will get you all the way out of the Dome, and you will have to find Bradwell and give him this message."

She lifts one of Freedle's wings, and through the thin casing of his light body, she can see the inner mechanisms. Lyda rolls the long thin message and fits it into the cicada's body, but she leaves a small tail—a little bit sticking out, something one of the others on the outside might notice.

The cicada opens his fine metal wings, flaps them, lifts from her hand, and flits around the room.

Lyda opens the closet door. She pushes through the maternity dresses, their hangers squeaking along the rod, but when she gets to the back of the closet, reaching for her handmade armor of woven hangers, there's nothing. It's gone.

Did they come in last night and take it? Have they known it was here all along? She feels invaded, betrayed—and stripped of the thing she'd made to protect herself.

She hears two voices in the hall talking quickly, urgently. Lyda presses her ear to the door. She recognizes Chandry's voice—high-pitched and whiny—and the guard's bass. She imagines Chandry coming in, pawing through her clothes, and ripping out the armor. It's probably already been thrown away.

The voices stop. There's a squeaking noise, something rattling along the wood floors—something on wheels? And then there's banging in the nursery. She knows what's happening. They're tearing it all down.

The noise wakes Pressia, who stirs and sits up.

Lyda presses her finger to her lips.

"What's going on out there?" Pressia asks.

"It's Chandry Culp. She's the one who's teaching me to knit and, well, trying to teach me how to be a good mother. She's taking apart the nursery. She's breaking it down."

"Your mother ordered Beckley to get everything in the nursery replaced."

"My mother," Lyda says. "She has the proof they'll need to put me away after they take the baby from me. My mother will report that I'm certifiably crazy. Maybe I am." She sits down next to Pressia on the bed.

"No," Pressia says. "Don't say that."

"Girls!" It's Chandry's shrill voice. "Girls, come out here now!" Is Chandry going to make Lyda take the nursery apart—as punishment?

Lyda clicks her tongue for Freedle again, who peddles through the air.

"Freedle!" Pressia says.

"He's fine!" Lyda says, and she quickly cups him and puts him in the pocket of her sweater. "Best to keep him hidden."

Pressia grabs Lyda's hand. "Is there a way?"

Lyda knows what she's asking—is there a way out of here? "There's always a way."

They step into the hall. The door to the nursery is open enough to see Chandry in a shiny blue pantsuit, leaning over a large rectangular bin on wheels. She's picking up a bundle of hand-whittled spears. The orb is gone. Chandry has been hard at work too. She's a little breathless and perspiring. She's muttering to herself angrily. "What a pretty mess we've made! What a pretty, *pretty* mess!" When they appear in the door, Chandry looks up. "You!" she says to Pressia. "Start helping!"

"And me?" Lyda asks.

"Someone reported the orb's broken. A repairman is here." Lyda looks at Pressia. She remembered to tell the guard! "He wants to know what's wrong with it exactly," Chandry says. "Personally, I don't think you should have access to that orb anymore! But does anyone ask my opinion? No! No they do not!"

"Okay," Lyda says. "I'll go check on him."

"And then come right back here. You have been wicked. Do you understand me? Wicked. And it has to stop!"

"I promise," Lyda says. "No more of it!"

Chandry gives a final nod, and Lyda walks quickly to the living room. There, at the dining room table, is Boyd, wearing a gray jumpsuit, working on the orb. "You came so quickly!" Lyda says.

He stands up and smiles. "Always at your service."

"Have you fixed it?"

"I'm working on it," Boyd says. "It's a wiring issue, I believe." There's nothing wrong with it at all, so does this mean he knows he's been called for a different reason?

"Well, I really needed your help," Lyda says.

"I'm smoothing it all out."

"Do you have to take it with you to the shop? I thought maybe it would need to be taken out." She means that she hopes he will help them get out—Pressia and Lyda together. But will he understand?

"I see your point," Boyd says. "Yes. And I've thought of that."

"You have?"

"I have."

Boyd screws a back panel onto the orb, tightens it up. He hands it to Lyda. "It's all better, though! See?"

She admires it. "Aren't you a lifesaver?" Lyda says, meaning, *Save us*.

"It was nice to see Chandry here this morning," Boyd says, idly packing his tools.

"Do you know her?"

"We're neighbors, actually. Mr. and Mrs. Culp are great people."

Lyda's alarmed. Is Boyd trying to tell her something?

"The kind of neighbors who help others. You know?"

"Really..." Lyda says.

"Really," Boyd says. "You can always trust a Culp." Is he telling her to trust Chandry? Lyda feels like crying. Is this a joke? Trust

Culp? *Chandry?* If she trusts Chandry, and Boyd is wrong, she'll wind up in the rehabilitation center. But if Boyd is truly part of Cygnus and so are the Culps, then this may be their only chance.

Boyd reaches out to shake her hand. He's leaving. She hugs Boyd and whispers, "Return him to the outside. He's a messenger. Let him go." She takes Freedle from her pocket and slips it into the pocket of Boyd's gray jumpsuit.

When she releases him, he looks confused, but she has to have faith that Boyd will find Freedle and do as she told him and that Freedle will have sense and strength enough to deliver the message. Lyda smiles at Boyd, pats his shoulder.

"Be careful with the orb," he says, but he glances at her belly. He means, *Take care of the baby.* Is he saying that he won't see her again—for a long time?

"I will, Boyd. Thank you," she says. "Thank you for everything."

"You're welcome. I hope it all works." He smiles at her—weary but with a hint of hope.

She smiles and then clips back down the hall.

When she walks into the nursery, Pressia is nowhere to be seen. The large plastic bin on wheels sits in the middle of the room. Chandry looks at her searchingly then glances at the cameras mounted in the high corners. The cloths hiding the cameras are gone, but one seems like it's been twisted so that it points mostly into a corner, leaving part of the room out of view.

"Are you just going to stand there?" Chandry says. "You should have been made to do all of this yourself!" Her tone is still harsh. Is she putting on a show? She picks up a spear. "Here," she says, nodding to the bin.

Lyda takes the spear and walks it to the bin. She looks into it, and there, amid all of the mess of her room—the remains of books and spears, pieces of Lyda's dress, the shell of a few books, even the bowl of ashes, now overturned, and all that's left of the crib—is

Pressia. She looks up and nods. *Trust Culp.* This is what she seems to be saying. Lyda drops the spear into the bin.

Chandry has a bundle of spears in one fist. She backs up close to the wall that the camera isn't filming. "Bring that bin closer," Chandry says. "Stop lazing around!"

Lyda complies. She pushes the bin to the spot Chandry is now pointing at. Once there, Chandry gives a nod. She means, *You're out of view now. Get in.*

The bin is dark and cluttered with the debris of her room. As Lyda climbs in, Chandry keeps talking. "I don't know what possessed you to make such a disgusting mess! A child is a holy, holy gift."

Soon, Lyda and Pressia are sitting on the floor of the bin. It's dusty with ash, like home.

Chandry is dropping in the last few spears, saying, "You were going to bring this child into this awful place? What were you thinking? Your mother was right about you."

This stings. What did Lyda's mother say about her?

"You need help! Real professional help! You'll probably never be right in the head. It's a permanent condition!"

Lyda closes her eyes. She knows why Chandry is saying this; it's a warning. She means that Lyda has to get out now. Her mother will be coming back for her with a team of professionals. She'll be taken into the rehab center and never allowed to leave. A permanent condition. Lyda thinks back to what she read in her psychological evaluation: *lifelong institutionalization.* She opens her eyes. Pressia reaches out and grabs Lyda's hand. She must know this is hard for Lyda. It's like losing a mother, in a way. Maybe it's worse. A rejection. Pressia squeezes Lyda's hand, and Lyda squeezes back.

Chandry closes the lid, and the bin goes dark.

The bin starts rolling. Lyda can feel the jostling wheels. She listens to their light squeaking.

Chandry has taken them out of the room. She stops in the hallway for a moment. Has she left them?

No—she's back, humming a little tune, pushing the massive garbage bin.

She says to the guard, "The poor girl has had a shock. We don't want her to lose the pregnancy. Let them both sleep the rest of the day. They've eaten. They're tucked in. Do not disturb them. Do you hear me?"

The guard must nod because Chandry starts moving again, the wheels catching and jittering beneath them. Lyda reaches down to steady herself and feels the tightly woven metal—her armor. It's here. Maybe Chandry knew this was the way for Lyda to keep it.

EL CAPITAN

ANGEL

EL CAPITAN'S ARMS ARE CORDED, and he hangs on the metal frame of what used to be a tall swing set behind an elementary school. Helmud is gripping his neck. There's a line of people waiting their turn to beat the two of them with sticks. He can only see through the puffed slit of one eye; the other is swollen shut—this was from the earlier beating: a free-for-all. The survivors' bodies are bent and warped, but the blurring of his one weeping eye takes away the details of their scars and fusings, which is a mercy.

They've chosen their own sticks—some thin and whiplike, others heavy as two-by-fours. One survivor is armed with what looks like an old golf club, bent and kinked. El Capitan and Helmud are covered in a mix of bloody cuts, deep bruises, and welts. El Capitan's body burns hot and bright with a pain so sharp and deep that his mind feels loose.

And he remembers being little—he was blindfolded, given a stick, and told to beat a brightly colored donkey strung to a tree branch. It was a birthday party. He'd worn new corduroys that swished with each step. His mother stayed the whole time, which was strange, and she held Helmud's hand instead of letting him wander.

El Capitan knew the birthday girl was from a rich family because they had a swimming pool—though it was fall and the pool was capped.

They'd already opened the presents, and the kids at the party had made fun of his gift—a plastic doll. It was a cheap present, and the birthday girl was too old for it. And so when his turn came, he beat the donkey as hard as he could. And when they said his turn was over, he kept beating it. He beat it and beat it until he heard a pop and the candy rained down, spraying everywhere as the donkey gaped and swayed.

He took off the blindfold and watched the kids scramble. Helmud wrestled loose from his mother's grip and joined them, but El Capitan was even angrier now. The kids had been rewarded for laughing at him. "Go on and help yourself," the girl's father told him, pushing on his back.

He refused. He wasn't going to dive for some rich kid's scraps. He stood there and watched. Later, he stole some of Helmud's candy; someone owed him something.

Now he's the donkey.

Even if he had no other fault or sin, he deserves this beating for losing the bacterium alone.

He hears people calling his name—jeering. His vision is blurred by sweat and blood. He blinks into the bright light of day. The sun—even clouded as always—sears a burning pain into his skull. He sees Dome worshippers mostly, but some of the mothers have also wandered in. They hate him plenty. He recognizes a few OSR soldiers too. Hasn't he done good things for them?

Their gaunt faces jump into focus then out again. His recruitment posters promised food without fear and that solidarity would save them. He left, and they were ravaged. They've come to view his violent execution because El Capitan abandoned them, because a lot of them have died and those who are still holding on are starving to death. He knows what it is to be abandoned. As a kid, he searched the sky for airplanes, hoping for some small connection to his father, a pilot who left the family before El Capitan could gather even a few memories of the man.

Still, the soldiers look almost happy. Survivors love a beating. There's so much to pay for. Whenever anyone is chosen to shoulder some blame, it's a relief. El Capitan knows that feeling. He killed people and sometimes thought, quite simply, *People deserve to die.*

But he said he was sorry. And whether it was God or Saint Wi or some spiritual force he can't even comprehend, he felt forgiven. Why are they letting him suffer like this? Does he deserve this beating? Has God already given up on him?

Some of those who stand in line are wiry and stronger than he would think, while others wear their strength with hardened shoulders and beefy guts. El Capitan and Helmud aren't blindfolded, which seems unfair, as none of them ever just swing at the air. But they are only allowed to hit him three times each. If someone winds up to strike a fourth time, Margit is there to keep the line moving. "Hold it," she says. "Everybody here wants theirs, so back in line."

He looks for Bradwell. He was forced to watch the free-for-all, but he wasn't beaten in the process. The survivors still hold him in some regard. He's gone.

Some of the survivors say a name when they beat him—someone dead, someone El Capitan killed or could have saved if he hadn't helped set up such an evil regime as the old OSR. Each name rings in his mind. At first, he arched and fought the blows then only braced for them, and now he accepts them.

A short man with wide-barreled ribs strikes El Capitan's thighs with a two-by-four. "Minnow!" he cries. "Minnow Wells. My Minnow!" It sounds like the pet name for a child—like the way El Capitan's mother in some deep way changed who he was when she stopped calling him Waldy. Was Minnow this man's daughter or son? His sweetheart?

El Capitan takes the blows. "Minnow. Minnow Wells," he whispers.

He knows there will likely be a final blow, like the one he dealt the piñata. He'll probably die of internal wounds rather than blood pouring from him. Will his heart stop first or will Helmud's?

He once imagined what it would be like to tell Pressia that Bradwell was dead. Will Bradwell be the one to tell her that he and Helmud are dead? He hopes that in that moment she realizes that she loves him. That's all he's wanted. He imagines that she'll cry and that Bradwell will be the one to comfort her.

In this scenario, they might be sitting inside of a cracked Dome.

They might have made it all the way to that reality—without him.

He got close.

Someone hits him so hard that his body arches and then sways. The crowd—now hundreds of them—cheers. But El Capitan remembers being weightless—up in the sky on that airship. If he has a soul, and if the soul leaves the body once someone dies, he'd like it to take off like that airship.

I'd like to fly. It's a new prayer. *I'd like to fly just once more.*

He's fighting to stay awake. He feels a dull shade being drawn over his eyes. Darkness. He fights it. His body bucks. His hands are blue claws strung over his head. He tries to wet his lips and tastes blood. He hears his brother's voice humming in his ear—a dim song, one El Capitan can't place.

The beatings have stopped. There's a rush of wind in El Capitan's ears. Things have gone quiet and still.

Except there's a voice.

El Capitan forces open one eye.

He sees Bradwell's wings arching over his shoulders. The wind buffets the feathers. The survivors are still holding on to their sticks and clubs, but they've gone quiet.

Bradwell has a way of talking that makes people listen. He always has. Shadow History. The underground. He had a following. He led a movement.

Has Bradwell convinced Gorse to let him talk to the people? Is he making a case on behalf of El Capitan and Helmud? Is Bradwell trying to save them?

He hears the word *evil*. Maybe Bradwell isn't trying to save them at all. El Capitan knows what evil feels like—on your skin it feels like hatred, but when you find it riding low in your gut, it's really fear. Fear is where evil comes from. And hatred always came so easily to El Capitan because he hated himself—so deeply, so thoroughly, like he'd been shot through with self-hatred, a spray of buckshot.

For a vengeful second, he thinks, *Let them beat me to death. Let them beat their hate into me.* He knows that beating him to death will be their punishment. Killing someone—that can't be washed away. They'll have to carry it around—easier in a group, easier to shift the sin from one person to the other, but never painless. They'll have his death forever.

Helmud's too.

Equality—that's what Bradwell is talking about now. In this world?

But whatever he says, it works. Someone has climbed the top of the old swing set and is sawing at the ropes with a knife. Other survivors have wrapped their arms around El Capitan's legs so he and Helmud are caught once the ropes snap.

Their lives have been spared. By God? By Saint Wi? By Bradwell?

And then Bradwell is there. He hugs El Capitan and Helmud.

"What happened?" El Capitan whispers through his swollen, split lip.

"I struck a deal with Gorse. I promised to take him to his sister if he'd give me a couple of minutes to address the crowd. And then I told the people I was sent from God. An angel."

El Capitan smiles even though it hurts. "The wings helped."

"Finally they're good for something," Bradwell says.

"Good," Helmud says.

Bradwell calls some survivors over. "Get them cleaned up. El Capitan was lost, but now he's found."

The survivors start giving each other orders. They gaze at El Capitan and Helmud, perplexed but a little awestruck too. The look makes El Capitan nervous. He always preferred fear to admiration, but maybe it's the same thing. Power. For a second, he wonders if Bradwell really saved him and Helmud because he loves them like brothers or because of some other more complex reason. Maybe he knows Bradwell needs El Capitan to get what he wants. And what does Bradwell really want? To take the Dome down or to get Pressia back before she decides to stay there?

"What's next?" El Capitan asks Bradwell, but Bradwell can't understand him. El Capitan's voice is so raw he can only whisper, and his lips are so puffed his words come out garbled.

Bradwell kneels down and lays a hand on his chest. "What did you say?"

"What's next?" Helmud says, speaking for his brother.

Bradwell says, "We await word."

"From Pressia?" El Capitan asks.

"We await word from on high," Bradwell says loudly so everyone can hear. "Who else? Where else?"

The brightness zeroes in on Bradwell's face. Blackness swallows the edges of El Capitan's vision. He blinks and blinks and tries to say something. But then the world is dark.

Partridge

DREAM

Partridge wakes up; a figure's looming over him. He jerks, sits up. "What the hell?"

He's on the couch in his honeymoon suite. The curtains are drawn except for one small inch of light...and there's Foresteed, staring down at him. He's wearing his military uniform—an old one from the days of the Righteous Red Wave. A red armband is cinched around his bicep, medals glint on his chest, and a cap sits slightly cockeyed on his head.

"What the hell do you want?" Partridge says.

"This is what we've been waiting for, Partridge. All these years. It's time." His voice sounds almost nostalgic.

"Time for what, Foresteed?"

"They're coming for us. Your father is dead. It's just us now. Just us."

"Who's coming? You're not making sense. Jesus. Where's Beckley? Where's Iralene?"

"I wanted us to talk alone," Foresteed says, reaching into the pocket of his dark uniform jacket. "I have another little recording for you, Partridge." He pulls out the handheld and gives it to Partridge. "Press play."

"I don't want to hear any more recordings. You got me?"

Foresteed unbuttons his jacket, reaches into a holster strapped around his chest, and pulls out a small pistol—again, it looks like it's from the Before. He holds the gun at his side, pointed at the floor. "Press play." It's the calmness of his voice that scares Partridge the most—detached, bloodless.

Partridge swallows dryly. He touches the play button. The screen remains dark, but he hears voices—lightly muffled but still distinct.

"We have to get you out." It's Pressia's voice, unmistakably. "They're going to put you away and take the baby once it's born."

Partridge glances at Foresteed, but Foresteed has his back turned. Pressia isn't talking to Lyda, is she? *They won't take the baby*, Partridge wants to say. *That's crazy.* Where did Pressia come up with that? His pulse quickens.

"I want to go back to the mothers," Lyda says. "This place— it can't be saved." Partridge almost laughs. Lyda can't want to go back to the mothers. She's here, safe. But he knows that Lyda didn't want to come in in the first place.

"Listen," Pressia says. "We have the means to take down the Dome."

"Do you hear that?" Foresteed mutters, turning back to Partridge. With a stiff arm, he starts banging the pistol against his leg.

"Are you really going to?" Lyda says. "Can you?" She sounds hopeful. My God. Why would she want to take the Dome down? Is she just jealous of the wedding? Has she believed Pressia about the baby being taken away? Has she gone crazy?

"If Partridge has turned on us," Pressia says, "we might have to."

That's it. The sounds fade away. Partridge stares at the black shiny screen. "Turned on them?" Partridge says. He feels utterly betrayed. "She walks in here, sees a wedding, and thinks she's got a handle on the whole situation?" Partridge is stunned, but then he hears the beat of Foresteed's pistol steadily banging against his leg. Foresteed thinks Pressia's going to take down the Dome. *This is what we've been waiting for, Partridge. All these years. It's time.* He thinks the wretches are coming for them. "Listen, Foresteed. They can't take down the Dome. There's no way."

"You don't know anything. That trip to Ireland put her in contact with a very advanced people who might see us as a threat."

"No, no." Partridge rubs the back of his neck. "Something's wrong. You've taken this recording out of context."

"We have to put a stop to her," Foresteed says. "She can't be allowed to gain any momentum. I've had to take action."

Partridge stands up. "Foresteed...what did you do?"

"I'm arming our militia in the Dome."

"You're giving out guns to people who've been killing themselves?"

"Only our militia—able-bodied men. We must defend what's ours. The Special Forces troops out there now are pathetic. They were rushed—a bad batch. We have no one protecting us anymore. Not really. I had to open up the stocks."

"This is crazy. Let me talk to Pressia and Lyda. I can set them straight. It's just a mix-up."

"You can't talk to Pressia and Lyda," Foresteed says.

"Why not?" Partridge says, feeling threatened.

"They're gone."

"What? Are you kidding me?" Partridge walks to the curtains and pulls them wide open. There's a view of the street. He sees people bustling below, running in all directions. Panic. Are they carrying guns? It's a disaster. "Gone where?"

"If we knew where they were," Foresteed says, "you'd be able to talk to them."

Partridge turns to Foresteed. "Have they gotten out of the Dome?"

"We have no evidence that anyone has escaped. We think they're here somewhere."

"It's a Dome, for shit's sake! It can't be that hard to find them!"

Foresteed lifts the pistol, rubs it gently. "You know what we could be in for..."

Partridge takes a deep breath. He imagines the Dome being infiltrated by Beasts, Groupies, the mothers, the OSR... He sees the Pures—pale and dazed, completely unprepared, walking around in their cardigans, their boat shoes. They'll be bludgeoned to death. The Dome will be ransacked. Special Forces will only make things bloodier. The inferior race—Pures. The wretches will bring diseases with them—ones they've already survived but that the Pures won't have immunities to. If the Dome's seal is broken, the air itself will choke them. Chaos. Bloodshed. A huge death toll. And then it hits him. "If my sister says she has the means, it's the truth."

"We have outside confirmation," Foresteed says. "We've captured the traitor who led them to the airship. We've gotten enough data from him to confirm that they have some kind of agent—chemical warfare of some kind."

"What traitor?"

"A Special Forces soldier who went rogue."

Not Hastings. Not Silas Hastings. Please, no. "Who?"

"Someone you once knew well, it turns out. Hastings."

Partridge tightens his grip on the curtains. "You didn't torture him to get—"

"No. He tried to fight it, but there was only so much he could do. He's programmed to give in to us. Behavioral coding," Foresteed says wistfully. "If only your mother hadn't blocked yours."

Partridge is thankful for that. He can still make his own decisions—for better, for worse. "Can I talk to him?"

Foresteed walks up to Partridge, stepping into the beam of fake sun streaming through the window. Foresteed is glazed in sweat. He lifts the gun and positions it in the soft pocket behind Partridge's jawbone. He says, "We are going to be ready. Your sister, if found, will be executed. And you, Partridge—you'd better do the right thing and help draw her in. Because you know what happens in a revolution?" Foresteed pushes the pistol in deeper. "The wretches will chop your head off first, but not if I'm moved to do it for them. Do you know what I'm saying?"

Partridge nods, and then, like a shot through his gut, he thinks of his own baby. Will his child be strong enough to survive if the Dome is taken down? Just because the child was conceived out there doesn't mean it will be tougher or more immune.

"Do you have a plan?" Foresteed asks.

"I need to get her grandfather for her. I need that." Could he trust Arvin to send word out among Cygnus? Did they help her escape? Or are they looking for her too?

Foresteed squints. His eyes tighten to watery beads. He says, "Can I trust you?"

"You already said it. My father's dead. It's just us now, Foresteed. You and me."

Foresteed smiles with one side of his mouth and lowers the gun. His eyes quiver over Partridge's face. "That's right. You and me." Foresteed straightens his Righteous Red Wave uniform with a few quick jerks. It's possible that Foresteed is looking forward to this, as nostalgic as he is for the good old days of the Righteous Red Wave. He gives Partridge a quick salute and then walks to the door, his pistol still held in one hand. Without looking back, he says, "Get the old man." And then he walks out the door and down the hall.

Partridge tries to rub away the lingering feeling of the gun pressed under his chin.

Beckley appears. "Report went out. State of emergency. Recorded message from Foresteed. He said the wretches are going to rise up. He said the time is now. Is it true?"

Partridge studies Beckley's face for a moment. "I know what you think of me."

"You do?"

"You think I'm in too deep. You think I have no idea what I'm doing. You think I'm going to drown. Sink or swim, and you're betting I sink."

"Are those metaphors? I don't understand metaphors."

"Knock off the bullshit. You think I'm sinking, don't you?"

"Partridge, we don't have time—"

"I can't even tell if I'm sinking or the water's rising all around me." He looks around the room seeing none of it, feeling blind.

"Partridge, what can I do? Give me an order."

That's right. Partridge is supposed to be in charge—even if he has no power, Beckley's on his side, isn't he? "You've got to get me to Peekins—the chambers."

"We should go fast. It's starting to get chaotic out there."

"Iralene's coming with us. And no one can see us."

"I'll figure it out."

"Glassings. I need him safe. I need to talk to him too."

Beckley shakes his head and looks out the window, as if he's trying to figure out the weather—as if it could change. The skin around his eyes is dark—sleeplessly so.

"Beckley. What is it?"

"Glassings."

"What about him?"

Beckley looks at Partridge. "He died in the night."

"What do you mean? Was Foresteed involved? Did he do it?"

"Blood clot. In his heart. Foresteed's men were moving in to interrogate him about Lyda and Pressia, but he was gone."

Partridge wonders if he knew on some level that they were coming back for more, if he willed himself to die because he couldn't take another round. "I should have gone to see him. I went to the Personal Loss Archives to see my brother's box—it was empty. I could have been there. Maybe I could have . . ."

"He's gone, Partridge. Now you have to concentrate on the living."

Partridge feels fatherless—an orphan who's been orphaned again. "But I need to see him. I need Glassings. I can't do this alone..."

"You've got to have some faith in other people."

Partridge sees a man running diagonally down the street, a rifle strapped to his back. Militia. Partridge looks up and sees his own reflection. *I'm not my father*, he wants to tell the hazy image of his own face. *I'm not my father.* But then he remembers the clerk's vibrating hand again. Yes, his brother is everywhere. His mother is everywhere. But so is his father. He says, "I'm Willux's son. What have I ever learned about having faith in other people?"

Beckley walks over and grabs him by the arms. "Get Iralene. We have to go. Now."

Partridge walks quickly down the hall to the bedroom. He feels robotic. He can't process Glassings' death. He grips the cool knob. He opens the door. He thinks of life and death—a thin membrane that separates the two. A doorway...sometimes closed, sometimes open.

Iralene is sleeping peacefully, her light curls covering the silky pillow.

He walks to her, sits on the bed, and gently shakes her shoulder. "Iralene," he whispers. "Iralene, wake up. Iralene."

She opens her eyes and rolls to her back. "I was having a dream," she says. "I'm still not used to how real they are, Partridge. It was so real."

"A good dream this time?"

She nods.

He rubs his fists together—knuckles bumping over knuckles. "I'm scared, Iralene. Foresteed's told the people that there's an uprising coming."

She sits up and puts her hand on his chest. "We'll be okay, Partridge. No matter what."

"No," Partridge says. "If they come at us, people are going to die, Iralene. Do you know what I'm saying?"

She wraps her arms around him. She whispers, "In the dream, we were happy. We had a house, and it had flowered curtains. You built the house, Partridge. It was in a field, and the wind blew through the grass. I think it was the future."

"I don't think that's how dreams work, Iralene."

"It was so real. It was better than the orb. We walked from room to room and peered out the windows. What would you say if I made a place like that real?"

He likes the sound of Iralene's voice. He closes his eyes for a moment and imagines the house.

"Tulips," she says. "That's what was stitched on the curtains. Tulips—thousands of them. I could touch the stitches with my fingertips, and then when I looked outside of another window, there was a field of tulips, bobbing their heavy heads in the breezes."

"It wasn't just an orb?"

"No, it was real. Do you think I haven't heard about the home that Lyda made for you, that dark ashen world from the orb? She's not the only one who can make a home for you, Partridge."

"Who told you about that?"

"I know things—more than you give me credit for."

"I didn't mean it that way. I just...What home are you talking about making for us?"

"What if they could create a home for us where we'll all be together? All of us. Even those you've lost, Partridge."

A world with his mother and Sedge? Not his father—not him, no. "Glassings died in the night." He can only whisper the words.

"Glassings could be there too," Iralene says, as if she's not afraid of death, and maybe she isn't.

"That's what they call heaven, Iralene."

"But what if it could be here, in the Dome?"

"It's not possible. You're still dreaming."

"We could be happy there. It's the future that we could walk into one day, if we want. Lie back," she says. "Lie back with me and dream a little." She looks dreamy. Her eyes are so crystal clear and beautiful.

He can't dream—not even a little. He has to bring Pressia's grandfather back up for air. He has to find Pressia and Lyda—that's who he's supposed to walk into the future with. "No." He's already wasted too much time. "You can't be here alone. It's no longer safe. Come with me."

"Where else would I want to be?"

"I'll let you get ready," he says.

She promises to be quick.

He walks to the door, closes it quietly, and jogs down the hall, hoping Beckley's found a way to get them out of here without being seen.

As he walks into the suite's living room, he sees a stretcher, covered in white sheets. It's not logical, but he thinks of Glassings; this stretcher can't be for him. He's dead...

The door to the suite opens. Beckley's talking to someone in the hall, thanking the person in a hushed voice. He shuts the door and, holding two lab coats on hangers, turns to face Partridge, who says, "What's wrong? Who's sick?"

"Not sick," Beckley says. "Dead."

"Who?"

"For now," Beckley says, "you."

PRESSIA

ANOTHER SKY

THE AIR IN THE BIN IS CLOSE and warm because of their bodies. Pressia and Lyda have shifted so they're sitting side by side. They hold hands like sisters. Pressia would have liked to have had a sister. She remembers what it was like to hide in the cabinet in the back of the burned-out barbershop, alone.

As Chandry pushes them along, Pressia tells Lyda about Ireland—the boars; the blind, vicious creatures in the woods; the thorned ivy. She confesses what she did to Bradwell, and as she does, she can see his large, dark wings. She says, "I want to get back to him." In fact, right now, trapped in this bin, moving to some unknown location, she would leave if she could. The vial, the formula, saving lives…Sometimes she wishes someone else could take over for her. Maybe she's just being a kid, but she misses being protected, watched over. She misses her grandfather.

She doesn't tell Lyda that she and Bradwell are married. It's not something anyone else would understand. Can a forest be a church? Are two people's whispered promises enough?

Lyda squeezes her hand in the dark. "I understand," she says. "Right now, it's like I can sense my other self still out in the woods—running through the trees. I want to be her again…"

"It's not the same out there," Pressia says, and she explains the effects of the most recent attacks from the Dome—the fires, the destruction, the Special Forces who are younger and rawer and easier to kill. And the soldiers who are like Dusts. The deaths on both sides of the battles.

"And the mothers?" Lyda whispers.

"They've survived better than most. Mother Hestra wanted me to tell you that she misses you, that you're like a daughter to her."

Lyda sighs. "I can't live in here for the rest of my life, Pressia. You have to understand. This place has to be stopped. You remember me when I first made it out—pale and weak. I was bred to be pale and weak," Lyda says. "I was raised to be quiet and sweet. I didn't know what I was capable of. You go around thinking that it's not fair that the wretches have to live out there. But I know that it's not fair that the Pures have to live in here—behind glass, batting around in our little fake world. If the Dome fell, it would be a mercy—not for the wretches, but the Pures."

"I don't know…" Pressia says. "Are you sure about that, Lyda? Do you really believe it?"

"It's something you might never understand. But that's my truth. Mine."

"I have the cure, Lyda. I have what they need to help survivors, to save them. Can't we try to…"

Lyda squeezes her hand in the dark again and tells Pressia about the inner chamber in the war room. "There's a button. It can release a poisonous gas and kill the survivors. All of them."

"Who has access to it?"

"Only Partridge."

"He'd never do it," Pressia says.

"Even if he thought he was saving people in the process?" Lyda says. "Don't you think he might be able to rationalize it?"

Pressia says, "I don't know what's going to happen, but I promised the mothers I would try to get you out. That's what you want?"

"More than anything."

The bin comes to a stop.

"One more thing, Pressia. Partridge can communicate with other people in distant places. If your father is out there..."

Pressia isn't completely surprised. The communication system is how Bartrand Kelly knew that Willux was dead and Partridge was in charge. "If I could talk to my father, I'd want to hear his voice. I'd want him to know I'm here. But I can't think of any of that now. I can't."

"I want to think about what it was once like between Partridge and me—how we loved each other. But I can't think about that either."

They hear the squeak of door hinges. And then they're moving again down what seems to be a ramp.

The cart stops once more.

Chandry pulls open the lid, and there, overhead, are stars—thousands of them. Miraculous, inexplicable stars like bright pinholes into other distant worlds. They both stand up, and Pressia expects a gust of wind.

But no, they're not outside. The image overhead is not the sky. They're in a theater with curved rows of seats. The sky is only a ceiling—darkness dimpled with bulbs of light.

EL CAPITAN

WORD FROM ON HIGH

THE PLAYGROUND WHERE El Capitan and Helmud were strung to a swing set frame and beaten is part of an elementary school, and El Capitan is lying on his side on a moldy handmade cot in what must have once been the library, now roofless with just the beams and rafters left behind. They're surrounded by metal bookshelves, some of them still clotted with hunks of char and dust—what used to be books? Helmud is taking up most of the flat, dank pillow—so foul it's not really worth the slight comfort. Sometimes an ex-OSR soldier comes in, gives them sips of water, and quickly leaves.

El Capitan hears voices, smells the smoke of campfires. How many people are out there? He hears sheep. No—a baby crying. His eyes are nearly swollen shut.

Where's Pressia gone? To the Dome. Where's Bradwell? Not here. Did he just leave them, surrounded by shelves of dead books? El Capitan gets tired again. He dozes and dreams.

He remembers the way his mother read to them, remembers the big wide pages in the books. El Capitan on the top bunk, Helmud below. Each of them cocooned in white sheets. Summer. A box fan in the corner chopping air—a constant whir. The moon locked in the window.

When she got sick, he wanted to save her. When she was gone, he took over. He sat in her chair and read books to Helmud. One cocoon empty above. When Helmud slept, El Capitan put his face in front of the revolving fan, let it stutter his voice—singing into it from behind.

He's being prodded. Helmud shifts on the cot behind him.

"A few broken ribs. Mostly contusions. All the cuts have been stitched. Hopefully internal bleeding has stopped." The voice is rough and low. "Maybe a few fractures in the legs. Hard to say."

And then there's Bradwell's voice. "How soon before he's able to get up and move?" El Capitan can barely see their faces through the slits of his eyes.

"They suffered dehydration. But they're taking fluids. They should be on their feet soon—or *his* feet, I should say."

The dust in the air—the char of pages, bindings. How much time has passed? El Capitan can't tell if it's been hours or days.

Bradwell is at his side, kneeling. The other person leaves. Bradwell straightens El Capitan's jacket. "How you doing?"

"Fine," he mutters.

"Helmud? You okay?" Bradwell says.

El Capitan feels the bob of Helmud's head.

"Good," Bradwell says, and he backs up and takes a seat on his footlocker.

"Where did that come from?" El Capitan asks.

"I had to go and get it from headquarters. You know how I am about it."

"One day, you'll let it go," El Capitan says. He's let go of his own past. He's clean of it.

"One day." Bradwell raps his knuckles on the top of it. "In this footlocker, my parents are still alive in a way. I started rewriting their manuscript. We have more proof. I wrote a lot of stuff, Cap. I needed to. I'm glad you're better." Bradwell stands up and shoves his hands in his pockets. "I was worried."

"You're still worried," El Capitan says. "I can tell."

Bradwell looks around the room, crosses his arms on his chest. "I went back to the vault."

"Why?"

"I hid the bacterium there in one of the slots that used to be a safety deposit box."

El Capitan feels like a balloon has erupted in his chest. "Thank God!" He feels like crying. "I thought..." He decides not to confess to losing it. Why admit such utter failure? "That was smart."

"I got the bacterium off you while you were drunk. Didn't think you were in the best shape to keep it safe. And I had just enough time to hide it as they came storming in."

"Thanks and sorry about that," El Capitan says.

"Well, there's just one more thing," Bradwell says.

El Capitan knows he doesn't want to hear this. "What?"

"It's gone."

"Gone?" Helmud says.

"Are you sure you checked the right slot?" El Capitan says. "The wall was filled with slots."

"I checked them all." Bradwell runs his hands through his hair. "Someone took it."

"Gorse?"

"I've talked to all of the people who were in that vault. They're on my side now. They're acting like I'm a god. It wasn't any of them. I'm sure of it."

He'd like to reach out and choke Bradwell—an ancient instinct. But, of course, he thought he was the one who'd lost it. He can't really blame Bradwell, and he doesn't have the strength to choke anyone right now anyway. And then he realizes how he really feels about the bacterium. Maybe he actually wanted it gone. "I'd be relieved that it's out of our hands," he says, "except that means it's in someone else's."

Bradwell looks at him, confused. "Why would you be relieved?"

"We can't take down the Dome."

"What?"

El Capitan wants to tell him that he's been forgiven. He's clean. "I can't go back."

"Back to what?"

"Who I used to be."

"We have to do it, Cap."

"Why?"

"So there is no divide. Aren't you tired of being nothing? Of being something left to die?"

El Capitan can't look at him. He's been nothing for so long he can't imagine anything else. "There will always be a divide. There will always be us and them. And if this divide disappears, there will be another us and them."

"They have to face up to what they did."

"Why?"

"They're all waiting for me—Dome worshippers, revolutionaries, OSR, even some of the mothers. Solidarity will save us—you said that. Even the Dome worshippers believe that this could be a way for them to join the Pures, in their own screwed up way. They've come down from headquarters and up from the city and out of the woods and Meltlands. They want me to lead them."

This hurts. El Capitan has been trying to amass an army all these years, and Bradwell comes along and takes it from him. He knows it's not the point, but still. "How many are there?"

"Too many to count. And now I've got nothing."

El Capitan sits up, leaning Helmud's back against the wall.

Helmud says, "Count." Maybe Helmud thinks they need to know exactly how many they'll have if they end up heading into some kind of battle.

"Now is the time," Bradwell says. "We need the bacterium. How else will the Pures learn?"

"Do you mean how else will you get a chance to punish them? Are you really playing God?"

"Willux played God—not me." He grinds his boot heels into the dirty floor. "Pressia's locked in there, Cap! You want me to just abandon her?"

"Are you doing all this just to get her back?" Will Bradwell be the hero in all of this? Pressia has pushed El Capitan to do the right thing. Isn't he finally doing it? Isn't that worth something?

"I'm doing this because it's the mission. Up until now, it was *your* mission."

"You said you taught Shadow History because we had to learn from the past so we wouldn't repeat it. Isn't this just another apocalypse, a smaller one—on your own terms this time?"

Bradwell sits on the ground, lowers his head into his hands. His wings fan out on the floor around him. He rubs his eyes. Is he about to cry?

"What?" El Capitan says. "What is it?"

"I lost the bacterium. We got drunk, Cap. We got drunk. We woke up. We got captured. I tried to hide it. It's gone." He looks at El Capitan. "What am I, Cap?"

"What do you mean?"

"Am I a human being? An animal? Am I even still my parents' son? What do you think I am?"

"It doesn't matter what I think."

"It does to me."

"You're a prophet. That's what some say. An angel, maybe, with those wings. You believe in the truth. That's why Pressia loves you."

"How could she love me like this?"

"Now you know how I feel."

"How I feel," Helmud says. Is he in love with her too?

"You really do love her, don't you?"

El Capitan nods. Bradwell seems to accept this. For some strange reason, he even seems like he's glad to hear it. "She hasn't sent word yet, right? We have time. Maybe we can find it."

"Maybe," Bradwell says.

"Word from on high," El Capitan says, remembering how Bradwell put it. "There's still some time."

Helmud says, "On high." El Capitan can feel him arching his back, looking up through the roofless library at the sky. "On high!" he says again.

"We know, Helmud. We know. Shut it, okay?" El Capitan says.

"On high!" Helmud says again, and then he grabs El Capitan's chin and pushes it upward.

"Get off!" El Capitan says.

Helmud points at the sky.

El Capitan looks up grudgingly. Bradwell does too.

And there is a small dot, jittering in a circle, fluttering down.

"What's that?" Bradwell says.

The little thing sputters and spirals closer.

They all stare at its fine metal wings as they flit and flit closer to them.

Freedle.

He lands on the bottom of El Capitan's cot, lifts his wings. Helmud reaches out. Freedle hops up on his hand. Helmud lifts him up. And El Capitan sees the small white edge of a piece of paper that's been slipped into the cage of his body.

A message.

PARTRIDGE

EVERYWHERE

Partridge is strapped onto the stretcher and covered entirely by a white sheet. They're out of the hotel now. Iralene and Beckley, dressed in white lab coats and surgical masks, guide the stretcher down side streets, the wheels rattling over the pavement. He can only see the lit-up sheet, sheer and bright over his eyes. He knows people are running nearby. They pass clusters of voices. A fight breaks out—he can hear two angry men shouting.

There's a scream then more distant shouting—a few gunshots.

He's supposed to be dead, but he feels very alive—his heart is sore, each beat like a punch inside of his chest. Glassings is dead. They might all die. Could his sister really be conspiring to take down the Dome? Is this sheet that covers his face—the thin, white sheet drawn into his mouth each time he takes a breath—a warning? Death—is that his near future?

He hears Beckley shout, "Watch the curb!"

The stretcher swerves, slams onto concrete.

They're moving as quickly as they can. They hit divots, jerking his body around. There's no car waiting for them this time. Luckily, they're on the same level in the Dome as the high-rise with the suspension chambers.

Partridge can't stand not being able to see. He pinches the sheet, inches it up on one side, and turns his head. He has a sideways view of it all, the streets jammed with people. Some are running, trailing kids, carrying jugs of bottled water and boxes of soytex pills. They're packed into stores with lines that snake around the block. Some are busy sealing windows with tarps and duct tape out of fear that the protective Dome will be broken. Because of Foresteed, some have rifles strapped to their backs.

Still, they push along. As a dead man, he's ignored. The Pures have gotten used to death. They're bracing for more. Their faces are a mix of fear, panic, and a strange resignation—as if something they've been waiting a long time for has finally arrived.

But then he sees someone writing on one of the posters, Partridge and Iralene on a date—a man scrawling in dark red paint across their faces: SCUM MUST DIE.

Partridge is shaken. These people loved him and Iralene. They were why he got married—to keep them happy, to give them a reason to live. And now they're scum? They must die? He lets the sheet fall. Is he going to be killed by Pures? Is this how it's going to go?

Once inside the building, Iralene and Beckley quickly unstrap Partridge. They all run through what's becoming a more familiar series of passages and long eerie halls, passing dimly lit rooms buzzing with the machinery that keeps the suspended people alive.

"Just up ahead," Iralene says.

Partridge follows her and Beckley around a corner and sees a door, the light spilling out of the room into the hall. Iralene and Beckley slow. Partridge reaches the door, pauses, and then knocks. Peekins and a nurse look up from a chart.

"Ah, good to see you, Partridge," Peekins says. "I'm glad you could make it under the ... circumstances."

The room is surprisingly bright and warm. Beckley and Iralene hover near the door, keeping an eye on the hall.

Partridge walks up to the capsule and can see the fogged outline of Odwald Belze's face—his stiffened white hair, his closed eyes, his sallow cheeks—crystallized with a thin layer of ice. The scar on his neck is red, preserved when it was a fresh surgical wound. Partridge remembers the small blue box that held the fan removed from his throat, and Pressia's face when she realized that this meant her grandfather was dead.

"Things are breaking down fast," Beckley says.

"We've got to move quickly," Iralene says.

"How do things look?" Partridge asks.

"Just a little longer, and we'll know if there's any long-term damage," Peekins says.

"Damage? I thought he either survived or he didn't."

"There are a lot of scenarios in between," Peekins says, obviously frustrated with him. "Quiet, please."

Peekins and the nurse work quickly. They move the capsule into a horizontal position. The bright, incubated heat defogs the glass. The heartbeat on the screen near the capsule picks up speed. In fact, Partridge worries the heart is beating too quickly now. The beeps come fast.

With an electric hum, the glass retreats into the capsule, revealing Belze's face—rigid and wet with melted ice crystals.

"Engaging full lung capacity," Peekins says, and he inputs data into the computer, his face fixed with concentration.

Belze's rib cage heaves, jerking up and down, and then he pulls air in through his nose. His head kicks back, his cheeks and jowls bobble, and then his face flexes. His eyes clench. His lungs seem locked.

"He's not breathing!" Partridge says.

"Hold on," Peekins says, his eyes ticking over the control panel. "Just hold..."

Belze's heart starts to race—the beeping is shrill and relentless—but he lies there rigidly.

"He's going into overdrive," the nurse says.

Partridge shouts, "Do something! We can't lose him!"

And then Belze takes another breath in, which seems impossible. He's now holding too much air. His face flushes a deep purplish red.

"Hold on," Peekins says. "Hold, hold, hold."

Belze's lips start to turn bluish.

"Jesus. He's dying," Partridge cries out. "He's dying right here in front of our eyes!"

Iralene tries to pull Partridge back from the capsule. "Partridge," she says softly.

Peekins suddenly looks panic-stricken. "I don't know what more to do! I've never done this with someone so old!"

And then the heartbeat goes flat. The beep turns into one solid, deadly note.

Partridge reaches out and grabs Belze's shoulders, which are still cold.

"Get back!" Peekins shouts, but Partridge pushes the old man's body enough to wedge his knee onto the capsule then leverages himself onto Belze's rib cage. He pushes down on his chest with all his strength.

Nothing.

Beckley shouts, "Partridge! Let him go!"

Partridge pushes on his rib cage again.

"If you're going to do it, do it right!" Peekins shouts and points to the spot where Belze's ribs join at the center of his chest.

Partridge rears and pushes down, his elbows locked. The old man is still rigid.

Partridge shuts his eyes and does it again and again. "Don't die!" he shouts. "Don't die!" He can feel the old man's thin skin, the bones of his chest, the give of his ligaments.

"He's gone," the nurse says.

"Partridge," Peekins says. "Stop!" He shoves Partridge in the shoulder. "Stop!"

Partridge, breathless and sweating, keeps going.

"It's a lost cause," Beckley says.

"Stop, Partridge," Iralene says. "Please!"

And Partridge wonders if they're right. He opens his eyes. The old man's face is taut. He is already dead. Partridge keeps going. He feels like crying, but then the machine skips. There's a heartbeat... and another. The man's eyes flit open and lock on to Partridge's.

Belze's chest jerks up and down. His eyes are wide. He breathes out a deep, rattling wheeze.

"Odwald," Partridge says. He leans in close to the old man. "Odwald! You're here! You're okay!"

Partridge hops down. Peekins and the nurse work quickly now, stabilizing Belze. Not long after, he's calm. His breathing and heart rate are steady. Partridge says softly, "We're going to get you together with Pressia, okay? She misses you. She wants to see you. Okay?"

"Pressia," the old man says, his lips trembling with her name.

"Yes. She misses you."

"My wife."

Partridge shakes his head. "No, your granddaughter."

The old man looks at him confused. "Where am I?"

"It's okay," Partridge says. "It's okay."

"Where's my wife? Where's Pressia?"

"Your granddaughter," Partridge says.

"I don't have a granddaughter. How could we when we couldn't even have our own children?"

Partridge looks at the others.

"He's disoriented," Peekins says. "Maybe it's temporary."

"This happens sometimes," the nurse says.

Partridge walks to a wall and leans against it, trying to clear his head.

"Where am I?" Belze says.

"You're in a hospital," Peekins tells him calmly. "You're going to get well."

Partridge says, "He wasn't her real grandfather. He found her after the Detonations and took care of her as his own. He must have named her after his wife. She was like the child they never had."

Peekins is explaining things to the old man. "You've been through an operation, and you've been in a kind of coma, but you're going to be okay."

Beckley says, "He's here but he's gone."

Partridge stares at the floor. He's not finished here. He walks out of the room and down the halls. He's running even though he feels dizzy. With one hand along the wall, he pushes off of it as he makes a turn.

Iralene and Beckley are following him. "What's going on, Partridge?" Beckley shouts. "Where are you going?"

"Partridge!" Iralene calls.

They know where he's going. He keeps running jaggedly down the halls until he comes to the high-security chamber—the one that's all locked up and waiting for Partridge to figure out some code, some password.

Partridge stares at the door, breathless, as Beckley and Iralene catch up. "What you got in there? What have you left for me?" He's speaking to his father directly. He's *everywhere*; he's inside of him.

"Maybe you don't want to know," Iralene says.

"Maybe you can't know," Beckley says.

Partridge turns around and shoves Beckley. "Pressia's grandfather doesn't remember her. I brought back her grandfather—but part of him is still dead. You try to hand that over to Pressia as a gift! You try it."

"Easy now," Beckley says, raising his hands.

"What if her father's in there? Hideki Imanaka is the person my father most hated in the world. My father loved his little relics. He'd have kept a relic of Imanaka if he could. And he could do anything just about, right?"

Beckley walks up to the heavy metal door.

"I've done everything I could to make progress. I need this to be Pressia's father. I need this."

"We've tried a lot of combinations, Partridge," Beckley says. "We can't get it open."

"Blow it up."

"Your father made sure that this wasn't about a show of force," Iralene says. "It was about a secret. Something that maybe only the two of you would know."

Partridge runs his hands through his hair. "My father and I didn't share secrets! We didn't share anything." Not even love, Partridge thinks. His father didn't even love him. That's what Partridge said to him before he killed him. *You'll never understand love.*

Does his father want love?

Partridge looks at Beckley. His hands still hold the memory of compressing Odwald Belze's ribs. They're shaking, like his father's once did. It's like the old man won't ever leave him. It feels for a brief moment like his father got his way, that he transferred his brain into Partridge's skull and is inside of him forever. He hates his father more than ever, and he knows what his father wants now—what he's demanding.

"I have to know what's in there, Beckley." He grips the sleeve of Beckley's lab coat. "I have to tell him I love him."

"What?"

Partridge knows that his father wants it to come from Partridge's own mouth. "There's a speaker," Partridge whispers, his back turned to the sealed door. "He wants me to say it."

"You sure that's it?" Beckley sounds unconvinced, but he doesn't know Willux like Partridge does.

Iralene puts her hand on the cold metal of the door.

"The room inside the war room was filled with old pictures, love letters—written to each of us. All the things he never said. Because he never said them, he never heard them back. I know what he wants. I've never been so sure of anything in my life."

Partridge knows it because his father is inside of him—a haunting from within. That's what he can't tell Beckley.

"Say it," Iralene whispers.

Partridge turns toward the door. He walks up to the small speaker. He clamps his mouth shut and shakes his head. He won't say it. He can't. He wants to say, *Leave me alone.* Is this what happens to all murderers? His body is a prison. Partridge slams his fists on the wall over his head.

Partridge tries to think of someone else. He can fake it. But his father is there in his head—his curled, blackened hands, his hissing breaths. A wretch in the end. And then, he's not sure where it comes from, but he says, "A wretch like me." There's a song about being a wretch, about the grace of God. He wants to tell his father we're all wretches. We all need saving. He puts his mouth to the speaker. "I love you," he says. "You're my father. I always loved you. I had no choice but to love you."

Somewhere inside of his father's elaborate locks, his words meet some criteria. Was it just his words? Was it the ache in his voice that activated something? He'll never know.

The clicking begins. The door finally gives. Its seal is broken. Cold seeps from the chilled room. Fog rolls into the hallway.

Partridge puts his hand on the door and slowly pushes it open.

An overhead light flickers to life, illuminating four small capsules.

Partridge walks up and sees infants in each of the capsules. They lie on their sides. They have tubes in their mouths. Their skins are all lightly crystallized and tinged blue, the way Jarv Hollenback's was when Partridge first saw him down here. The room also has one table in the corner with a metal box sitting on top of it.

"Four little babies," Iralene says, walking into the room and leaning in close to one of them.

"My God," Beckley says as he steps through the door. "My God."

Partridge doesn't understand. He looks at Beckley who blanches and backs away.

Beckley grips the doorframe and looks at Partridge, wide-eyed. "Jesus, Partridge. Don't you know?"

Partridge shakes his head and looks at Iralene. He watches the realization wash over her face too. He looks at the capsules again. This time he searches the edges of them for nameplates. He finds a small silver tag on the front of each capsule with initials: RCW, SWW, ACW, ELW.

RCW—his initials: Ripkard, his real name; Crick, his middle name; and Willux.

SWW—his brother's initials: Sedge Watson Willux.

He grips this second capsule, and then moves quickly to the third nameplate: ACW. Aribelle Cording Willux, his mother.

He says, "No, no," as his eyes dart to the final nameplate: ELW. His father. Ellery Lawton Willux.

Could this be his family—rebuilt?

He thinks of the premature babies behind the bank of windows in the nursery. Clones—made from the genetic coding of Pures and wretches.

Is he looking at his mother and father—as infants? Is he looking at Sedge and himself? Is this what his father has given him? His family, returned?

One of his knees buckles. He grabs the edge of a capsule and walks to the metal box on the lone table. He stares at it for a moment. His ears are rushed with blood. His eyes blur. He blinks, and the box clicks back into focus.

He has to open the lid.

"Don't," Iralene says. "Leave it."

But he can't. He pushes the lid off with his thumbs. It clatters against the table.

Inside, there are medical instructions—a schedule for aging the specimens so that they will eventually have the correct age differences to be a family again. ACW and ELW have to be brought out and aged for twenty-five years, and then SWW can be brought out.

Partridge's mother and father had Sedge when they were twenty-five years old. RCW can be brought out two years later.

And then...what did his father have in mind? They would be a family? A normal family? Reunited and whole?

Maybe his father didn't regret killing his wife and his oldest son because they were still alive.

Partridge walks back to the capsules—the tiny infants. What will he do with them? This is his inheritance.

Beckley's radio squawks. Has Partridge's sister set her plan in motion? Are the survivors invading? Is this the beginning of another bloody war? He says, "Iralene, tell me something in this world matters. Tell me something is sacred."

"You matter," she whispers. But this isn't what he needed to hear.

Beckley walks back into the room. "Lyda and Pressia have been found."

"Do you think it's started?" Partridge asks.

"A group has formed not far from the Dome," Beckley says. "According to reports, they seem to be moving."

Iralene and Beckley step into the hall, and for a moment, it's only Partridge and the infants. His father thought he was doing the right thing too. But now Partridge knows he isn't his father. His father will always be foreign to him. Partridge is going to try to save the Dome, not because of what it stands for or what it aspires to be but because each person matters. He can try to save lives.

Iralene tries again. "Home is sacred, Partridge."

"We have to bring Lyda and Pressia into the war room. Odwald Belze too."

"Family is sacred," Iralene whispers. "A home filled with family."

He walks into the hall. The lights in the room flicker out. The door automatically closes. The only noise is the sound of the locks clicking into place.

EL CAPITAN

FITTING

OUR LIVES AREN'T ACCIDENTS. *This is the beginning, not an end. Do what you have to do.*

Bradwell reads it over and over, aloud, his fingers pinching the edges of the small strip of paper. His hands are shaking so badly that the hand-drawn swan looks like it's shivering. "How the hell are we going to take it down with no bacterium?" Bradwell says.

"Hell if I know," El Capitan says.

"Hell!" Helmud says angrily.

Outside, the people have started buzzing with noise—there have been a few shouts and unclear chants.

From his bed, El Capitan finds a view of the gathering crowds through the blackened bookshelves and the crumbling wall.

"What's going on out there?" Bradwell says.

"No idea," El Capitan says.

But then, the crowd parts, and Our Good Mother, flanked on all sides by mothers, is striding toward the remains of the elementary school. She's bundled in fur except for the bare skin on her bicep where the baby's mouth is lodged, and he knows that she's coming to find El Capitan and Bradwell, and once she's in the room, he'll be able to see the baby's small pursed lips.

The baby scares him most of all.

"She's here," El Capitan says.

"Who?"

"Our Good Mother. I feel like I'm about to get in trouble," El Capitan says. "I hope she's not armed."

"She's always armed," Bradwell says.

"Always," Helmud says.

El Capitan pulls a thin sheet up over himself, as if this will serve as some kind of protection. "I hate it when the mothers call us Deaths."

"I hate it when Our Good Mother calls us at all."

The tarp flap set up between two bookcases is pulled back. Our Good Mother walks through it followed by three other mothers who then stand by the doorway.

"Leave us alone for a moment," she says. "Guard the door." They glare at El Capitan and Bradwell, then leave reluctantly.

"I don't think you've ever paid us a visit before," Bradwell says. "What's the occasion?"

"Don't take a tone with me, Death. I'm here out of the goodness of my heart." She looks at El Capitan, his face mottled with bruises. "So they finally got their revenge."

"Maybe not all of it," El Capitan says.

"All of it," Helmud says, disagreeing.

"Well, you can't blame them," she says.

El Capitan doesn't respond. He blames himself, and the feeling is new and strange. He doesn't like it.

"Why are you here?" Bradwell says.

"I'm here because you need me," Our Good Mother says.

"Really?" Bradwell says. "Because I feel like we've gotten a pretty good show of people here. We might be set." El Capitan knows Bradwell doesn't want to be indebted to Our Good Mother. She has brutal ways of settling debts.

"Please—you're disorganized, unarmed, and weak. And I think you're missing something very precious to you. Am I right?"

Bradwell opens his mouth to say something, but El Capitan cuts him off. "What's that? What have you got?"

"We've been trailing you—just keeping tabs. And you left something behind. You know what it is," she says coyly.

"You're missing my point," El Capitan says. "I'm not convinced that *you* know what it is."

"I know it's small. I know it's powerful. I know it's essential to your plan. I know that if one of you starts off for the Dome alone, or even if you go together, you'll likely be killed in the process. Have you noticed the shiny new guns that are now on top of the Dome's roof—a wreath of weaponry?"

"What?" Bradwell says. "New guns?"

"They're preparing for war," Our Good Mother says. "Are you?"

Bradwell's massive wings unfurl and twitch.

"This will be a massacre either way. Why don't we help you take down the Dome and make it a fair fight?" Our Good Mother says.

El Capitan shakes his head. "I can't go in fighting," he says. "I won't. That's not who I am anymore—not ever again."

"This doesn't have to be an act of aggression," Bradwell says. "We don't have to be attacking them. We're attacking the Dome itself. We could be setting them free."

"You're hoping to approach with your small special delivery, correct?" Our Good Mother begins. "We have to be prepared for the possibility that Pressia has let it slip—or had news of your *weapon* beaten out of her. They might know a good bit, in fact. If we surround the Dome and come all at once, they won't know which one has this special delivery. It could be any of us. Where to start shooting? How to begin the massacre? We all arrive and circle in tight. We live as a mass; maybe we will die as a mass. But at least we are all together. To kill the right one, they'll have to kill us all."

"They'll start mowing us down with machine guns," Bradwell says. "They won't care who they shoot."

"Only those who want to circle will circle," Our Good Mother says. "No one will be forced."

"If Partridge is truly in charge," El Capitan says, "he won't have the stomach to kill all of us."

"And if he's not really in charge?" Bradwell says.

"We'll find out, once and for all," Our Good Mother says. She reaches into her animal skins and pulls out the square metal case containing the bacterium. "Are you in?"

Bradwell looks at the crowd through the crumbling wall. "I'm in only if I'm the one who brings the bacterium to the Dome," he says.

Our Good Mother shakes her head. "They'll aim at you first, Bradwell. They'll suspect you most of all."

"I won't have to get in too close." He walks to the bookshelf where Freedle sits on his small pronged legs. "If I get shot, we can still make sure the bacterium makes it."

"That little creature?" Our Good Mother squints at it. "I remember it now. This was a gift for Pressia from her mother, right? It was how her mother knew that Pressia was being taken care of?"

"Right," Bradwell says.

Our Good Mother leans in close to the delicate metal cicada. "Her mother is still with us. This is what mothers do. We watch on—even from the grave." She gives a nod. "This is fitting. Yes. I approve." With that, she moves to the tarp flap, but before she leaves, she turns back and says, "I had a husband once. You must know that. He left me before the Detonations hit. He's inside of the Dome, my Death is. Do you know what I'll do once the Dome falls?"

"What?" Bradwell asks.

"I'll hunt him down like an animal and kill him in cold blood— preferably with my bare hands." She smiles. "Mrs. Foresteed killing Mr. Foresteed. I confess, some aspects of war can be very intimate."

Pressia

DOLL HEAD

CHANDRY, LYDA, AND PRESSIA stand in the center of the planetarium on a small circular stage, with the bin that delivered them here between them. The theater is darkened as if it's dusk. The stars glint overhead.

"Everything has shut down—stores, schools, restaurants," Chandry says. "That's why we could arrange a meeting here."

"Shut down?" Lyda asks.

"They know what you have," Chandry says to Pressia. "They know your plan."

"What are you talking about?" Pressia says, refusing to let on. She's not convinced she can really trust Chandry. She trusted her enough to get into the bin because it was their only way out, but giving up this secret is different.

"Your revolution. They know."

"Revolution?" Pressia says. She's never thought of it as a revolution before, but of course Chandry is right. That's exactly what it could be.

"We are preparing," Chandry says, "for the worst, which might be for the better, in the end."

"Preparing how?" Lyda asks.

"With military force, of course. Armed militia. The Righteous Red Wave is needed once more." Chandry looks at her watch nervously. Pressia knows the stories of how the Righteous Red Wave took power before the Detonations—a rule of terror and oppression; she wants to know who they're waiting for. "Who's coming?" Pressia says.

"A doctor," Chandry says, and she glances at Pressia's doll head, as if the doctor is coming to cure her.

"Arvin Weed?" Lyda asks.

Chandry nods.

Pressia knows the name. "He came up to me at the wedding reception." She feels immediately guilty for bringing the wedding up in front of Lyda. She can sense Lyda's bristling. "He wanted to talk to me."

"He was desperate to get you to a safe place to talk," Chandry says. "And here you are."

"What does he want?" Pressia asks, aware of the metal box still pressed safely against her skin.

"He thinks you might have something. Something…" Chandry searches for the right word. "Essential."

Pressia's stomach flutters. Could this be the person she's wanted to meet? "You know him? Is he trustworthy?" she asks Lyda.

"I don't know who to trust. Isn't that obvious by now?" She's looking up at the fake stars.

"Is he part of Cygnus?" she asks Chandry. "Like you?"

"I knew your mother," Chandry says. "We were in a playgroup together—a cover for meetings."

Any mention of her mother makes Pressia feel physically hungry. She tries not to sound too desperate. "My mother? What was she like back then?"

"She was amazing. A thoughtful sharp mind, a deep heart. I thought the world of her," Chandry says, staring at her hands. "I thought she could save us." She looks at Pressia. "Maybe you can."

Pressia isn't sure what to say, but there's no time anyway.

They hear a click. The planetarium's emergency-exit door opens. A wedge of light slides into the room, and then the door clangs shut.

It's the young man she saw at the wedding reception—yes, she recognizes him immediately. He walks to the stage and then stands there awkwardly for a moment. "I've been trying pretty damn hard to get a minute with you," he says. "Finally had to do this the hard way." He looks at Chandry. "Thank you," he says. "Much appreciated."

"The least I could do," she says, and Pressia wonders if she's indebted to Weed.

He looks at Lyda and smiles. "Been too long," he says.

She says, "Whose side are you on? Just tell us the truth."

"I'm on my own side," he says. "Each one of us is. If you think any differently, you're delusional."

"What do you want then?" Pressia asks.

"I know the trip you've been on. I know what you may have had access to. I know you might be more like your mother than Partridge ever dreamed you could be."

"What's that supposed to mean?" Pressia says.

"You want to do the right thing."

"I want a lot of things," she says.

Weed locks his hands behind his back. "Tell me what those things are, Pressia. Maybe we can work a deal."

"I don't know if I can trust you."

"What do you want? Start there."

"I want Lyda to be able to get out of here. I made a promise."

Weed shakes his head. "I don't get it. You want to live out there, Lyda?"

"I don't care if you get it or not."

"Is that why you turned your back on Partridge? Because you wanted to leave him behind?"

"I never turned my back on him."

"You didn't return any of his letters, though."

"Did he send me letters?" Lyda asks. "Arvin! Did he write me?"

"Lots of them," Weed says.

Lyda takes a deep breath. She holds it in her lungs. Her eyes flash around the room. "I need to see him. I need to see him before I leave. Now," she says. "I need to see him now!"

"Wait, Lyda." Pressia turns to Weed. "I know that you Purified people here. I know that you created Special Forces but that those enhancements turn on people. The children you Purified…"

"What about them?" Weed says.

"They're dead. You killed them. You have the ability to Purify, but that process…"

"It erodes the body's most basic functioning." Weed holds his hands out flat in front of him, palms down. They tremble, ever so slightly. "Willux made me take the brain enhancements. He wanted me to use my mind to save him." He reaches out and holds Pressia's wrist, lifting the doll head. "Maybe it's not too late for either of us."

Pressia is breathless. Her heart feels like it's rising weightlessly in her chest. "I have what you need—a vial of my mother's serum and the formula. You can Purify, and I have what it takes so the process doesn't have any deadly side effects. There was another piece. That's what the formula is for and—"

"We have all we need, Pressia," Weed says. "I could start with you."

This is the moment Pressia's been waiting for. The doll head can be removed. She can be free of it. She can be whole again—herself, completely. And they can save the other survivors.

Lyda interrupts. "There's no time."

"We don't know when they're going to attack—if they even have the courage to try it," Weed explains, shoving his hands in his pockets. "Maybe we have time. Maybe we don't."

"They haven't gotten a message from me yet. They're waiting," Pressia says.

"No," Lyda says, looking away from them all. "The message has been sent."

"I didn't send it," Pressia says defensively. Does Lyda not believe her? "I didn't!"

"I did," Lyda says quietly.

"What did you tell them, Lyda?" Pressia says, grabbing her by the elbow. "What message did you send?"

"You know what I told them," she says, pulling her arm from Pressia's grip. "I told them to do what they had to do. I used the words you told me to and I drew a picture of a swan—so that Bradwell would know it was from you."

"Lyda, why? Why did you do that?" Pressia stares at the ground, trying to process everything—the shifting facts, the repercussions outside of the Dome—and coursing through it all, she feels betrayed. "You got me to tell you the code words. How could you do that to me?"

"I did it for all of us," Lyda says. She reaches into the bin, pulls out two spears, and hands one to Pressia.

"I'm not taking a spear, Lyda. Do you even know what you've done?"

Lyda reaches into the bin again and pulls out a piece of metal knit out of hangers. She puts her arms through the straps she's rigged. It fits snugly over her chest and stomach—where the baby is just starting to take shape. It's armor, handwoven. Lyda had to have made this—how? Pressia doesn't know, but it fits her perfectly. "I've done what I had to do," Lyda says.

"We've got to get you two to safety," Weed says, rubbing his jaw, obviously trying to piece together a strategy.

"I have to see Partridge," Lyda says again emphatically.

"That's where I'm sending you. But first"—he looks at Pressia—"I can protect the research labs, Pressia. There's an extra protection built in. If you give me what you have, I can keep it safe."

Pressia can feel the metal box against her ribs. "Do you promise to do the right thing?"

"I promise."

Pressia looks at Lyda. "Do you trust him?"

Lyda says, "Trust requires a leap of faith. Right now, what else do you have?"

Pressia reaches up under her uniform jacket and pulls out the box. When she hands him the vial and the formula within it, she's stricken with fear. Her hands shake as if she, too, is breaking down.

"Partridge is going to want you to call off the attack. The Pures have everything to lose, so he's going to throw everything at you—everything you would ever want. Be ready for it."

How could she prepare for being given everything she's ever wanted? "Be good to your promise, Arvin Weed."

"You know, Willux killed my parents too," Weed says. "I'm supposed to say that my little sister died of complications at birth. But she was a hostage. My parents did what Willux wanted, but he killed her anyway. And then when I was a little older, they caught colds and didn't recover, as if something benign as a cold killed them. I've played along, Pressia. I've played and played and played. And now I just want to save them."

"Who?"

"So many of them—too many to count..." Weed can't speak for a moment. His voice is choked by sadness. He coughs and says, "Willux made me create them. Now it's my responsibility to keep them alive." He looks at Pressia and Lyda suddenly as if so deep in thought he'd forgotten they were there. "I'll send word to Partridge that you're coming." He grips the metal box, raises it in his fist. "Thank you," he says, and as he walks back to the door, he shouts over his shoulder, "Take the spear, Pressia. At some point, you're going to need it."

EL CAPITAN

HEART

THEY'RE MOVING—ALL OF THEM: Groupies, mothers, OSR soldiers, Dome worshippers, even a few Basement Boys, and families that were smoked out of the city and headquarters and the outposts. There aren't many Special Forces left, but every once in a while, one will skirt the edges, sniff the air, and before getting shot, dart off.

The survivors crowd into the woods at the edge of the barren territory, which rises uphill to the Dome, gleaming white and crowned with sleek black weapons, its cross piercing the dark clouds.

El Capitan is propped on either side by OSR soldiers, who are shouldering his and Helmud's combined weight. His bones ache, especially his broken ribs, and his skin is turgid from bruises and deep swelling. Where the ropes dug into his wrists there are now bandages.

Bradwell is talking to a group of mothers. Everyone moves with quiet intensity, hushed electricity. El Capitan's relieved that their unifying purpose is no longer killing him and Helmud.

The mothers have been organizing the herd. Survivors fan out in either direction to circle the Dome. And they've sorted out the ones who will stay—children, those who will watch over them, and those who are more burden than help. They're putting up a few makeshift tents to cut the wind and cold, and that's where the two OSR soldiers stop.

"This one will work," one of them mutters.

"I'm not going in a tent," El Capitan says.

"Not going!" Helmud says.

"Sir, we were told to set you up in a tent."

"No. I'm staying with Bradwell. He goes. We go."

"We go," Helmud says.

"But you can't really walk, sir," the OSR soldier says.

"Bradwell!" El Capitan shouts, breaking the quiet.

Bradwell walks over. "What?"

"We're not sitting this out in a goddamn tent."

"Cap, you're not in any condition—"

"We're coming with you. Even if I have to crawl, we're coming."

"Seriously, you can't even—"

"I'm not going for the reasons I always thought I would. I'm going because I'm not letting you go alone. We're like brothers."

"Brothers," Helmud says.

Bradwell looks up into the tops of the stunted trees. "Fine," he says. "If you're coming with me, I want you to promise me something."

"What?" El Capitan says.

"If I don't make it," Bradwell says, "I want you to check my heart."

"Your heart?"

"Just make sure it's no longer beating. Make sure it's stopped."

"If you die, you want me to put my ear to your chest and make sure your heart's not beating?"

"Yeah. And take Gorse to his sister. That's what I want, and don't ask me anything more about it."

"Okay," El Capitan says. "You're not going to die anyway, Bradwell."

Bradwell doesn't respond to that. Instead, he says, "The wind is strong today. Isn't it?"

El Capitan nods. "Pretty strong."

"Hopefully it'll keep up," Bradwell says, and he walks away.

"The wind?" El Capitan says. "We're talking about the wind?"

"The wind," Helmud says.

Partridge

Tied With String

THE LONG MAHOGANY TABLE is actually a screen. It's projecting a live map—the Dome sits in the center. Partridge looks down at the image. Small dark flecks have circled the Dome, and more are coming—flecks are pouring out of the woods.

"It's produced through a compilation of various cameras that tag movement and follow it," Beckley explains.

"Each fleck is a survivor?" Partridge says. It's really happening. He realizes now that he never fully believed it.

"Correct."

Iralene hooks her arm around Partridge's. He's so disconnected that her touch surprises him. "There are so many of them!" she says.

Partridge's heart thuds in his ears. He feels a surge of pride. He can't believe they've organized and joined together like this. He imagines what El Capitan and Bradwell are feeling now. Are they at the head of this? Has it happened around them? But at the same moment, that surge of pride quickly switches to fear. They're gathering because they're expecting entrance. This isn't a feel-good mission. This is the beginning of a revolution.

"We have to communicate with them," Partridge says. "There's still a way to slow it all down! We have to do this peacefully. Do we have an update on Pressia and Lyda?"

"They're on their way," Beckley says.

The thought of Lyda makes his chest constrict. Why didn't she ever return his letters? Has she fallen out of love with him?

"You can talk Pressia into calling a truce. I know you can," Iralene says. "She comes from those people. She'll know how to communicate with them, right?" Wretches—that's what Iralene means.

Beckley's talking to someone on his walkie-talkie. "He's ready? Here now?"

"What's going on?" Partridge asks.

"I hope you don't mind," Beckley says, "but I took the opportunity to get someone who could be a liaison."

"A liaison?"

"You'll need someone on the ground to serve as a go-between. I thought of the perfect person. Someone who might seem... trustworthy to them." Beckley walks to the door, opens it, and in walks a tall, lanky Special Forces soldier hobbled by a sleek prosthetic, the soldier's leg ending in the thigh. The soldier stares at Partridge, and Partridge knows him.

"Hastings..." He tries to see his old friend, goofy and easily embarrassed. He misses him.

"Partridge Willux." Hastings' voice is more robotic than ever, but there's still something deeply human inside of him, something they can't erase.

Iralene is afraid of Hastings. She tightens her grip on Partridge's arm and shifts so that she's standing slightly behind him.

"What happened?" Partridge asks about Hastings' leg. The last time he saw Hastings, Partridge had told him to go find El Capitan. Did that lead to his loss? Is Partridge to blame? It wouldn't surprise him.

"An incident." Hastings has been shut down. He can only give short answers—the least revealing kind. He went rogue and they recoded him.

"I'm sorry about that," Partridge says.

Hastings nods. They're still old friends. Some loyalty remains.

"Hastings," Beckley says, "we need you to be our eyes and ears." Hastings is fully bugged. "We'll set you up with communication so we can speak directly to who's in charge down there."

"El Capitan and Bradwell," Partridge says.

"We'll give you a handheld that will transmit our voices from here," Beckley explains.

Hastings takes a deep breath. His bulky shoulders rise and fall.

"Beckley brought you in because you'd be the one they might trust out there, but really you're the one I trust, Hastings," Partridge says. "We go way back."

"You don't have to play on your old ties," Iralene says softly, recognizing something in Hastings. "He's programmed to obey you."

"She's right," Beckley says. "Foresteed doubled up on his behavioral coding. He'll never go rogue again."

"I want him to have a choice!" Partridge says. "Damn it! I want people to make up their own minds!"

Beckley walks up to Hastings. "Can you make up your own mind, Hastings?"

Hastings looks at Partridge and then at Iralene. He shakes his head. "No, sir."

"We have to get him out there fast," Beckley says, "if we've got any hope of negotiating."

"Okay, Hastings, go on out. Find Bradwell or El Capitan. Pressia will be here soon," Partridge says, hoping it's true. "When you find them, we'll be ready to talk. We can still turn this around."

Beckley walks to the hall and picks two guards to escort Hastings out of the Dome.

Before Hastings leaves, he glances over his shoulder. He gives

Partridge a look—it's all he has, an undeniable humanity in his eyes. The look is both accusatory and full of suffering. It's sharp and quick and sends a shock through Partridge. It's as if Hastings knows the future, and it's worse than Partridge could ever imagine. But before Partridge can say anything—and what would he say?— Hastings has walked out of the room, half lumbering, half limping.

He remembers Hastings talking to a girl at the last dance he ever went to, the one where Partridge danced with Lyda. How did they end up here—each newly broken in ways they never could have predicted?

"There's one more thing," Beckley says to Partridge as he steps back into the room. "Cygnus decided it was better if you and Lyda were split up." He reaches into the pocket of his uniform jacket and pulls out two bundles—stacks of folded paper, each tied with string. "Letters—from you to Lyda and from her to you."

Pressia

SACRED

PRESSIA AND LYDA ARE RUNNING along the streets of the
Dome toward the war room. Their spears are tucked into their
belts. Pressia took one that was small and sharp, just six inches
long and easier to hide. Lyda is wearing her armor. Everyone is
so panic-stricken, so dazed and angry and hopeful and lost, that
they don't even notice. A shop window has been shattered, and
people are on the street, fighting over flashlights and batteries.
Another group has blocked an official Dome truck and is looting
gas masks, blankets, bottled water. Pressia remembers the stories her grandfather told her about what happened just after the
Detonations—fights in mini-marts and sprawling superstores. The
posters announcing Iralene and Partridge's engagement, plastered
in storefront windows, have been defaced, their faces x-ed out,
DIE written in thick ink above their heads, along with nooses and
skulls.

"He's the goat," Lyda says. "Partridge is the goat!"

"What do you mean?"

"The scapegoat. They're going to blame him for everything!"

Pressia's scared. These people want blood. She knows that look
in their eyes. She remembers it from the survivors who took to the

streets during the Death Sprees. People can only suffer for so long before someone must pay.

She and Lyda cross the street to avoid the Pures, who are brawling in their overcoats and pantsuits and sliding around in their thin-soled loafers.

They head into a cloud of smoke. It's billowing up from a crowd in front of a church up ahead, roiling and roiling with nowhere to go.

"It's starting to smell like home," Lyda says. "Not just the smoke but the desperation."

They cover their mouths and noses with their sleeves and press on.

As they pass the church, Pressia sees that the crowd is burning an effigy—a stuffed suit with a crackling face. "Par-tridge! Par-tridge! Par-tridge!" they shout. Pressia can barely breathe. She's lost faith in her brother, but burning him in effigy?

She looks at Lyda, who's stricken. Pressia shoves her away from the crowd. "Just keep your head down," Pressia says. "Keep going."

Lyda stumbles a little, but they press on.

When they turn the final corner, Pressia slams into a guard. He grabs her by the arm. "Where the hell are you going?"

A woman is standing nearby. She sees the doll head before the guard does, and she screams.

"They're here already!" she screams. "Wretch!" the woman screams louder. "Wretch!"

The guard sees the doll head and falls backward, clawing for the rifle on his back. "Stop!" he shouts through the thickening smoke. "Stop now!"

But they keep sprinting as fast as they can. Pures around them are running and shouting. A gunshot goes off. Was it from the guard shouting at them through the smoke? Someone else?

Lyda pulls Pressia into a building, and they run across a broad, airy lobby with mirrored walls and beautiful gold trim. Another guard shouts, "This way!" They run to a sole elevator and step inside.

The guard hits a button. "He's been waiting for you."

"Which one of us?" Lyda asks.

The guard shrugs as if he doesn't even really know who they are, and now Pressia can tell that he's young—younger than she is. "Do you think I should stay?" he asks quietly. "I'm worried about my sisters. Should I leave? It's getting bad, isn't it?"

"Are you related to the Flynn girls?" Lyda says. "Did you go to the boys' academy?"

"Aria and Suzette," he says. "My parents are gone. They didn't make it much past"—he lowers his voice—"the speech. They did it in a good way—really well planned. No blood, and they arranged it so the maid would find them, not us. They were good parents." The boy shivers.

"Of course they were good parents," Pressia says. "I'm sure they loved you very much. They'd be proud of you now, thinking of your sisters." She knows what she always wanted to hear from her mother and father—*I love you. I'm proud of you.* She's hung on to the idea of them watching over her for so long...She can't imagine if they'd killed themselves.

Lyda reaches out and grabs the boy's sleeve. "You should go. Now's the time for people to talk about love. There might not be much time left."

Pressia thinks of Bradwell. She can't help it. Love. There it is. She'll always love him. Will they have more time together?

The elevator rocks to a stop. Pressia will never get used to elevators. The doors open, and Lyda and Pressia step out.

"This way!" another guard calls to them down the hall.

"I'm sorry about your parents," Pressia says, turning to the boy in the elevator.

His eyes tear up. "No one ever says anything like that here. No one talks about them anymore. It's like they disappeared."

"They aren't gone," Pressia says.

The guard lowers his head, and the doors glide shut. Pressia knows she'll probably never see him again. This is how everything feels now—a first time and a last, all in one.

Lyda runs down the hall. Pressia follows after her. As they pass a series of doors, Lyda ducks into a hall and presses her back against the wall.

"What are you doing?" Pressia asks.

Lyda wraps one arm around her ribs. "I just need a moment. Go on."

"Are you sure?"

She nods.

Pressia continues on. A door opens up ahead. Partridge steps into the hall. Pressia remembers the first time she ever met him—how, with his scarf unwound, she knew that he was the Pure that she'd heard about, the Pure with the short hair and the perfect skin let loose from the Dome. He reaches out—to shake her hand? Is this going to be formal? "I saved your life before I even knew who you were," she says. She doesn't accept the handshake.

Partridge puts his hands in his pockets. "That's right," he says. "Groupies were about to take me out."

"They wouldn't have, though, right? We were being herded together then, and we're being herded together now," she says.

"Maybe that's true."

"I have a feeling it's going to be different this time."

"We're in a lot deeper," Partridge says. "As deep as it gets."

"What have you done here, Partridge? Who have you become?"

"What about you? You turned on me. You gave up on me."

"No, you gave up on us," Pressia says.

"You have to call off the attack," Partridge says coldly. "We're getting a location on Bradwell and El Capitan and are setting up communication. Hastings is the messenger. It's all coming together. We'll be in dialogue—real dialogue—for the first time in the history of the Dome."

"And in this dialogue, you tell them what to do? Is that a dialogue?"

Partridge looks down the hall, and Pressia knows by the changed look on his face that Lyda has appeared. And then he says her name. "Lyda. Lyda Mertz." He starts to walk toward her, and then he starts running. Lyda stands completely still. Pressia doesn't know if she'll accept him or not. Does she really still love him, or does she just have to know whether he loved her at all—really and truly loved her?

At the last second, he slows. She says something that Pressia can't hear, and he says something back. He reaches up and touches her cheek with the back of his fingers. She hugs him then, whispering something to him.

Pressia hears a noise behind her and turns. There's a woman. She stares at Partridge and Lyda, and she takes a sharp breath in and a ragged breath out.

"Iralene," Pressia says, recognizing her as the bride at the wedding.

Iralene nods. "I have something that will change your mind." Iralene looks down the hall, and Pressia follows her gaze to Partridge, who is now holding Lyda's face in both hands, talking to her in a rush of words. "It was a wedding gift."

"Iralene," Pressia says again. "Are you okay?"

Iralene grips the doorframe. "It's heaven," she says, and she smiles at Pressia as tears slip down her cheeks. "I had them make heaven. Here. Right here. Because it's the safest place in the world. Here," she says, "let me show you heaven."

As she steps into the hall, her ankle buckles, and she teeters for a moment in her heels. She whispers so softly Pressia can barely hear her. "Come with me. I want to show you why you should tell them to stop. This will change everything. It will make everything right. You'll see."

Iralene walks a few feet down the hall. Partridge and Lyda notice her now. They look up, holding hands, just as Iralene opens a door, and suddenly she is aglow in a bright wash of light. It's as if she's opened the door to a room containing the sun itself. "Pressia," she says, "you're family. Family is sacred. What's a home without family?"

EL CAPITAN

EYES

THE CROWD IS QUIET. They march silently. El Capitan sees their faces—the shining plastic and glass, the bright burns, and the tough and knotted scars. Their jaws are set with grim determination. They lurch and shuffle and limp. Some are fused together but stride just the same. No guns, no rifles, no knives. Up ahead, there stands Special Forces—their bodies look overworked, too weighted with guns and rigid with fusings. Some are bent and their arms and legs look uneven. They stand at twenty-foot intervals, ringing the Dome's perimeter. Regardless of how they look nearly crippled, they are prepared to open fire.

El Capitan can't keep up. Every step shoots a series of pains through his body. And yet, he feels a strange surge of strength. The Dome looms larger and larger. The wind is cold and sharp. And for some reason, it's all beautiful.

The shifting veils of ash.

The gauzy dark sky.

The sun a smear of light.

And then everyone stops. Voices begin to whisper and hiss. What's going wrong? El Capitan pushes through the crowd, his body screaming in pain. "Bradwell!" he shouts. "Bradwell!" He gets to the front and sees Hastings emerge from behind the row of Special Forces protecting the Dome.

Bradwell steps forward to meet Hastings, who lopes downhill, a slightly uneven jerk in his gait.

"Hastings is bugged," Bradwell says. "They see what he sees and hear what he hears."

But now that El Capitan sees Hastings' face clearly, he knows something's wrong. "Hastings," El Capitan says. "What'd they do to you?" El Capitan can tell that, despite the deep emotion in his eyes, Hastings has been through more coding. "They reprogrammed you, didn't they?"

Hastings nods.

"Worse than before?"

Hastings nods again.

"Partridge!" El Capitan shouts. "What'd you do to him? Jesus Christ! He's a friend of yours!"

Hastings says, "Partridge and Pressia are going to talk to you soon. Please stand by."

Bradwell looks at El Capitan. "Are you ready?"

"Ready for what?" El Capitan says.

"What comes next."

"What comes next?" Helmud says.

PARTRIDGE

ROOMS

SUN. CURTAINS WARM WITH IT. Lit up. It's how he felt when he saw the letters and then Lyda herself—as if he had suddenly filled with light, as if the sun were blazing in his own chest.

She didn't stop loving him. The letters were proof, but she said it herself. "Even though I thought you'd abandoned me, I still loved you. I always will."

And now here she is with him, wandering this kitchen in the house that Iralene designed, the one she started to talk to Partridge about as if it were a dream, but it was already in the works—for how long now?

Butter glistens in a glass dish. A toaster shines on the counter. A woman stands at the sink, her thin back, her flower-print shirt.

He knows this is an image of his mother. He wants to reach out and touch her shoulder. But he knows there is no shoulder. No woman. He wants her to turn and look at him. But he has no mother.

Lyda reaches out for a milk glass, beading water. Her hand glides through it.

Iralene walks into the room. "Do you like it here?" she asks.

Can he love both of them? His love for Lyda runs deep. But

he's grown to love Iralene. She's steadfast and true. They all move around the kitchen where his mother—the pale image of her at the sink—reaches into the sudsy water, swirling a white dish, humming to herself. She's so real he can't bear to look at her for too long. He wants her to see him there, to treat him as her own—returned.

But does he like it here? Can he answer that? It's a mirage. It's not real. Doesn't Iralene know the difference? He doesn't tell her any of this. He says, "I do like it here." It's a half-truth.

Why is there so much sun? It pours into the windows, fills the room so brightly that it blots the details. Maybe the details aren't finished.

"How did you do it all?" Partridge asks.

"Purdy and Hoppes have access to all these files. They thought it might convince you. There's more," she says. "So much more."

Lyda isn't moving. She stands in the sunlight thrown from the fake window. "Birds," she says. "In the rehabilitation center, they had birds flutter past the fake windows of light just like this."

"We didn't have much time!" Iralene says angrily.

"I didn't like the birds," Lyda says. "They reminded me I had nowhere to go."

Lyda told him that Arvin had let it slip that the letters weren't passed between them, that she thought he'd abandoned her. Partridge explained to her that he wasn't allowed to see her; Foresteed had taken control of his life. After she confessed to him that she'd always love him, he told her that he wanted to be with her. She said, "I understand." But what does that mean—*I understand*? What had he wanted? For her to say that she'd been wrong to let him go the last time and that from now on, they'd always be together?

"Partridge!" It's Pressia, calling for him down a hall. He follows her voice, passing a bedroom with bunk beds.

He stops, doubles back, and looks inside. There, sleeping in the bottom bunk, is his brother. *My God, it's Sedge*—before the enhancements and all the coding. He's not a Special Forces soldier. He's just a kid—maybe fifteen or sixteen. He's sleeping even though the sun is streaming in the window. Partridge wants to wake him up. He wants to hear his brother's voice. But he knows that this was a rushed job. This is probably all his brother does—he sleeps, as he once did, a boy in a bunk bed. Partridge leans his head against the doorjamb. He says, "Sedge, Sedge. My brother."

And then Pressia calls for him again.

He pushes himself from the door and walks, unsteadily, into a bedroom. A pink ruffled skirt, a canopy. A stuffed giraffe. A long inlaid mirror on the door of a wardrobe. Pressia stares at herself in the mirror. She pulls her hair back. The crescent scar around her eye isn't there in the mirror image of her face.

And then she stands back and raises her doll-head fist. But in the reflection, it's gone. She raises both hands and flexes them—open, closed, open, closed.

She stares at Partridge through the mirror. "Why would anyone make a place like this?"

He doesn't have an answer.

A chorus of voices. Pressia recognizes them. She can tell that Partridge does too. He freezes, and she pushes past him. She feels like her heart has swelled and might explode. She follows a hallway into a parlor. And there, as if waiting for her, are three men. Bradwell, El Capitan, and Helmud. Three *separate* men. They're talking, joking. Helmud smooths his hair and rubs his knees. He's nervous. El Capitan gives Bradwell a slap on the back. They all laugh.

She can't make out their words. They're still just voices—the kind heard down a long hallway through the walls and doors. They don't seem to know she's standing in front of them either.

"Bradwell," she says.

His face is clean. No scars. His knuckles aren't nicked. He's wearing a suit jacket—a fitted one. There are no massive wings. No birds in his back at all.

"How did they do this?"

Partridge is now next to her. He crouches and looks up into their faces. "Jesus," he says. "Look at them."

Pressia can't look at them. "They're all wrong," she says to Partridge. "They aren't themselves—not like that, not without any past."

She can see a small eye on a round apple-sized object on the floor. An orb, like Lyda told her about. Each room must have an orb, creating each of the images. None of this is real.

She runs from the room and back down the hall, but it's changed a little. There's a door where before she's sure there was no door. It's open—just a crack. She lifts her doll head, relieved it's still with her, and pushes the door wide.

There's her grandfather, pillows plumped behind his back. A crossword book sits on his knee. She can see that he only has one leg still, and a fake leg—shiny and pink—with a small black sock and shoe stands in the corner. The fan that had been lodged in his throat is gone. In its place, there's a jagged cross-shaped scar.

He isn't like Bradwell, El Capitan, and Helmud in the parlor. He seems to know that she's here. But then he says, "Can I help you?" as if she's a stranger.

"It's me," she says.

"Hello," her grandfather says, but his tone is embarrassed as if he's never seen Pressia before.

"Pressia," she says. "It's me. Pressia."

He closes his eyes for a second, tightly, as if the name itself causes him some pain. When he opens his eyes, he's smiling. "That was my wife's name," he finally says. "She died some years ago."

Pressia walks up to her grandfather then. She lifts her hand, reaches out to touch his but hesitates. She wants to feel the warmth. What if this is just a trick—a cruel trick?

She fits her hand over his—and feels the dryness of his skin, the give of his arthritic knuckles. "You're real," she says. "But you don't know me."

He smiles at her.

Her eyes burn with tears. "Partridge! Lyda!" she shouts.

Lyda appears at the door.

"He's real," Pressia says. "We have to get him out of here. He has to be with us."

Lyda's shaken by the sight of the old man.

"Partridge!" Pressia shouts. "Where are you?"

Pressia reaches out and touches everything now—the wall, the pictures, doorknobs, a vase. Sometimes things are real, and sometimes her hand passes through them like air. "Partridge!" she shouts. "Partridge!"

There's no answer. She runs to the kitchen, which she passed through quickly the first time.

A woman is standing at the sink doing dishes, and Partridge is sitting at the kitchen table.

"You brought my grandfather back."

"Except his memory," he says.

"But he's alive," she says. "You did that. Thank you."

He glances at the woman at the sink and says, "Don't you know who she is?"

Pressia walks up to the counter. She tilts forward and sees her mother's face, the profile of her delicate nose and chin. Her eyes are gentle. Her lightly freckled arms are bare. The soap bubbles shine on the surface of the water. She then lifts a bubble on her palm and blows on it until it lifts and glides and then pops.

Pressia reaches out to touch her.

"Don't," Partridge says. "Don't touch her."

Iralene walks into the room, smiling. "This is worth keeping, isn't it? A home full of family. All those you've lost, perfected. You can't bring down the Dome now. Not when this place exists! You can call it home, Pressia."

"Do you think I'm going to want to save this place? It's not real."

"No, no," Iralene says, wringing her hands. "We can program them better. We can make them interactive. You can have conversations with them eventually. You don't understand."

"*You* don't understand. They aren't real people."

"That's why you can't take down the Dome, Pressia," Partridge breaks in. "It's filled with real people. They'll die out there. And you know who'll be killed first? Us. You and me and Iralene and Lyda. Lyda and our baby. And more..."

"More?"

"Babies," he says. "Tiny babies in incubators. What will happen to them?"

"Babies in incubators?" She imagines the mothers finding rows of babies in warm plastic boxes. Mother Hestra and the other mothers would pick them up by the armfuls, strap them to their bodies—a familiar comfort of closeness—and take care of them. "If there are babies who need mothers, Partridge, I think you should know who'd take care of them."

"You would trust the mothers? The ones who chopped off my pinky?"

"Things have to change," Pressia says. "I know that. They have to!"

"Well, it gets worse. There are people in cold storage. You can't imagine..." Partridge stands up, staggers, and walks out of the door of the house and back into the hall.

Pressia follows him, shouting, "Partridge, what are you doing? Partridge!"

He is bent over, trying to catch his breath, but as she reaches him, he straightens and walks into a conference room, stopping at the table in the center of the room.

She moves to the table. There's a map of the area around the

Dome, but it's a living map. Black marks are moving uphill in every direction, getting closer and closer to the Dome. Is one of those marks Bradwell? Are El Capitan and Helmud among them? Who has the bacterium?

"The survivors are on the move," Partridge says.

"They're closing in," Beckley says.

"Jesus," Partridge says.

"Is this...?" Pressia isn't sure how to finish the sentence. Is this *the revolution?*

"It's what you think it is." He puts his hand on a dark shining pad next to a door. The door opens. "My father's chamber. Come in. I've got something else for you to see."

Pressia steps into the darkened room. The lights turn on. The floor is covered with photographs of Partridge and his family—holidays, school pictures, vacations—and handwritten letters. Pressia sees one that's clearly signed "Your Father." Is this how Willux chose to decorate his office?

Pressia sees a picture of her mother. She kneels quickly and picks it up. Her mother is sitting by a fireplace with a newborn in her arms—Partridge or his brother Sedge? She only knows that it isn't her as a baby.

Iralene walks in and starts picking up the papers and photographs as if she's embarrassed by the mess. Partridge walks to a large desk in the middle of the room.

"There's a communication system here," Partridge says. "It connects us to the other places in the world that survived." He touches the desk, and a screen lights up on its surface, like the mahogany table in the conference room, but this one is of a map of the world. "If the Dome goes down, so does your shot at finding your father." He points to Japan. "His heart was beating," Partridge says. "He's alive somewhere..."

"Weed told me you'd throw everything at me to get me to call it off."

"Why won't you?"

"Why do you think I can?"

"Let me tell you what my father figured out. The wretches are the superior race. They've been tested and tested and tested by all the horrors they've been through and are now toughened. And the Pures? They're weak—coddled and protected. They have no real immune systems anymore. You know what will happen if the Dome no longer exists and the Pures have to live out there, breathing ash and fighting Dusts and Beasts and Groupies?"

"Yes," Pressia says. "I know exactly what will happen. Have you forgotten? That's my childhood."

"And do you want that to play out again?"

Pressia shakes her head. "I wanted Pures to help the survivors. I wanted to even the playing field with the cure. I wanted to erase all the scars and fusings and have everyone be whole again. But I don't want that anymore. Bradwell was right. We should never erase the past even when we wear it on our skin."

"I know where the button is, Partridge." Iralene points to a small metal square embedded in the wall. "This is it, isn't it? Save us, Partridge."

There's a knock on the open door. A man's voice says, "Bradwell is standing by. Are we ready?"

"We're ready," Partridge says.

A screen lights up one wall. And there is Bradwell's face. His eyes are squinting. The wind is whipping his shirt, his hair. He turns and looks to one side—showing the double scars running down one side of his face, his dark wings.

Iralene gasps. She's not used to ash, scars, and fusings.

The cameras that are lodged in Hastings' eyes take in El Capitan and Helmud, who look pale and weak. El Capitan has two black eyes and a crooked jaw.

"What happened to them?" Pressia says.

"Are those two fused together?" Iralene says the word *fused* as if it's new to her. She's horrified, and Pressia remembers what Bradwell said about what he thought the Pures would think of him—that disgust, that horror.

"I'll explain it later," Partridge says.

Pressia wonders if there will be a later...

"Tell Bradwell to call it off," Partridge says to Pressia. Would Partridge hit the button? Would he kill all of the survivors once and for all?

Pressia slips her hand in her pocket and grips the top of the spear that Lyda whittled from the crib slats.

"Bradwell!" Pressia says. "Can you hear me?"

"Yes!" he shouts into the wind. "Are you okay?"

"Are you?" she says.

He nods. He glances at El Capitan and Helmud. "We're okay. I wish I could see you!"

"Tell him, Pressia," Partridge says.

"Is that Partridge's voice?" Bradwell asks.

"It's me," Partridge says.

"What do you have to tell me?" Bradwell asks.

Pressia knows that she's supposed to tell Bradwell to call off the attack, but instead she says, "Partridge can kill all of you. He can push a button of his father's design and send a gas out across the wind that will put you all to sleep forever."

Bradwell takes a deep breath. "We're unarmed," he says. "El Capitan said that was the only way to do this. Unarmed. All of us together."

"If you bring down the Dome, Pures will die. They can't live outside the Dome. Most won't make it," Partridge says. "So you seem pretty well armed to me."

El Capitan starts to speak. Hastings' eyes quickly focus on him, and his face fills the screen. "You'd choose to kill survivors to save Pures?"

"Don't you see the death toll on either side?" Partridge asks.

"Do the deaths of wretches count for less?" Bradwell says.

"None of you can understand. I'm going to be a father. I've got a baby on the way—you don't know what it's like to worry about raising a child out there."

"Partridge," Bradwell says, "we were children out here. We know what that's like, and you never will."

"My own child!" Partridge says. "My own child has to be able to breathe and grow and thrive. He can't do that out there."

"*Your* child?" Iralene says, as if it's just now dawning on her how much this child means to him. Does she think she'll be the mother of the child? Or is she talking about Lyda?

Pressia says, "The baby isn't just yours. In fact, right now, the baby isn't yours at all."

"They'll kill me—you know that. I'll be the first to die. They'll kill Iralene too. Pures and wretches—it doesn't matter who. They'll kill us. You know what we represent." He presses his hands against the wall. "He's in me. He's inside of me. My father. He's not just in the air all around us. He's inside of my body. His blood is my blood."

Pressia watches his hand, the one with the pinky that's now fully grown back, the one dangerously close to the command button. She can't rush Partridge with the spear. He's been coded for strength and speed. He'd overtake her easily.

But she glances at Iralene. She's a Pure—she's the weaker race; that's what Willux came to believe. And so Pressia reaches for Iralene's pale wrist. She grabs it and spins her around, twisting her arm and jamming it up between her shoulder blades. The letters and photographs that she'd collected in her arms fall to the floor, a spray of faces, birthdays, bicycles, Christmas trees, and handwritten notes—pages and pages of them. Her skin feels thin and chilled. Pressia shoves Iralene's face against the wall, pinning her other arm with Pressia's hip and holding the spear tip to her throat.

"Walk away from it," Pressia says, "or I'll kill her."

Partridge glares at Pressia. He clenches his fists and stands completely still. "Hastings," Partridge says. "Get Bradwell."

Partridge's voice is tinny and cold. *Get Bradwell.* The words are a sick echo in Pressia's head, a ringing that won't stop.

Hastings has no choice.

He pushes Bradwell to the ground, puts his good foot on Bradwell's chest. Bradwell's wings splay beneath him. Hastings aims one of the guns lodged in his arms at Bradwell's heart.

There's the red bead of light.

Bradwell stares into Hastings' eyes, but he's only talking to Pressia. He says, "I'm sorry."

Pressia can't breathe. She knows what he's sorry for—not what's happened, no. He's saying he's sorry for what's about to happen.

"No!" she screams, still holding Iralene tight. "No!"

And then Bradwell starts to fight back. He bucks. He kicks Hastings and tries to wrestle himself up from the dirt. His wings beat against the dirt, filling the air with more dust and ash.

The screen darkens. Bradwell's face is lost in the dark cloud.

"Stop resisting!" Hastings orders. "Stop now!"

Pressia shouts at Partridge. "Do something!"

But Partridge doesn't understand, does he? Bradwell is fighting to the death. He's fighting, knowing he'll die.

The screen goes black.

Hastings has shut his eyes.

And then there's a gunshot.

Just one.

A few survivors scream.

And then silence.

And then there's a cry—loud and long.

It's followed by another cry—just as loud and just as long.

An echo of the first.

Pressia drops the spear. She loses her grip on Iralene, who remains completely still, her body leaning against the wall.

"He's dead," Pressia whispers.

—∞—

Hastings is stiff, his guns poised on the crowd. He is a soldier. He stands his ground.

El Capitan kneels next to Bradwell. He's terrified of all of the blood, so sudden and quick, spreading across Bradwell's chest. Helmud holds on to El Capitan's neck. He grips his shirt in his skinny fists.

"Bradwell," El Capitan says breathlessly. He's supposed to check his heart. But the blood has soaked his shirt. There can't be much left of his heart.

El Capitan's hands are shaking so badly he can barely get hold of Bradwell's shirt. But when he does, he rips it wide open.

The wind gusts.

Small sheets of bloody paper lift.

El Capitan sits back as the wind collects the papers and sends them out over the dry dirt.

Hastings' boot steps on one, its edges soaked red.

El Capitan picks one up.

```
    We are here, my brothers and sisters,
  to end the division, to be recognized as human,
    to live in peace. Each of us has the power
                to be benevolent.
```

There is no cross on the bottom of the message. Only random splatterings of Bradwell's blood.

The survivors pick up the sheets. They gather around Bradwell. His body lies on a blanket of his black-feathered wings. The bloody white sheets of paper keep fluttering up from his chest like an unending ribbon pulled by the wind.

His arms are spread wide, his hands open—and from one of them, Freedle appears. Nearly lost in the spinning, swirling sheets of paper, Freedle spreads his mechanical wings and takes flight, heading toward the Dome.

———ooo———

Pressia can't breathe. She can't cry. Bradwell is dead. He knew that he was going to die. *If we don't see each other again...* She should have stayed with him. She shouldn't have left. He knew, and he didn't tell her—not the whole truth. He said *if...* if, if, if... She thought it was just the beginning.

She can still remember his kiss. Will she always remember it? Is it burned onto her lips? This is why he made her promise to be together here, now, and beyond—in case there's a heaven... in case of what might lie ahead.

She puts her fist to her heart. She and Bradwell are still locked together. There is no better church than a forest. In the end, a wedding is between two people—what they promise in a whisper.

She isn't sure why, but now she feels fear. It seizes her chest. She knows what it is to feel the shock of grief, what it's like to mourn. But what she feels is terror. He is gone. The realization that the world still exists and he doesn't—this is what she's been most afraid of. And here it is.

She looks at the ground littered with the photographs of Partridge's happy childhood.

Partridge walks toward her. "I killed him," he says.

"Don't touch me. Don't look at me."

Partridge is a ghost.

Iralene says, "You didn't kill anyone. You didn't. You didn't kill him. Hastings did it!"

"Shut up," Pressia says. "Shut up!"

Iralene slides down the wall and sits on the floor. She stares blankly.

"Pressia," Partridge says, "I did the right things. I swear. I didn't know that Hastings was going to kill him."

"Hastings was programmed to kill anyone who resisted. Bradwell knew it. It's why he fought back."

"I gave the order," Partridge says, his voice so hoarse it's barely audible. "I could have called Hastings off. I could have done something."

"You got us here," Pressia says. "You drove us all to this moment. You've done worse than not calling off Hastings."

"I wasn't going to push the button," Partridge mutters. "I wouldn't have done it. I wouldn't have."

"No," Iralene says. "You wouldn't have. I know you wouldn't have." Then, with hope in her voice, she adds, "Maybe that stopped them. Maybe they'll turn back now."

"Freedle," Pressia says. "Didn't you see him? He's carrying the bacterium. It's coming. It works fast."

There's pounding on the door. They hear Beckley's loud, urgent voice. "The people are rising up in the streets! They want blood!"

"They're coming for us," Iralene says.

"They'll find us here," Partridge says. "I know they will."

The screen is still playing out the scene. Hastings' eyes are wide open. He scans the crowd of people. El Capitan is shouting, "We keep going. This is what he wanted. We move forward. Together!" His face is streaked with black ash. He's wiped his bloody hands on his shirt.

And then Hastings turns. He walks toward the Dome and stands in line between two other soldiers.

"The Dome is coming down, and when it does, I'm getting out and going home," Pressia says. She walks to the door, opens it, and stands in the conference room. Beckley is standing next to Pressia's grandfather, who sits in one of the leather chairs, Lyda at his side.

"You'll come with us," Pressia says to her grandfather. "We'll keep you safe."

He's scared, but he nods. Once upon a time, he was the stranger who took her in. This time, she'll be the one to take care of him.

⸎

Partridge stares at Lyda, still shocked that she's here, so close, and yet she's still distant. Things have changed between them. What has this been like for her? He remembers Pressia telling Lyda that they were going to take the baby from her. Did she believe that? Was it the truth? He doesn't know what's true anymore. Maybe he never has. Pressia will tell her what happened in that room. She'll tell Lyda that he could have saved Bradwell and that he failed. His friend is dead. Partridge hesitated. Why? Out of anger, spite, or did he really think he was doing the right thing, trying to save his people? Deep down, is that the way he thinks of the Pures—as his people? He may never know his own truth. Maybe this is how it began for his father—one act that he couldn't ever take back and he had to decide what kind of person he was. Partridge wants to be good. He's always wanted to be good, hasn't he? Right now, he has to decide how they're all going to try to survive. "You could have run. You probably should have. Why'd you stay?" Partridge asks Beckley.

"We're friends. Friends stay."

Partridge didn't realize that he'd been waiting for this, but now that he hears it, he's happy. He grabs Beckley and hugs him. "Thank you," he says.

"We have to move now. If you don't go," Beckley says, "they'll find you here. You can't lock yourselves away. They'll only wait you out if you stay in your father's chamber."

Partridge looks at Pressia. He knows that he doesn't deserve to come with them. He shakes his head. "They'll just tear us apart out there," he says. "One way or another..."

"We have to move now," Beckley urges.

"Come with us," Pressia says. "We can find a way to get you out of the Dome; then we can find a hiding place for you on the outside."

Beckley and Lyda help Pressia's grandfather. They move to the door. Pressia follows. "Come on, Partridge. Bring Iralene. Getting out is her only chance. Let's stick together." He can tell that it pains her to say this. He knows what he must seem like to her. He hates himself. He hates both worlds—inside the Dome and out.

Iralene and Partridge walk into the hall, following the others to the elevator, Lyda and Beckley supporting Pressia's hobbled grandfather.

Then Iralene stops. She looks at the door to the house she designed. It's still open—just a crack. Light is pouring from it.

She grabs Partridge's arm, holds it tight. "Remember," she says, "you still owe me a favor."

"Iralene," Partridge says softly.

"You made me a promise," she says. "Will you stand by it?"

"Please..." he says.

"Are you a man of your word?" she says. He knows what she wants, and he doesn't want her to say it aloud, but she does. "I built a home for us."

Pressia holds the elevator door open. "Hurry," she calls to them, as the others turn and look back.

He shakes his head. "I can't." Iralene lets go of his arm and heads toward the door filled with golden light. He grips Lyda's letters.

"Don't, Partridge," Pressia says.

Lyda says, "There's nothing real in there. It's emptiness."

"I can get you out of here," Beckley says pleadingly. "Iralene, tell him to come with us!"

"One minute," Partridge says to Iralene. She gives a nod. He walks down the hall to Lyda. He reaches into his pocket, pulls out the stack of his letters, and hands them to her. "Here. These are yours."

Lyda takes the stack and holds the letters to her chest. "I can't stay and you can't go?" she says to Partridge.

"You never know what will happen. One day..."

"If you come looking for me, you know I'll be out there..."

"Both of you," he says. Mother and child. "This is a ship. I think if it goes down, I should go with it."

He walks back to Iralene, takes her by the hand, gives one final wave. He and Iralene step into the glowing room, into its blinding light—and he closes the door behind them.

—❀—

A group of survivors stands watch over Bradwell's body as El Capitan and Helmud lead the others. The circle grows tighter and tighter until only ten yards stand between El Capitan and the Special Forces soldiers, Hastings among them. El Capitan gives a shout, and the survivors around him stop. His command travels around the circle, and soon all of the survivors are locked in place. Hastings looks at El Capitan. Has Hastings lost contact with those inside? What's going on in there?

No one moves. No one speaks. They stand there in the wind, Bradwell's sheets still spinning in the ashen air.

And then it happens.

A creaking noise, low and deep, like something heard on a massive ship.

There's a pop, and then a crack shivers up the side of the Dome like a crack through the ice of a frozen lake. It shoots across the surface, sending out fissures.

And then a piece of the Dome shifts, tilts, and then falls into the Dome itself.

Our Good Mother walks uphill, protected on all sides by mothers. The cross of the window casing in her chest keeps her posture stiff. She holds her head high. When she sees the splinters run across the white surface of the Dome, she whispers to the baby mouth lodged in her arm, "Let's go find Daddy, dear one!" And she tightens her grip on her spear. "Let's go find your papa."

The lights flicker then fade. Arvin waits. He holds his breath, closes his eyes—and when he does, he sees his parents' faces. He's followed orders so that he could stay alive. He's made himself valuable, indispensable. But now, he's finally free. The generator hums to life. The lights brighten overhead, and he hears the buzzing noise of the laboratory being sealed. He won't leave until he has a cure.

When the lights flit out, the hum of machinery dies inside of each chamber—up and down the halls. It's deathly silent. Peekins has been working in this one chamber, trying to save a family—four stiff infants, the pale blue tinge fading from their skin. He fumbles in his pocket for a flashlight. He pulls it out and shines it on the babies before him—the Willuxes. One set of eyes flutter. The eyes open. It's the little girl. Partridge's mother. Maybe she'll be the only one to survive.

The orbs light each room. Iralene has chosen the music—the same song they danced to at the picnic, which seems so long ago. It seeps in from unseen speakers. They hold each other in the living room—they're swaying more than dancing. There are voices in the hall now, thudding footsteps.

Partridge whispers, "The sunlight isn't warm. It's not real."

"What is reality anyway?" Iralene says.

"They're coming for us."

"Let them come."

"Iralene," he says. He cups her face and touches her cheeks with his thumbs.

There's banging on the door, a heavy body throwing itself against it again and again.

By the time they reach the street, they can see the sky through the gaping hole. The ash swirls in.

Pressia says, "It's happening."

"Ash," Lyda says.

Beckley is carrying Pressia's frail grandfather on his back. "I will remember what it was like, won't I?" Beckley says.

Pressia's grandfather lifts his hand in the air and catches light flecks of ash in his palm. He looks at Pressia, a shocked expression on his face, and says, "My girl."

Pressia starts to cry. "Yes," she says. "I'm here." Her mother is dead. Bradwell is gone. And Partridge has chosen his own ending. But she has gotten one person back.

There are others on the streets. Some are screaming and crying. They grip their children to their chests. Some are holding on to their valuables—gold candlestick holders, boxes of memorabilia, their guns. In fact, at this distance, they're holding on so tightly that they look fused to their earthly possessions.

Some start to run—but to where? There's nowhere to go.

The electrical grid has been compromised. The lights flicker and die. The monorail has come to a grating stop. Beckley leads them to the set of hidden stairs along the secret elevators, now stalled like everything else.

They get to the ground level of the Dome and walk through the vacant grounds of the academy, past dormitories, the darkened windows of classrooms, even across a football field—its white lines striping the fake turf—and by a basketball court behind a chain-link fence. Once upon a time, she'd been told her father was a point guard. Her real father—she'll probably never hear his voice...He's out there.

Finally, they come to the soy fields, which are green and leafy. The rows curve with the shape of the Dome. They walk and walk. Pressia can feel the wind sweeping in from somewhere unseen.

Lyda pulls out her spear. The soot is thicker now, whirling in the wind. She says, "It's snowing."

Close to the ground, a triangle of the Dome has fallen onto the soy fields, onto the plants with their green leaves and yellow seedpods. The ground, littered with broken shards, crunches under their boots. They walk toward the hole itself and to the edge of the Dome. Pressia looks out into that ashen world, her homeland. Trudging up the hill are the survivors, coming to claim what's theirs. She starts to run toward them and searches the faces for Bradwell, knowing he won't be among them.

But there are El Capitan and Helmud—soot streaked and pained. When El Capitan sees Pressia, he stops and falls to his knees. A white piece of paper is clenched in his fist. He raises it over his head like a small white flag.

There is no victory. There's always loss.

This is his surrender.

This is her surrender.

Her heart is saying, *Enough, enough, enough. I give.*

And she expects her heart to stop beating.

She's lost too much.

And she knows that out there, she will find Bradwell's body. It will hit her again and again that he's dead. How many blows can she take?

But her heart beats in her chest and keeps beating.

It beats her back to life.

Her own heart will not surrender.

And so this isn't the end.

This is only another start.

She stops and looks back over her shoulder. Walking through the black snow toward her are Beckley, carrying her grandfather, alive after all, on his back, and Lyda and the baby inside of her, protected under her handmade armor. She turns back to El Capitan. He staggers to his feet, Helmud weighty on his back, and walks toward Pressia. He hugs her. When they were in the fog surrounded by creatures they thought would kill them, El Capitan said, *If you were the person standing there with me, I'd always, always stay.* This is the promise she needs to believe in. *Stand with me. Stay.*

This is her family now.

She and El Capitan and Helmud turn and look at the Pures who are heading into the fields, the green soy leaves shimmering around their ankles. They're pale and wide-eyed, moving like timid ghosts toward the broken edge of their world.

Somewhere, Partridge and Iralene are sitting at a table in a fake kitchen swollen bright with fake sunlight—while batteries inside of orbs are slowly winding down. If people come after them, she hopes that they'll at least fight. This is the final bit of faith that she must have in him.

But she's chosen this truth—grotesquely beautiful and beautifully grotesque—*this* world.

"What are we going to do now?" El Capitan whispers.

"What now?" Helmud says.

"No more blood," Pressia says.

Her heart beats and beats and beats—each time like a detonation in her own chest—and every moment from here on out is a new world.

The End

ACKNOWLEDGMENTS

I want to thank so many people who endured this ashen world with me for so many years—my spouse, my kids, my loving and generous parents, especially my lead researcher, Bill Baggott; it's been a lot of welding and soldering and making from cinders. Thank you for your patience.

I'm thankful to my editors, Beth de Guzman, Selina McLemore, and Jaime Levine, as well as all of my overseas editors, especially Hannah Sheppard, Frankie Gray, Florence Lottin, Louise Loiselle, and Patricia Escalona, and my translators who bring this work to life in other languages, in particular Laurent Strim. Thank you to the voices in the audio version—Khristine Hvam, Joshua Swanson, Kevin T. Collins, and Casey Holloway—for adding layers to the narrative. And of course, I'm deeply thankful to the art departments for creating such striking covers. Thank you to the publicists who put so much heart and muscle into getting these books into the world—Linda Duggins and Ben Willis most of all. And I'm thankful for Clare Anne Darragh—for all of her sisterhood and support! I'm thankful to Karen Rosenfelt, Rodney Ferrell, Emmy Castlen, and all of those at Fox 2000 for their vision and conviction. And, welcome in, James Ponsoldt. I'm so glad you're here.

I want to thank Cheryl Fitch at Florida State University's Biological Science Department in the Molecular Cloning Facility for letting me see firsthand the work they do. I'm thankful to Margaret McKeown Henihan, who once told me an old Irish tale that made me tear up; it never left.

I'm deeply indebted to Nat Sobel, Judith Weber, the whole crew at Sobel Weber, and Justin Manask. A million times, thank you.